Going Dark

A crime novel

Neil Lancaster

Burning Chair Limited, Trading As Burning Chair Publishing
71-75 Shelton Street, Covent Garden
London WC2H 9JQ
www.burningchairpublishing.com

By Neil Lancaster
Edited by Simon Finnie and Peter Oxley
Book Cover Design by ebooklaunch.com

First published by Burning Chair Publishing, 2019

ISBN: 978-1-912946-06-8

Praise for Going Dark

"A tense, edgy debut that captures the mind and captivates the reader."
- Ian Patrick, author of the Sam Batford series

"A great read. Lancaster clearly knows his stuff."
- Stephen Leather, Sunday Times bestselling author of the Dan 'Spider' Shepherd series

"A geniune, gripping page-turner from a new author with real insider knowledge... the pace and tension are relentless."
- Alex Waters, author of the DI Alec McKay series

"A gripping page-turner that drags you in and won't let you out until you finish it."
- Paul Harrison, author of Mind Games, Dancing With The Devil, and Chasing Monsters

"If you enjoyed my Manhunt look out for this. A novel written by a bloke who actually worked on my investigation."
- Colin Sutton, author of Manhunt - How I Brought Serial Killer Levi Bellfield To Justice

Dedication

This book is dedicated to my late Mum, Brenda Lancaster, who started this whole journey by throwing me my first adventure book when I was twelve and saying, 'You'll love this.'

1

November 2005
1600hrs
Basra, Iraq

Tom strode down the side road towards Al Saadi Street, past the burnt-out husk of a car, the remnants of a recent improvised explosive device. The war in Iraq was decimating the country but people still needed to eat, work, and make money and no number of bombs or mortars would stop them from doing so. The street was bustling and alive with the noise and smells of a typical Arabic city: a mix of petrol fumes, cigarette smoke, and roasting coffee.

His covert earpiece crackled with Buster's cockney voice. 'We are parked nearby, Borat. No more than a minute away if it all goes tits-up. Now try not to kill anyone today, old son.'

Tom smiled, pressed his transmitter and muttered back, his lips barely moving, 'I always try not to kill people, Buster. It just happens.'

'That's why none of us want to work with you. You're a shit-magnet,' Buster countered.

'That's unfair. I haven't killed anyone for ages.'

'That's because we haven't let you out on your own for ages.'

Tom smiled again at his friend's banter as he entered the café. 'Anyway, I'm going in, so shut the fuck up, you cockney twat. I'm a busy man,' he whispered, his lips only moving slightly.

The Metro Café was a large establishment mostly occupied

by groups of men chatting, smoking, drinking tea and playing dominoes. Tom sat at a small table with an overflowing ashtray that afforded him a clear line of sight to the barber shop and the green-doored entrance to the meeting place.

No one took any notice of him; he was one of a million people just going about their business as normal. The words of his surveillance instructor still rang in his ears, even after all those years. 'You've as much right to be there on the street as anyone else so, if you act normally, no one will notice you. It's only when you bob and weave and skulk about that you stand out like a bull dog's bollocks.' It was true; nothing attracted the eye more than someone peeping, known in the trade as 'chadding', around a corner.

A waiter approached him, a groaning tray of small glass cups balanced on his hand and a cigarette dangling from his lips. The man did not speak, instead raising his bushy eyebrows questioningly.

'Mint tea, please,' Tom said in Arabic. He'd completed an intensive course in Arabic prior to deployment to Iraq. He wasn't fluent by any means, but his aptitude for languages meant he was confident he could manage the level of interaction required for the job at hand.

The waiter disappeared without a word. The place was busy, and the deafening roar of the traffic made conversation pointless anyway. Tom found the buzz of the café almost comforting; his confidence rose that it would be pretty easy to remain anonymous. He produced some Islamic prayer beads and began to finger them absent-mindedly, further assimilating into the tableau of the café.

The waiter returned as quickly as he'd departed and unceremoniously deposited a small glass of dark tea full of mint leaves, sugar crystals visibly sinking into the depths. Tom sipped the scalding-hot amber liquid, trying not to screw up his face at the overpoweringly pre-sweetened flavour. He picked up an Arabic newspaper from the empty table next to him and settled in, while he watched the door and waited. Through his jeans pocket he pressed the transmitter tone switch twice to indicate to control that he was in position.

'Two tones received; do you have a clear eyeball?'

Tom replied with two tones.

'Two tones, Roger. Wait. Out.' The tinny voice of Damien, the boss at the control centre at Basra Palace was clear in his ear.

Tom sat with his tea, looking at the newspaper as if he was deep in thought while twirling his prayer beads, his eyes fixed on the green door across the street.

The tinny voice sparked up in his ear again.

'Alpha One Foot, stand-by. Friendlies approaching venue. We understand the package is already in place,' Damien said.

Tom replied with two tones.

'Two tones. Roger. Stand-by,' relayed Damien.

Tom's senses were at their peak as he waited for the two CIA agents to arrive at the premises. He had not seen any obvious signs of surveillance on his journey from the palace to the café, nor were there any on the target premises opposite. He casually surveyed his fellow café-dwellers; if he'd been able to identify the café as the best vantage point for the rendezvous, then so could any hostiles. His brief survey didn't reveal anyone of concern, the tables mostly occupied with small groups of elderly men all chatting amiably or playing dominoes.

A crackle erupted in his ear. 'All units … package moving up towards target premises. With you in two minutes, Alpha One.'

Tom remained impassive, his eyes ostensibly on the newspaper, but peripherally covering the door. He was well-practised at being able to closely observe a target point without necessarily staring directly at it.

The operation had been sold to them as a simple counter-surveillance operation to watch the backs of the CIA agents, Mike and Hamed, as they met a potential asset in the apartment above the barber shop opposite. The powers-that-be wanted to make sure that the agents were not being followed ahead of the meeting, given that they were in a very dangerous part of Basra, with militia groups and criminal kidnap gangs active in the area. As the Special Reconnaissance Regiment (SRR) unit currently in Basra, Tom's team was the best one for the job: hugely experienced in covert surveillance in hostile environments. The operation was meat-and-drink to them.

After a few moments he saw Mike and Hamed approaching the barber shop from their Subaru, which was parked about twenty metres away on Al Saadi Street. Mike was wearing a blue jacket and had a red and white shemagh round his neck, a dark baseball cap pulled low over his face, with sunglasses just peeking out from beneath. Hamed was dressed in chinos and a blue fleece to protect against the early evening chill, and also had a shemagh around his neck.

Tom could see no obvious watchers; the pair didn't seem to be attracting any unusual attention. The plan was that they should be visible and in the open for the least possible time between exiting their vehicle and entering the premises.

Tom affected a yawn, covered his mouth with his hand, and without his lips moving said, 'From Alpha One: you're clear to proceed.'

He received two tones of acknowledgement in his ear from Mike or Hamed. He kept his peripheral vision on the pair as they pushed the green door open and went inside.

He transmitted once more, again with minimal lip movement and his newspaper high. 'Package is complete, and I have the visual on the door. Stand-by.'

Tom kept up his observation of the green door while apparently studying his newspaper, the seconds ticking off in his head and his senses heightened. Mike and Hamed were badly exposed: in hostile territory, meeting a violent Jihadist, and without any secure knowledge of the target's intent. Tom felt the comforting presence of the Sig Sauer P228 pistol in his belt and the weight of the flash-bang in his pocket. There was nothing he could do but wait.

Out of the corner of his eye he noticed a silver Land Cruiser pull up outside the front of the barber shop. It had tinted windows, but Tom could see the outlines of two occupants. He tried to read the registration plates, but his view was obscured by other vehicles.

He pressed the transmitter. 'Land Cruiser outside front of shop, two fighting-age males in front seats, no registration. Be aware.'

Tom heard two tones in his ear, signalling that the Americans understood.

As he watched the car, both front doors opened and two men got out to stand outside the barber's shop. One man had a mobile phone clamped to his ear, the other stood close by, keeping a watch on their surroundings. They were both in their thirties: one in a tracksuit, the other in jeans and a Barcelona football shirt. They had the look of hard men who had seen combat close-up. Tom felt his stomach lurch at the sight of them. There was no way they were casual shoppers; they were there for a purpose. The one on the phone had long, collar-length hair and a full beard, the other had cropped hair and heavy, dark stubble.

Long Hair finished his phone call, and the pair fixed each other with a knowing look, conversing quietly.

'Two males on pavement outside barber's, one in Barcelona football top, the other in a blue Adidas tracksuit. This doesn't look right. Beware inside,' Tom whispered, his lips barely moving. The urgency in his delivery was not matched by the calm manner he continued to outwardly project. The clock was beginning to tick faster in Tom's head as he worked out the angles, coming up with a plan of action if the men went into the flat. He surveyed the street in front of him, seeing no other suspects, no one else other than the two who didn't belong.

'Alpha One received,' replied control. 'Stand-by but do not engage unless shots fired.'

Long Hair raised his mobile to his ear again and began talking, his lips moving rapidly, tension clearly etched on his rough face.

The call finished quickly, and he spoke to his colleague, both men reaching into their waistbands almost simultaneously. To Tom's eyes this indicated one thing only: they were checking sidearms. It was a habit for all soldiers and operators before any planned situation: a reassuring check that their weapons were still secure. Tom had done it himself in the café, leaning into his Sig in a more covert style.

There was a brief nod between the two before they turned to the door and purposefully strode inside.

Tom threw a crumpled banknote on the table, stood, and walked away from the café, keeping his eyes fixed on the door. His eyes rose to the first-floor window, which was obscured by dark curtains.

'Two suspects into premises. I'm sure they're carrying sidearms, acknowledge?'

A double tone spoke dispassionately, conveying nothing of how the agents were feeling.

Control barked in Tom's ear. 'Stand-by. Alpha One Zero, move up, move up for possible exfil.'

Buster's voice crackled in Tom's ear with a trace of frustration—or was it panic?

'We're blocked by a lorry, we can't advance. Do you want us to deploy on foot? We're four minutes away.'

'Negative, we need the vehicle. Get up by any means possible,' Damien replied calmly.

Tom crossed the busy street and took up a position to the left of the green door, ready to intervene if this was a kidnap attempt. He wouldn't allow the agents to be taken hostage under any circumstances.

Over the roar of the traffic, Tom heard the unmistakeable crack of a sidearm firing—9mm by the sound of it—coming from the upstairs of the building. An un-silenced pistol report is loud and hard to mistake, particularly if you're listening for it.

'Shots fired, shots fired,' said Tom, still calmly, although he was churning inside. Clearly a major drama was unfolding upstairs.

Damien came in on the net. 'Mike, Hamed: acknowledge!'

Silence.

Damien repeated the urgent missive.

Silence.

'Alpha One mobile, how far away?' demanded Damien, still ostensibly calm.

'Three minutes,' said Buster, screaming engine-noise audible over the radio static.

Three minutes is too long, thought Tom. He had no choice.

He moved through the door drawing his Sig in two hands and pointing it at the floor. He quietly ascended the staircase, using the edges of the treads to minimise any creaks.

At the top he was faced with three doors along a short corridor. The closest was ajar and he could hear faint, low voices from within.

Moving slowly, he edged his back along the wall until he reached the door, which was open just a couple of inches. He peered in and quickly took in the scene. Time seemed to slow to a syrupy crawl as he edged closer to the door jamb.

Mike and Hamed were both face-down on the floor, wrists secured behind their backs with zip-ties. Long Hair and Barcelona were stood over them with automatic pistols drawn. Long Hair was speaking in rapid Arabic on the mobile again, his pistol covering the agents with his free hand. Tom's mind flashed back to the earlier briefing given by Mike Brogan, the smiling and personable leader of the CIA pair.

'We are hoping that Bashar Al-Ahmed is considering coming over to the good-guys. He's a well-placed mid-ranker close to the Shia militia leader. His recruitment would be a coup, as I'm sure you can imagine.' He had handed photographs around to the team.

Prone on the floor to the side of them was a straggly-haired Arabic man who Tom immediately recognised as Bashar Al-Ahmed. What he didn't recognise from the photo was the dark red hole in the centre of the man's forehead and the blood circling the floor around his head like a macabre halo.

Tom pulled the flash-bang from his pocket and, with his pistol still extended, pulled the pin out with his teeth. He opened the door an inch further and rolled the grenade into the room. Both men turned in the direction of the noise as Tom flattened himself against the wall, ready for the explosion. The one-second fuse delay seemed to go on for an age.

The report, when it came, was deafening, accompanied by a

blinding white flash as the magnesium and ammonium nitrate combined. If the targets are not prepared for it, the combination can temporarily blind those within a few feet and cause serious disorientation. Tom rocketed in after the explosion, his Sig extended. He first encountered Barcelona who was flailing his arms, his gun pointing away from him. Tom responded with a quick double-tap into the man's central body mass and Barcelona dropped like a stone. Tom immediately turned to Long Hair, who was bringing his weapon to bear unsteadily in his direction. Tom dived to the side as the man blindly loosed off a round, feeling the scorched air of the bullets trailing past his cheek. As he hit the floor, he turned in the direction of the insurgent and let off another double-tap, the first round hitting the man in his left shoulder and spinning him, the second hitting him smack in his right ear and blowing off the top of his head. The man collapsed like a puppet whose strings had just been cut.

The silence was suddenly deafening and overpowering.

The whole encounter had taken less than two minutes, but to Tom it felt like an hour had passed since he'd entered the building.

He pressed the transmitter and spoke calmly, feeling no panic, just strangely relaxed as he always felt in situations like this. His heartbeat remained only slightly elevated and his breathing was steady and even.

'Two suspects down, exfil, exfil! One of the players was on the phone and I think we can expect company.'

He reached down and cut Mike and Hamed's zip-ties with his pocket knife.

'You okay, guys?'

'Holy fuck! Jesus fucking Christ, those bastards were going to fucking ice us!' said Mike. His eyes flashed with fear and his usual warm and easy smile was replaced with panic and alarm as he twisted to look at Tom, breathing heavily.

'It's all cool guys, but we can't hang about.' Tom managed what he hoped was a reassuring smile.

Both agents were shaken and disorientated, but their positions on the floor—face-down—had protected them from the worst effects of the grenade.

Tom quickly checked both insurgents. Long Hair was dead; most of his brain was decorating the wall behind them. Barcelona was still alive but it seemed unlikely he would stay that way for long, as he had two clean holes in his upper chest and was barely breathing.

Hamed said, in a panicked and trembling voice, 'We gotta get out. He was calling for reinforcements to come get us. Let's get the phones and weapons from them and fuck off.'

They searched the insurgents, retrieving their phones and pistols before leaving the building as calmly as they could manage. They walked to the parked Subaru and drove off, Tom behind the wheel.

'Control from Alpha One Foot. Package secure, no injuries and we're exfil in vehicle. All units will RVP back at the palace,' said Tom.

'Thanks, man. I thought we were toast,' said Mike in between heavy breaths, the panic and shock still visible on his face.

2

Tom, Damien, and Buster met with Mike and Hamed back in the briefing room, all clutching large mugs of tea. The atmosphere was thick with a mixture of tension and relief. Both CIA agents seemed to have visibly aged since the pre-deployment briefing with the strain of their recent experience. Tom yawned as he leaned back in one of the cheap chairs.

'So, what went wrong, then?' Damien asked.

'Al-Ahmed must have been compromised,' said Mike, his blue eyes etched with a mixture of relief and regret. 'He was terrified when we got there, saying that they were on to him and we must get him out. He wasn't making much sense when the other two goons turned up; they iced Al-Ahmed without a word and, before we knew it, we were screwed,'

'They were on the phone straight away to someone,' added Hamed, 'saying they had American kuffars, and telling someone to send people to come get us. They were delighted and clearly expecting plenty dollars for us. Thank fuck you got us out, Tom.'

'Forget about it,' said Tom with a half-smile.

'Seriously, Tom,' said Mike, 'I've been a CIA agent for long enough to have seen some bad shit and seen some bad mother-fuckers do some bad stuff to bad guys, but I've never seen anyone as icy and calm as you. It was like you were just taking out the garbage, or something. Which I guess, in a way, you were!'

Tom shifted, feeling a little discomfort at the American's words, his awkwardness made stronger by a snort of amusement from Buster.

Buster smiled. 'They used to call Tom "the Balkan Psycho", or "Bootneck Robot", after he killed loads of Taliban when he was sniping in Afghan. He doesn't show much emotion, does our Tom, and he's not prone to panic.'

Tom gave a half-smile that he hoped hid his disquiet. It was true that he had killed many times over in Afghanistan as a sniper with the Royal Marines, and each time had not felt even a flicker of emotion. No revelling in the red mist of an exploded Taliban head from a thousand metres. No regret, no celebration, just... Nothing. It didn't make him feel comfortable with himself. It was the reason he had quit being a sniper and moved to SRR. He wanted to be a door-watcher, not a door-knocker. He hadn't wanted to confront that absence of emotion, the void he felt in spite of having just killed once again.

Buster continued, a look of embarrassment now in his grey eyes. 'I'm sorry we took so long, guys. We were happily parked up nearby when a fuck-off big lorry blocked us in at the off-side and an SUV came right tight up our arses. I had to pull a bit of pavement-mounting action, pissing off lots of pedestrians.'

'Our regular army reaction force got in pretty quickly and must have scared everyone else away,' said Damien. 'The two bodies are being tagged and bagged, and hopefully we can get an ID on them.'

Mike nodded. 'The phones are hopefully going to give us some leads on who ordered this. The intel will be valuable ... but, fuck, that was too close. I had visions of us in some video in orange boiler suits getting our heads cut off.'

'We have to get back to the Embassy,' said Hamed. 'Everyone is jumping up and down and wants to know what happened. The President wants updating,' he added, with a trace of nervousness.

The group stood and there were handshakes all round.

Mike gripped Tom in a hug, the emotion detectable in the tension of his muscles. 'Tom, I'll never be able to repay you for what you just did. You saved our lives, man. You ever need anything—I mean anything—you call me. I'll always owe you.' He handed Tom a business card on which was listed two phone numbers and an email address.

'No worries,' grinned Tom. 'Orange wouldn't have suited you two.'

'I mean it, Tom: I'll never forget this.' And with a nod they left.

Buster smiled at his friend. 'Good work, Borat. But can we try and have a week or two now where you don't kill anyone?'

'Buster,' Tom said.

'Yeah?'

'Fuck off.' Tom smiled as he delivered the insult. Buster was a piss-taker, but he was a good man, a good operator, and a very good friend. He clapped Buster on the back and left the room to search for a phone.

It was a familiar urge he had after every violent contact he was involved in: he just wanted to hear his foster father, Cameron's, voice.

The piss-taking that Tom received from comrades about his lack of emotions had caused him some reflection over the years. Tom would laugh along with his friends, but it concerned him enough to make him google the traits of a psychopath. Ticking off these traits didn't make things any clearer, though: he wasn't cruel, he had morals, and he believed he always wanted to protect the innocent, but he still felt nothing. Maybe all those good things were just learnt behaviours; after all, he had always followed Cameron's mantra: 'Always do right, boy.'

He soon found the troops' welfare phone, a secure mobile phone that was cleared for use for personal calls, with each soldier given a limited allocation of minutes to use.

'Hello?'

'Hi, Cameron, it's Tom,' he said in a cheery voice. 'Just checking in.'

He hadn't spoken to his foster parents, Cameron and Shona Ferguson, for a few weeks, given the humdrum chaos of deployment without action. But at that moment, with Buster's words still ringing in his ears, it was the only thing he wanted to do.

'Hey, son, how's it going?' Tom could imagine the big grin splitting his foster father's rugged face.

'All a bit boring here, to be honest,' Tom said. Cameron knew not to press: an ex-bootneck himself, he knew he wouldn't get an answer.

They talked about nothing in particular for about ten minutes, with Cameron boasting about some enormous trout he'd allegedly recently caught. As always, discussions were a front for the comfort of hearing each other's voices. Tom rang off and stepped out into the cool air

He thought about Cameron and Shona and when they had taken him in, a scared twelve-year-old boy from Bosnia. They lived in a beautiful little farm cottage on the edge of the Cairngorm mountain range. On arrival he had felt like he'd arrived home after the fog of the city, and was happy to have left that sense of claustrophobia behind.

Life had been wonderful and, sometimes, Tom had managed to forget the pain of losing his parents that still sat deep in his chest. Life went on, as always, and Cameron had known that keeping Tom busy and active was the only way to keep the boy moving forwards.

Tom shook his head and cleared the moment of reflection. He was hungry and needed something to eat. It wouldn't be long before they were back out on the Basra streets once again.

3

14 years later
London

Tom drove his anonymous hatchback along Kilburn High Road, following a Friday late-shift as Duty Detective Sergeant. It had been a busy night with two stabbings and a raft of domestic assaults, meaning that by the end of the night every cell in the nick at Kilburn was full. He was supposed to finish at 10pm but it had been closer to midnight before he managed to get the decks cleared and handed over to the next Duty DS. It had been frustrating and for a moment he once again cursed his decision to take the promotion.

His previous job on the Homicide Task Force, part of the Homicide and Serious Crime Command, had been far more interesting and, he had to admit, a damn sight sexier. Lots of surveillance work against some very bad people: covert operations and man-hunts for murderers. But his attitude towards the job had been tainted thanks to some of the managers he'd worked for, who were ambitious just for the sake of ambition. They would use any situation simply as another means of furthering their career, and as another addition to their portfolios. Tom found all that self-serving to be so different from the military, and not in a good way. So, as he couldn't beat them, he decided to seek promotion so that, maybe, he could balance the careerists out by being the best DS he could. In essence, he wanted to make a difference. But he was quickly finding that he'd wasted his bloody time.

In the name of ambition, he'd given it all up for the chance to manage a ridiculous case-load with insufficient resources. His team consisted of just him and a handful of DCs and trainees, all trying—and barely managing—to handle crime in a very busy London borough. It was the same all over in the age of austerity. Sod-all cops, rising crime, and forever shifting priorities from virtue-signalling senior officers. It was hard not to get cynical and jaded.

In spite of all that, he'd grown to enjoy living in London. He liked that he was close to work and didn't have to commute. He actually enjoyed the contrast with his earlier life in Scotland and Bosnia before that. He'd kept a foothold in Scotland with a small bothy he'd bought cheaply years ago that was perched on the side of a Munro in the Cairngorms, and which he loved dearly, spending his precious leave up there shooting and fishing with Cameron.

As he drove, he continued to listen to the Airwave radio he always took home with him. He switched to the Camden channel as he left Brent. He'd been accused on many occasions of being job-pissed: Met vernacular for being a little over-keen. It was probably a fair comment, he conceded to himself. He'd never grown tired of locking up bad guys during his eight years in the Met and couldn't really understand those that had.

As he drove along West End Lane, he heard the Camden radio channel spark up with a fairly stressed-sounding transmission from an old colleague, Sergeant Dale Rogers, calling for assistance. It seemed that he was having difficulty arresting Tony O'Reilley, who was wanted on a recall-to-prison order. Tom knew O'Reilley well: an absolute monster of a man with a long criminal history almost exclusively for violence. 'Ten Man Tony' was his nickname, owing to the fact that ten officers could be needed to nick him if he wasn't being cooperative. Tom had had dealings with him when in uniform at Camden and later as a Detective Constable and had always managed to get through to him. From the radio chatter, it became clear that no backup was imminent, and he could hear an unusual note of concern in Dale's voice. Tom picked up the radio.

'Echo Kilo from DS Novak. I'm close by: show me assisting.'

A minute later, Tom pulled up outside a drab terraced house on a side street just off Haverstock Hill.

A response car was pulled up outside, its blue lights strobing. Tom walked up the path to the door, where he met Dale.

'Anything I can help with, Dale?'

'Blimey, Tom, what are you doing here?' He was a stocky Londoner with a cheerful smile and receding hair. At his side was an impossibly young-looking PC who looked like he was going to faint through fear.

'This is Steve, my newest probationer,' said Dale. 'Ten Man Tony is inside and refusing to come without a tear-up. You know what he's like. There's only me and Steve; everyone's tucked-up at a huge fight in Camden Town.'

Tom smiled. 'I've not seen Tony for ages; want me to have a word?'

'Be my guest, but he's in a right fucking mood tonight. He's probably looking at another year inside, minimum, and I reckon he doesn't fancy it.'

'Turn the blues off then, Dale; no need to up the ante. I'll go and have a word with him. He knows me.'

The front door was slightly ajar, so Tom rapped lightly on it, noting that it bore all the hallmarks of previous damage: probably the result of a police battering ram.

A loud, aggressive 'Fuck off!' bawled from within in a familiar cockney/Irish brogue. Tom smiled to himself, gently pushed the door open, and walked casually inside. O'Reilley sat in the kitchen with a scowl on his face, stripped to the waist to show off his torso, an assortment of badly-worked tattoos across his arms and chest. The layer of flab on display couldn't disguise the power that lurked within his huge physique.

'Hey, Tony. Long time no see.'

O'Reilley's scowl immediately softened, replaced by uncertainty.

'Mr Novak, what you doin' here? I thought this weren't your

manor no more.' His face turned puzzled and slightly introspective at the sight of Tom.

'I'm just passing and fancied a chat, as I've not seen you for ages. So, what's the problem, Tony?' Tom said in a soft, steady voice. 'There's a warrant, fellah: no point taking it out on these two officers.'

He paused as he faced Tony, taking care to appear unthreatening and projecting no emotion. Tony O'Reilley was like a dog: he could smell fear. They stayed like that for a full two minutes. Tom never feared a long pause in a conversation, remembering his foster father's words: 'Don't let someone else's discomfort in a silence encourage you to say something unwise, my boy.'

'It was that fucking child-in-uniform, Mr Novak,' O'Reilley spat. 'I promise you, if he tries to lay his hands on me again, I'm gonna knock the fucker right out. I'm not getting nicked by him, not even for you, Mr Novak.' He was still fuming, but Tom thought he could detect some of the man's anger beginning to ebb away.

Tom didn't reply, instead picking up an upturned kitchen chair, placing it back down the right way up and sitting down with a sigh, his arms folded in front of him. He crossed his legs and fixed O'Reilley with a calm and even stare, his face relaxed and calm.

O'Reilley spoke once again, still angry but the fight starting to dissipate from him. 'He was taking a right fucking liberty, thinking he could lay hands on me like that. Nearly shit himself, mind.'

'Tony, I'm tired. It's been really busy and all I want is to go home and have a whisky. Are you really going to keep this up?' Tom spoke quietly but firmly, with a half-smile on his face.

O'Reilley puffed out his cheeks in exasperation. 'Fuck's sake. I don't want to go to jail again, not now.'

Tom fixed O'Reilley with a direct stare for another full minute.

'Right, Tony, here's the deal. You're going to go outside, quietly, let that young officer cuff you, and you're going to have to go to the nick. There's no alternative, fellah: there's a warrant. If you play the big fight-and-roll-around game, then they're just going to call

all sorts of cavalry with tasers and CS gas. You'll get hurt, and no doubt some of them will too, but you'll still end up in the nick. The only difference will be that you'll be facing all sorts of assault charges, and your six-month recall to Pentonville will end up as two years, pal.' Tom spoke in almost mesmeric tones.

O'Reilley sighed and paused for a further full minute. 'You always talked sense, Mr Novak. I guess you're right; I can't be arsed with another two years in the nick.' His shoulders sagged a little before he hauled himself up and pulled his sweatshirt back on.

'Come on, then. Let's fuck off,' he said, resignation in his voice.

They left the house together and O'Reilley walked up to the young constable, his arms held out passively in front of him.

'Sorry, officer. I can be a bit of a dick sometimes.'

The young, quaking officer snapped handcuffs on O'Reilley, only just managing to encircle them round his thick wrists. O'Reilley then meekly clambered into the rear of the police Astra, the officer joining him in the back before formally arresting and cautioning him.

'Cheers, Tom,' said Dale. 'You ever considered a career as a lion tamer, or hypnotist?'

Tom laughed. 'He'll be fine now. You okay if I bugger off? I'm on my way home.'

'Yeah, no bother mate. Meet for a pint next week?'

Tom nodded with a smile, got back into his own car, and drove off.

In the police Astra, the probationary officer turned to his superior. 'Jesus, Sarge, who was that and how did he manage what I just saw?'

His supervisor grinned. 'Son, DS Tom Novak could talk anyone down. He's apparently a hard man but no one's ever seen him in action; he always talks people into the car with a smile. He's a really cold fish, though. I could never work him out.' They carried on to Kentish Town Station, with O'Reilley silent in the rear.

4

Tom walked past the Wilsons Sheet Metal sign at the entrance to the converted warehouse, the sole reminder of the building's former life, and let himself into the ground-floor apartment. The sheet metal door clanged shut with a satisfying solidity as he keyed the code into the keypad. The alarm system was much more sophisticated than any of his neighbours' and that, combined with the industrial door and barred windows, formed his very own Fort Knox: his sanctuary from all the London stink and crime.

He was thankful for owning such a nice place: peaceful yet convenient, and close to all the amenities that Camden was known for. The legacy left by his Mama had been put to good use; Cameron was pretty shrewd and had seen the London property price rises ahead of everyone else.

The centrepiece of the big, open-plan apartment was a makeshift gym: a pull-up bar hung above a stretching zone, a punch bag, and a weights bench with a full selection of dumbbells. In pride of place on the wall was a silk escape map of a desolate part of Iraq, framed above the TV.

He'd bought the place when he was living with Bev in the even more North London area of Colindale but, as they'd split up while it was still being converted, he'd tweaked the plans to make it the ultimate bachelor pad. He sometimes missed Bev but, he had to admit, not a great deal: she'd wanted more that he'd felt able to give. He certainly didn't miss the constant arguments about how difficult he was to live with ever since he'd joined the CID. He'd left the Forces so they could give the relationship a proper go, but he had just replaced the constant deployments chasing dangerous terrorists with ridiculous hours chasing criminals. Bev had given him an ultimatum and, as much as he had thought he loved her, it wasn't a hard decision. He had chosen the job.

He went over to the battered oak sideboard and selected a bottle from a row of thirty alphabetised bottles of whisky. His time in Scotland and the influence of his foster father had given him an appreciation of fine, malt whiskies: the perfect tool to help put the world to rights.

He poured a good measure of a sixteen-year-old Lagavulin into a crystal glass and deeply inhaled the evocative, peaty aroma, instantly transporting him back to the Highlands. He added a couple of chilled, granite whisky stones and sat on the large corner sofa, nestling into the rich leather.

He sat for a few minutes, letting the stresses of a busy, frustrating day evaporate from his body. Promotion had seemed the right thing to do, but he was quickly finding the frustrations of man-management, targets, and performance criteria difficult to reconcile. He missed the adrenaline rush of a manhunt, the surveillance follows, collaring a villain. All of that had been replaced with target-driven monotony and performance indicators.

He switched on the TV and turned to the sports channels, selecting Cage Warrior's Mixed Martial Arts: a middleweight bout between two unnamed fighters. He was a big fan of the sport but quickly found himself getting frustrated. The defending champion was all over the place. 'For fuck's sake, get some side-control, you pillock,' he muttered at the TV.

His work phone winked at him, indicating that an email had landed in his inbox. He wearily picked up the handset and read the message from his boss, DCI Simon Taylor. Apparently DS Neil Wilkinson from SC&O35, the covert policing command, wanted to speak to him urgently the next morning about a potential deployment. There was a contact number in the email and Taylor signed off with, 'Don't think this gets you out of late-turn, Tom, we're short of manpower already.'

Tom allowed himself a wry grin. He knew Neil Wilkinson from previous operations; he was a good man who wouldn't take any nonsense from a desk-jockey like Simon Taylor.

He hadn't deployed undercover since promotion, and his interest picked up at the prospect. After the past few months staring at a computer screen and crime statistics, the prospect of a deployment caused a slow smile of anticipation to creep across his face.

He drained his whisky and headed off to bed.

*

Tom woke early and dressed in clean jeans and a dark polo shirt, selected from a meticulously-organised wardrobe holding a line of five identical polo shirts hanging on the rail next to several pairs of identical jeans. He didn't like wasting mental energy deciding what to wear. For business-wear, he had three identical blue suits together with five identical white shirts. There was another wardrobe in the bedroom that held a supply of more gaudy casual clothes, used for undercover work.

He ran his hand over his chin, noting the dark stubble pushing through his jaw line. He toyed with the idea of shaving and then shook his head; if deployment was likely, then some sort of beard gave him more options for his appearance.

Using his work phone, he called the number for Neil Wilkinson.

'Hello?' came the voice from the other end.

'Hello, boss, it's Tom Novak. You wanted to speak?'

'Tom! How you doing, mate? Not seen you since you jumped on the promotion bandwagon! How you been?'

'Fine thanks, boss. Up to my neck in petty crime and domestics. Plus for some reason the DCI is holding me personally responsible for the clear-up rate for hate crimes that aren't actually crimes.'

'Well I may have something to liven up your working hours, if you're interested. Can you get to ESB later today?'

'Well I'm late-turn but I could get to you a bit before then. My

DCI is being a bit antsy about manpower.'

'No bother. Say about twelve? Don't worry about Simon Taylor, my dad's bigger than his,' Wilkinson said with obvious amusement.

Just before 12pm, Tom sat in the canteen on the top floor of the Empress State Building: or ESB, as everyone referred to it. It was a large, twenty-eight-storey tower block near Earls Court, housing many differing Met units and HR functions. It had been gradually absorbing all sorts of staff as the old building at Scotland Yard was run down.

Unusually, it had a very good canteen—or restaurant, as management insisted on calling it—its revolving floor giving fabulous views of the whole of London, making it a popular location for impromptu meetings and pow-wows. Lots of deals, over and under the table, got done on the twenty-eighth floor of the ESB.

Tom sat in one of the booths cradling a coffee as he waited for Neil to arrive. He saw a few familiar faces and exchanged nods that displayed friendliness but didn't encourage any further approach. Neil Wilkinson only ever dealt in covert conversations.

Tom raised a finger in a subtle greeting as Neil approached his booth, smiling a greeting and clutching a Styrofoam cup. He was a slight, wiry man with neat grey hair and spectacles which seemed too large for his face. As usual, he was immaculately dressed in a well-fitting grey suit, blindingly-white shirt, and sober tie. He offered his hand and Tom shook it warmly.

'Tom, good to see you. How's life back in the real world of territorial policing?'

Territorial policing—or TP—was the business of day-to-day law enforcement across London's thirty-two boroughs.

Tom gave the expected raise of the eyebrows and replied, 'A little weary, if I'm honest, boss. I miss homicide but, for some reason, promotion seemed a good idea.'

'Had to be done, fellah, had to be done. Can't be a DC your whole life. Anyway, down to business. I understand you're Bosnian by birth?' Neil Wilkinson was famed for his lack of small talk and tendency to always get straight to the point.

'Yes, boss. Came over as a refugee as a twelve-year-old and got citizenship at eighteen.'

Neil paused a moment. 'We've received a request from Home Office Immigration Enforcement for an undercover officer to infiltrate a gang of Bosnian traffickers. They're bringing young girls over from Sarajevo, passing them off as Slovenians, and sham marrying them off for visas and prostituting them out.' He paused to take a sip of his coffee before continuing.

'It looks a good job on the face of it. May be a bit of travel. They're bad bastards and some of these poor girls have come over to the cops. One or two of the girls initially said they had been sexually assaulted but seem far too scared to put pen to paper. A couple of the traffickers have been nicked but the main players are still untouchable, and they have a bent solicitor helping them out as well. It's high-profile stuff and everyone's under pressure to stop these girls coming into the UK. Sound up your street?'

Tom pretended to consider for a moment. 'Sounds very interesting, boss, I'd be happy to have a look. Can you square it with my DCI?' He didn't want to appear too keen, but in reality he was trying not to give the impression of biting Neil's hand clean off.

'That's no problem, Tom. I know Simon well enough. Once he realises the level this is coming from, he'll have no choice. I understand the Home Secretary is taking a personal interest in the operation, what with trafficking being so current. What we need to do is sort out a meeting with the operational lead at the Home Office. He's an ex-superintendent from the Met who's landed himself a senior role setting up this new investigative team. I'll speak to him and organise a meet. How's your Bosnian by the way?'

Tom smiled. 'It's not too bad. I grew up speaking Serb, but I can get by in most of the languages spoken over there, they're all very similar.'

'That's great, Tom. I'll be in touch.' He stood up, draining his cup. 'Right, I have to run. I have an assistant commissioner about to kick the crap out of me about my ridiculous overtime budget, which I've smashed to bits as usual.'

With that, he shot Tom a smile and strode off. It was typical of Neil Wilkinson; he didn't waste time on the niceties.

Not for the first time, Tom was pleased that his foster parents had insisted he kept some link to his country of birth. While growing up in the Highlands he would often visit a very small resource centre in Inverness that offered support to refugees. There he'd met a kind, old Serbian man called Filip, who'd talked with him in Serbian about the old country once or twice a month. It had kept his grasp of the language intact, meaning that he could still converse well in Serbo-Croat even after all those years. Many of the adjacent countries' languages were based on the same Slav rules, which had proved useful in his career when investigating crimes among his countrymen.

Tom finished his coffee and left the building deep in thought. An undercover deployment? He'd done a few, mostly on drug buy/busts, but not for a while. He felt a slight prickle of excitement. It sounded like a tricky assignment, but he would've tried anything to get away from the mundane quest for clear-up rates and detections, even if it did piss his boss off. Especially if it pissed his boss off.

Anyway, there was every chance it would not come off. There were so many hoops to jump through to get assignments like those authorised, that they often got cancelled at the last minute. He put it out of his mind and made his way to Kilburn, ready for another weary late-turn, sat in front of a computer terminal, juggling too much crime with insufficient resources.

Like most undercover-trained officers, Tom had a day job: in his case, running a small team of detectives on a volume crime team dealing with day-to-day minor crimes. He could, however, be called on to fulfil an undercover role if one came up that suited his profile and legend, or back story. He hadn't had many deployments since completing his undercover course a couple of years before, and the prospect of a more involved spell undercover was appealing. It would certainly be a break from the deathly boring and frustrating crime-report-shuffling he was forced to do every day. Once again, he questioned his decision to get promoted. His skills and experience were wasted stuck behind a desk when he should be out there, nicking big villains.

He got to Kilburn just before 2pm. As he passed DCI Taylor's office his superior called, 'Tom, a minute please.'

Tom wandered in, trying to look innocent and hide his pleasure at his boss looking none-too-pleased. Taylor was quite young for a DCI: skinny-fat with sandy, thinning hair, a permanent air of panicky stress hanging round him like a cloud. Taylor was renowned for being ambitious and would do anything to get the next rank up, no matter who he had to trample on.

'Tom, I've been called by Detective Superintendent Wilkinson; you will be assisting his team on some deployment. I've told him it's not good at all, that we're strapped, and my clear-up rate will suffer. It seems, however, that you may be the only person with the requisite skills, despite the fact he won't tell me what it's about.'

It would have upset Taylor more than anything to not be cleared to know what his staff member was going to be doing. He didn't look happy at all. Tom tried hard to keep a straight face.

'So, it looks like you're going,' Taylor continued, 'but don't think this excuses you from your day job right now, so get cracking. There's been another raft of domestic assaults that all need supervising. I want a progress report by close-of-play.' The DCI turned back to his computer screen, indicating that the meeting was over. Tom walked out, unable to keep the smile spreading across his face.

He walked to his desk, offering greetings to colleagues as he passed them. He received a few nods and greetings in return; everything professional and distant, just the way he preferred things. In any case, they were all too busy to engage in much more than simple pleasantries as they beavered away on phones and tapped away at computers, trying their best to stay on top of the constant merry-go-round of territorial policing.

His phone buzzed in his pocket and he checked the screen to

see a message from Neil Wilkinson. '1100hrs tomorrow, Becket House, St Thomas Street, EC1 for meeting with Home Office, I've told your boss, rgds, Neil.'

Becket House! The memories from all those years ago swarmed into his head: his mother attending that very same immigration reporting centre, stood in the queue for hours, waiting to see if their application for asylum had been granted.

Game on, he thought with a smile.

5

Tom woke early, as normal, and launched straight into his morning routine: a forty-five minute hard run around the Kentish Town streets. He followed this with a high-intensity circuit in his indoor gym: a minute on the punch bag, a minute's skipping, a minute of push-ups, sit-ups, and burpees, with no rest between each set. And then repeat.

Fifteen minutes later he allowed himself to rest, breathing deeply as his pulse dropped back to normal before jumping into the shower. Pulling on clean jeans, a light shirt and a bomber jacket, he wolfed down a breakfast of scrambled eggs on toast with plenty of black coffee as he checked his phone for messages.

The screen lit up with a message from Neil Wilkinson.

'Still on for eleven?' Brief as ever.

Tom replied just as briefly.

'Yes.'

He thought about the task at hand as he nursed his coffee at the kitchen island, enjoying the feel of the cool granite against his arms.

Sham marriages were a big problem: female EU citizens trafficked to Britain and forced into marriages with non-EU men who were typically from India, Pakistan or parts of Africa. The marriages were simply for the purpose of keeping those foreign nationals in the UK for as long as possible. Once the ceremony was done, the girls were either forced to work as prostitutes, or just shipped back home. The sums involved were eye-watering, with as much as £10,000 a time paid by the grooms to secure their place in the UK. It was a trade in misery, with many of the women treated dreadfully and paid very little, if anything.

Tom thought of his previous undercover legend, which had been remarkably similar to his own story, as a Balkan orphan, living in the UK since age twelve. That and previous deployments so far had generally been in supporting roles: a bit of muscle, a drug courier and, on one occasion, buying £100,000 of moody—or more accurately, counterfeit—bank notes from a Kosovan dealer. This new assignment, though, sounded meaty: an infiltration. The thought caused a flicker of excitement to flush through his body.

He'd left the military to lead a more normal existence, to try to be a normal guy in a normal home with a normal relationship. He had failed on all accounts. Being a cop had gone from being a job to almost an obsession. On the homicide team, ninety-hour weeks were commonplace, and he had been too wrapped up in the job to realise that his relationship was failing.

He had simply failed to notice how dissatisfied Bev had been with his constant absences. He had obsessed about work even when he was at home, constantly researching on the internet, trying to understand every aspect of crime and criminals.

When Bev left him, he wondered whether he would always be on his own, and whether he was capable of maintaining a normal relationship or even leading a normal life, whatever that meant. It was confusing.

He did miss the adrenaline rush of his military days with the SRR, though. He certainly didn't get it shuffling virtual papers on computerised crime-recording databases, searching for extra clear-ups and detections. This new assignment could be just the ticket. He laced up his trainers, picked up his jacket, and left the apartment with a distinct spring in his step and a smile forming on his face.

*

Tom walked along St Thomas Street from London Bridge

station in the shadow of the thousand-foot-tall Shard tower, the bright morning sun reflecting off its brilliant, polished glass. He approached Becket House, a long queue full of so many different races and nationalities already snaking out of the door, all of them waiting to sign-on or for appointments to learn their fate. Frustration and desperation hung palpably over the line, hopes and dreams hanging in the balance. A few stared sullenly at him as he walked straight past them to the main entrance, where he showed his pass to the security guard on duty, who ushered him through and into a lift which ascended to the top of the drab, grey building.

He was shown to a secure office at the end of the corridor, inside of which was Neil Wilkinson with two colleagues.

Neil jumped to his feet, a bundle of energy as usual. 'Tom, this is Assistant Director Pete De-Glanville, who runs the North Area Crime Team, and this is HM Inspector Jean MacDonald, Senior Investigator on the job we're hoping you can help on.' Handshakes were proffered and accepted all round.

'Perhaps Jean can give you a little of the background, and we can go from there.'

Jean clicked a remote control, turning as a PowerPoint presentation sprang to life on a screen in front of them.

She was of slender build, with collar-length dark hair and a subtle air of confidence about her. She gave the impression of knowing her stuff, thought Tom: probably an ex-Customs investigator. When Customs and Immigration had merged into the UK Borders Agency a few years back, a lot of good investigators got spread all over the place into all sorts of roles. Tom had worked with a few 'Cuzzies' in the past and found them to be a mixed bag. They were red-hot with phone intercepts, though, and he wondered if one was being used on this job. He wouldn't ask as he knew he wouldn't be told. When the Government wrote the law on intercepts, they put strict secrecy rules in place; you weren't allowed to ask, and no one was allowed to tell. Everyone knew the score, however, and you could normally tell when a line was on:

intelligence of that quality doesn't just come from thin air. When there was an informant about then you knew about it; but when a line was being used, all you would get told was something like, 'Reliable intelligence suggests that Mr X is on his way now to pick up a great big bag of drugs.' It didn't take a genius to work it out. It often led to a bit of dancing around the issue at court, though, when defence barristers suspected the truth. They weren't allowed to ask, and it couldn't be used as evidence in any case: it could sometimes be quite amusing.

'Operation Springfield' was the headline on the screen. Jean cleared her throat and spoke in a broad Glaswegian accent.

'Op Springfield is the investigation into a Bosnian Serb gang that are trafficking vulnerable women into the UK from Sarajevo, mostly with the intention of working them as prostitutes and, as a bonus, using them for sham marriages to foreign nationals already here. Once married, they claim EU status and get a five-year stay. The grooms are charged a fortune, up to ten grand a pop.'

She pressed the remote, and the slide changed to mug-shots of four men and a woman.

'These are our main subjects. Sat at the top is Mira Branko, who is also the mother of Aleks and Luka Branko. Mira's husband, Zjelko Branko, is currently in jail in Switzerland serving a nine-year sentence. He was apparently very well connected and involved in high-value robberies of jewellers all over Europe and beyond. Interpol have him pegged as one of the Pink Panther diamond thieves who've been tearing the arse out of all the high-priced jewellers in Monaco and places like that, proper multi-million-pound thefts. There is intelligence that he was an active paramilitary during the Balkan wars and was responsible for some terrible acts. We also have some unconfirmed intelligence that he was responsible for a number of contract killings that took place across the Balkans. All-in-all, he is a thoroughly dangerous sadist. We have literally just managed to deport their footsoldiers: Zoran Radic and Mirko Zoric. All five came over in the nineties as refugees and one of our caseworkers managed to prove that Zoran and Mirko came over on false documents. This obviously leaves us in a position where they are now short-handed and may be looking for a new recruit to assist them. This is where we hope you can come in. Any questions so far?'

Tom had nothing yet, so Inspector McDonald continued.

'Mira tends to deal with the girls and acts as the Madam when they're working in the pop-up brothels. The brothers recruit them in Sarajevo and bring them over on forged or stolen Slovenian passports, which is handy for them with Slovenia being in the EU. They generally come overland by car and ferry, but sometimes by air. Mira can be particularly spiteful and treats the girls like crap once they're here.

'They've been using a dirty solicitor in East London to make the introductions to prospective grooms and submit the applications to Visas and Immigration once the sham marriage has gone down.' She pressed the remote again and an image of an African man in his thirties flashed onto the screen. He was slim, with thinning hair, a clipped beard, and moustache. He was smiling slightly at the camera; Tom guessed it was a publicity photograph. The man had deep-set, impenetrable eyes that projected no warmth to accompany the smile.

'This is Michael Adebayo. He is the sole solicitor at Adebayo Associates Solicitors, and he came to the UK aged eight with his parents. He's a Christian by birth but converted to Islam at university. His firm is an immigration specialist and the analysts looking at the applications he has submitted have raised some serious concerns. We think he is submitting hundreds of corrupt applications every year. It seems he is active at the local mosque and, as he's been so successful, he is inundated with clients of all nationalities. In the eight years Adebayo Associates have been trading, he has submitted over seven thousand applications, many with serious question marks about them. Financially, he is very wealthy and has made a fortune out of his trade. He's the only solicitor at the firm; the other staff are unqualified caseworkers. He's a clever man as he only employs local employees who are all multi-lingual, so he can see and deal with all types of clients. He is a terrible employer and a really nasty piece of work, apparently: everyone is terrified of him. He also has a brother, Emmanuel Adebayo, who seems to be his link to the underworld.'

A further image flashed up on the screen of another African male who looked similar to Michael Adebayo but with a much larger build, close-cropped hair and a short, trimmed goatee beard. His face was twisted in a grim, arrogant expression and his flat, dull eyes were so dark they almost looked black.

'We think Emmanuel sorts the forged documents required for supporting bogus applications and provides security and muscle if things get a bit lively with unsatisfied customers, of which there are lots. He got out of prison a year ago: he got four years for GBH after he battered one of his brother's customers to a pulp when he went to his office to complain that his application for leave to remain got refused—'

'Jean, do we have a source for any of that intelligence?' Neil interrupted.

'Not directly into the solicitor's firm, but there has been some anonymous intelligence, probably from ex-staff members and clients about his business practices. We can't just go storming into his offices: because of legal privilege we'd get our arses sued off. We need a solid, prima facie case before we go in. We do have a live informant on the periphery of the Bosnians. He's done some work with the Branko brothers, but he's not a hard man so is of no real use to them. I think they'll need some extra muscle and you could be that muscle, Tom.' She fixed him with an appraising look.

Not an intercept then, thought Tom.

'I understand from Neil that you're something of an expert in martial arts?' she asked.

Tom suppressed a grin. 'I wouldn't use the word expert, Jean. I've wrestled and boxed pretty much all my life and I've been doing Muay Thai and ju-jitsu for about ten years. I can probably hold my own,' he said modestly. The truth was that, had Tom led a more settled life, he could have achieved a great deal of competitive success in any one of his disciplines.

'How are your languages? I understand they speak English most of the time, having been here many years. But any ability you have could only help.'

'I'm okay in Serbo-Croat and can manage in most of the region's dialects,' said Tom. 'They're pretty similar.'

Peter De-Glanville piped up at last. 'How much more information will you need on the big picture?' he asked.

'I prefer not to know too much,' Tom replied. 'It makes it easier to be natural once I meet them. Who are your priorities here?'

De-Glanville paused for a moment. 'Ideally we want the lot of them, but with the amount of applications coming in from the solicitor, we want to take him down as a priority. It makes a better headline and will save us a lot of time and money. The Brankos would be a bonus; I have to say, some of the intelligence reports filtering through make it clear that the brothers are very nasty. Some of their clients have been sadistically beaten, particularly by Luka: it seems he enjoys inflicting pain. The victims are all too scared to come forward and go on record, given the reputation of the Branko family. It seems they have inherited their father's violent tendencies.'

'Any info on guns by the gang?' asked Tom.

'Not that we know about, although their father is heavily linked with firearms from his paramilitary days. My understanding is that they intimidate physically. The punters they engage with aren't villains, they're just desperate to stay in the UK,' Jean said.

Wilkinson nodded. 'I think we have enough background. We need to get a cover officer assigned and develop Tom's undercover legend, make sure it's all back-stopped. It's not bad already, but it needs some tweaking so it can hold water. Can the informant do an introduction into the Branko's gang for Tom?'

De-Glanville nodded. 'I'm told he's as reliable as any snout can be. The martial arts may be a good inner. Luka fancies himself as a bit of a cage fighter and he loves a tear-up. If Tom gives him a good bout, he'll be easily impressed and that might get him onside. We can arrange a meet with you guys and the informant and then come up with a plan. Jean will forward you by secure email a detailed briefing pack with all the photos and everything else you need.'

'Right,' said Neil, 'that's enough to be moving on with.'

*

Tom made his way back home, a briefing for the next day planned with his cover officer to iron out the plan around his legend. He would need to be ready for any questioning by the Branko brothers, especially as they were his countrymen. His interest in the assignment was high, especially as one of them was a solicitor. The fact that he had limited information didn't concern him; too much intelligence could be a dangerous thing and could cause unnatural reactions when deployed. If, for instance, he was told that one of the brothers always concealed a knife in his sock, it may cause him to react if a leg was innocently scratched. In many ways, it was safer not to know: if you could improvise, you could generally cope. Tom was confident in his ability to think on his feet; he'd had plenty of practise.

He got changed into his training gear and beasted himself with a punishing exercise routine for a full hour to clear his mind.

6

The gym was in a grubby Islington side street, just a stone's throw from Angel Tube station. Tom approached it with the informant, Ivan, a small, nervous young man in his twenties with sharp features and a wispy moustache and beard. He spoke good English, but they conversed in Serbian to maintain Tom's cover. They had already spent a couple of hours with Liam, the cover officer, coming up with a cover story which they'd deliberately kept very straightforward.

'I'm a simple man, Tom. You know my brain won't let me come up with a complicated cover story, so it won't,' Liam had said, exaggerating his sardonic Northern Irish accent. He was a funny man with a gentle, self-deprecating line in humour. He was very sharp, though, which contrasted with his rather hang-dog expression, messy greying hair and poor taste in clothing.

They agreed that Tom and Ivan's cover story was that they'd met in a pub and got chatting once they realised they were both Serbians. Tom was going to be known as Tomo Kovac, a refugee orphan from Sarajevo who had been more recently living in Glasgow, where he had done some security and door work before making his way to London to look for something new. He had in reality spent plenty of time in Glasgow and knew the city well, meaning that he could deal with any questions they may throw at him. He would present himself as being a bit dodgy and open to any offers that came his way.

The story was that Tomo was looking for a gym to train at for mixed martial arts, which would put him in the sights of the Branko brothers. Using his real first name would mean he would react naturally when it was used. He hoped that impressing the brothers in the ring would be the key to the infiltration. Ivan had said that Luka Branko was 'Good but not that good' at MMA fighting, but was good at Brazilian ju-jitsu and grappling. He liked to be tested but was in possession of a massive ego and apparently didn't react well if he lost. Tom was confident enough in his own ability to be able to take Luka close but still 'lose' by just enough to massage the Serbian's ego, and hopefully make the right impression.

In these assignments, legends were kept as simple and as close to the undercover officer's real history as possible. Simplicity made things easy to remember, especially when Ivan was introducing Tom to the Branko brothers. They wanted Ivan out of the picture pretty much straight away, as he wasn't a professional, would be very jumpy and, to be frank, Tom didn't trust him as far as he could throw him. Anyone willing to sell their friends and accomplices down the river for a few quid, or because of some pressure being applied, was at risk of switching sides back again if it was of some advantage to them. Informants were the lifeblood of covert policing, but Tom had never met one he could trust.

The cover story had been rehearsed and Liam, as cover officer, gave the official briefings, warning, as always, that Tom couldn't act as an agent provocateur. This meant he couldn't encourage others to commit a crime that they wouldn't have committed without his involvement.

They were ready.

As soon as they entered the gym, the smells and noises instantly relaxed Tom; it was an environment he'd known since childhood. Ever since his papa had taken him to wrestle in the gyms in Sarajevo, he'd relished getting involved in contact sports.

He'd carried this on after settling in Scotland and then into the military, practicing the disciplines of grappling, boxing, kick-boxing, and Brazilian Ju-Jitsu, or BJJ. BJJ had become popular in the Marines while he was serving and was his sport of choice. He enjoyed that it was highly technical as well as brutally physical.

Technique trumped size and power every time. The upside of BJJ was that you could practise all the time: something you couldn't do in boxing, kick-boxing, or MMA unless you wanted to spend all your life nursing concussions. You could go full-bore at BJJ and grappling and, every time you were locked or choked out, you learnt a little more. A smaller guy could easily defeat a much bigger guy simply through technical expertise.

When on deployments with SRR, BJJ practise had become a big part of their training regime. It could be practised anywhere, was relevant to the job, and was a good pastime in the long periods of inactivity that often blight soldiering.

The Islington gym was a large, cavernous area with big matted grappling zones, a weights zone, kettlebell racks, squat racks, and strong-man zones. Old tractor tyres, battle ropes, sledge hammers and atlas stones dotted the training areas. It was not a corporate gym with treadmills, cross trainers and weights machines, but a serious, no-frills establishment for dedicated trainers. Hard-core kit for hard-core workouts. Thumping heavy metal music shook the air, competing with the sounds of exertion, shouts and grunts from a mix of all types of people. City businessmen rubbed shoulders with rough looking, tattooed monsters and slim females, all training hard. The motto: 'Train Hard or Go Home' was emblazoned on a large poster on the wall facing the entrance. The painted walls streamed with condensation, rolling in rivulets down the chipped surfaces.

Ivan had a quiet word with the gym owner, a brute of a man in his fifties dressed in a grey sweatshirt and jeans, hunkered in front of a battered laptop. He looked Tom up and down, nodded and then said in a surprisingly light voice, 'I'm Tommy. This is my place. Have a trial week, mate, if you want. Ivan here tells me you're a handy MMA man. If you like it, we'll sort you out with a membership.' He winked and then turned back to his laptop.

Tom went into the changing rooms and emerged wearing shorts and a tight rash vest and trainers. He began gently warming up, going through a series of stretches and Pilates movements, while

Ivan kept a look-out for Luka. Tom's routine drew some quizzical looks from one or two of the guys pumping iron, but Tom smiled inwardly; he was always careful with his warm-ups and it helped him mentally. Once warm and stretched, he moved over to the squat rack and loaded up an Olympic bar and began his usual squat routine, loading the 20kg plates and increasing after every set. He started light, at 80kg, pushing the repetitions out with strict form, head back, pushing though the heels and lowering himself fully at the end of each repetition.

After a while he became aware that Ivan was watching him, accompanied by a well-built, muscular man with dirty blond hair and sleeve tattoos on both arms. He immediately recognised Luka from the briefing pictures. Ignoring both, he loaded the bar up with his working weight of 180kg, carefully pushed out a good solid six repetitions and then re-set the bar on the rack. As he finished, Ivan and Luka approached.

'Tomo, this is a friend of mine, Luka,' said Ivan. 'He loves a bit of BJJ and MMA. Luka, Tomo is a fellow countryman.'

Luka stepped forward, an imposing man with heavy Slav features and broad, muscular shoulders squeezed into a sweatshirt with the sleeves ripped off. He was powerfully built: a similar height to Tom at about six-foot-tall but at least twenty to thirty pounds heavier, mostly muscle. He extended his hand and gripped Tom's hand with a firm shake, smiling to show a row of crowded teeth.

'You any good at rolling, my friend? I always struggle to get someone to roll with, who can stay with me for more than a minute.' A glimmer of sarcasm was detectable in his deep, even voice. 'Rolling,' the term used by BJJ practitioners to describe practice bouts.

Tom met his stare. 'Good to meet you. I can roll pretty well; happy to help you out. I'll see if I can last more than a minute,'

'Where are you from, Tomo?' Suspicion and reserve deep in his face.

'Sarajevo. Came over when I was twelve at the start of the siege.'

'How come we've never met? Not so many of us Serbs about.'

A slight interrogation starting already, thought Tom. Not even a subtle one.

'I grew up in Scotland. I was an orphan and lived all over, but I've only been down here a couple of months. You want to roll, or talk?'

The Serbian smiled. 'Come on then, let's see if you're as tough as Ivan says.'

They moved through to the MMA area. Luka stripped off his sweatshirt and track pants, pulling on a skin-tight rash vest similar to Tom's. He was well-muscled but, Tom noticed with a touch of satisfaction, carrying a bit too much fat for proper efficiency. They faced each other on the matting in the dojo area, bumped fists, and then took the fighting stance.

BJJ is a little like a game of chess: move and counter-move, trying to lead an opponent down a particular route. It usually begins with standing holds, the aim being to take your opponent to the ground on your terms to try and get a submission from a joint-lock, choke, or compression-lock. Luka grabbed aggressively at Tom, trying to take the initiative and get him to ground quickly. As soon as Tom saw his opponent's approach, he knew he could beat him; Luka was rushing, and he was overly aggressive. He knew that he could easily counter and have him locked up in a heartbeat, but that wasn't the objective.

Tom let himself be taken down to the mat, falling into the half-guard. Luka pressed his weight across Tom's chest, trying but failing to get full control. It was an easy escape for Tom: he was much faster and fitter than the bigger man. Tom quickly got an elbow-lock in place—which he could have easily finished the bout with—but he kept it loose enough to allow Luka to escape and move into a dominant position. The bout continued in that way for a good six minutes: Tom allowing Luka to nearly win several times, before escaping and turning the tables for a brief moment. It prolonged the bout, but Tom knew he could have won several times over.

When Tom felt that Luka was tiring badly and at the end of his stamina, he finally allowed himself to be caught in a rear-choke, submitting with a double-tap of his hand on Luka's arm. Luka rolled off him with a huge gasp, exhausted. Tom exaggerated his breathing to match his opponent, pretending that it had taken him to the edge rather than just been a mild workout.

Luka looked delighted. 'Jesus, man, you're as tough as Ivan said. I struggled to beat you, took everything I know.' His sweaty face shone bright-red.

'Well done,' Tom gasped. 'You're a good fighter. I thought I had you once or twice.'

Both stood and shook hands. 'Come on, man; let's go and have a drink,' said Luka.

After showering and changing, both men left the gym. Ivan had excused himself, saying he had to see his woman, which suited Tom just fine.

They entered the Angel pub opposite the Tube station and both ordered pints of lager. Luka led Tom to a nearby table that was already occupied by a man of a similar size and build to Luka. Aleks Branko: Tom recognised him from the briefing photographs.

Luka introduced Tom to his brother. 'Aleks, this is Tomo, the first worthy opponent I've had for some time. I still kicked his ass though, eh, Tomo? This is Aleks, my older brother.'

Aleks fixed Tom with an even, unsmiling gaze. His face was scarred with old acne marks and he had the same blue eyes and stocky build as his brother. The coolness of his light eyes and his grim expression gave him an aura of barely-disguised cruelty.

Aleks nodded in Tom's general direction and said to his brother in Serbian, 'Who is he and where's he from?'

'He told you,' Tom replied in Serbian. 'I'm Tomo. I'm from Glasgow, but I was born in Sarajevo.'

Mild surprise spread across Aleks' face. 'I wasn't told you were a countryman. Bosniak?'

'Bosnian Serb, my friend, I just look a little dark; I think I've some Roma blood. But I'm an orphan; I don't really know.'

'You fight well, Tomo; where did you train?' asked Luka.

'Glasgow, mostly, but a fair bit all over. I started with boxing back in the homeland and wrestled at school in Sarajevo. I've always loved fighting sports. I also spent some time in Thailand at Muay Thai camps.'

'I've never been to Glasgow, or Scotland, for that matter. It's funny, I never met a Serb with a Scottish accent,' said Aleks.

Tom smiled and the tension dropped a notch. He had kept his normal accent for the deployment, but with just a touch more Slav. He knew from experience that it was too easy to slip back into his normal brogue after just a few hours undercover; Tom's usual accent was light Scottish with a trace of something else underneath.

'I like your T-shirt, man,' Aleks said, reaching across to feel the fabric of Tom's shirt. Tom tried his best to look comfortable in the gaudy Emporio Armani T-shirt, overly-designed stone-washed jeans and huge, glittering Brietling watch.

'Thanks. Armani is classy stuff,' Tom said.

'Where do you live now?' Luka asked.

'I got a place in Dalston. It's okay. Area's a bit of a shit-hole, though.'

SC&O35 had a small quantity of flats furnished and ready to go for undercover operatives to use while deployed. A very creative member of the team could very quickly personalise each flat to each individual officer with post and bills in the cover name and some personal effects to give the impression that the operative was living there. They would also stock the cupboards and fridge to reflect who was living there. In Tom's case that meant lots of beer and a few Pot Noodles. The whole place screamed 'Single Man'. It was fairly basic; Tom had stayed there a few times to make sure he was seen by the neighbours.

The three of them chatted amiably enough, mostly about MMA and fighting sports. Tom had no intention to raise the issue of trafficking or anything criminal: it was far too soon and would have to happen organically if he wasn't to arouse suspicion. But he was also determined to not forget that, in spite of the fairly friendly banter between them, he was dealing with violent, sadistic criminals.

After about half-an-hour, Tom stood and said, 'I have to go, guys. Good to meet you both and maybe we can roll again soon, Luka. I'll kick your butt next time.'

Luka snorted. 'In your dreams, skinny man. Sure, let's roll soon.'

They exchanged phone numbers and shook hands.

Tom left the pub and walked back to where he'd parked the old BMW he'd procured from the SC&O35 pool of covert cars and drove to the flat in Dalston. The car had been re-registered to his name at a Glasgow address which had been fully back-stopped to make sure that anyone investigating it wouldn't get any further. He really didn't fancy staying at the flat, but he couldn't risk going home at such an early stage of the assignment. He parked nearby, let himself in and made a cup of tea, sending a message to Liam updating him that initial contact had been made.

He was pleased enough that the introduction had gone well, although a little frustrated that there had been no mention of business. But he also knew that such things couldn't be rushed without arousing suspicion: a risk he couldn't afford to take. The Branko brothers had a sinister reputation, and his meeting with them had done nothing to dispel that.

He had looked into the eyes of evil men on many occasions in his career, both in the police and the military, but this was different. The Brankos transported him back to that day in Petrovici in 1992 where he had witnessed true, sadistic evil. The brothers radiated malevolence and cruelty and it disturbed him.

7

A Month Later

Tom woke early and headed straight to his workout zone to begin his usual punishing circuit training. He did a simple and speedy circuit, using all the equipment, and was soon bathed in sweat. He dived into the shower but didn't shave. His beard had grown substantially, and it gave him a slight feeling of anonymity, even if it was illusionary. That, plus the fact that his hair hadn't been trimmed for a while, made his appearance somewhat different from when he had accepted the tasking.

The past month had been a bit of a rollercoaster ride. He had been quickly accepted into the group as an acquaintance and training partner, but he'd not yet been approached about getting involved in any criminality.

He had been to the Branko family house, a tidy and over-furnished fourth-floor flat in a fairly run-down estate just off City Road, an area that the creeping London gentrification had not yet quite hit. There he had met the Brankos' mother, Mira: a matronly, heavy-set woman with dyed red hair, lots of costume jewellery and clown-like make-up. She looked older than the date of birth on the briefing sheet had suggested, and her lined face told the story of a hard-lived life. The brothers were deferential in her presence and she was clearly the boss of the small organisation. It was amusing to see that the brothers still had a room with single beds in it, despite both being in their early thirties.

Tom found his time with the brothers seriously hard work. Their enforced collegiality was wearing in the extreme; they both felt it necessary to put on a display of machismo all the time, unless they were in the presence of their mother. As a self-reliant person who used words carefully, the company of two such overly-macho, aggressive buffoons was torturous for Tom, but he was professional enough to play along, remaining sufficiently deferential to not be perceived as a threat.

He had dropped hints that he hoped would lead the brothers to believe he was approachable to any criminal enterprise but, so far, he'd had no bites.

He held regular briefings with Liam, reporting that he'd been accepted and seemed to be trusted to a degree. This he put down to the regular BJJ bouts where he kept taking Luka to the edge without ever quite beating him. Tom sometimes found this frustrating, knowing he could submit Luka in a heartbeat, but it kept the big Serb's confidence high; and in any case, being under-estimated could be a distinct advantage. Luka had such an enormous ego, it wasn't difficult to keep it massaged.

As Tom finished his post-workout coffee, his phone rang: Luka, summoning him to a meeting. Half-an-hour later he was sat in a café in Hackney, nursing a coffee with Luka and Aleks Branko.

'We need to speak, my friend,' said Aleks. 'We have a business opportunity for you.'

'Are you up for a bit of work if we need some help, Tomo?' asked Luka. 'We sometimes need a bit of help with our business interests, and Ivan says you can be relied on.'

'I'm listening,' replied Tom

'Has Ivan told you anything about what we do?'

'A bit. Not much,' Tom replied. This is perfect, he thought. The Brankos making the approach in this way couldn't be better.

The big Serb scowled. 'Ivan talks too much but we go back a long way. He always had a big mouth.' He shook his head and continued, a slight smile touching his blue eyes. 'We help people who want to stay in the UK I think we're like a dating agency!' He laughed uproariously at his own joke.

'Seriously,' he continued, 'we're making plenty of money. We have Bosnian girls at home who can use EU Slovenian passports. It's simple: we have someone who can do good photo-swaps in the passports. We then use them for paper marriages to men wanting visas. It gets them their visas and they pay us plenty for it. Some of our girls do escorting as well for extra cash. Most of them are working girls from back home who can make more over here.'

'What would you want from me then?' Tom said.

'We often have to move a lot of cash after a busy day with the girls and you know how it is: you have dodgy money, and dodgy people want to steal it from you. Maybe you mind the girls, maybe help us at a few meetings. We just lost two good men—the bastard Home Office deported them—and we need some muscle. You interested, Tomo?'

Tom flashed an easy smile. 'Yeah, I can help you out, Luka. As long as I get a few quid my way.'

'Good man. I trust you, Tomo. A fellow Serb who can fight. I'll give you a call soon, yeah?' Luka stood, indicating the meeting was over. They shook hands, and then Luka locked Tom in a light embrace.

Aleks stared at Tom and growled, 'Always remember though: you cross us and we will fuck you up. You wouldn't be the first. The Branko family won't be crossed. Ever.' He smiled, but Tom could feel the conviction and menace behind the expression.

Tom shrugged. 'Hey, guys. Look at my face: who wouldn't trust me? I'm a man of my word and we're all Serbs. If that's not enough, I can fuck off any time. A man can always find ways to make money.'

The brothers laughed and Aleks said, 'We'll be in touch. Stay available. We're busy, there's lots of money to be made.'

They nodded a farewell and left the café without further comment.

Tom sat with the remainder of his coffee, smiling to himself. He fished his work phone out of his pocket and tapped out a text to Liam.

'I'm in.'

8

Three Weeks Later

After the meeting in the café, Tom found himself accepted as a full member of the gang. The days and weeks of groundwork and detailed preparation had proven essential, fully validating the decision to go for a slow-time infiltration. It was perfect that the socialising and MMA had led to the Brankos approaching him to help with their criminality: not only from a legal but also a safety standpoint.

The past three weeks had enabled Tom to gather more than enough evidence of the family's trafficking and prostitution business, much of which he had captured on covert recording equipment, both video and audio. For a week or so, he'd performed a security role at a brothel in Hackney, where Mira had rented a first-floor, three-bedroom maisonette and installed three Bosnian girls in the bedrooms, all of them sad and tragic individuals. The girls were worked pretty much full-on and Mira didn't like them talking to Tom, so his conversations with them had been brief at most. They were all terrified of Mira and the brothers, a climate of fear keeping them very much in check. One of the girls, Ana, would often come out between clients to smoke a cigarette by where he sat. She was a funny girl, probably only eighteen but looking younger, full of life and with a great sense of humour. Tom always thought that with a change in life circumstances she could have made something of herself, but it seemed that the lure of drugs had put paid to all that. He couldn't help but feel sorry for her but forced himself to keep his mind on the wider job and maintain a respectful distance between them. She would often flirt with Tom but only jokingly; Tom reckoned the last thing she actually wanted was more sex, given she was at it almost constantly with the punters.

'Come on, Tomo. You know you want to; I'd be the best you ever have,' she joked with a happy smile that almost, but not quite, masked the hidden sadness that her grey eyes betrayed.

'Ana, you are on the go with men all day and night. You wouldn't want extra, you must be exhausted.'

'You'd be special, though. I will only charge half-price, as it's you,' she teased.

Tom laughed. 'What would Mira think of that, Ana?'

'She'd go crazy, the nasty bitch. But she has promised to get my passport back soon so I can go home.' Again she smiled, but the smile failed to touch her eyes.

The girls seemed to be high on drugs half the time: probably the only way they could get through the days and the constant stream of clients. His brief conversations with Ana established that they had been working girls in Sarajevo who had jumped at the opportunity to earn more money in London. They had come over together, driven from Sarajevo by the brothers and crossing over on the ferry; a similar route to the one he'd taken himself with his mama all those years ago.

Those who had been forced into sham marriages had done so with minimum fuss, with the applications to the Home Office apparently going in via the solicitor. They were all unhappy about how little they were paid and the fact that Mira had retained their passports but were too scared to protest.

Tom's team were delighted with his progress: all the covert recordings and forged documents had the Brankos bang to rights. They also had surveillance of the brothel as well as phone call and cell site information that plotted all the Brankos' movements from Sarajevo to London. It would be a watertight case against them, even if the three trafficking victims didn't want to give evidence.

What they didn't have yet was the final piece to nail the corrupt solicitor, Michael Adebayo.

They did have good supporting evidence that he was handling bogus applications, but not enough to prove that he was knowingly subverting immigration rules. Tom had been kept away from the lawyer, with the Brankos frustratingly not even having talked about him in Tom's presence. They needed more: Tom needed to get into the office and get something recorded to show that Adebayo had knowledge of the sham nature of the marriages.

Tom's phone buzzed next to him as he pondered the problem. Glancing at the screen, he saw it was from Aleks and groaned inwardly as he answered it. 'Aleks, man, how goes?'

'We are out of the country for a while on some business and will be away for about four days or so. Mama may need a little help with a few things, so can you be available if she needs you? The girls at the Hackney place are going home; I think we've worn them out and we want them out of the way.'

'Sure thing.' Conscious that every word was being recorded on an app installed on his phone, he added, 'What about the girls' husbands?'

Aleks laughed coarsely. 'Who gives a fuck about them? Their applications are in, if they don't get granted, we've already been paid. What they gonna do? Go to the police?'

Tom laughed along. 'No problem, Aleks. I'm about if your Mama needs anything. Tell Luka I was gonna kick his butt on the mat this week as well.' More laughter as Aleks rang off.

Tom was thankful they were going to be away, as it gave him a break from their bullshit. Mira had never called him before, so he reckoned he could have a few quiet days. He decided to go for a run; he was full of energy and wouldn't be able to sleep later if he didn't burn some of it off.

He quickly changed into his running gear and set off along the Kentish Town streets, heading towards Hampstead and the Heath.

He enjoyed his solitary runs, relishing the time to think and reflect. This reclusiveness was probably another reason Bev had called time on their relationship. He thought of her again: slim, pretty, with a big laugh and a big heart. He had enjoyed living with her and enjoyed the brief foray into normal life she gave him, but his fractured upbringing, nomadic military existence, and total commitment to the job had made things difficult. Could he ever completely trust anyone? Bev had got sick of the fact that something stopped Tom giving all of himself to her, so she left. The split had saddened him, he supposed, but a part of him felt like he should have been affected more than he was. A bigger part of him relished the comforting fact that he would continue relying on himself. He picked up his pace, feeling the burn in his legs and the tension dissipate as he pounded the streets.

*

Michael Adebayo pushed back his chair from the desk and stretched. It had been a long morning seeing clients at the busy office in Ilford. It was like a sausage factory, desperate immigrant after desperate immigrant, all with the same thing in mind: staying in the UK. Most of them were students who wanted to stay beyond their visa. Some were asylum seekers not yet granted, all with the same bullshit stories. He thought of his last client, a Pakistani with years of rejected applications-to-remain behind him. He almost laughed at what the wretch wanted to claim, even if it was at Adebayo's suggestion. He was going to try to convince the authorities that he needed asylum as he was gay and would be killed in Pakistan as a result. This was despite the sham marriage application the same man had made and had had rejected just a few months before, claiming undying love for a Hungarian girl half his age. He laughed at the audacity of it, but he just took the money and, if applications failed, he couldn't care less.

He stared out of his window onto Station Road. The sunlight streamed through the window as he watched the bustle below him. A grimy, poor area, but one he loved well enough.

He had been aged eight when he had come to the UK with

his parents from a small village outside Lagos. His father was a natural businessman who had managed to set up a small chain of printing and photocopying shops that were moderately successful and afforded them a comfortable lifestyle. His parents were decent, God-fearing Christians who were not best pleased when he had converted to Islam at university. It was an easy conversion for Adebayo: most of his friends and associates were Muslims and, even just for business reasons, it had seemed the natural choice.

He had been a bright boy who had progressed well at school and qualified as a solicitor without difficulty, specialising in immigration law after doing his articles at a solicitors firm in Plaistow. His mentor was a clever and cunning man who made good money progressing applications to the Home Office with no regard for the client. 'I mean, who are they going to complain to when they get deported?' the man would laugh.

The business model was simple: start the client's fees at a low level, then increase them as the applications progressed. Make applications that were doomed to failure, safe in the knowledge that the client's money would be in his pocket before they got deported. He had cared little for any of his clients, viewing them as rats to be exploited. Adebayo had learnt well from his mentor. There was money to be made in their business; you just needed the desperate clients to come through the door.

He had started Adebayo Associates seven years previously and was immediately successful after advertising heavily on local Urdu radio stations and in the mosques. He promised success in Home Office applications at rock-bottom prices, and the clients descended in droves. He had no associates; he was the only lawyer. The rest were caseworkers paid minimally and treated with disdain. The applications were simple, and he quickly realised he could charge hundreds of pounds simply for form-filling. Soon he was making more money than he knew what to do with, and each morning the queue stretched out the front door and his reception area was always full.

His brother, Emmanuel, had not had such an easy childhood.

He was a much rougher boy, always in fights, always bullying, cajoling and stealing, leading to trouble with the police a few times. Adebayo had always found it easy to manipulate Emmanuel, who in turn just wanted to please his older sibling. The benefit of this was that the bigger boy always protected his brother, keeping any bullies away.

Things hadn't changed all those years later. Adebayo kept Emmanuel happy with cash and his brother repaid him by keeping him safe. Emmanuel's links to the underworld were useful; Adebayo didn't like dealing with criminals—he didn't trust them—but he appreciated the need to sometimes get things done by less conventional means. He needed a good proportion of his clients to be successful to keep the business going, so forged documents were sometimes needed. Emmanuel was his link into this world: he could call on good forgers of identity documents, supporting paperwork and passports, all with one phone call.

Adebayo smiled to himself. Business was good and life was good. He lived in a large house in the best street in Ilford. He could have moved to a better area, but this was his home, where he was known and respected by all. He owned other properties in the area that he rented out and he also owned a large house in the prosperous area of Lagos. He felt like the King of Ilford.

A knock at the door jolted him from his daydream: his brother, as always slightly deferential.

'Brother, that fool Rizwan Khan is here to see you, shouting nonsense about the Home Office refusing his claim,' said Emmanuel. 'He's getting quite stroppy in reception and threatening to expose us and call the police. What shall I do?'

Adebayo considered for a moment. 'He is from Karachi, no?'

'I think so.'

'Tell him I will see him in one hour and refund his money.'

His brother nodded and left the office. A cold, hard fury gripped Adebayo. Who the fuck did that bastard think he was, threatening him? He remembered Rizwan Khan's application well: a sham marriage to a Hungarian girl supplied by a trafficking gang.

She was a very pretty little thing, who he had fucked in his office. A perk of the job. He smiled at the memory; the girl did whatever her traffickers told her, she was so frightened: a vulnerability that just excited him even more.

He dug the man's file out of the teak cabinet and picked up the phone. He knew just the person to call to get the job done.

An hour later there was another knock at the door and his brother entered once again, this time accompanied by a small, wiry Pakistani man dressed in tracksuit trousers and a threadbare sweater, leather sandals on his sockless feet. His hair was fashioned into a greasy side-parting and he wore a scraggly beard with no moustache.

'Yes, Rizwan Khan, what can I do for you?' said Adebayo, his voice slightly condescending.

'Mr Adebayo-Sab,' the man said, nervously using the respectful suffix. 'My case has been refused; the Home Office say my paperwork is false and I must leave. They have been looking for me. I cannot go to Pakistan, and I owe the moneylenders for the money I paid you for my application. I must stay to send money home to my family.' Flecks of spittle flew from his mouth as he stuttered.

'How is your situation my fault, my friend? Why do you threaten me, after all I've done for you?' Adebayo's voice was even, his eyes locked on Khan.

Khan looked sweaty and his breathing was shallow and rapid as he fidgeted with his prayer beads. 'I've no more money, Mr Adebayo. None. You must give me mine back; my case is gone, I will be deported. I don't want to get you into trouble, but I will tell the police if you don't.'

Adebayo held the nervous man with a fixed, dead gaze.

'Sit,' he commanded, indicating the chair in front of his desk. He did not answer but picked up his iPhone and dialled a number, holding the phone in front of him. The handset sprang into life, voices clearly audible. Adebayo turned the screen to face Khan. Visible on the video call was the green door to a small, one-roomed house in a dim terrace. A military fatigue-clad arm stretched out and knocked at the door. The door was answered by a young girl, aged about twenty and dressed in a threadbare Shalwar Kameez.

She looked terrified. 'Yes?' she said in a voice so quiet it was barely audible.

'Rayaan!' screamed Khan. 'My sister! You fucking bastard!' He leapt to his feet but was restrained from behind by Emmanuel, powerful arms wrapping him in a bear-hug, forcing him to watch. On the screen a fist rocketed into view and connected with his sister's nose, knocking her to the floor, blood immediately streaming. The girl let out a piercing scream and the picture disappeared. Adebayo set the phone down quietly on the desk and fixed the babbling man with a glare.

'If you ever come to my office again or if you go to the police or anyone, I will have her fingers removed and posted to you. She will be violated by many men and the house burnt to the ground. You dare threaten me, you fucking worm!'

Khan was sobbing now: unrestrained, destroyed, all options gone, all hope gone.

'Get him out of here.'

Emmanuel dragged the smaller man out of the office and, as the door closed, Adebayo smiled his cruel smile and picked up the phone again.

9

It was a month since Tom had last been to Kilburn nick and he entered the building reluctantly, knowing his boss would have the hump with him. DCI Simon Taylor didn't like it when his staff knew something he didn't, although Tom of course had no intention of enlightening him.

He went up to the canteen on the second floor and bought a cup of tea, steeling himself for the inevitable supercilious attitude his DCI would no doubt heap on him.

Sat alone at one of the tables was an old friend of his, Stan Munro. Stan was a legendary ex-Marine Sergeant Major and Falklands Conflict veteran, who now worked as the Kilburn CID Office Manager. He managed the vehicle fleet, answered the phones, took messages, and generally made sure everything ran smoothly. He was a nice guy in his sixties with a bald head and long bushy beard, a man who didn't take his job too seriously but did it very well. Despite his low-status job and unusual appearance, it was always wise to keep Stan on your side.

For reasons no one really knew, Stan wielded significant power at the station, being one of the few people who could walk into the Borough Commander's office without knocking and speak freely. It was, though, a testament to Stan's character that he never misused this power, simply seeking to make sure that any injustices were resolved without the need for management intervention. He was also responsible for issuing various enquiries and investigations, and anyone foolish enough to piss Stan off would find themselves on the receiving end of a paperwork body-blow within minutes.

He had an enormous presence, and some younger officers would cower in his formidable presence. Perhaps because of this, few cops took the time to speak to Stan, not knowing that he was also a Military Cross recipient, following some serious bravery on Mount Two Sisters during the Falklands Conflict.

Since joining, Tom often passed the time of day and shared a tea—'a wet'—with Stan, talking about their Bootneck days. They had soon discovered that Stan knew his foster father well, having served in the South Atlantic together, and this had deepened the bond between them.

'All right, Royal,' said Tom, using the universal greeting that all Marines traditionally used when addressing a fellow Green Beret holder.

'Royal. Where you been, mate? I've missed our little sandbag-sitting, lamp-swinging sessions,' said Stan in that booming, sonorous voice which was once so feared among the tough commandos.

'Oh, you know, sneaky-beaky stuff.' He knew Stan wouldn't press. They shot the breeze for about twenty minutes until they were interrupted by Tom's operational phone ringing. He didn't recognise the number but answered it with a 'Hello?'

A gravelly female Serb-accented voice barked at him. Mira. 'I need you to help us. You must take a girl to the lawyer's office later today after they close.' It was an order, not a request. 'I give her your number, you meet her later, and take her to office in Ilford. Wait for her, then take her back to me, okay?'

'Sounds fine. What's her name?'

'Jeta. I text you the lawyer's brother's number and address of office. Get her there for seven, stay out of the way, and let the lawyer do his thing. She is meeting new husband.' She rang off without further comment.

It was goldmine stuff, and all recorded on the phone's covert app. Maybe it was the break he'd been waiting for: a chance to get into the solicitor's office and gather some proper evidence. He needed to speak to Liam.

'I gotta run, Stan. Business to attend to, mate. We'll have a beer soon.'

'It would make the decade worthwhile, Old Fruit. Whatever secret-squirrel stuff you are doing, be careful.'

'Always careful, Stan.'

*

Tom drove from Jubilee House in Putney, where SC&O35 was based, having put together with Liam a snap briefing with the Home Office operational team. He was wired up with a covert camera, the lens concealed in a button on his lightweight jacket. The hard drive with a micro-SD card was secured in a holster at the small of his back. This would give more than enough recording for the deployment. A wireless remote was located in a key fob attached to the car keys: all he had to do was press the button and recording would commence. He'd used that kit a few times before and it had always provided excellent quality images. If the job went as planned, Adebayo would be caught bang-to-rights within a few hours.

In case he got into any problems, the Home Office had supplied a backup team which would stay close by, following his progress on a small vehicle tracker hidden in the BMW, but with no radio communications between them. They weren't planning to arrest Adebayo that day, even if he did incriminate himself. Better to wait until the evidence was all in good order and ready to go, so that when the bust went down it would be a simple interview, charge, and remand in custody.

Jeta had called Tom about an hour earlier, a quiet, nervous voice at the end of the phone. 'Tomo?'

'Yeah, is that you, Jeta?' Tom asked in Serbian.

'Mira says I must meet you and we go to lawyer's office. I'm in Hackney. When can you get here?'

'I'll be there in about an hour, we need to get you to the lawyer for 7pm, so meet me at Hackney Central and I'll wait by the newsagents. Call me when you get there.'

He rang off and immediately called the number given to him by Mira. It was answered after eight rings.

'Yeah?' A mix of cockney and African accent questioned.

'Is that Emmanuel?' asked Tom, slightly upping his Serb accent.

'Yeah, who is it?'

'It's Tomo. Mira asked me to call you. I'm delivering a package to you this evening.'

'No problem. Call when you're outside and I'll bring you in. Get here for seven o'clock.' And he hung up.

Tom rang through to Jean MacDonald and updated her with the plan. It was all looking good, although there were variables, as always. The girl sounded pretty fragile, so he couldn't be sure how she'd react when they got to the office. As always on undercover meetings, he'd have to be flexible. The key was to keep on his toes throughout, always think of the evidence, and stick to the rules.

Tom smiled at the prospect of deploying right into the heart of the conspiracy, right under their noses.

*

Tom saw Jeta as soon as he pulled up outside Hackney Central. She was tiny and almost child-like, but Tom guessed she was about twenty. She had short, choppy, dark hair that framed an elfin face, with a slight, waif-like body in a short, floral sun dress and pink Converse trainers. If he didn't know better, he would have thought she was waiting to go to a youth club disco. Tom pressed the record button on the car fob and said quietly, his lips barely moving, 'My name, for this operation, is Tomo. I'm an undercover police officer and I'm about to meet Jeta and take her to Adebayo Associates Solicitors. The time is 1830 hours.' That effectively began the undercover deployment; everything from then on would be recorded and evidential.

Tom waved and she walked over, smiling shyly as she opened the car door. 'Tomo?' she said in a light voice, a hint of nervousness in her pretty face. She had very dark eyes and an equally dark complexion, and Tom recognised some Roma in her features.

Tom smiled and said in Serb, 'Yes. Get in, we're going to be late.'

'Wow! I love your car! I've never been in a BMW before,' she said as she got in. 'Where is Mira? Do you have my passport? I really want to go home as soon as this is done.'

'How long have you been over here, Jeta?'

'A few weeks. Mira flew me over. I'm a hairdresser in Sarajevo but I'm not making enough money. Mira told me I would get good job over here, but nothing so far. She wants me to be a prostitute, but I don't want that.' Sadness tinged with fear was etched over her face.

That was often the trick with traffickers: exploit vulnerable young girls with false promises, make them totally dependent on you, then force them into the trades of misery, be it prostitution or unpaid work of some type. Tom shook away his rising anger. He had to look at the bigger picture; taking out this group would benefit many girls and keep them from the situation Jeta had found herself in.

Jeta continued, 'Aleks and Luka get very angry with me when I don't be prostitute, tell me I can't have my passport until I do. I just want to go home now. Luka keeps trying to get me into bed as well, but I don't like him.' Her voice cracked, and tears brimmed in her dark eyes.

Tom forced himself to keep his voice level. 'Look, just get this business out of the way, then you can go home. You know what we're doing today?'

The girl blinked the tears away and regained her composure. 'Mira says I must do a paper marriage with a Pakistani boy, so he can get a green card for the UK. She says it won't be a real marriage and, when I go home, it won't count. I think I'm meeting my husband today. They say I'm a big prize for a Pakistani as I have a real EU passport because my mama is Slovenian.' She forced a smile at the ridiculousness of the statement.

That was the story often told to the victims in those cases. Unfortunately, it wasn't true: the marriages were binding and in most cases the girls would need divorces or annulments. Tom also made a mental note that the girl was using her own passport, not a forgery as the others had.

'Let's just get today out of the way, then we'll see about getting your passport back from Mira. Just sign what the lawyer wants you to sign. Let me do the translating so you don't get ripped off.'

Tom tried to reassure her, but he was also aware that he was supposed to be playing a bad guy and the overriding objective was to get Adebayo on film.

They drove the rest of the journey with little small talk, arriving in Ilford just before 7pm. Tom parked in a street just over the road from the offices and they both got out of the car.

The lawyer's premises were above a parade of shops typical of areas like Ilford: mostly Asian food stores, African haircare shops, and mobile phone outlets. The windows above the parade of shops were stencilled with lettering proclaiming 'Adebayo Associates Solicitors and Commissioner for Oaths', with the door just to the left of a newsagent's entrance. He sent a one-line text to Emmanuel. 'We are outside.'

Two minutes later the door opened and Tom recognised Emmanuel straight away. The first thing that struck him was that the other man was bigger than he was expecting: at least four inches taller than him and probably four stone heavier. He was wearing a slim-fit polo shirt that stretched across his muscles, his wide expanse of back testing the strength of the fabric everywhere. His biceps forced the sleeves wider than the manufacturer had clearly expected, giving the man an intimidating look. It had the look of chemically-assisted muscle and Tom couldn't help but notice the layer of fat that caused the shirt's fabric to stretch in a less flattering way across the stomach. All that was topped by a scowl in a face that may have been described as 'striking' or 'ugly', depending on your point of view. His hair was cropped close to a scalp which was shiny and reflected the evening sun. The big man nodded at Tom and jerked a thumb, indicating that they should follow him.

Once upstairs, they followed Emmanuel through the reception area to a closed door that bore a brass plate: 'Michael Adebayo, Solicitor and Principal'. There was no doubting who was in charge in that little empire.

Emmanuel knocked once on the door and stepped through, leading the way. The three of them entered a large, well-furnished office where Michael Adebayo sat behind an ornate, teak desk. The knot of his tie was pulled down from the collar of his pink shirt, sleeves rolled up to show slim, hairy arms, one of which was adorned with a thin, gold chain. Tom saw the family resemblance immediately: only the disparities in size and hair set them truly apart.

The lawyer did not look at them but continued to talk on the phone in a language Tom suspected was Yoruba, a half-smile on his face.

Sat in the corner of the office was a middle-aged, Asian man with a long beard, wearing Islamic Shalwar baggy trousers. He looked nervous and was clearly intimidated in the presence of Adebayo.

Adebayo finished his call and fixed Tom with a steady gaze. 'You must be Tomo. Mira told me you were coming with the girl,' he said in barely accented English, a half-smile touching his broad lips, more condescending than genuine. 'Where are the brothers?'

Mindful of the recording running, Tom replied, 'You mean Aleks and Luka?'

'Of course, who else?'

'Overseas looking for more girls for you, I imagine.'

Adebayo smiled. 'They're good boys, their mother must be so proud. I have many prospective husbands waiting for beautiful Slovenian girls.' With his fingers he mimed over-exaggerated quotation marks either side of his head, his over-pronunciation of the words making his meaning clear.

Gold dust, thought Tom as he laughed along. This is too easy, and all caught on camera as well. With the evidence they had gathered already, that was almost enough. He just hoped that the video was recording everything.

'Who is this lovely creature you have brought to see me?' Adebayo smirked, eyeing Jeta, his gaze a little too lingering for Tom's liking. 'Does she speak English?' He carried on staring at her, and Jeta shifted uncomfortably under his penetrating gaze.

'This is Jeta. Her English isn't so good; it's best I translate for her.'

Adebayo nodded. 'Tell her that this is the man she is going to marry. His name is Sohail Ali and she will be helping him to stay in the UK.' Adebayo pointed at the man sat in the corner of the room, who jumped to his feet and nodded, his big smile almost hidden by his beard. He looked with interest at Jeta, who seemed a little perplexed.

Tom explained to Jeta in Serbian, 'Jeta, the man in the pyjamas is called Sohail Ali and you're to marry him to help him stay in the UK.'

'How old is he? I hope I don't have to live with him, he's ugly.'

'Jeta is okay with this,' translated Tom, 'but she doesn't want to live with him. I don't think he's her type.'

'She doesn't have to, unless she wants to. The paperwork will be prepared to show that she is living with him. I have a man who can sort it, so her name will be all over it. We just need to convince the Home Office and registrar that they are together.'

Tom translated this to Jeta, who nodded with relief. Clearly the prospect of living with a fifty-year-old Muslim was not appealing to the young girl.

'We need a few photographs of the happy couple together, but not in here. Can you take her over to the park with Sohail and take half-a-dozen photographs? Make them look like a couple.' Adebayo threw a small digital camera at Tom, which he caught.

'Okay, no problem. We can do that.'

Tom, Sohail and Jeta left the office wordlessly and went to the park just a short walk away. He took a series of photographs of them together in various poses: sitting on a bench, gazing into each other's eyes lovingly, holding hands by the swings, leaning against a tree. He was sure the photos looked utterly ridiculous, but it didn't really matter as they would never make it to the Home Office.

Back in the office, Adebayo looked through the pictures on the camera's screen and chuckled. 'How do those fools ever accept nonsense like this?'

'You go now, Sohail,' Adebayo said. The man left the office, shooting a deferential look back in Adebayo's direction as he did so.

Adebayo waved a hand dismissively. 'We don't need him anymore; he has signed the forms, we have the pictures, so we just need to go through the forms with Jeta and get her to sign. The next thing will be to go to the registry office and book the wedding, but Emmanuel will help on the day for that. We have a friendly face there who doesn't ask too many questions. Will you be her witness on the day to translate?'

Tom shrugged. 'Maybe. Depends on whether the brothers are back from overseas.'

'Whatever. Anyway, I just need Jeta to hang around until these papers are finished so she can sign, and then you're done. I have her passport: Mira was good enough to post it to me. I tell you what, Tomo, can you run and get us three coffees from over the road and I will do this now, so it's all done. We don't need an interpreter for this bit.' He smiled a slightly unpleasant smile.

Tom thought it through. It didn't sound quite right, but he didn't want to risk a confrontation in the office while the camera was rolling.

'Okay. I need to make a call, anyway.'

Tom descended the shabby staircase, an uncomfortable feeling in his stomach; he didn't trust Adebayo or his brother one bit. Rather than let the door lock behind him he propped it open with a doormat, so he wouldn't need to be buzzed back in. He went and picked up three coffees from the nearby shop that had a Costa machine and paid at the counter. He returned to the office within ten minutes and climbed the stairs quietly. Something wasn't right. He had a niggling feeling that had been bothering him since he left the office. Then it hit him. There was only one reason why Adebayo would want Jeta alone, and it wasn't a good one. He walked quickly towards the office and was met by Emmanuel, stood outside like a bouncer at a nightclub door.

'How did you get back in?' he asked with a note of aggression in his voice.

'Door was open. Where's Jeta?'

'In with the boss, do not disturb just yet.'

'I'm not happy about that, Emmanuel. She's not a working girl,' said Tom, not taking his eyes off him.

Emmanuel just laughed. 'She's a whore just like all the others, Tomo. Mira always lets the boss sample the goods: perk of the job.' He sneered at Tom, almost challenging him to try to get past him.

A scream of, 'Molim vas pomozite, ne, Tomo! Help, please, no, Tomo!' erupted from within the office.

'Step aside, Emmanuel,' said Tom in a low, impassive voice, fixing the other man with an even, unrelenting gaze. He was getting Jeta out; no way would he let her get raped in there.

Emmanuel said nothing, but his eyes narrowed and his muscles tensed, ready for whatever was about to come his way.

Tom threw the three cups of scalding coffee straight into the other man's face. Emmanuel screamed and put his hands up to his eyes as Tom followed up by driving his right elbow straight into the bigger man's solar plexus with devastating force. The elbow is often a far more effective striking weapon than a fist, and the kinetic energy which was concentrated through the small surface area caused Emmanuel's breath to leave his body with a whoosh as he doubled over and hit the floor, gasping. Tom jumped over him and burst through the door, taking in the scene in front of him.

Jeta was bent over the teak desk, her sundress hitched up over her hips, her briefs discarded on the floor. The dress front was ripped away, and vivid red weals were visible around her bra strap. She looked utterly terrified, her eyes wild with fear. 'Tomo, Tomo, molim, molim!'

Adebayo's eyes widened in shock at the sight of Tom. His trousers and boxers were down by his skinny ankles. He began pulling away from the girl, his rapidly deflating penis clearly visible.

'What the fuck do you think you're doing? Emmanuel, Emmanuel!' he screamed, his face a mixture of fear and anger. He grabbed a letter opener from the desk and waved it threateningly at Tom. 'Keep the fuck away from me, you fool! Do you know who you're fucking with? I'll have you killed, you impudent Serb fucker!'

Time slowed for Tom, as it always did in circumstances like this. Jeta was the priority: he had to get her away from there, now. He had everything he needed on tape to put both brothers away for a long time.

Adebayo continued to threaten him with the letter knife. 'Come near me and I'll cut you,' he snarled, more out of fear than anger, but Tom saw it in his eyes that he was defeated.

'I'm taking the girl. Come on, Jeta.'

The girl picked up her underwear and ran to Tom's side, rearranging her sundress as she did so, her movements shaky with terror and her breathing rapid. She was showing all the signs of shock and it was only at that moment that Tom saw the livid bruise and swelling forming at the corner of her left eye.

'Take the slut then,' yelled Adebayo. 'You'll never get my business again. Plenty of people like you, you fuck. You mean nothing!'

Tom slowly approached the lawyer, his eyes fixing him with an even gaze, full of contempt. Adebayo raised the knife and continued to wave it threateningly at Tom.

'I'll stab you, I promise, you bastard,' he hissed, his voice full of fear and loathing.

Tom paused just out of the blade's reach, aware of the impediment Adebayo faced with his trousers round his ankles. Tom gave him a slow, even smile.

'You know, Michael, you're not the first man to hold a knife towards me. I wasn't scared then, and I'm not scared now; you may want to ask yourself why?'

Doubt flashed across the lawyer's face; the calm aura that Tom projected was disconcerting. He jabbed the knife half-heartedly in Tom's direction, the blade pointed directly towards his stomach.

Tom gave Adebayo a slight smile and delivered a sweeping roundhouse Muay Thai kick with his right leg, a vicious blow into the nerve bundle just above the lawyer's knee. Adebayo dropped as if he had been shot, screaming in pain and clutching his leg. Tom turned to Jeta, who was staring open-mouthed at him and smiled, icy calm.

'Come on, let's get out of here.'

'My passport, Tomo; I need my passport.' Jeta pointed at the desk where her Slovenian passport lay.

Tom considered for a moment; it was now officially a crime scene, and everything should have been left as evidence. However, he knew how the police property systems operated and it was likely that, once seized as evidence, she'd be unlikely to see her passport again. He figured that the poor girl had enough to contend with without the complications that having no passport would cause her. He grabbed it and handed it to her.

'Right. Let's go.'

They stepped over Emmanuel, still gasping on the floor and clutching his face, and descended to the street. Tom called Jean on his mobile and she answered immediately.

'Jean, it's Tom. Get someone to me now. I'm going to be outside the station entrance in one minute. I have a rape victim with me. Get the arrest team to move in to the office: Emmanuel and Michael Adebayo need to be arrested for rape and immigration offences. All the evidence is there, and I have it all on tape. I need to get out of the way or my cover will be even more blown than it is now.'

'On our way. Fortunately, we have two of our seconded cops with us,' said Jean and she hung up.

'Come on, Jeta,' said Tom in Serb, 'we're here to help you.'

'He raped me. The bastard raped me and punched me when I said no. Thank you, Tomo, you saved me from him.' She fought back tears, a lost and faraway look of hurt and pain deep within her eyes. For just a moment, Jeta reminded him of his mama all those years ago. Tom swallowed heavily at the memory.

'The police will be here soon, Jeta. They will help you,' he said, putting his arm on hers. Jeta flinched, just slightly, at his touch.

'Who are you, Tomo?'

He smiled. 'Just a friend.'

10

Jean arrived at the railway station within a couple of minutes, accompanied by two officers wearing police baseball caps. That was good news: they would need the local borough cops, as the office was a crime scene and there was a victim to look after. They also had two rape suspects to process and get safely to the local nick. This is going to get heavy quickly, thought Tom. The crime would be investigated by the local sexual offence specialists and a whole new set of procedures were about to begin.

Even though Emmanuel wasn't in the office with his brother at the time of the offence, he was just as culpable. It was as clear a case of Joint Enterprise as was possible to imagine. Even better, it was all recorded.

Tom explained to Jean what had happened. He needed to get away from there; his cover was essentially blown and, once word got back to Mira and the brothers, there would be recriminations all round. He could give his statement under his pseudonym, though, and the recording would tell the story.

'Jean,' said Tom, 'can you and your man here take Jeta and get her to the closest cop shop, probably Ilford. Tell them she's been raped and assaulted. Tell the custody officer I'll make a statement soon and I'll deliver the SD card from my camera with all the evidence they need. Get your arrest team in and nick them in the office and secure the scene. Forensics for the rape will be the priority but you will be able to move in after securing evidence for your investigation. Best call the local police to get some support here as well.'

Jean nodded. 'You okay, Tom?'

'I'm fine. Adebayo is a horrible bastard; make sure you nail his arse to the wall. It's all on the tape, he's proper screwed to the wall. They'll be feeling a bit under the weather: I had to get a bit lively with them,' he said, his face impassive.

Jean nodded. Tom explained that he would get out of the way to try to preserve his anonymity as best they could while things calmed down.

*

Tom ran back to his BMW and drove away, keen to be as far from the situation as possible. That was not how it was supposed to go down; he should have calmly delivered the evidence into the hands of the investigating team via his cover officer and then melted into the background.

That would have then allowed them to plan a clear arrest strategy that preserved his cover for as long as possible, and maybe even kept him out of the evidential chain. No chance of that now, though. The pervert Adebayo had forced his hand; he could hardly have stood back and let that poor young girl be abused like that.

He called Liam, who wasn't best pleased, as it meant a load of work for him to try and preserve what little remained of Tom's cover. Liam promised to call Neil Wilkinson and fully appraise him of what had happened, and they agreed to meet at Forest Gate nick, only fifteen minutes away, to plan the next move.

Tom sat in his car, the tension rising as he thought the whole thing through. The potential for everything to blow up was huge. He had just violently attacked a solicitor and his brother in their office and deposited a vulnerable rape victim into the hands of unknown officers. He was very reliant on the actions of his colleagues, and his general mistrust of others began to rise to the surface.

The realisation of how easily he had just used serious violence in despatching two criminals also flashed across his mind. He knew he had been justified in the circumstances but how was it that he, as always, felt nothing? No excitement, no fear, no satisfaction: in fact, no emotion at all. He forced those thoughts back down. Now was not the time.

He needed to see what the recording held before handing it over. That was not totally in line with the rules: the evidence should have been duplicated immediately on an official police copier, then the original bagged in a tamper-proof bag. But if he did that, he might not get to see it for ages, and he wanted a view before he wrote his statement. Adebayo was a rich man who would no doubt be employing high-priced defence teams to pick over every bit of what had happened. Knowledge was power in cases like that.

Tom went to the boot of the BMW and retrieved his messenger bag which contained, among other things, a camera case which held an SD card reader that would enable him to view the footage on his iPhone via the lightning port.

He extracted the SD card from the hard drive in its holster at the small of his back, slotted it into the cable port and opened the photos app on his phone. He then clicked 'import' and watched as the familiar egg-timer ticked through the transfer of the footage to his phone. Once complete, he pulled out the SD card, tucked it in his shirt pocket, and packed the cable back into his camera bag before tapping the icon on his phone to view the recording.

He watched himself walk into the solicitor's office and was happy with the quality of the recording: the audio was clear through the tinny iPhone speaker and the footage of the Adebayo brothers was, in general, pretty good. The look on Adebayo's face when Tom had burst through the door was priceless and there was more than enough evidence to sort the job out, once and for all.

Satisfied, Tom packed his bag back in the boot and drove up to Forest Gate nick to meet Liam.

*

Liam was already sitting at a table in the corner of the deserted canteen, nursing a tea in a Styrofoam cup, when Tom arrived fifteen minutes later. He looked up as Tom approached and offered a slight smile.

'Jobs never go as planned, do they, fellah?' he said as they shook hands.

'I didn't have too much choice, Liam. I wasn't about to let him continue raping that poor girl. Hopefully it's all recorded and should cause him a little problem.' He didn't mention he'd already scanned the footage; it wasn't strictly correct procedure.

'Talk me through it then, mate,' said the Irishman.

Tom went through the whole series of events, giving all the details, including the direct evidence of the trafficking and immigration law breaches, plus what the tape should show relating to the sexual assault.

Liam paused before answering, as if weighing up all the possibilities.

'It sounds a done deal, mate. Right, you got the SD card?'

Tom plucked it out of his shirt pocket and handed it over. 'Should all be on there, in HD resolution. Make sure they destroy that fucking creature; he is not nice at all.'

Liam took the card and popped it inside a small, self-seal evidence bag. He tore off the protective strip and sealed the bag, exposing the unique serial number. Tom signed the exhibit label on the bag and gave it his exhibit number, TK/1, making a note of the seal number on a scrap of paper. He would need to refer to the serial number in his statement to keep the evidence legally watertight. The card was of paramount importance, especially in this case when the defendant was a rich solicitor.

'Right, pal, best get started on your statement. Once you're done, I'll whizz it all over to Ilford with the card. I assume the team there will be desperate for it: the PACE clock is ticking.' PACE: the Police and Criminal Evidence Act, dictated how long a suspect could be held after being charged. Liam handed him an undercover officer's notebook.

Tom found an empty office on the second floor and spent

the next hour making detailed notes in the book, giving precise information about the sequence of events: from his briefing all the way through to extracting the SD card. Together with the card, those notes would comprise the evidence he would supply to Jean and her team, as well as whoever was investigating Jeta's sexual assault.

Tom wondered how the girl was doing. The Met had vastly improved its handling of sexual offences over recent years, and he assumed it would be one of the Sapphire Teams that would investigate. Jeta would hopefully be at one of the rape suites: so-called havens, where she'd be forensically examined and emotionally supported. Tom had found that the quality of the investigators varied widely on Sapphire Teams, but there were some good cops who specialised in dealing with the victims.

He couldn't help but feel sorry for Jeta. She'd seemed so naïve and vulnerable, and the process of a rape investigation was intrusive, to say the least, with a medical examination as well as her having to re-live the incident in detail as her statement was taken.

Tom found Liam again, still nursing a tea in the canteen that was now a little busier, being close to the end of late-turn.

He handed his notebook over and said, 'It's all in there, Liam. Hopefully, with the recording, that's more than enough.'

Liam briefly looked through the book without comment. It was fully accepted that, after a stressful incident, an undercover officer's notes may suffer a little and a second pair of eyes were always valuable.

Liam seemed satisfied, however. 'That's fine, Tom. I'll get these over to the team at Ilford. You may as well go home. I doubt much will happen with the prisoners at this time of the night; not until they've done the first recall with the victim and she's been examined. I'll call you tomorrow. Leave the liaison with the team to me: you're a bit too close to this job. It would have been nice to distance you before the team struck.'

Tom had to agree on that point. On other deployments he had been able to muddy the waters a little and create some distance from the informant. It wasn't so troubling in this particular case as Ivan had only introduced Tom to Luka as a potential sparring partner, and that was quite a few months ago. It had been Luka himself who had made the offer of participation in crime, so the informant had a big outer on that front. Ivan just needed to say that he didn't know that Tom was working with the brothers: he just thought they were fighting partners.

'Hey-ho,' said the Irishman. 'Not much we can do about it now. Good job, Tom. Now get yourself home: you look tired.'

Tom did feel a little jaded. It had been an unusual and tiring deployment; the brothers had been stressful company and he would be glad to be away from them. One thing he was sure of, though, was that Adebayo would be moving heaven and earth—whether in prison or not—to find out how an undercover officer had ended up in his office.

11

A few hours later, Michael Adebayo was sat in the solicitor's consulting room at Ilford Police Station. He was still in pain; his leg was throbbing evidence of the encounter with Tomo at his office. He was both angry and extremely worried about the events that had led him there, but the presence of his old friend and solicitor was a welcome development.

Asif Khan sat across the desk, looking at him with those familiar hard eyes. He was immaculately dressed in a tailored grey suit with a blindingly-white shirt and conservative tie. They had been friends at university and immediately gravitated towards each other, especially once their mutual desires to make money became obvious. It had been Khan's suggestion that Adebayo take the plunge and convert to Islam. They shared the same taste in women: particularly feckless white women of questionable morals who were amenable to their advances after a few drinks.

After university, both men went on to be solicitors: Adebayo specialising in immigration and Khan setting up his own successful criminal defence practice. Part of Khan's success story was down to his morals. He had none whatsoever; he would represent anyone and use any tricks—fair or foul—to keep them out of jail. He and Adebayo had remained good friends and associates ever since going their separate ways after university, often feeding work each other's way, their practices complementing each other perfectly.

'Right, I've had the evidence disclosure from the officer in the case,' said Khan. 'It doesn't look good. They have the girl secured away at an examination suite and I think—although they won't admit it yet—they had an undercover officer, or they've recorded you at the office. Basically, my friend, you're screwed and I don't think normal tactics will work here. If it was an undercover officer, he would have been wired as well. They also have you bang to rights for organising sham marriages.'

Adebayo didn't answer, instead slumping against the desk with his head cupped in his hands. Tears seeped out between his fingers and spotted the dark Formica table. He pictured everything he'd worked for falling around his ears.

Khan spoke after a second, 'We say nothing for the time being. I will demand the information about the undercover officer and the details of the girl. I will also demand to see the footage in full before we comment.'

'I knew I shouldn't have agreed to let the new face bring the girl,' said Adebayo. 'He seemed just like the brothers, though. I didn't think for a second he would be an undercover officer, the bastard. Police were there within minutes after he fled with the bitch; he must have been a cop.' The thought pushed away his self-pity, resolve suddenly returning with a vengeance. 'Get hold of Mira, find out what the fuck is going on and where this bastard came from. I want to know everything about him. Also, call the Brankos' police and Home Office sources, see who knows what. Money is no object, I'll pay whatever. The girl will respond to money; if not, do we know where she's from and where her family are? Then do whatever you can to get me and my brother out on bail.' Spittle flecked from Adebayo's mouth as he barked furiously.

'It won't be easy, brother,' said Khan. 'If the girl gives them a statement and they have undercover recordings you will be charged with rape and remanded. If the Home Office can only charge you with the immigration matters, then I may be able to make the case for bail.'

'Make it happen. I need to get back out so I can straighten this mess out. Go and speak to Mira and the sources, then come back. I can't go to prison; not a fucking chance.'

12

Liam Devlin used his warrant card to swipe himself into Ilford Police Station and ascended to the first-floor CID office to hunt for the officer on the case.

Liam found the officer glued to a computer terminal with a phone held to his ear. He acknowledged Liam as he approached his desk with a harassed half-smile.

'Okay, let me know once she's done and I'll get someone along,' the man barked into the phone and hung up. He was a tired-looking man in his late forties wearing a rumpled, ill-fitting suit. An air of weariness surrounded him like an aura.

'DS Liam Devlin. I come bearing gifts, my friend.' Liam smiled a greeting. He handed him a brown envelope containing the notebook and the bagged SD card.

'I'm DS Pete Lyons from the Sapphire team. I'm taking the rape job over, unfortunately. Are you from SC&O35? I'm hoping you've got some evidence with you, as right now I haven't a fucking clue what's going on.'

'The UC is away but we have an audio and visual record of what's happened. I've not seen it, but I'm assured it has captured everything. We also have other recordings from previous deployments, but they don't relate to Adebayo. The UC went to Adebayo's offices today in relation to a sham marriage job and the victim was supposed to be a bride. Unfortunately, Adebayo decided he was at liberty to help himself to the merchandise.'

'How many copies of this are there?'

'Just that one: no copying facilities at Forest Gate and we

wanted you to get hold of it right away. I assume Mr Adebayo is a bit pissed off?'

'That's a fucking understatement. Screaming about assault and entrapment and breaching legal privilege and all sorts of shit. He has a twat of a brief as well; the smarmy fucker is demanding bail before we've even got to the fucking bottom of what's happened.'

'How's the girl?'

'Not particularly injured, but she's shaken up as fuck. She won't stop crying and panicking about her family back in Bosnia or wherever. She's only just cooperating with the haven staff and has threatened to fuck off several times. I've got a SOIT investigator with her, but it still wouldn't surprise me if the girl fucked off given the chance.'

Devlin smiled to himself at the DS's command of old English oaths. It probably explained why the actual liaison with the victim was being left to one of the Sexual Offences Investigative Trained— or SOIT—officers.

'Okay. Well, the Home Office investigators are dealing with him for the immigration offences, which seem pretty tight. It would be really good if the sex offences stuck as well, as my man has intervened and blown his cover wide open.'

'We'll do our best, mate, but if she doesn't want to know, we're fucked anyway. Happens too often in sexual offences.'

The men shook hands and Liam left. Once in the car, he called Tom.

'I've delivered the SD card and your statement. It's up to them now, although it doesn't sound like the victim is being cooperative. They think she's scared and just wants to go home.'

'That wouldn't be good, Liam. I've assaulted him and his brother and I'm far too exposed on this job. We need Adebayo locked up.'

'Not much we can do about it now, mate, just got to let it ride out. Your recording keeps you well in the clear.'

Tom agreed, and they rang off, promising to speak the next day. Devlin started his car and drove off, looking forward to a pint after a difficult day.

*

Tom couldn't face going into Kilburn the next morning, so he phoned up and asked for a day off. He had worked extra hours recently so had lots of time to take. Simon Taylor was his usual blustery self but eventually agreed with a sigh, saying, 'We really need to speak about your career development, Tom. You've not had your shoulder to our wheel recently.'

That pissed Tom off, but he was too tired to argue with the senior officer. He knew from experience it wouldn't get him anywhere, so he kept his feelings to himself.

He made himself a strong coffee and ate some toast while the morning news played in the background. The job hadn't gone as well as he'd hoped. Adebayo had made a sensible arrest strategy impossible. The Home Office would be under severe pressure and it was in no way a sure thing that the CPS would authorise a charge on the immigration matters alone. The CPS wanted everything gift-wrapped, especially for an immediate charge. Home Office investigations were always drawn out, as they were so reliant on documentation that took time to assemble. Often that meant long periods of bail while all the paperwork was prepared to the CPS's exacting standards.

The telephone buzzing on the coffee table started him out of his reverie: it was Liam.

'They've bailed him.'

'What?'

'The girl is refusing to do a statement at the moment. She was too upset and just wanted to sleep. They've got her in a refuge in Clerkenwell until she feels up to it, but she's saying she wants to go home. They've just bailed Adebayo after a 'no comment' interview. The CPS won't authorise a charge on the immigration matters either. They've asked for loads more evidence before they'll authorise it. He has all sorts of bail conditions, but he's out on the street. I'm sorry to say though that's not the worst news I have.'

Tom felt a sick feeling in the pit of his stomach but said nothing, waiting for Liam to continue.

'The SD card was blank. Nothing on it, nada. You sure you set it up right?'

Tom felt like he'd been punched in the gut. He clearly remembered copying the file onto the phone, leaving the original footage on the SD card. This meant only one thing. The card had been wiped.

'Liam, I know I set it up right, I know it.' He thought the possibilities through. No one knew he had a copy of the footage, not Liam and none of the investigation teams. So it had either been deliberately or accidentally erased. Wiping the disc could be done simply enough on a computer just by formatting, or it could potentially be done with a strong magnet or extreme heat. But by who? Who could he trust? He had handed it to Liam, who said he had handed it in turn to the investigators.

'Who did you give the card to?' Tom asked.

'Some DS from Ilford called Pete Lyons. I don't know the bloke. What are you thinking?'

'Somehow, it's been wiped. But by who? Was it sealed when you handed it over?'

'Yes, mate. I sealed it at Forest Gate. You were there.'

'This is fucked up, Liam. It gives Adebayo a massive loophole to jump through: he can claim destruction of evidence and allege that it's all been concocted and a fit-up, for fuck's sake!'

Tom's head spun as he realised he didn't know who to trust. He recalled Liam sealing the bag, but that was the last he saw of it. Plenty of people would have had the opportunity, possibly, to interfere with the bag. He made a snap decision.

'I copied it,' he said. 'I put it on my phone to review it and check it had recorded okay. I watched it in the car before I got to Forest Gate.'

He heard a sharp intake of breath at the other end of the phone, followed by a pause.

'Jesus, man, that's good news. Defence may have a little go at a procedural breach but it's better than having nothing. When can you get it in?'

'I'm being careful with this one, Liam. I'll copy it and deal with it myself. I don't know who to trust here; someone has deliberately erased an exhibit, and there's only one reason. There's a fucking leak.' He hung up.

Tom's mind reeled. A leak, a corrupt officer somewhere. But who?

He didn't know Liam personally, but he had a very good reputation and a long and distinguished history with SC&O35. The bag had been sealed when he left Forest Gate, but Tom had no idea what had happened to it following that. Tom had the only copy of the undercover footage that would sink Adebayo and the Serbs. They would obviously be desperate to keep it under wraps; who knew what they were capable of to get it erased permanently? Without the footage there were so many holes in the case for a good lawyer to exploit, so it was unlikely that Adebayo and his brother would be convicted.

He went to his operational bag and retrieved his camera case, picking out a new SD card. Using the same lightning SD card port he had used the day before, he transferred the footage from his phone onto the blank card. The evidence contained on that small square of plastic and metal now held enormous importance and he had to protect it at all costs.

Who could he trust? The only name he was confident in was Neil Wilkinson, the head of the undercover unit. He picked up his phone and dialled.

'Tom, where are you?'

Not even a greeting. Neil was always to-the-point, but that was brusque even for him.

'At home. What's up?' asked Tom, feeling a rising sense of unease.

'We've just received a credible threat against you via the main informant's handler. The Serbs had Ivan up against a wall at some point overnight. He's played dumb but they know you're an undercover and, even worse, they know your true identity and that you live in Camden.' Neil's normal calm manner was gone, replaced with urgency and concern.

This is a fucking disaster, thought Tom. He wasn't safe, and he had to get out: now.

'How quickly can you get yourself to a nick? I'm calling witness protection now. We need some time to assess the risk and get something sorted. Liam's just told me about the SD card and your copy: do you still have it?'

Tom paused, his mind ticking over, assessing all the options. The SD card; that was what they wanted, and he knew they would do anything to get it.

'I still have it, it's safe,' he said, calmly. 'Who got hold of Ivan?'

'The Brankos. They were fuming, apparently, and he only just managed to bluff his way out of it. They said they have men out looking for you and you're going to get silenced permanently. Adebayo is making it clear there's money on your head. Jesus, this is fucked up, Tom. I'm sorry.'

'I thought the Brankos were out of the country? That's what they told me.'

'Well it seems they're back and it also seems that their dad, Zjelko, is with them. He got out of jail in Switzerland on early release. This ups the ante. He's very well connected and is a fully made member of the Serb mafia.'

Tom replied calmly, 'I'll get up to Holborn. Who shall I go and see?'

Neil sighed, the stress obvious in his voice. 'Get yourself to the Borough Commander's office. Mark Willis: you know him?'

'I know him, he was there when I was; he's a good guy. I'm leaving now.'

'Get out of there now, Tom: they must know your address by now. Talk to no one but Mark Willis; we don't know who we can trust.'

Tom hung up and paused for just a second, gathering his thoughts. If they knew his real identity, it wouldn't be difficult to trace him. If you have money, anyone can be traced if they live a normal life.

He stood and strode to his bedroom and the built-in wardrobe, removing the suitcase from the floor and peeling the carpet back from the suspended floor to reveal a recessed trapdoor. He lifted the particleboard hatch to reveal a small black Nike rucksack: a legacy from his days in the military, his grab-bag. All Det members had one, to be used in the case of a compromise or emergency that required them to escape and evade. Tom didn't know what the immediate future held, so some preparation could only be a good thing. After tucking the SD card into his sock, he grabbed his jacket and left the apartment.

*

Tom drove the short distance from his apartment to Holborn Police Station on the edge of the City of London. He decided not to go into the underground car park in case a swift exit was needed. He pulled over on Emerald Street and locked the car up, paying for an hour's-worth of parking at the nearby meter. The wardens were particularly zealous in that part of Camden and getting towed away at that point was not a great prospect. Hoisting the grab-bag over his shoulder, he made for the rear entrance of the nick by the roller-shuttered underground car park.

He felt calm, despite Neil's alarming call. He felt sure there would be some exaggeration involved: Ivan had always seemed a bit of a dramatist. The news that Branko senior was out of jail was disconcerting, though; the boys didn't worry him a bit, but their dad was a different prospect.

He went to the side door adjacent to the vehicle access roller-door and used his warrant card to swipe access into the pedestrian door. His first swipe led to a blinking red light on the keypad. Frowning slightly, he swiped again with the same result. The card entry systems in the Met were notoriously fickle, but he'd never had a problem at Holborn. Swiping again only produced the same blinking red light. He pushed the intercom button and listened to the repetitive tone indicating he should wait while the reception officer got to him.

A voice behind him said, 'DS Novak?'

Tom turned to see a well-built male, about his own age, smartly dressed in a blue suit and grey tie, with dirty blond, buzz-cut hair.

'Who wants to know?' said Tom, suspicion prickling his senses.

'I'm DS Martin Green from Witness Protection. I was coming to meet you here at the Borough Commander's office, but I'm glad I caught you now; we don't think it's secure here at Holborn.' He had a deep, resonant voice with the slightest tinge of a vaguely familiar accent.

He proffered the familiar Metropolitan Police warrant card with its standard-issue leather wallet and metal crest with braille underneath. Tom looked closely at the card: it looked brand new, the leather wallet still stiff, the plastic photocard inside shiny and unmarked. Looking at the warrant number Tom was able to estimate that the DS had a little more service than him. The name read 'Detective Sergeant Martin Green' and bore the familiar logo and embossed signature of the current Commissioner.

Tom took a long look at the man, noting the strong features and prominent forehead. Familiarity niggled.

'Have we met before?' Suspicion prickled in Tom's mind.

'I don't think so. Listen, you should come with me. We don't think it's safe here and it may be that Holborn is the source of the leak. My car is nearby and we have a safe house we can get to quickly. I can fill you in on what we know when we get there.' The man spoke quickly, and Tom thought he detected some urgency: or was it nervousness?

'I'm supposed to see the Borough Commander. Neil Wilkinson made it clear.'

'Change of plan. There's new intelligence from Ivan that the threat is imminent. Come on, I'll explain in the car. Neil is coming to the safe house too.'

The man turned as if to go. Tom hesitated, conflicted. He was suspicious, but he couldn't put his finger on entirely why. How else would the DS know he had been heading there if not from Neil?

'Okay, let's go then.'

They walked side-by-side along Emerald Street towards Rugby Street.

'You're definitely familiar, Martin,' said Tom as they walked. 'Were you on my promotion course last year?'

'No. I've been a DS for a few years now. I don't think we know each other.'

Tom's mind began to work systematically. The warrant card was brand new, as in just issued; the poor quality of the materials used in the cards meant they always deteriorated quickly. Something wasn't right: the accent wasn't right, he didn't look right. Tom got a sinking feeling in his gut, aware he may have made a big mistake.

'Where are you based, Martin?'

'At the Yard,' the man replied, keeping his gaze straight ahead. 'But I came here straight from home on a call-out. Busy day, eh?' He offered a slight but uncertain smile.

Tom cast his mind back to the man's brand-new warrant card, the photograph of the smartly dressed man, in a blue suit and grey tie.

Blue suit... grey tie... The same blue suit and grey tie the man was wearing right now.

*

Martin produced a car key from his trouser pocket as they approached a blue Audi Q5 parked on Emerald Street by the dead end, unlocking the car with the remote.

'We'll get your car later, once you're out of the way.'

Tom stopped and squatted down in a show of tying his shoelace, but more to have the opportunity to assess Martin from behind at a slightly longer distance. Was it just his imagination that there was a slight disturbance in the suit's line at the back? Was that a small bulge in the base of his spine? A pancake holster? Tom knew for a fact that witness protection officers were not armed, instead availing themselves of SCO19—the specialist firearms unit—when required.

Tom wondered if he was being paranoid, but thought the consequences through quickly.

Martin turned, suddenly aware that Tom was no longer next to him, a slightly impatient look showing in his light-blue eyes.

'We must get a move on,' he said, the slight but familiar accent barely discernible but ringing further alarm bells in Tom's mind. It was time to act; no turning back.

Martin moved to the front passenger door, opening it for Tom as a chauffeur would, jerking his head towards the leather seat.

Tom shrugged his grab-bag from his back and went to the rear passenger door, opening it and casually throwing the bag on the rear seat. He slammed the door while mentally preparing his next move, knowing he probably only had one chance. Martin was a big guy and Tom instinctively knew he would be problematic without the element of surprise.

Tom shaped his body as if to lower himself into the Audi passenger seat. As he did so, Martin turned to cross in front of the car to the driver's seat. Tom raised his right hand in a club fist and drove it hard, four inches below the big man's ear, smashing into the vagus nerve chain. Martin's knees buckled, and he hit the floor in a crumpled heap.

It was serious now. If Tom was wrong, he would be in big trouble for knocking out a colleague. But he was certain he wasn't. He searched the man's pockets and found that his instincts had been correct. Under his left armpit was a handgun, secured in a concealed holster.

Tom looked at the Sig Sauer P226. Not police issue, certainly not with the silencer attached to the front: an assassin's weapon. With the subsonic ammunition that Tom was willing to bet the weapon was packing, it was very quiet. The 9mm round it fired was designed, even at low speeds, to bounce around inside the body, ricocheting off bones but staying inside, causing maximum damage.

A ticking clock in Tom's head told him that only a few seconds had passed and, as there was no way of telling how long Martin would be out, he had to move fast. In the man's inside jacket pocket, he found a set of plastic zip-ties. He heaved the big man up and deposited him in through the passenger door, lying him prone over both seats. He jammed the man's legs into the passenger footwell and zip-tied his hands to the steering wheel as tight as he could manage.

Whoever Martin was, he began to stir slowly, his face pressed into the driver's seat. A slight groan, no more than a murmur, emitted from him.

Tom continued to search his pockets and produced the warrant card, a small, fat brown leather wallet, and an iPhone. A small, zipped-up leather folded case was in the other jacket pocket. Tom grabbed his bag and put all the items inside apart from the iPhone. The bulge Tom had noted in the small of the man's back revealed two spare clips for the Sig, which he also threw into the rucksack. He took the iPhone and pressed the home button to reveal the time and a locked screen. It was an iPhone 7 with fingerprint recognition, so Tom leant over and pressed the man's right thumb against the reader. 'Try again' blinked up on the screen. He tried the left thumb and the phone unlocked, revealing minimal apps loaded. He quickly went into the phone's settings to disable the key lock, but it required a code. Tom scowled. The phone may have elicited contacts and clues that would be useful, but he assumed it would auto-lock after a given period, normally less than a minute.

He checked the phone's contact list, which was empty. He checked the call history: empty. Emails: empty. SMS history: empty. WhatsApp was installed but, again, was empty.

'Damn, damn, damn!' he muttered under his breath. This man was a professional. The deleted calls and messages could probably have been retrieved but only with a forensic download. He engaged airplane mode on the phone, so it couldn't be remotely wiped, and threw it in his bag.

'You've no idea what you're doing or who you're fucking with,' slurred the man, contempt in his voice, the accent a little stronger now.

'Well, I hope they're better than you, sunshine. Look where you are now.'

The man strained his head up and fixed Tom with a defiant stare. 'You'll regret this. These people have reach everywhere. There's nowhere they can't find you. Give them the card and they'll leave you alone.'

'Well, forgive me if I don't believe you on that one, pal.' Realising that time was limited and any further discussion was pointless, Tom produced his own iPhone, enabled the camera function and said, 'Smile, sweetheart.' He took a headshot of the man, forced his feet fully inside the Audi and slammed the door shut.

Tom estimated that the whole encounter, from incapacitating Martin to slamming the door, had taken approximately three minutes. He needed to get moving quickly as, inevitably, Martin would not be alone.

He slung the now-heavier rucksack over his shoulder and made his way back to his car. The street was clear and he looked around, hoping he hadn't been spotted. He made a snap decision; he had to get off the street somewhere safe, to get his thoughts together and plan his next move. One thing was clear: he couldn't trust anyone in the job. There was at least one bent bastard and probably more. Given that they'd managed to track him quickly, they were also probably highly placed, with access to all police systems. Worryingly, they also had to have the highest levels of clearance and the ability to use the most secret and sensitive intelligence tools available. His mind raced, and only one name hit him as someone he could trust and who might be able to help.

Mike Brogan. Mike still owed him a big favour from that day in Iraq.

13

Tom planned as he drove along Grays Inn Road towards Kings Cross. First job was to get off the street and out of the area. He couldn't go back home; not at that moment in any case. Whoever was tracking him would surely have it staked out as the first port of call. He needed somewhere anonymous, preferably in an area unconnected to him where he could blend in while he collected his thoughts.

He had only once chance of survival at that moment. By going dark.

He didn't know who was his ally and who was his enemy. All the normal methods were redundant; the people looking for him clearly had access to all the resources he'd normally use to track down the most serious criminals.

He made his way out west through the heavy traffic towards the A40 and decided to head towards Uxbridge. It was conveniently placed for him to head wherever he needed to go once he'd spoken to Mike. It was an area of London he'd never worked in but was familiar with from his military days. On occasion he'd flown from the nearby RAF base when deploying on snap operations around the world, and he knew that the area was busy enough but not so rampant with CCTV as Central London.

His journey took longer than normal owing to the anti-surveillance tactics he used. He circumnavigated every roundabout fully once before exiting. He stopped and observed frequently and practised the old technique of 'blocking': leaving the main routes and driving around residential blocks repeatedly, looking for any followers. By the time he got to Shepherds Bush he was sure he hadn't been followed.

He needed to lose his car. He was aware that whoever was feeding the Brankos information could, with just one phone call, have his car followed using automatic number plate recognition. He drove off the A40 towards Shepherds Bush and into the NCP car park right by the Empire Theatre, where he parked it on the first floor. Putting his car in a pay-on-exit car park would ensure it would be safe and unnoticed, unlike if it was left on the street. Parking enforcement in London was so stringent that it wouldn't last a day without getting towed. Using a car park would also add to any confusion of those tracking him.

He picked up his grab-bag containing the liberated Sig and other items taken from Martin Green and made his way out onto Wood Lane.

He hailed a black cab and asked the sullen driver to take him to Hillingdon Station, just off the A40. He wanted to blur his trail a little further before holing up somewhere.

Traffic was busy but not solid, so the trip took about forty minutes in almost total silence, which Tom was thankful for. The last thing he needed was the archetypal London cabbie talking non-stop. As they drove, he dug out the leather wallet he had taken from his attacker. It contained a fat wad of bank notes, a credit card in the name of J Vele, and a driving licence in the name of Martin Green.

Tom was no forgery expert, but he'd received some input from the Home Office experts at the beginning of an undercover forgery investigation into fake documents in the past. He studied the card and noted that the ink quality looked faded and that the corners of the cards were slightly unevenly cut. Genuine driving licences were machine cut, giving perfectly curved corners. That was puzzling; an apparently genuine warrant card with a forged driving licence, both produced that day if the suit was anything to go by. His puzzlement began to shift to concern as he realised the resources his enemies seemed to have access to. He couldn't rule out that his phone was being intercepted, which would give away his exact location. At the very least, they could be tracking his position and direction of travel by using the cell sites as his and Martin's phones tried to connect with the masts as he passed. Both phones would have to remain in airplane mode until he was more prepared.

He pulled out of his bag the fat leather pouch that he'd taken from Martin. He unfastened the side-zip and examined the contents. A syringe was secured by a leather loop with a sheathed IV needle already attached. Alongside was a small bottle marked with Cyrillic script with an English translation underneath: Sodium Thiopental.

His concern deepened even further. He had received significant medical training when he was in the military, including on the use of drugs and intravenous injections. This was a fast-acting barbiturate that would render its victim unconscious very quickly. So Martin's intention was clear: overpower Tom, inject him with the sodium thiopental and secure him properly. Then probably interrogation until Tom revealed the whereabouts of the SD card. The silenced Sig was probably for despatching him once he had handed over the card. His wary respect for his adversaries raised another notch: they not only had resources but also the skills to obtain and administer dangerous, stupefying drugs.

He asked the taciturn driver to drop him on the approach road to the station, paying him with the notes taken from Martin's wallet. He stashed all the items away back in his bag and got out of the car, walking briskly away.

He decided he needed a drink and a phone as he spotted The Swallow Public House just off the Uxbridge Road. With its Tudor-style beams and floral window boxes and baskets, it looked like a perfect, anonymous bolthole to plan his next move. He needed a firm plan; he was now being sought by Serbian Mafia who clearly wanted him dead.

*

It was just after 11am, so the pub was empty aside from a fat, middle-aged barman leaning against the bar reading a tabloid newspaper. He glanced up at Tom as he walked in and subjected him to a cool appraisal before returning to his paper. It was a typical West London suburban pub struggling to make a living, if the décor was anything to go by. The sour smell of stale beer was strangely comforting to Tom as he approached the bar.

'You have any malts?'

'Just White Horse or Bells, mate,' replied the barman, not looking up from his paper. Tom smiled lightly, wondering how long the pub would last in business with the guy's charm.

'Lager it is, then. Fosters, please.' He wasn't a whisky snob, but it had to be single malt or he wasn't bothering. 'Do you have a payphone?'

'By the bogs.' The barman nodded to the toilets at the back of the pub.

Tom paid for the beer, set it down on a table and made his way to the door marked 'Toilets', finding the payphone on the wall on the other side. He imagined that the phone was particularly popular with local drug dealers trying to keep their conversations away from the ears of law enforcement officers.

Tom fed a few coins into the slot and dialled a number from memory. The receiver emitted several clicks before transferring to a long, high-pitched ringtone. After a few rings it was answered with a familiar Californian drawl. 'Hello?'

Tom recognised the voice straight away as Mike Brogan, memories returning of their time in Iraq as he pictured the handsome, tanned face.

'Mike?'

'Yeah, who's this?'

'It's Tom. Tom Novak.'

'Tom, my man, where you been? I've not seen you for like three years and you call now. Everything okay?'

'Not really, mate. You remember you mentioned if ever I needed a favour? Well, I need one now. Badly.' Tom was surprised at the slight hint of emotion in his own voice.

'Where are you calling from, Tom?'

'I'm in a pub on a payphone,' said Tom, 'I needed to get off the street.'

There was a slight pause that seemed an eternity.

'I'll call you on this number in ten minutes. Stay there and stay outta sight,' said Mike in a firm, calm voice before hanging up.

Tom returned to his beer at the table closest to the phone. He sat and took a long pull on the cold lager; the liquid was soothing in the way that only cheap lager could be, calming his parched throat.

He thought through the events of the past two days. It was clear that someone with police or other law enforcement resources was tracking him to recover the SD card and probably to silence him for good. The suppressed Sig was good enough evidence for that, given that it was a perfect assassin's weapon. Martin had said enough for Tom to realise that the threat emanated from Adebayo. The question was: who was tracking him? He needed more information, but who could he trust? A wave of loneliness swept over him as the reality of his situation hit home.

That all just reinforced the fact that he needed help from someone who had access to all of the intelligence systems that weren't available to him now he'd gone dark.

After a few minutes, Tom returned to the payphone to wait for Mike's call.

Exactly ten minutes since he had ended the call, the phone rang again.

Tom picked it up. 'Mike?'

'Sure, buddy… I've checked this number out; it's safe for a short time and we've put an electronic disruption around it. Anyone listening wouldn't hear shit, man. But we only have five minutes, max.'

'I was on an undercover op against some Serbs and a Nigerian lawyer,' Tom said, getting straight down to business. 'I've been compromised and there's at least one highly-placed dirty cop feeding back on me. I've just had a serious attempt on my life that probably came from my phone being intercepted. I've gone dark and I'm laying low until I can figure this out.' He spoke calmly but his words were tinged with rage.

'Okay, man, that's a bad situation. What do you need? I'll do anything I can, but I can't give you boots on the ground. It's very touchy politically at the moment between the UK and US.'

'I need some IT capability to try to figure out who is working against me. It's at least one but probably two corrupt individuals. I need access to systems to find out who's bugging me, who's tracking me, and who wants to kill me. I'll also need someone with the kit to interrogate the phone I liberated from the guy who tried to take me out. I could also do with some tactical gear, surveillance, and maybe some weaponry. I've liberated a Sig from the hit man, but it's a dirty gun so I don't want to use it.' Tom knew he was asking a lot, but he had to try.

'Okay, Tom, I'm going to send someone to see you who's already in London. They work for us as a consultant, of sorts. They are awesome at hacking and anything you need on that front. Tactical kit I'll have to think about. I'm in Paris at a conference right now. I'd be over there myself but I'm section chief at Brussels now, so I gotta tread carefully or this could be a major diplomatic incident. Where are you staying?' Mike's calm control was comforting.

'Nowhere yet. I can't go home as I'm compromised. I'll get a hotel nearby; I can be anonymous as I still have my alternate ID driving licence from my SRR days, and I have a safe credit card.'

Tom could hear the tapping of a keyboard over the phone line.

'Okay, get yourself to the Ramada in South Ruislip. Get a burner phone on the way and send me a text with your room number and name you're using. My contact, Pet, will be with you early evening. Stay safe, man; I'll never forget what you did for me and I will be as good as my word.' With that, he rang off.

*

Tom found a mini-cab by Hillingdon Station, driven by an elderly Pakistani man only too glad of a fare. He was a pleasant enough guy who engaged in small talk with Tom on the short journey to South Ruislip, dropping him off by a small parade of shops.

Tom crossed over to the Asda superstore and made his way straight to the electronics section to purchase a simple Nokia phone and a £50 top-up voucher, paid for with cash so that nothing could link him with them. His iPhone and the one taken from Martin remained in airplane mode, safely stashed in his bag. His route had been circuitous, and only paid for in cash; he was off-grid and hiding in plain sight.

He strode up to the check-in desk at the Ramada Hotel. It seemed clean, modern, and anonymous and perfect for Tom's purposes. He fixed the smiling, pretty receptionist with his most self-effacing smile. A name badge announced her as Beata, her smile was wide and genuine, and she had dark curly hair and vivid blue eyes.

'May I help you, sir?' she said in a Polish accent.

'I'd like a room for a night, please.'

Her smile widened. 'No problem, sir. We only have a queen-sized room left at one hundred and ten pounds with breakfast. Is this okay?'

'Fine,' said Tom, handing over a pre-paid MasterCard in the name of Tom Johnson. The name was replicated on a genuine driving licence that bore his picture, issued to him while he was in the SRR.

He had obtained the bank card a while ago as an insurance policy for events such as this. His time with SRR had made him very careful, always expecting the worst. The work had been such that, if his identity had become known in some circles, then contracts on his head would have followed. He had killed two prominent Republicans in Northern Ireland, as well as the two Al-Qaeda operatives he'd despatched in 2005 while rescuing Mike Brogan. Tom was a careful man by nature, and the option of £2,000 in untraceable funds was attractive. Using his own credit card at that moment would have been akin to painting a target on his chest and waiting for the bad guys to come. Not for the first time he silently thanked his own in-built caution.

It was a lesson he had learnt from his childhood: life can take a turn at a moment's notice. Some lessons you never forget.

Beata handed over a plastic card room key accompanied with a brilliant smile. 'Room 231, Mr Johnson. Enjoy your stay.'

*

The first-floor room was just as Tom had expected: clean and tidy, with two huge beds alongside each other and a spotless bathroom. It overlooked the front of the hotel, giving Tom a good view of the road in front as well as South Ruislip Station.

Tom sent a simple text to Mike. 'Room 231, Tom Johnson'.

Within a minute the reply came in from the familiar number.

'Affirmative. Pet visiting you 1900hrs. We'll speak soon. Stay safe, buddy.'

Tom reached for his grab-bag and took a closer look at the items liberated from Martin Green. He first checked the Sig, handling it with practised ease as he ejected the magazine and worked the action, expelling the round in the chamber. The weapon was clean, well-oiled and, tellingly, had a machined gouge where the serial number would have once been. The suppressor was of a professional grade and not one of the home-made varieties he often encountered. He examined one of the 9mm rounds and made an educated guess that they were subsonic hollow points. It was an ideal assassin's weapon: light and easily concealed, quiet but with enough stopping power for the task. Not readily available in the UK, and very few were encountered on the black market.

Tom rifled through the wallet but found nothing of any further interest, taking out the banknotes totalling £350, and adding them to his own stash. He took another look at the warrant card, the image of 'Green' glowering out at him. Tom was sure it was genuine. The warrant number was a little older than Tom's: no more than a year though, he estimated. It could be the key to unlocking who was helping Adebayo from the inside, so he needed to know more about it.

On an impulse, he picked up the burner phone and dialled a London number.

'CID Office Kilburn, how may I help you?' boomed Stan's familiar voice.

'Stan, it's Tom. Don't say my name out loud. Just talk some crap for a second and call me back on this number when you can talk,' said Tom. The office at Kilburn was small and anyone could have been listening.

'I'm sorry, my dear. I don't think DC Yeung is working today. Can I leave a message for him? I can call you back in five minutes if I can find out exactly when he's back?'

'Five minutes. This number, Stan: it's important. You trust me, right?'

'Of course, my dear. I will speak to you as soon as I have more information for you.' The phone went dead.

Stan was a first-class liar and wonderful at placating irate victims, witnesses, and suspects.

Exactly five minutes later, Tom's phone vibrated.

'What the fuck's going on, Royal?'

'What have you heard?'

'Something about you going rogue, some shit about a death threat, and you've run off with the evidence. Glenda's been going on at me, asking if I've heard from you.'

Stan couldn't stand DCI Simon Taylor, hence the 'old woman' nickname: Glenda. They had often clashed but the DCI was fearful about Stan's influence wrecking his career, so those clashes had been fewer of late.

'That's partly true. I got compromised on a UC job. There's at least one corrupt cop passing info to some properly nasty Serbs, and some bastard tried to terminate me with extreme prejudice this morning when I tried to get into Holborn nick. I don't know who to trust, Stan. They have serious reach. I think they have intercepts on me and possibly surveillance. The guy who tried to take me out was a DS Martin Green, warrant number 203745, allegedly of witness protection. The warrant card is genuine, but he has a fake driving licence.'

Stan exhaled heavily. 'What can I do?'

'I need you to check out Martin Green and the warrant number; I think the card was issued today and is genuine. Find out what you can, eh?'

'Leave it with me. Anything else?'

'I may need a job car with covert blues-and-twos.' He figured an unmarked car with the under-grille flashing lights and siren would be useful if the situation went as he thought it might.

'Righto, Royal, I'll see what I can do. Stay by the phone and I'll get back to you.'

'Thanks, Royal,' Tom said, hanging up.

He looked at his worn and scuffed watch; it was only one o'clock. He couldn't stand the thought of waiting around in the room for another six hours. The time could be used a little more fruitfully, and he wanted to get a better idea as to who was following him.

Time enough to test his hunters, see who he was dealing with and, more importantly, how good they were.

A tinge of excitement began to push the mix of fear and rage away. He'd gone up against serious bad guys in the past and he wanted to see who was out there this time.

*

He left his hotel room and crossed over the road to the Asda superstore, an idea forming of how he could draw his pursuers out into the open. His hair was currently longer than average for a police officer, he had a heavy stubble and was casually dressed in jeans and trainers. Given that that was what his pursuers were no doubt looking out for, a change of appearance was in order.

After entering the store, he browsed for five minutes at the magazine racks and leafed through a copy of a magazine, keeping a peripheral view of the CCTV monitors on the wall by the entrance security station. He didn't think he was being followed, but a little anti-surveillance could only be a good thing. He saw no one suspicious: only shoppers.

He made his way to the clothing section and selected a simple navy-blue suit and a white shirt-and-tie set. He picked up a pair of plain black shoes and went to the checkout, grabbing a pack of disposable razors and some shaving foam on the way.

He was not a habitual suit wearer; despite the CID dress code, he normally found an excuse not to dress smartly, much to the chagrin of his boss. He was amazed that for less than fifty pounds he'd purchased full business-wear. It was not Savile Row but he didn't think anyone would be looking that hard.

Having paid, he made his way to the toilets and slipped into the disabled cubicle. He stripped to the waist, lathered and shaved his face clean, and then changed into the newly acquired suit, shirt and tie.

He then headed to the Turkish barber shop on the small parade close by for a short-back-and-sides. As the silently scowling barber went about his work, Tom watched the transformation before his very eyes. From his inside pocket he produced a pair of clear glasses he'd retrieved from his grab-bag, put them on, and checked himself in the mirror. He couldn't have looked more different from the slightly scruffy, bearded man of just an hour before.

The art of disguise is not radical: just don't be what people are looking for and your disguise is complete.

His haircut complete, Tom made his way to the Tube station and used his pre-paid Oyster card to beep through the barrier. The card was fully cash-paid, with no audit trail: unlike the police issue card that left a big computer footprint. To the letter he was using perfect tradecraft, employing the military mantra of the seven Ps: Prior Planning and Preparation Prevents Piss-Poor Performance.

*

He took the underground to Ealing Broadway, a typical busy suburban London shopping area which was not too swamped by CCTV.

He located a Cash Converters store near the shopping centre where, for £100 cash, he purchased a second-hand Sony digital SLR camera with a 300mm zoom lens thrown in. It was an old-style model but would be more than adequate for the job he had in mind. Even more conveniently, the guy behind the counter was happy to throw in the scruffy-looking shoulder bag which the items were displayed in.

He made his way to the Town Hall: a grand, Grade II listed building set back away from the main road. It had lots of meeting rooms and dining suites, as well as the usual council facilities and registry functions. More importantly for Tom, it had several meeting rooms at the front of the building overlooking the Broadway. He had once used them as an observation point when involved in a manhunt for a murder suspect.

He approached the receptionist who greeted him warmly, produced his warrant card and, flashing his most charming smile, said, 'Hi, I'm DS Novak; I wonder if I could just borrow one of your front-facing meeting rooms for an hour or so. We are waiting for a suspect to show up at the pub over the road. I'll be discreet and won't get in anyone's way.'

The receptionist smiled politely as she looked at the warrant card. 'I'll have to get it authorised by the building manager, but I'm sure it's okay.'

She made the call while Tom stared out of the window to the front of the building.

'The manager says that's fine. Take room 125 on the first floor. Here's the key, if you can just drop it back when you're done. Can you sign for it here?' She indicated a key list on a clipboard.

Tom scribbled an illegible scrawl on the form.

'I'll be back in ten minutes if that's okay,' he said. 'I just need to grab something.'

Tom left the building, crossed the road to the Café Nero

opposite, and went inside.

He ordered a black coffee and a panini, which he paid for with his personal credit card. He sat at a table at the rear of the busy coffee shop and switched his iPhone on for the first time since disarming Martin. As the buzz of several missed calls and text messages broke the phone's enforced silence, he imagined the signal hitting the nearby cell masts, announcing his phone's presence back in cyberspace. He was now visible to the world, just as he wanted: now he could see who was doing the hunting.

He switched the phone back into airplane mode, silencing its presence once more. Most of the text messages had been from Neil Wilkinson, one from Liam Devlin, and a haughty one from Simon Taylor demanding to know where he was. A couple of voicemails were also showing as received, but he wasn't willing to come off airplane mode to listen to those. He doubted anything of value would be on them in any case.

Tom left his coffee and panini behind and left the café, surprised to see a phone box a short distance outside. Finding a working payphone was a rarity, so Tom felt that at least something had gone his way today. He went into the booth, fed a coin into the slot and dialled the number for Neil Wilkinson, knowing that the number of the payphone would be visible at the other end.

'Neil Wilkinson, can I help you?'

'Neil, it's Tom.'

'Jesus, where are you? Everyone's been crapping themselves.' The emotion in Neil's voice seemed genuine.

'Never mind where I am, who did you tell I was going to Holborn?'

'Just witness protection, Simon Taylor, and the Borough Commander.'

'How did they get to me then?'

'We've no idea; we don't know how you've been compromised. Look, just come in, we can keep you safe.'

'I don't trust you, Neil, I don't trust anyone.' And he hung up, his presence now marked for everyone to see.

Tom crossed the road and re-entered the Town Hall, smiling at the receptionist as he passed her on his way to the lifts. Making his way up to the first floor, he unlocked room 125 and entered a small meeting room, which had a large central table and a spider conference-call phone in the middle. The projector and big screen marked the room's purpose as the home of many a pointless meeting.

He went to the window and surveyed the scene in front of him about 100 yards away. He had a perfect view of the café and the phone boxes. Now he just had to wait.

*

He didn't have to wait long.

He recognised the blue Audi Q5 pulling up outside the café, clearly unconcerned about traffic wardens, as the one Martin Green had tried to force him into.

He raised the camera and began snapping away as he saw 'Martin' leaving the driver's seat, a hard look on his face. He was joined on the pavement by two other males, both Slav-looking with jutting cheekbones. One had short, cropped, blond hair; the other collar-length and untidy hair. Both looked lean and had a military bearing. Tom continued to snap away as they entered the café three abreast, looking as tough as possible.

Tom checked the photos he'd taken in full zoom, giving him good headshots of all three men. Other than Martin, the men were not familiar. He noted the registration of the Audi: brand new and, he guessed, rented.

While the three were out of sight in the café, a large, powerful, motorbike arrived in the front of the café and mounted the pavement close to the Audi. The leather-clad rider dismounted and removed his helmet, revealing a middle-aged man with cropped blond hair and a rough Slavic face. Even at that distance Tom saw the piercing blue eyes. He zoomed the camera in and snapped a full-face shot. He paused, a flicker of recognition itching a corner of his brain as he lowered the camera and watched the man surveying the scene in front of him. At one point it seemed to Tom that the man was staring straight at him, those pale blue eyes impassive and tinged with cruelty.

His reverie was broken when the three men came out of the café and joined motorbike man on the pavement for a short conversation. Motorbike man seemed to be the boss; the body language of the others was certainly deferential as he barked orders at them. Motorbike man then produced a mobile phone from his pocket and spoke on it for a minute while the others stood by, scanning the area carefully.

A distant siren seemed to spook the four men. A decision made, Martin and his cohorts got back in the Audi and sped off. Motorcycle man paused for a moment, looking at the phone in his hand before pocketing it, replacing his helmet, and roaring off. Tom photographed the retreating motorbike, capturing the number plate as it disappeared down the Broadway.

Interestingly, no one took any notice of the payphone Tom had used. That could have been an indication that Neil Wilkinson wasn't involved, although he'd need more conclusive evidence to be sure.

Tom smiled to himself. Putting his head above the parapet had been worth it: photos of four of his pursuers and registration numbers for two vehicles.

14

Michael Adebayo sat in his office in Ilford with his brother, Emmanuel. The atmosphere had been thick with tension ever since they received the call from Zjelko Branko. A dense fug of cigarette smoke hung in the air as both men chain-smoked in a forlorn attempt to dissipate the stress.

As soon as he'd heard about the situation with the undercover cop, Zjelko had taken charge, coming over to Adebayo's office. He was an overpowering character and, frankly, he terrified Michael. He had pale blue, ice-cold eyes that barely concealed the venom from within. Michael had heard all about his past as a suspected Balkan war criminal: a high-class jewel thief with a direct line into the Serbian Mafia, a terrifying thug who had accepted Adebayo's contract to silence Novak.

'One hundred thousand pounds, Michael,' Zjelko had said. 'No one else will be able to do it. We have a tame senior cop who has access to all the databases, banks, phones, the lot. Only we can find the bastard and silence him for good. Good people don't come cheap and the cop isn't cheap; neither are we,' he had said with a sneer. 'If you'd have kept your cock in your pants, you wouldn't be in this situation, would you?'

Adebayo had said nothing, just looked at his brother who met his glance evenly.

'If you find him and silence him and get me the SD card, then £100k is okay; just do it quick.'

That was yesterday, and they'd just received a call from Branko.

'He's just surfaced in Ealing. Used his credit card and phone in a café. We're going after him now.'

Adebayo couldn't hide his excitement.

'Once he's gone and we have the card, then we're home and dry. Just the bitch to deal with—and she'll say fuck-all, she'll be so scared!' he said animatedly to his taciturn brother.

An hour later, another call came in from Branko.

'He wasn't there. No sight of him and the staff didn't recognise the photo of him. The cop assured us that he'd spent seven pounds on his credit card and his mobile phone went live and received some messages. It hit a cell phone mast close to the cafe so, unless it was someone else using his card and phone, he was there.' Branko spoke in a matter-of-fact tone that infuriated Michael.

'For fuck's sake, I thought you had him. This isn't what I'm paying you for, you fool. He must be caught now!'

There was a pause that seemed endless to Michael.

'I would advise you not to speak like this to me, Mr Adebayo. I don't like being insulted. It makes me sad.'

The tone was full of menace and immediately Adebayo regretted his words.

'I'm sorry. I'm just stressed.'

'We are on the trail and we have some other options to bring him out of hiding. Don't worry, we'll find him.'

15

Tom returned to his hotel room at about 6pm, after a circuitous route back using public transport to make sure he hadn't been followed. He felt secure in the hotel for the time being, knowing it could have no links back to him.

Feeling uncomfortable in his cheap suit, he ripped it off and hung it in the wardrobe before taking a long, hot shower, grunting as the jets washed away some of the stress of the last few days. He towelled-off and dressed in his casual clothes to await the arrival of the CIA consultant.

He switched on the TV and turned to the twenty-four-hour rolling news programme. Nothing of any interest was showing; the usual threats of terror and political malfeasance. It always amazed Tom how quickly deplorable situations became the everyday norm in the UK.

His burner phone buzzed on the bed. He picked it up and answered with a 'Hello?'

'Tom? Stan. You free to speak?'

'Crack on, mate. I'm clear.'

'Right, your friend Martin Green doesn't exist. There's only two in the Met, neither of which are your man. The warrant number is a dead one from a PC who transferred to North Yorkshire a good while ago. Her name was Jill Buchanan. With me so far?'

'Yes, mate. Go on.'

'I made some calls and called in a favour or two. The warrant card was issued first thing this morning. My mate knows the main man at the Passes and Permits Issue desk at the Yard. He's let me know that a guy came in with all the paperwork present and correct and a temporary pass was issued. He can't remember where the temporary pass was issued or who countersigned the paperwork. This stinks, Tom. Someone with a bit of clout has organised a genuine pass to be issued to a fucking imposter. I could find out more: my mate is the head of security at NSY. You want me to?'

'No. I want to keep this tight until I know more.' The more people who got involved, the greater the risk of him being exposed, especially if they got New Scotland Yard involved. 'Any luck with a car?'

'Of course. I thoroughly enjoyed relieving our favourite DCI of that car he likes to monopolise. He wasn't pleased, but I convinced him it needs servicing. It's yours for a few days at least; just don't crash it.' Tom could almost hear the delight in Stan's voice. 'Where do you want it? I can leave it anywhere. It's a newish VW Passat with covert blues-and-twos. It really irritates me that Glenda monopolises it.'

Tom knew that Stan lived in Greenford, not that far from his hotel.

'Can you park it in McDonald's car park at the roundabout off the A40? Leave the keys in the exhaust pipe and I'll get a cab up to it,' said Tom.

'Consider it done, dear boy. You take care and call me if there's anything else I can do. Some bastards have it in for you and I don't want you coming to any harm.'

Tom smiled to himself at his friend's concern.

'Just give me the heads-up on this number on anything you hear, mate. And mention to no one that we've spoken. I'll call you soon.'

16

The senior police officer sat in his office with the door shut, worry etched across his features. He reached into his bottom desk drawer, pulled out a half-bottle of Jameson's whisky, and poured a large measure into his empty coffee cup. He took a sip and felt the comforting burn of the liquor sliding down his throat and into his stomach. The stress of the last day had been unbearable ever since the Brankos called him about Novak's activities. They wanted help, and lots of it. They wanted evidence stealing and information about Novak. He initially refused, told them to fuck off and no mistake.

That was a bad idea. They got hold of him as he had left the police station; worse still they had their father with them. He was a nasty bastard who scared the shit out of him. He looked dangerous and what the officer had since found out about him—a Serb paramilitary and war criminal suspected of multiple killings over the years—meant he was right to be scared. A mate on Interpol had looked into him and what he found out was shocking: Branko was a sadistic psychopath.

It was fine when he used to just keep the Branko brothers informed of any police activity into their brothels, but this was different; this was big league.

He had got caught up with the Brankos when he found himself invited to one of their party nights. It was just so decadent that he couldn't help himself, and he recalled the incident with the impossibly-young girl who had sidled up to him after a brief conversation with Mira.

'Hey, baby. Mira tells me I show you good time,' she whispered sexily, showing even, white teeth in a broad smile. He had pretended not to notice that her pupils were as wide as saucers, evidence of recent use of a stimulant. He recalled the lurch of excitement in his stomach as she spoke. He just couldn't believe he'd allowed himself to be so weak; in his heart he knew they were trafficked girls and he was behaving like a fool.

He shuddered at the memory of one of the big minders, Aleks, smiling at him while studying the warrant card that he'd plucked out from his discarded trousers. 'Well look what we have here: we have a Detective with us, and a senior one, as well.' He had guffawed drunkenly, showing his crooked teeth.

'We won't tell a soul, my friend. Just keep us informed of any interest in us and maybe check out an enemy if we need you to,' had said the big, ugly bastard Aleks.

It had gone on for a little while; he would periodically check the databases but got no signs of them being investigated, which reassured the brothers. Once or twice they had asked for vehicles to be checked, but nothing too serious and he had started to relax. He had even allowed himself a couple of visits with one of the prettier young girls, Ana, who always made him feel wonderful and who the brothers allowed him to visit for free. More recently he had tried to pull away from the Brankos and hadn't visited any of their brothels for a few months. He had started to believe that maybe he was free of them, as he hadn't heard anything for a while.

And then it happened. Out of the blue the father, Zjelko, had pinned him to the wall outside the police station in a side street.

'You'll help us find Novak, as you didn't tell us about the operation into my wife and sons.'

'But it wasn't a police enquiry, it was immigration looking at the solicitor,' he had whined, his lips quivering in fear.

'You will help us or your bosses will see this.' Branko had produced a smartphone and played a section of video back to him. His heart had sunk as he watched.

The pin-sharp images on the small screen were of him, naked

with Ana, clearly snorting cocaine from her tanned belly. The scene was so seedy it almost made him want to weep. Why was he so weak? He knew how the scene would be viewed. A saggy, middle-aged man with a barely-legal prostitute; the drugs would just be the icing on the cake. He could all-too-easily imagine the headline in the red-top press: 'Senior Cop in Seedy Drug Vice Sting.' He had shuddered at the prospect, feeling a cold sweat breaking out. His career would be finished and he could even end up in prison, his pension gone.

'You either help us find Novak or these go to your bosses and the newspaper,' Zjelko had growled, his blue eyes boring into him. 'I don't care how you do it; you get him for us. You have the connections, you're a senior officer. Tap his phone and get into his bank accounts, whatever. Just get us leads on where he is. Adebayo will even pay you if you succeed. But if you don't, you'll have me to answer to, little pig.'

So that was it. He was fully committed and in way over his head. He didn't feel that bad about Novak: the stupid little refugee had brought it upon himself. His motivations were the preservation of his career, avoiding imprisonment, and even worse: after all, he couldn't imagine Branko letting him live if he didn't find Novak.

He'd made the calls, called in favours and misled a few people into tagging extra phone and account numbers onto intercept applications and account monitoring orders. Fortunately, he had a friend at Ilford who he'd partied with in similar situations to that which had caused his predicament. That friend was able to take care of the SD card.

His other friend, at the National Crime Agency, was very helpful once he led him to believe that Branko had images of them both at the brothel. They shared similar tastes in women, so he was scared into helping him, and he had access to more intrusive tracing methods.

He'd passed on the information when he realised Novak was going to Holborn, but then the bastard had escaped and disabled the hit man. The Brankos insisted he kept looking but Novak had gone dark and off the radar completely.

So he felt huge relief when, earlier that day, he had got the call that Novak's phone and bank card had been used in Ealing. He'd phoned Branko immediately with the news and was fervently hoping they'd get him.

His mobile phone rang causing him to jump out of his daydream.

'He wasn't there: no one seen him, not even the owner. Are you wasting our time?' Branko growled down the phone.

'All I know is what I'm told. His card was used, his phone was switched on, and it was for you to find him.'

'I'm not interested in your fucking excuses, piggy! Find out where he is or you'll be fucking sorry. We know where you live, we know everything about you. Find out now or your life collapses.'

'I tried my best, I tried everything, I promise.' But he realised he was talking to a dial tone.

His face crumpled and he began to weep, his shoulders heaving, tears spilling through fingers that covered his eyes.

He rubbed his hands through his thinning hair and sat up straight. He looked up at the line of commendation certificates and photographs on his ego wall in front of him. 'For dedicated and resourceful leadership in a complex murder enquiry.' The photograph of himself shaking hands with the Commissioner a few years ago on his Senior Command Course. All would be for nothing if he couldn't locate Novak. He'd need to think of something new.

17

Tom lay on the bed in his room, his eyes closed but not sleeping as he contemplated the events of the past few hours.

The test at the café had shown that they had access to his bank accounts and, in all probability, his mobile phone and cell site data.

As always, the basics of an investigation came to the front of his mind.

Motivation: either financial or duress?

Opportunity: who could it have been?

How was it done?

From what Tom had seen of Michael Adebayo, he easily had the necessary finances to bribe a corrupt police officer. He and the Brankos may also have had enough dirt on someone to coerce them into doing their bidding. But who was in a position to access the SD card, tap phones, access bank accounts, and obtain a brand-new warrant card for a hit man?

It had to be someone senior who not only had serious influence, but also had knowledge of ongoing major crime investigations. So probably a senior detective. Probably more than one person, as the processes for obtaining all that information were handled by very different departments.

Intercepts were usually handled by the National Crime Agency, account monitoring by financial crime units, and phone data by a single point of contact for each force or agency. Who could access all those disparate agencies?

Who had the opportunity to access the SD card, which should have been locked away in a police store? How was it wiped clean?

Police stores were very secure, but transit storage outside of office hours? Not so much. It would probably have been locked in the custody office where anyone could have got to it, or maybe in the CID office with the investigating officer prior to it being reviewed. Again, anyone could have got to it.

Also, to sort everything against him in a matter of just twenty-four hours was seriously impressive and realistically unheard of, so whoever it was definitely had influence and ability.

All-in-all, Tom couldn't come up with any cogent theory other than that it had to have begun with Adebayo and the Brankos. So that was where he'd start. One of them must have contacted the corrupt official, and that was his one opportunity: if Mike Brogan and the CIA had the resources Tom imagined they had.

A quiet knock on the door pulled Tom from his thoughts. He checked his watch: exactly seven o'clock.

He held the Sig in his right hand, concealed behind his back. He didn't use the peephole in the door. If the caller was an enemy, the light shift in the peephole prism would show them exactly where his head was, enabling them to make a very effective assassination by a single shot through the door.

Instead, he unlocked the door then quickly backed into the room, ducking into the bathroom to the right.

'Wait there,' he called, his grip firm on the Sig.

A lightly-accented female voice replied, 'Okay.'

'Pet?' asked Tom.

'Yes. Mike sent me,' the voice replied.

'Come in.' He didn't move from the bathroom and instead aimed the Sig at the door.

The door swung open and a small woman slowly walked in, carrying a heavy bag over her shoulder and a rucksack on her back.

'My hands are up, I'm not armed.'

Tom fixed the Sig on her. She was in her late twenties, of slight build, with short, choppy, auburn hair. She wore geek-chic spectacles and was dressed in a funky style with her slim frame clothed in green combat trousers, a denim jacket, and Converse

All-Star sneakers.

'Please don't shoot me, Tom. Mike asked me to come help you out and these bags are really heavy,' she said, giving him a shy smile.

'Walk over and sit on the armchair,' said Tom, lowering the pistol but keeping it by his side, following her as she walked past the bed and sat calmly on the chair.

'Who sent you?'

'Mike Brogan, CIA Section Chief in Brussels with responsibility for counter-terror liaison in France, Belgium, Netherlands, and Germany. He asked me to help you out with IT, phone interrogation, communications, and shit like that. He loves you because you pulled his ass outta the fire a few years ago. His words, not mine, by the way.' Her smile widened. 'Anything else, Tom, or can I relax? I'd love a cup of tea. That's what you English do, isn't it, in times of stress?' Her English was faultless, with a mixed German and American accent.

'I'm not English,' Tom said, tucking the Sig in his waistband.

'I know. You were a Bosnian refugee. Orphaned in London, brought up in Scotland, army at nineteen, and then police. You've been a bit busy, I hear.' She smiled once more. 'Don't worry, Tom. I can find out anything about anyone; it's a gift and why the CIA pays me.' Her smile widened a little more. 'Now, how about that tea? I can see a kettle from here.' She nodded at the desk.

'How do you like it?'

'Just milk.'

As Tom made the tea he asked, 'So how did you end up working for the CIA?'

'I don't, officially. In reality, it was that or they'd put my ass in jail. They caught me looking at the CIA mainframe when I was younger. I just wanted to see if I could breach their security. I got in quite easily, but in those days I wasn't good enough to get out again without getting caught. They traced me to my parents' house in Germany and they were so impressed that, rather than jail, they offered me a job.'

Tom stood to make the tea, tipping a mini capsule of milk in each. Handing Pet a cup of the scalding tea, he said, 'Pet?' a quizzical look on his face.

'Petra. But that sounds like a dog's name.'

'So you decided on 'Pet' instead?'

'I know, it's supposed to be ironic,' she smiled. She sipped her tea and pulled a face. 'I hate UHT milk. Why can't hotels do proper milk?'

'No idea.'

Pet smiled again, looking directly at him with eyes that sparkled like jewels. 'So what do you need, Tom?'

'I need a locked iPhone interrogating and some photographs putting through facial recognition software for a start. Can you do that?'

Pet gave him an almost offended look. 'Is that all? That's child's play.'

'For starters, we'll see after the phone has been looked at. I managed to get a brief look before it locked, and it seemed all the history had been erased.'

'I doubt it's fully erased. I can probably recover most of it, so let's start with that. I'm the CIA's most prized deniable asset.' She smiled at her own self-confidence.

She heaved up her bag and extracted a slightly battered-looking laptop and a small vulcanised case. Tom was certainly no computer expert, but the laptop looked quite old and was festooned with various stickers.

'I expected more modern tech,' Tom said, slightly puzzled at the archaic-looking machine.

'Detective, this is state-of-the-art, trust me. I built it myself with the help of some of the finest tech minds in the CIA. Don't let appearances fool you.' She opened the other case and pulled out a small, nondescript metallic box which she attached to the laptop using a cable, before plugging both machines into the wall socket.

'Okay, where's this phone you want looking at?'

Tom produced it from the bag on the bed.

'It's been on airplane mode since I relieved it from the owner. It's fingerprint and passcode protected as well. Is that a problem?'

'Please, Mr Novak, all this talk of end-to-end encryption only goes so far. I can get into any phone. Handset manufacturers won't admit there are back doors into the phones but, if they want to trade in the US and lots of other countries, they sometimes make exceptions.'

Tom tossed her the iPhone which she caught with ease. As she switched it on, she said, 'I'm going to assume that there is a remote wipe enabled on the phone so, if we disable airplane mode, all data will be wiped. If we had a faraday cage, we could disable it, but I don't see the risk is worth it. There may be all sorts I can learn with the handset in its current state.' She connected the phone to a cable and pressed a few keys on her laptop.

'Done,' she said after about thirty seconds. 'That's the contents of the phone downloaded onto the hard drive. I've enabled it to recover deleted items, so it shouldn't be a problem. I have e-discovery software, so we can run lots of cross-checking to come up with any links.'

'How the hell did you break the password that quickly?'

'I didn't need to.'

Tom raised an eyebrow. 'Can I see what's on there?'

'Let's see,' she said. Her fingers blurred over the keyboard with practised ease. As he moved behind her to see the screen more clearly, Tom noticed a small tattoo of three stars below her left ear.

'He's been careful,' she said. 'There's very little on here. I suspect it's recently been purchased. Hold on.' Her fingers danced across the keyboard again.

'Okay, the phone went live two days ago. No calls, no SMS, no social media accounts. I've recovered two deleted messages and two deleted calls. One from a landline; one from a mobile. The messages are from UK-based cell phones. I'll retrieve them.'

More tapping of keys. 'Okay, there was a call from this number this morning at 0700 hours lasting two minutes.' She pointed at the number on a chart on the screen.

'I recognise that number,' said Tom, shocked. 'That's the Met switchboard number at Scotland Yard. Can we find out extension numbers or where it came from?'

'Not from this phone. I'd need to hack into the systems and, even then, there's no guarantee.'

Tom clenched his fists, 'Okay. Carry on.'

'A ninety second call was received from a cellphone number ending in 219 at 1105 hours. We can check these out once we've finished the download.'

Tom nodded as she continued.

'Okay. Two SMS messages: one sent at 0820 hours from this handset to 219 saying, "Card obtained, I'm ready when you hear". The next one was at 0835 hours which includes a photo of you, your name, date of birth and an address in Camden. See?' She pointed at the laptop screen.

Tom was shocked to see his warrant card photo staring from the screen at him. It was also disconcerting to see his home address in the text. Jesus, how much influence did these people have?

It made some degree of sense. 'Martin' received a call from someone at Scotland Yard at 0700 hours, possibly arranging to get the warrant card. He then sent a message at 0820 hours, seemingly once he'd got the warrant card, saying he was ready to go, and received a reply at 0835 hours with photographs and details of Tom's movements.

The crucial call was then made at 1105 hours after he received the call from Neil Wilkinson about the threat.

The key was the phone number: who had 219? That person was at the centre of everything, coordinating the activity against Tom.

He looked at Pet. 'Can you get me phone call data for that mobile? I need in-and-out call and message data with cell sites.'

'I reckon so, but it will cost you something to eat. I'm starving,' Pet said with a grin.

'In a minute,' said Tom. 'Can you overlay GPS data for the phone with the calls?'

Pet's fingers flashed across the keyboard again, pausing only to brush her fringe to one side, a look of fierce concentration across her fine features.

'Here,' she said, pointing to the screen, where a map showed the route the phone's GPS function had tracked since being switched on. The highlighted route first appeared close to City Road in Central London, adjacent to the flat shared by the Brankos. The first call at 0700 hours was received there almost as soon as the phone was switched on. The phone remained static for a while before going to Victoria Embankment and into New Scotland Yard. It remained static before sending the message saying the card had been obtained at 0820 hours.

It moved again just after the text attaching the photograph of Tom was received at 0835 hours. The GPS signal then travelled north towards Camden, crossing Blackfriars Bridge and heading towards Kentish Town. Traffic was always painfully slow at that time of day.

The signal then remained static until the call was received at 1105 hours, when it travelled to Holborn Police Station, where Tom had met Martin.

'This is great, Pet, thanks. I can trace the sequence of events now. I just need to find out who was using the phone number that called Martin,' he said.

'You know the problem with all this data I'm giving you, don't you?'

'If you mean I can't use it as evidence as you're a deniable asset and this is an unlawful extraction of data, then yes, I do,' said Tom grimly. 'I'm not worried about that. I'm just trying to stay alive.'

'Now that I understand, Detective. I'm hungry, can we get pizza?'

'Sure. Why not,' Tom said, suddenly realising he was hungry.

*

The small pizza restaurant was only a short walk from the hotel so they walked slowly, enjoying the cool night air after being cooped up in the stuffy hotel room.

On the way Tom told Pet an abridged version of what had happened. He figured someone with a logical brain might be able to offer valuable insights into his next steps.

The restaurant was a typical London chain, with faux Italian prints hung on the walls and staffed by Eastern European waiters. It was almost empty, which suited Tom perfectly.

They both ordered margherita pizzas and beer from the extensive menu.

'So what next?' asked Pet as they clinked bottles together.

'Investigate that phone number. If you can get into the relevant databases, see who has been calling and been called by it. Then we can start getting a bit proactive against them. I need to know who the bent cops are, so I have some leverage going forward. I've also got some photos I want you to run through facial recognition.' He sipped his beer.

Pet nodded. 'I can get you the data and run the pictures, but I don't think Mike will give you any surveillance kit or weapons; it's too risky with the political situation. They couldn't risk US kit falling into the wrong hands, not with relations between the UK and the new president being what they are.'

'Then I'll just have to improvise, I guess. I have a few tricks up my sleeve. I also want to try to get hold of Ivan, the informant, and find out what happened when he got challenged by the Branko brothers. He may know something about how they found out about me.'

'I understand from Mike that you are a man of many talents.'

Tom looked at Pet, wondering how much she actually knew. 'I've been about a bit,' he replied cautiously.

'So, tell me about your childhood then. Why the UK from Bosnia?' she asked casually, taking him by surprise.

He certainly didn't want to talk about his full backstory with someone he'd just met and so he quickly changed the subject. 'How did you get so adept with computers? You'll have to be patient with me, I am a Luddite.' When she frowned at the phrase, he explained, 'I'm useless with computers.'

'Just came naturally. My parents bought a second-hand computer and I almost instinctively knew how to operate it. I found a new world in the internet where it didn't matter that I was a nerd. Before I knew it, I was learning all sorts of techniques on the hacking forums and practicing them on small institutions. I never looked to steal anything, I just got a kick out of breaching security systems. It felt like I was striking back against all the bullies, for some reason.'

'Impressive. I genuinely don't have a clue. I spent all my childhood outdoors, fishing and climbing.'

'Ugh. I hate outdoors, especially when it's cold. I hate the cold as well.'

'So, are you living in London?'

'For two years; my paymasters find it useful to have someone with my skill set available here in case anything comes up.'

'Like what?'

She raised an eyebrow at Tom. 'Come on, DS Novak, I could tell you...' She winked and held his gaze just a little too long with her sparkling, green eyes.

'...You'd have to kill me,' said Tom, finishing her sentence for her, slightly uncomfortable at the look in her eyes. He wondered if she was flirting as he shifted uncomfortably in his seat.

'Come on, we've work to do,' he said.

*

Back in the hotel room, Tom handed the memory card from the camera over to Pet. Within seconds she had the photographs imported to her computer.

'I'm running them through the CIA and NSA facial recognition database to see if we can ID these guys. It shouldn't take long.'

The silence was broken by a low-pitched buzzing from one of Pet's bags. She picked up a bulky mobile phone from within and answered it.

119

'Yeah? Okay. He's here.' She looked at Tom. 'Mike wants to speak. This is a secure line, so you can talk freely.' She tossed the phone to him and returned to the laptop.

'Mike.'

'Tom, how's it going?'

'Making progress. Pet knows her stuff.'

'She's the best there is; an amazing resource, and she's security cleared so you can tell her anything. You want to tell me the whole story now I have the time to listen?'

Tom sat on the bed and talked Mike through everything.

'Jeez, Tom. What a fucked-up situation. Look, this is off-books for me. I've sent Pet because she's deniable but, with the political tension at the moment, I can't do anything traceable back to the agency. This means no weapons, no surveillance kit, no boots on the ground. No evidence, just intelligence. I'm sorry, my friend, but it could cause an international incident,' he said, with genuine remorse in his voice.

'Information is fine, Mike. I don't want this to end up in court. I'm bringing them down, all of them. By whatever means.'

'Well, be careful and don't do anything stupid, like getting killed. And stay with Pet; she has access to most databases and those she doesn't she can hack into anyway.'

'I'm always careful, Mike.' Tom hung up and handed the phone back to Pet, who was still busy at the laptop. Within a minute, a series of images and data erupted on the screen.

'Whoa, Mr Englishman, you're messing with some major criminals here! All Serb mafia, all with multiple convictions, all ex-military or paramilitary. I can't give you any copies in case you get taken and these fall into the wrong hands, but look at the profiles while I go to the washroom. Don't write anything down.' She stood and walked across to the small bathroom.

Tom sat in front of the computer and took in the individual subject profiles on the screen.

Martin Green looked back at him from the screen. Real name Bojan Dedic, aged forty-two, ex-army, discharged under a big cloud. Convictions for robbery, racketeering, and firearms offences; suspected of a number of murders. Current location unknown.

The passenger from the Audi was named as Filip Stevanovic, aged thirty-nine, also ex-army, with convictions for manslaughter, drug trafficking, and jewel theft. Escaped from a Swiss prison in 2015. Current location unknown.

Finally, as Tom scrolled down, Zjelko Branko appeared on the screen. He saw the man he had photographed on the motorcycle outside the pub in Ealing, the picture staring back at him from the CIA database clearly a few years old. He looked at the pale blue eyes, pock-marked face, and contrasting light scar from his left ear to his bulbous nose. The recognition that he felt earlier flared in his mind. He read the biography impassively: former Serb paramilitary, suspected of war crimes including multiple civilian murders. The description noted an identifying mark of a tattoo on his left wrist of a Serb white eagle crest. He sat back, stunned, with realisation finally hitting home. He was cast back twenty-five years, once again a child in his family home. His dark eyes fixated on Branko's pale, cruel eyes.

Pet appeared behind him. 'Are you okay, Tom?'

Tom's eyes did not move from the screen.

'Tom?'

'This man killed my father,' he said, his voice low and even, giving no indication of the fury that gripped his insides like an ice fist driving through his ribcage.

18

Tomo walked home from school back to his tiny home in the shadow of the Trebivic mountain, whistling and kicking a stone along the dusty track. He was looking forward to the twelve-kilometre drive with his papa to Sarajevo later that day, where he would join Papa's wrestling class. The full group of other embryonic wrestlers would all be star-struck by the ex-Olympian wrestler teaching them, with Tomo the proudest of them all.

He arrived home to a sight he truly was not expecting. Every instinct told him that something was wrong, very wrong. Four burly men in rag-tag camouflage uniforms were stood outside the cottage smoking: all Serbs, laughing at a shared joke, cruelty leeching from their pores. Every window in the house had been smashed, and the garden was strewn with his family's belongings; clothing and papers fluttered in the stiff breeze. Even the chickens were gone, just a trail of feathers and blood on the grass where they should be.

The largest approached Tomo with a nasty smile on his pocked face, his vivid pale blue eyes staring directly at the boy. His nose was bent to one side and blood was smeared on his lip. His bull-neck gave way to a muscular body that spoke of hours in a gym and a thin scar traced from his left ear across to his nose. He squatted on his haunches and offered his hand to Tomo, who remained rooted to the spot, ignoring the shovel-like hand. He was transfixed by the tattoo on the man's wrist: a white, double-headed eagle.

'You must be the great Jacov Novak's boy. Are you a wrestler too, like your papa?'

Tomo stared at the man.

'Never mind, son. You'll get another man for your whore of a mother. Your father could have joined us in glory, not consorted with Roma and Bosniak scum.' He patted a crest patch on his right shoulder that showed the same two-headed white eagle as that on his wrist. Fury and a maniacal gleam shone in his eyes.

His mama appeared at the cottage door and rushed to meet Tomo, shooting a look of utter hatred at the intruders as she took him in her arms, protectively. Her face was bruised and bleeding, her dress ripped, and she shivered, her tear-stained face radiating fear and desperation.

Of his papa, there was no sign.

His mama sobbed as she clutched him protectively, quivering with emotion.

The big Serb guffawed, got to his feet, and marched off, barking orders at the other men. They all climbed into a battered Toyota Land Cruiser and sped off in a cloud of dust.

'Mama, what have they done with Papa?'

His mama couldn't answer. It seemed as though words wouldn't leave her mouth, instead remaining at the back of her throat, choking her.

'Gone, little one,' she said eventually. 'He's gone.'

*

The next day
Sarajevo

The crowds thronged the packed streets, an air of tension lingering, palpable in the cold, crisp afternoon sun. The smell of fear and uncertainty was almost visible, hanging like a fog above the human tide. Long queues formed outside banks and stores as people attempted to fill larders and empty bank accounts. Cash was king, and credit was a memory.

Soldiers lounged on every corner and by every queue, heavily armed with automatic weapons and hard faces. Mistrust lay everywhere. Mistrust between Serb, Croat, Bosniak, Roma, Muslim, Christian, and Orthodox. The community, once tolerant, was dividing before their very eyes. The buildings either side of the street showed the aftermath of a mortar attack. Shattered windows, strewn glass, and deep scars were gouged in the facades on both sides of the road. The siege of Sarajevo, the city known as The Jerusalem of the Balkans, was taking hold.

Aishe, a tall, lean woman, fought the tide of bodies while clutching Tomo's hand. Both were dark in complexion, their brown eyes betraying their Roma lineage. A livid bruise coloured her cheek and a trace of blood remained on her lip. She carried a rucksack almost as large as herself and was dressed simply in a blue cotton dress and woollen coat. The boy looked bewildered and frightened, his world turned upside down.

'Mama, what is happening? Where are we going?'

'Hush, little one. We must hurry,' she replied, a haunted look in her dark, glittering eyes. The mask of fear couldn't quite disguise her classic bone structure and innate beauty.

'But why have we left our home? What did those bad men want? Where's Papa?'

'Papa has gone, Tomo. He's gone…' Tears coursed down her cheeks, fear and fatigue etched across her features. 'We must leave this place; we're not safe. Keep up. We must hurry.'

The enormity of what had happened to her Jacov hit her so suddenly, it took all her resolve not to collapse.

Jacov had warned her they were at risk in the political turmoil of Bosnia and the wider Yugoslavia. Their mixed origins hadn't endeared them to anyone: he was a Bosnian Catholic and she was of Romany gypsy heritage. Jacov's work as an English interpreter with the government had raised his head firmly above the parapet and into the sights of the Serbians and the Bosniak Muslims.

Just the day before, he had told her that only in England could they be safe. 'The Bosniak Muslims hate us because we're Catholics, and my Serbian countrymen hate us because you're Roma. I won't join paramilitaries in the killing of innocents, so we will never be left alone.'

'They should love you, Jacov,' she had protested. 'You were an Olympic hero for Yugoslavia.'

He had shaken his head. 'That only makes them hate me more. No, the Yugoslavia I loved is gone. We have to go too. Don't worry, the arrangements will be made.'

Jacov was a taciturn man who wasn't given to panic, so his words had resonated with her. He feared no one, but she could see he was terrified for his family.

Their home was in the high ground south-west of Sarajevo. The area would clearly become the focus of intense military activity as the opposing forces tried to gain an advantage. No one would be safe when the paramilitaries came, particularly the Roma and their children.

When the opposing forces clashed, as they surely would, Jacov had feared he wouldn't be able to protect them, so he'd made his plans to get them all out safely... But before Jacov could do anything, they'd run out of time.

She shuddered at the memory of the day before, when the gang of Serbs had come to their home and tried to get Jacov to throw in his lot with them.

'Join us, Jacov,' the grinning leader had said. 'Join us in ridding our country of the Bosniak scum and non-believers. Do that and we will forgive you for marrying a Roma bitch.'

Jacov had launched at the man, breaking his nose with a thunderous right hook. And after that... It had all happened so quickly after that. A rifle butt to the back of Jacov's neck dropped him to the floor, and he was dragged outside. Aishe was left alone with the leader. He had looked her up and down and her stomach had churned, the silence in the room overpowering as she had realised what he intended.

He had approached her, fumbling with his trousers, a pistol in his free hand. As she shook her head, the crack of a gunshot from outside split the silence in two.

The memory welled up, threatening to overwhelm her, but she forced the horror down. Only now mattered, only right now and the chance she had, her one remaining chance, to get a future for little Tomo.

The arrangements made by Jacov had amounted to a scrap of paper with a name and telephone number scribbled on it. She'd made the call which had led them to a cab office in a grimy side street in downtown Sarajevo. Aishe and Tomo entered a tired and scruffy office where an elderly woman manned the desk.

Thick dust lay everywhere, and an ancient calendar of Sarajevo's historic buildings hung askew on the wall. Peeling linoleum covered the sticky floor. The silence was only interrupted by a ticking clock which showed it was 3.49pm.

Aishe approached the desk. 'I've been told to ask for Braslav.'

'Who are you?' The woman's scorn was evident with every syllable.

'I'm Aishe and this is my son, Tomo.'

The woman surveyed them, her eyes showing the greyish bloom of cataracts, and her face heavily lined, her make-up only serving to make her look more hag-like. 'Roma?'

'Yes,' Aishe said quietly.

The woman stood up slowly, her heavy frame disappearing through a beaded curtain to a back room, muttering as she went.

The silence in the room was cloying, punctuated only by the rhythmic ticking of the old clock on the wall. Tomo stared at the clock, his face a mask of confusion.

Aishe looked at her son's dark, handsome face. His cheeks were stained with fat tears that carved trails on his grubby skin. His near-black eyes were impassive and her heart ached for him. The enormity of his father's death had not yet arrived, but it would soon. And how would they cope then? They'd have to. She'd have to. Jacov's legacy must be protected. Nothing else mattered but Tomo now; his future was all that concerned her. Grieving could wait for another day.

Her thoughts were interrupted by the entrance of a sturdy, grey-haired man with sharp green eyes and a kindly face, with a monstrous grey moustache that totally dominated his upper lip and cheeks. He wore dark trousers and a short-sleeved, crisp cotton shirt.

'Aishe?' he asked, grunting when she nodded. 'And you must be little Tomo?' His eyes held a smile as he looked at the little boy.

'Yes, sir.'

'I am Braslav, an associate of Jacov's.' He started to ask when Jacov would arrive but the desolate look on Aishe's face told its own story.

'When?'

'Yesterday,' Aishe replied, casting her eyes down to hide the welling tears.

Braslav shook his head. 'This is happening too often. What will become of our country? I promised Jacov I would help him, and I will,' he said firmly. 'You have everything you need?'

Aishe looked sadly at him. 'We have nothing else. They took everything.'

Braslav shook his head again. 'Do you have money and papers?'

Aishe nodded. 'We have enough money for the journey only and we have our papers. We also have these.' She reached into her pocket and produced a small, soft leather bag. Tipping the contents into her hand, she proffered them to Braslav.

Three small stones glittered in her hand, given to her by Jacov only three days before.

Braslav looked at the diamonds with a mild expression of wonder.

'Hide them well, my dear. Men will kill for such a prize. These are Jacov's legacy to you to start a new life in the free world,' he said as Aishe returned the stones to her pocket.

Braslav looked firmly at Tomo, his green eyes shining with tears.

'Your father told me much of you, my friend. "The next Yugoslav wrestling champion," he would say. We will get you to England in his memory. Tomo, your papa was a great man. Maybe Yugoslavia won't survive, but we will make sure you do, Tomo Novak.'

19

'I need to speak to Ivan,' Tom announced as he paced the floor of the hotel room.

'Is it worth the risk?' asked Pet.

'I have to. I don't know if he has any leads on where the leak came from. The Brankos had him up against a wall and the information had to come from somewhere. He may know something, even if he doesn't know it himself.'

'Okay. How are you gonna call him?'

'With that sat-phone I just used. It's untraceable, right?'

'At least from this end, yes. But if they're listening to him or tracking him, then it doesn't matter if it's untraceable, does it?'

'I think it's worth the risk. If he has information, then we need it.' He picked up the chunky sat-phone and dialled Ivan's number, which he'd retrieved from his own iPhone.

'Hello?' Ivan answered.

'Ivan it's Tomo. Can you speak safely?'

'Man, where you been? People looking all over for you.'

'We need to meet, now. Where can you get to?'

'Man, I'm scared. I thought those bastards were going to kill me. And it's late as well,' Tom could hear the naked fear in his voice.

'Come on, Ivan. We have to meet. I need to see you now: it's urgent. I need to know how the Brankos found out about me. It's important and I don't want to talk for long on the phone.'

'Okay, okay. I'm in Willesden Green. Can you meet me in Gladstone Park? Benches by the kids' playground. It's quiet there this time of night.' He was slurring as if he'd been drinking.

'I know where it is. It's ten-thirty now; I'll meet you there at midnight. Don't let me down, Ivan,' said Tom, hanging up. 'Do you have a car?' he asked Pet.

'No. I got an Uber here,' Pet replied.

'Okay, how do I do that then?'

'You don't know about Uber?'

'I thought it just meant something was really good in German.'

'You really are a Luddite. You know about the internet, right?'

'Obviously.'

'Well you know smart phones have these things called "apps"?'

'Are you patronising me?' Tom affected a hurt expression.

'No, just fucking with you, Detective. Uber is an app that means you can instantly call a cab. Where do we need to go?' Pet smiled broadly at Tom's mild embarrassment.

'Target roundabout on the A40.'

Pet clicked a few times on her iPhone. 'Done. It'll be outside in six minutes. I'm coming with you.'

'No way. It could be dangerous, and I don't know if he's alone. He won't talk in front of you. You're not a field agent, you're a consultant. No chance.'

'Don't be stupid. I can keep watch. I can also track Ivan using my iPad, so we can see where he is.'

'How?'

'Easy. I have his phone number. A simple hack and I can use his phone's GPS to track him. It will take me about three minutes to sort out. You gotta admit that's good tradecraft, being in control of your informant.'

Tom paused for a second. He couldn't deny that it was perfect tradecraft that many a specialist agent-handler would use. Be in control of your informant, not the other way around, was the mantra of safe informant-handling. Tom wondered just how much she knew, and how much of 'just a consultant' she was.

'Okay. I can't fault your logic.'

'Sure thing, boss man,' she said as she returned to her laptop and produced an iPad from her holdall. She began tapping at the keys with the look of intense concentration he'd noticed before, her tongue slightly protruding from the corner of her mouth.

Tom picked up the Sig, tucking it in the rear of his waistband, and also took his burner phone and his iPhone. He then secreted the SD card behind a loose edge of carpet. There was nothing to link him to the hotel but why take the risk? The SD card was the only bargaining chip he had left.

'Okay. I have him live now on GPS. He's at an address at Melrose Avenue in Willesden.'

'Blimey. You're better than Mike gave you credit for. Do you know how long that would take me through official channels?'

'Never, would be my guess.'

'Come on, let's go and get this done. I'm tired and need to sleep.'

*

The cab arrived outside the hotel exactly six minutes later: a beaten-up Nissan driven by a Pakistani driver who, it seemed, spoke little English. That was perfect; a chatty driver was the last thing they needed at that moment.

After being dropped off at the Target roundabout they made their way on foot to the McDonalds car park, where the VW Passat was waiting: exactly where Tom had asked Stan to leave it, with the key secreted just inside the rim of the exhaust pipe.

They got in and Tom took a moment to familiarise himself with the controls and the location of the blues-and-twos. Pet fired up the app on her iPad.

'He's not moved yet. He's still at the address in Melrose Avenue, so we have plenty of time.'

Tom set off, keeping well within the speed limits, fully aware that he was carrying an illegal firearm. He also had no idea if the Sig had been used before, which could make life difficult if he was found in possession of it and it had been used in a murder.

Forensic testing on firearms was of such high quality that it only needed one shell casing or intact bullet to link a crime conclusively to an individual weapon.

He certainly didn't need to be getting arrested at that particular moment, not with whoever was feeding information to Branko and Adebayo still somewhere out there. At the very least, he'd be staring at a charge of unlawful possession of an illegal firearm, which could again land him in jail. The realities and seriousness of his situation threatened to overwhelm him again, but he quickly shook it off, the memory of what Branko had done to his family overtaking any doubts. He would see it through and bring those people down, no matter what the cost.

'He's still static at Melrose.' Pet's lightly-accented voice cut through his ruminations.

'That's good: at least we know he's close by. When we get there, I'll approach the meeting place and you take up a position and keep an eye open. If you see anyone else approaching, send me a text to the burner phone.'

'No problemo.' Pet touched a finger to her brow in a mock salute. 'Have you worked out what you're going to do once you catch up with these guys?'

'You really want to know?'

'Maybe not.'

'I have to find out who the bent cops are first. After that, we'll see.'

'Do what makes you happy, Tom. Are you sure that killing Branko will make you happy?'

Tom didn't answer. He just continued driving in silence, his eyes focused on the road ahead.

*

They pulled up at the side of the road a short while later and took up a position with a view of the dimly-lit playground and reasonable visibility to the benches. They had good cover between a parked van and a car about a hundred metres from the meeting point. Tom switched off the engine and extinguished the headlights.

'What now?' asked Pet.

Tom looked at his watch: fifteen-minutes-to-midnight.

'We wait until he shows, so I can make sure he's alone.'

'Classic tradecraft, Detective. Always arrive before the informant.'

'What kind of a consultant are you?'

'Just an IT geek, Detective. Just IT, but I've hung with enough spooks to know about agent tradecraft.' She looked at her iPad. 'He's not moved. Still in the address.'

Tom shrugged. 'It's still early, and he's only five minutes away.'

He scanned the area with practised efficiency, looking for signs of any watchers. It was unlikely that the call had been intercepted but he wasn't taking any chances. He also wasn't sure if he could trust Ivan, but he needed to speak to him; there was no telling what he knew and where it might lead.

'So, is there a Mrs Novak?'

Tom moved his gaze to meet hers, the question hanging in the air.

'No. I don't do so well in relationships. I'm not so easy to live with.'

'Always put career first, yes?'

'Something like that. Work complications I can handle; relationship ones, not so much. Still no movement?' he added quickly.

'Way to change the subject, Detective.' She smiled. 'No, no movement.'

'It's five-past, he should at least be moving by now.'

'Maybe he fell asleep?'

Tom grabbed the satellite phone and redialled the number for Ivan. The phone rang and rang with no reply.

'I don't like this. Something's up.'

'GPS puts him in a house in Melrose Avenue still. Maybe give him a minute?'

'No. Something's wrong. Can you isolate an exact house?' he said, starting the car's engine.

'It's about halfway down on the right-hand-side if we go from here.'

Tom drove steadily along Anson Road adjacent to the park and turned right into Melrose Avenue.

'Talk to me, Pet. Where's the signal?' he asked, his voice still calm.

'On the right any time now.'

Tom strained his eyes as the car crawled down the suburban street with its Victorian terraces, looking for anything to give him a clue as to where Ivan might be.

'It has to be this house here.' He pointed to a dilapidated terrace with an overgrown privet hedge and an overturned bin in the front garden, the bin's contents strewn across the decaying concrete in front of the bay window. A light shone from within, obscured by grimy curtains. Two bell-push buttons to the right of the door indicated that, like most of the properties in the area, it had been divided into two dwellings: one upstairs and one down, with a shared front door leading to separate doors where the hallway had once been.

Tom pulled the Passat over into a vacant space on the other side of the road, a short way from the address.

'Wait here,' he said. 'I'm going to check it out. Get in the driver's seat. If you hear shooting or any other significant commotion, drive off, dial 999 and get the police here. Understand?'

'Okay. Maybe I should monitor you, so I can hear what's going on. Hold on one second.' Pet clicked at some icons on her iPad and the satellite phone buzzed. She accepted the call and passed the handset to Tom. 'Keep the line open and I can monitor in real-time. If you get captured or something, I will know about it and can call help.'

'Good idea,' Tom said, putting the phone in his jacket pocket.

'What are you going to do in there?'

'I'm not sure yet. Depends what I find,' he said, opening the car door and getting out.

The issue was that Tom had no idea what the next few minutes would bring, but his gut told him that it wouldn't be good.

He strode across the road towards the property, walking past and giving it the merest of glances, noting that the door was part-glazed and appeared shut. He walked to the access alley four doors down and turned left down an alleyway cluttered with rubbish and a discarded mattress. Gentrification had not quite hit Willesden Green yet, and most of the houses looked tired and shabby.

Now in the shadows, stealth took over. His trainers made no sound on the path as he made his way down behind the gardens. None of the back gates were numbered and, by counting back, he was able to identify the rear of the flat, which had a completely demolished fence. Picking his way silently through the debris, he made for the rear of the property. Dropping to his knees, he crawled the final few feet to the rear window. Very slowly, he inched his head up to look through the window and into a small, shabby bedroom with no lights on, the flicker of a computer monitor giving the room an eerie glow.

The door was open and gave a partial view into the front room. He couldn't see fully inside but could observe the rear of an ancient leather recliner chair parked in front of a TV that was switched on to a sports channel. A single leg was visible, stretched out from the chair as its occupant apparently lounged in it watching the programme. There was a scuffed Nike trainer that Tom couldn't recall Ivan wearing but, in reality, he hadn't taken any notice of his chosen footwear.

Tom dug out his burner phone and pressed the last number dialled function for Ivan's phone. He immediately heard it faintly ringing from within the house. Peering into the bedroom, he saw the light of the smartphone screen illuminated on the bed but there was no trace of movement from the chair in the living room. With a cold feeling of dread, Tom realised he was going to have to affect an entrance.

He had no lock picks with him, but the Sig dug comfortably

into the small of his back. He edged his way over to the rear part-glazed door that, he guessed, went into the kitchen. He reached up and tried the round doorknob, withdrawing the silenced Sig with his other hand and holding it by his side. His senses were alive to all the sights and sounds around him. The faint murmur of the TV from within competed with a distant barking somewhere outside.

The doorknob turned and the door began to give slightly. Keeping his body to the side of the door, he slowly inched it open, peering through the crack as it widened. A messy kitchen emerged in the half-light from the living room, the TV getting louder with excitable commentary. Tom tuned out the noise, his ears and senses searching for any other presence within the flat.

Once the door was sufficiently ajar, Tom inched his way into the kitchen, his feet silent on the linoleum floor, the Sig pressed tight to his thigh.

A metallic smell assaulted his nose, a copper-like stench familiar to every police officer. Emboldened, Tom strode through the kitchen, the Sig in both hands in a close-quarter battle-grip, still treading lightly but quickly as the dread began to course through his body. He moved to the threshold leading to the living room and entered at speed, the Sig stretched out in front of him. As always, time slowed as he took in the scene before him. First priority: clearing the rest of the room for any other occupants. There were none. He then turned his attention to the chair.

Ivan was sprawled in the cracked and ancient armchair, his arms either side of the armrests, his feet splayed out in front of him. Blood covered the front of his white-and-blue Bosnia and Herzegovina football shirt like a gory bib. His eyes were half-open but no light shone from behind them. A long, ragged incision stretched across his neck, almost from ear to ear, the faint white glint of his windpipe visible in amongst the gore. The nature of the wound was not clean but had clearly been hacked at until he had choked to death or bled out. Once the carotid artery had been severed, as the enormous puddle of blood indicated it had, death would have been only moments away.

Tucking the Sig back in his waistband, Tom approached Ivan and touched his forehead: it was still warm. There was no pulse point to feel in his neck: it had been destroyed by the inexpert hacking of the killer.

He felt nothing other than a familiar cold, hard rage. The smell of the blood assailed his nostrils, added to by the loss of bowel control that Ivan had clearly experienced in his final moments. Tom swallowed bitterly, fighting to stop the bile rising in his throat.

He felt rather than heard the creak behind him: almost a disturbance in the quality of the air that alerted him to the fact that he was not alone.

'Mr Novak, how nice to see you,' spoke the voice in glottal Serb.

Tom turned to find Filip Stevanovic pointing a large-barrelled revolver at his chest, a slight smile on his face. Tom saw that the hand gripping the gun was bright red with Ivan's blood, and a large stain covered the other sleeve.

Tom said nothing, just fixed Filip with his even stare, feeling the familiar calmness sweep over him.

'Where is the memory card?' asked Filip, not moving the revolver from Tom's chest.

'Why did you kill Ivan?'

'He was a traitor. Now where's the fucking card?'

'You look nervous, Filip. You're sweating, your pupils are dilated. You're breathing heavily as well.' Tom's voice was eerily calm.

The Serb shifted on his feet and firmed his grip on the pistol, his eyes widening at the sound of his name.

'How do you know my name?'

A smile spread across Tom's face. 'Why are you so nervous, Filip? Is it because you think I'm dangerous? You can't just shoot me because you need the card and I don't have it with me. If you shoot me without the card, then Branko will want to know why. Who knows what I've done with it? I could have left it anywhere for people to find.'

'How do you know my fucking name?'

'Come on, Filip, you can't be that nervous. You've got a great big 44 Magnum, or whatever that is. You were in the army, for God's sake. I bet you weren't this nervous when you broke out of that Swiss jail, were you?' Tom continued to fix Filip with his dark brown eyes. 'I'm not nervous, Filip, not at all. You want to know why?' Tom advanced a step.

'Shut up and don't move or I'll shoot you, fucking pig!'

'I bet you won't. You see, I've had guns pointed at me loads of times but most of those guns were automatics, not a revolver. The benefit of an automatic is that I can't see if it's loaded or not.'

The smile on Tom's face widened a little before he continued. 'But with a revolver I can see whether you're loaded. Now you're mostly loaded but I don't think you used a speed loader. I can see that on your next shot the chamber is empty. I reckon you only have five rounds in there. Your first pull of the trigger won't work, which means you have to pull twice to kill me. How fast do you reckon I can move?' Tom smiled again, projecting utter confidence.

Uncertainty spread across Filip's face and his eyes flicked down to the revolver.

Tom lunged forwards, thrusting a hard, right-footed kick into Filip's arm, jerking it violently upwards. The pistol roared and bucked with the heavy-grain .44 round smacking into the ceiling. Tom closed the space between them and delivered a devastating elbow-strike which connected with Filip's temple.

The big Serb crumpled to the floor like a broken chair.

Tom quickly searched the man's pockets, finding only a single car key and a set of zip-ties. He quickly secured the man's wrists to his ankles, saying as he did, 'Pet, I'm coming out. Can you watch out for anyone on the street?' He stood and lifted the phone to his ear. 'Pet, you there?'

'Yes, I'm here. Are you okay?'

'I'm fine, but we need to get out of here quickly. I've taken one of them out but there may be others. Am I clear to come out?'

'Yes, it's all quiet out here at the moment.'

Tom quickly left the house via the front door, jogged across the road, and climbed into the Passat passenger seat.

'Let's get out of here quick, Pet. I really don't have the time to speak with the local constabulary.' Tom smiled at her as he slipped his seat belt on.

'Are you okay?' she asked staring directly at him.

'Eh?' Tom didn't seem to understand what she was asking.

'Tom, I heard everything you said. I heard that Ivan's dead. I'm asking if you're okay?'

'Of course, it's a bit annoying, but it's not me that's dead. Listen, Pet, much as I'd like to give you a full debrief right now, we probably have police on the way right now. So we really ought to get weaving.'

'I'm just a bit surprised, Tom. You've just seen a man dead and been held at gunpoint, and you're acting like you've just come back from a stroll in the park.'

'Pet, I'm fine, seriously. Please can we go. Like, now?'

Pet put the car in gear and drove away, but something seemed to be bothering her. She was agitated and looked scared, her eyes wide with alarm. Tom felt a definite atmosphere in the car which had not been present before he entered the flat.

'What's up?' Tom said.

'You, Tom. What the hell are you? I was listening and I've never known anything like it.'

'I've no idea what you mean, Pet,' Tom said, looking confused.

'You just saw a man killed in cold blood. You just killed a man and you seem like you've just been playing dominoes, or something.'

'What do you expect me to do? Cry? Flap and panic? Not my style, Pet. Also, I didn't kill anyone. Ivan was dead already and I just knocked Filip out. He'll be fine, more's the pity.' Tom didn't know where Pet was going with this.

Pet suddenly wrenched the steering wheel violently, turning left onto a side street and pulling the car over at the side of the road.

She looked directly at Tom, her eyes alight with alarm. 'Tom

I've been doing this work for a while. I've worked with CIA wet-work specialists, Special Forces soldiers and rogue agents. I've never met anyone as cold as you. Just who or what the fuck are you?

'Pet, we don't have time for this. A big bullet has just gone through a floor and there is a dead man and an unconscious man in a flat I've just come out of. We need to get the hell out of here. Now can you stop pissing about and drive?'

The momentary silence was fractured by the distant wail of sirens that seemed to be getting stronger.

'Pet, seriously. We can talk about this later if you like, but not now. We need to get the fuck out of here.' Tom spoke urgently as strobing blue lights flashed along the road behind them in the direction of Ivan's flat.

Pet wordlessly turned away, engaged the gears and drove off.

*

They travelled back to the hotel in Ruislip in near-silence, a palpable atmosphere of mistrust between them.

Back in the room, Pet sat on the bed and asked, 'What happened in there?'

Tom sat next to her, pretending not to notice as she edged slightly away. 'I went in the back door, which was open, and found Ivan there in an armchair, his throat cut. I heard a creak behind me, and Filip walked in. We had a fight. He came off worse.' His voice was flat and empty, as if describing a poor-quality snooker match.

'I heard you speaking in that room. You have ice in your veins, Tom. I heard no panic, not even a little fear. What are you?' she said looking directly at him.

'I'm just a cop, nothing else.'

'Did he only have five bullets in that revolver?'

'Nope. I lied.'

She breathed out heavily. 'You are a weapon, Tom. A deadly, emotionless weapon.'

'I'm just a cop, that's all, Pet.'

She stared right into his eyes, clearly evaluating him.

'You scare me, Tom. I don't frighten easily but you frighten the fucking life out of me.'

'Pet, I don't understand. I encountered a situation and did what I had to do. What do you want from me?'

'I need to understand if I'm safe. If I'm to help you I don't want to be frightened, but you're the coldest, most emotionless man I have ever encountered. How? Why?' Tom was surprised to see genuine concern on Pet's face. He was genuinely perplexed as to what could have caused such a reaction.

'I really don't want to talk about it,' Tom said, coldly.

'Well I am getting the fuck out of here unless you level with me. We can do this job together. I can and want to help you, but I need some honesty. Why are you so emotionless?'

Tom sighed and massaged his temples with his fingers.

'Look. I don't like talking about it because it scares the shit out of me.' The words came slowly, as though he needed to drag each and every one out. 'I don't like what I am, but I've learned to deal with it. I deal with it by always thinking what my foster father would want me to do. That way I always do the right thing.' He spoke quietly and evenly, avoiding eye contact. He wasn't usually given to many emotions, but a feeling of anxiety was beginning to bubble in his stomach. He hated confronting who he was.

'Because of what happened to me in Bosnia I have no feelings, Pet. Nothing. In Afghanistan I killed twenty-eight people and I didn't feel a fucking thing. Nothing. Not once. No elation, no remorse, no fear. Nothing. I don't like talking about who I am because I have no. Fucking. Idea… Who I am.'

Strangely and unusually, Tom almost felt a sense of relief at blurting out his deepest demons, even to a near-stranger.

Pet's face softened visibly. 'Jesus, that explains it. You can't blame yourself for this, Tom. You are a good man and your foster father is obviously a good man.'

There was a long silence as they both looked at each other, the tension in the room dissipating palpably. Tom let out a sigh before breaking the impasse.

'We should get some rest. It's after two and there's a lot to do tomorrow. I can run you back home if you like?'

Pet paused for a second. 'If it's okay with you, I'll stay here. I don't fancy being alone and it's late. I'll take the left-hand bed.'

Tom shrugged with a smile. 'Fine by me.'

Avoiding Tom's gaze, Pet removed her jacket and cast it on the floor. She sat on the bed and removed her combat trousers and sneakers and climbed beneath the duvet, taking her glasses off and setting them on the bedside table. She snuggled down beneath the bedclothes and said, 'Goodnight, Detective.'

'Goodnight, Pet.'

Tom removed his shoes, socks, and trousers, climbed under the covers and settled down. Once again, he considered his actions that day. Was Pet right? Was he really a cold, emotionless machine? It wasn't a comforting thought, but he still felt nothing, despite seeing what he realised must have been horrifying sights. Resisting the urge to replay the day further, he relied on his military ability to sleep, whatever the circumstances. As expected, it came to him immediately.

20

Tom woke at seven, dressed quickly, and crept out of the hotel room, leaving Pet sleeping peacefully, her face almost child-like as she dozed.

He walked to the local shops and bought toothbrushes and toothpaste for them both. He also picked up two large coffees and muffins from the nearby coffee shop.

Key-carding his way back into the room, he found Pet dressed in a hotel towelling robe, her hair damp from the shower. She was sat in front of her laptop with an intense look of concentration on her face.

'I'm just accessing the phone databases. I've searched for the 219 number that sent all the damning texts to your friend Martin Green, aka Bojan Dedic. Thanks,' she said with a smile as Tom handed her a coffee and a muffin.

'And?'

'219 is an unregistered pre-pay, no top-up data. Nothing, nada, nix,' she said, sipping on the coffee. She broke off a piece of the muffin and put it in her mouth.

'I've got in-and-out call data with cell sites which shows limited use only, most of which we know about from Dedic's phone. But the cell sites put it close to the City Road address you said the Brankos lived at, so I imagine that's their base of operations.'

'There is one other number it calls and is called by: one ending 079. That's also a burner phone with nothing known about it. But that number made the call to 219 just before your photo got sent to Dedic by 219. That number has been hitting cell sites in SW1 when it calls into 219.' She was obviously proud of the speed of her work.

Tom thought it through. 219 received a call from someone at Scotland Yard about the warrant card. 219 then sent Dedic to get the warrant card. He then sent a photograph of Tom with his personal details after 219 received a call from the new number in London SW1, presumably despatching Dedic to intercept Tom.

'Bring me up a map of the cell site in SW1.'

Pet's fingers sped across the keyboard and brought up Google Maps, with an arrow pointing at a street in Central London.

Tom stared at the screen, a knot forming in his stomach.

'That's a National Crime Agency office. They run intercepts from there. Jesus, they've had my phone hooked up.'

The realisation of the true scale of the resources being deployed against him struck home. Intercepts were only used in terrorism cases and the most serious of life-threatening crimes. They needed enormous resources to apply for and obtain the warrant, which then had to be signed by the Home Secretary.

Just who was leading all this? Tom's mind raced.

'I need to hear what the Brankos are talking about. Can you sort an intercept?'

'No. No chance. I just can't get access to that; we don't even have a back-door route,' she said apologetically. 'You could bug their house easily enough.'

'No. Mira never leaves home, and we don't have the resources to do it safely. I'll have to improvise then, I guess. I'm going for a shower,' he added, stern-faced.

He went into the bathroom, stripped, and stepped under the needle-sharp jets, enjoying them beating against his tired body. As he dried himself a plan began to form in his mind. He was going to listen in on the Brankos by whatever means necessary. If he could do that, he'd be closer to finding out who the corrupt officers were.

He dressed, becoming aware of the need for some fresh clothes, and returned to the bedroom where Pet was already dressed, sitting clutching her coffee.

'So, what now, Detective?'

Tom smiled. 'Let's go shopping.'

21

The senior police officer sat nervously in a café in a down-at-heel suburb of East London. His breathing was erratic, and he was sweating despite the morning chill.

He was casually dressed in jeans, trainers and—ridiculously—a NY Yankees baseball cap in a poor attempt to fit in and look inconspicuous. He was practically shaking as he tried to drink the stewed tea which the unsmiling Eastern European waitress had dumped down in front of him a minute earlier.

Madness being here, he thought to himself. But Branko senior had insisted, the edge of threat ever-present in his gruff voice.

The door of the café opened and the big form of Zjelko Branko stepped in, surveying the scene before him. Making eye contact, he strode over and sat in front of the officer, the chair creaking beneath his weight.

'Tea!' he barked at the waitress, who nodded hastily.

He fixed the officer with a direct and nasty stare. 'So, my friend, what do you have to tell me? I'm hoping you're about to tell me where Novak is.'

'No sightings of him, I'm afraid. His phone is off, his bank accounts inactive, nothing on ANPR for his car, and he's not been home. I'm afraid there's nothing more we can do. Also, the murder squad is looking for him because of Ivan's murder.' he said, his voice shaking slightly.

'That doesn't make me happy, my little porky friend. Your career and your liberty depend on you finding him. Have you tried his family?' the big Serb asked.

'He has no family; he's an orphan, brought up with foster carers since he was about twelve. No wife, no kids. He's known as a bit of a dark horse, ex-army type,' he said, trying not to babble, almost close to tears.

'Is he still close to the foster family?' asked Branko.

'He visits there regularly enough. They're in Scotland, in the Highlands,' he said.

'Hmm. Get me the address and everything you can find out about them straight away. It may be just the place for a man to hide.'

The senior officer paused, in two minds. 'I may have something of use,' he said tentatively.

'What?' asked Branko, fixing him with that unpleasant stare.

'The address of where Jeta's being kept safe. You know, the girl who Adebayo assaulted,' he said, self-loathing coursing through his veins.

He slid a small slip of paper across the table which Branko picked up, looked at briefly, and then tucked in his shirt pocket. He smiled at the officer, showing discoloured and uneven teeth, the scar vivid on his cheek.

'Helpful, my little friend, but doesn't get you off the hook. Just buys you a little more time. Now fuck off.' He produced his mobile phone from his pocket and began tapping at the keypad, no longer looking at the man in front of him, the meeting finished.

The senior officer stood and hurried from the café, not looking back.

22

'So where are you taking me, Detective? Dior, Mulberry, Hermes? What lovely designer items are you planning on buying me?' Pet asked with her impish smile.

'Tandy. Then, after that, I may treat you to a new T-shirt and pants from Asda.'

'You're too kind. It's fine: designer labels are for the emotionally weak. Tandy?'

'Electrical supplier. I need to do a bit of DIY if the CIA won't give me listening devices.'

The Tandy outlet store was on the trading estate close to Asda and sold all types of audio, visual and electrical items. They entered the large warehouse-sized store and Tom busied himself in the self-service racks with a basket until he was satisfied.

The only items Pet recognised were a half-sized mini camera tripod, a full-sized tripod, and a pair of binoculars. The other items were smaller and just looked like electrical wires and components.

'So, what's the plan then?' Pet asked.

'A little trick I learnt in Northern Ireland, once upon a time. We didn't always have the resources we needed, so we learnt to improvise.'

Tom went and paid for the items while Pet waited by the exit.

'All done, Detective?'

'Yep. I could just do with clean pants and socks and some stakeout provisions; it could be a long night. Do you need anything? My treat.'

'From Asda? You are so kind. No wonder you're single,' she said as they deposited the items in the car and walked to Asda.

They took a small trolley and Tom bought boxer shorts, socks, a plain grey T-shirt, a new baseball cap, and a selection of sandwiches, drinks and crisps. Pet shyly added some new socks and underwear and a tiny-looking Superman T-shirt to the basket, raising an eyebrow at Tom as she did so.

'This is a weird-ass shopping trip, Detective.'

'Stick with me, Pet, and I'll show you a good time,' he said, returning her smile.

Tom paid for the items using his untraceable card and they left the store, got into the car and drove back to the hotel. Once there, Tom unpacked his purchases and began sorting through the electrical items.

'You going to share the plan with me?'

'I'll show you once it's done. You probably won't believe me otherwise.'

Tom took out a roll of cable with a jack plug at each end, the type that would be used to connect an electric guitar to an amp. He stripped one of the plugs and took a small electrical component from the bag.

'What's that?' Pet asked.

'It's a photodiode, it focuses light into this sensor. Now, please let me work; I need to remember how to do this.'

Pet feigned hurt and turned to her laptop screen.

Tom got out a roll of lead strip and a soldering iron, which he plugged into the wall socket. He soldered the connection terminals onto the exposed jack plug wires, filling the room with the smell of scorched lead.

He used insulation tape to secure the end of the lead where the photodiode was exposed, and taped the whole thing to the top of the full-size tripod. He then removed a small pen-shaped object from a blister pack and connected it to the smaller tripod using a plastic G-clamp.

'A laser pen, before you ask. Do you have audio software on the Mac?'

'Of course. It has Wavepad installed. I can record and manipulate sound however you like on it.'

'Perfect.'

He went to the window which looked out onto the main road. In direct line of sight was a row of 1930s semi-detached houses about a hundred metres away. Perfect for the test, thought Tom, picking up his binoculars. Fortunately, the weather was dark and overcast.

He took the smaller tripod and set it on the window ledge, pressing a switch on the side of the laser pen. He began making slight movements while looking at the houses in front with his binoculars.

'I didn't know you were a Peeping Tom, Tom.' Pet smiled at her own joke.

'Look at the wall behind us and tell me when you see the reflection of the laser dot.' He began adjusting the pitch-and-tilt function of the tripod.

After about five minutes, Pet said, 'It's here now, four feet up the wall.' Tom turned and saw the laser dot on the wall behind them, clearly visible. Perfect.

He took the larger tripod and lowered it so that the electrical component was visible, facing forwards by lightly bending the connector strips upwards so it resembled a forward-facing torch. Tom carefully adjusted the tripod's height until the laser dot hit the photodiode face.

Holding the other end of the wire, he took a jack plug adapter from his bag, snapping it into place so it was compatible with the headphone port on the laptop.

'Right, time to see if this works. Open Wavepad and let's see what we've got. I reckon the window I have it trained on is a living room in an upstairs flat.'

Pet looked at Tom with a slightly puzzled look. 'Is this a bug of some type?' she asked, realisation dawning on her face.

'Hopefully.'

The programme opened on the laptop screen and a hissing

erupted from the speakers, the equaliser audio waves dancing across the screen. Pet played about with the on-screen controls, trying to filter out some of the extraneous noises. Tom saw that the laser dot on the photodiode was slightly off-centre and made a small adjustment until it was dead centre. Suddenly the hissing was replaced by the tinny tones of Jeremy Kyle haranguing some poor unfortunate individual.

A broad grin split Tom's face. 'Bingo. Thank goodness for the unemployed daytime TV watcher.'

'I have to say, Detective, I'm impressed. A listening bug from a laser pointer. You are a resourceful dude. How the hell does that thing work?'

'Simple enough: the laser bounces off the window and onto the photodiode receiver, which is translated from light waves into sound waves from the speech inside the room vibrating the window pane. It's all about getting the trajectory right so it bounces back at the right angle.'

'Well, I'm impressed.'

'We just have to find somewhere to set this up near the Brankos' address. I also think we should get out of this hotel, Pet. We've been here long enough.'

*

They drove along City Road in the Passat, fully aware they were in the Brankos' stomping ground. Tom felt safe in the knowledge that he wouldn't be expected in that area, but nevertheless kept his senses honed for any unexpected sightings.

He needed to fully scout the area around the Brankos' maisonette so he could secure a suitable listening post in direct line of sight and on the same level. That way he could ensure that the trajectory would be appropriate to deploy the laser listening device.

He parked the car on the opposite side of the estate, on a side street off City Road. He put on the cap and spectacles in the hope it would alter his appearance as much as possible.

The premises occupied by the Brankos was in a small quadrangle. There were four storeys of dwellings, all accessible by a communal external door with lifts and stairs to each level. Each level opened onto a walkway with individual flats side by side. In the middle of all that was a neglected green space with a small swing set in the centre.

The Brankos lived in the middle of the fourth floor, overlooking the quadrangle at the front and the hustle and bustle of City Road at the rear.

There was no possibility of being able to utilise the device within the quadrangle, even if Tom could get access to one of the flats. It would be far too risky to attempt, as he had no idea what relationships the Branko family had with their neighbours. In any case, in his time at the flat while undercover he never saw them congregate anywhere other than the over-furnished lounge at the rear of the property, overlooking City Road.

The listening point, therefore, would have to be in line of sight of the rear of the flats.

He needed to get onto the fourth floor so he could identify an ideal location to site the laser-listener. That meant getting up close and personal with the Brankos' flat, which could be dangerous but no more than other things he'd done before. It was behaviour, not presence, that caught the eye. If Tom acted like he belonged, no one would question why he was there.

'Right,' said Tom, fixing Pet with a stare. 'I have to get out and recce now. I need you to go and have a coffee while I do it. I may need you in front of a computer, so I can find somewhere to set up, okay?'

'Whatever you say, Detective. I could just go get a coffee, anyway.'

'There's a Café Nero just five minutes away by the Old Street roundabout. I'll meet you there when I'm done,' he said, getting out of the car. Throwing her the car keys, he said, 'If I'm not back in an hour and you've not heard from me, get out of here and tell Mike.' He turned and walked off towards City Road.

He wandered into a Tesco Metro Store on City Road and made straight for the till area, where there was a rack of business cards for local enterprises in the area. He helped himself to a large stack for a local mini-cab firm and slipped them into his jacket pocket before walking out.

Workmen were digging up the pavement on the approach to the estate, presumably working on subterranean digital cabling. The hole was protected with red and white plastic mobile barriers and the usual warning signs. A neon hi-visibility vest was draped over one of the barriers, discarded by a workman who was probably underground working on the unseen cables that kept the digital world turning.

Without hesitation or missing a beat in his step, Tom casually snatched the vest and slipped it on: perfect urban camouflage.

He walked across to the quadrangle, entering it through an alleyway from the adjacent side street. He reached into his pocket and pulled out a small pack of paper tissues. Balling up three, he stuffed them into his mouth and positioned them down between his lower molars and cheek. That had the effect of rounding out his fine jaw and making him look jowly and fatter-faced. He pulled his cap low over his eyes, rounded his normally-square shoulders and walked in a more loping manner than he was accustomed to. Those slight alterations to his appearance and gait, while not significant, had a far greater effect than they had a right to, and would hopefully be enough if Mira happened to be looking out of the kitchen window as he went past.

Tom strode straight up to the stairwell door for the property, one of the new types with entry controlled by intercom buzzers for each flat. This door would be used by residents and visitors to flats 20-40, who could gain access with a magnetic fob or by pressing the correct flat number to be allowed access via intercom. It was a good, secure system if maintained well and not neglected: thankfully, this one was not. The door was slightly ajar, and the graffiti-daubed control panel had clearly not worked properly for some time.

Ignoring the lift, Tom ran up the stairs two at a time, pulling out the stack of business cards as he did so. A golden rule of surveillance is having a reason to be in the location. With the hi-vis on and a stack of business cards in his hands, Tom now had that reason: a delivery guy who would attract no attention and would cause no gossip on the walkway.

Reaching the fourth floor, he began going door-to-door, posting mini-cab cards through letterboxes as he went. Before he reached the Brankos' flat he came across a fire-break between the flats which was lit by daylight from a corridor window overlooking City Road. He took out his iPhone, still in airplane mode, and quickly took a series of pictures from all angles, capturing the skyline of the buildings around him. He noted a large tower block of modern flats directly in front, just fifty metres or so away.

He returned to his delivery task, putting a business card in each letterbox, including number thirty-seven where the Brankos lived. Stealing a quick glance through the letterbox, he was able to see down the hallway and into the lounge. No one was visible and no sounds came from the flat, but he was able to see the yellow floral curtains of the front room. Satisfied, Tom retraced his steps and descended the staircase, continuing back out into the quadrangle.

*

Pet was sat in a booth in the corner of the Café Nero, her laptop in front of her and a large, empty cup in her right hand.

'More coffee?' Tom asked as he walked over to her table.

'Why not? It's not like I'm jittery enough, is it?' she said, her eyes wide.

Tom bought two cappuccinos and sat opposite her.

'Nice vest,' she said. 'Got a new job?'

'Urban camouflage,' said Tom. 'You got 4G on the Mac?'

'I have more than you would probably understand, Detective,' she smiled with mock smugness.

'Good. Can you get me the name of the large block of flats in the tower block up the road? It's modern and brand new by the look of it.'

Pet's fingers tapped at the keyboard, and Tom could vaguely see the reflection of the screen in her spectacles as she typed.

'I assume from what you've said it's Canaletto Tower. It's a thirty-one-storey building, finished recently. It was in the news a lot as most of the flats were sold to foreign investors; half of them are never lived in.'

'We need to get in there: it's going to be perfect for our purposes. Are there any we can rent or am I going to have to break in?' he asked.

'Hold on, Detective, I'm sure we can come up with something,' she said, tapping at the keys. 'It's fully managed with twenty-four-hour concierge and looks busy. You want an easy option?

'Of course. Easy options are my favourite.'

'There's one to rent with Airbnb. On the sixth floor. We can get in by three this afternoon.'

Tom paused. There would definitely be an appropriate vantage point within the building, even if it wasn't in the flat they rented. Once safely inside he would have free rein to find the perfect location. The surfeit of empty properties left vacant by foreign investors would work well for Tom's purposes, if not the capital's housing crisis.

'Book it. We need somewhere to stay in any case.'

She tapped on the keys some more.

'Done. I've booked two nights and my employers are even going to pick up the tab. We are lucky that Mike has access to some deniable funding that won't attract anybody's attention. Don't ask how much it cost.'

*

Tom and Pet walked into the reception of the stunning thirty-one-storey building, marvelling at the sweeping glass and steel structure stretching up more than a hundred metres above London. Tom lugged a holdall in which he'd secreted the laser device, together with his grab-bag and a few items of clothing.

The reception was all sleek surfaces and polished teak, with a shiny marble floor and a hushed atmosphere of style. Even more of a bonus had been the underground car park he'd deposited the Passat in, keeping it off the street and out of sight.

Pet approached the receptionist and collected the keys while Tom watched the flat-screen TV on the wall, which was showing the rolling news.

Pet came over. 'Room 618, overlooking City Road. One of the least desirable apparently, but it will have to do.'

They took the elevator to the sixth floor and then Pet unlocked the heavy wooden door to reveal a small, one-bedroom apartment. It was sparsely but stylishly furnished with a cosy leather corner couch and a bright, modern kitchen. Floor-to-ceiling windows gave a fine view over City Road and across to the Brankos' block of flats.

Tom pulled the sliding doors open and stepped out onto the balcony, feeling the late afternoon chill and hearing the roar of the rush hour traffic below him.

Pet joined him. 'Is this okay?'

'The angle's too steep. I won't be able to bounce the laser back to here without mirroring it somewhere else, which we don't have time for. I need to be two floors down.'

'So it's useless then.'

'Not exactly. We are in and past security. I just need to site the laser and receiver further down and then feed the wire up here. Let's go and eat. I can think about it and then do some more research. I think there's a café on the twenty-fourth floor.'

He rummaged in the holdall and took out a small leather pouch, which he tucked into his jacket pocket.

They left the apartment and took the lift to the twenty-fourth floor, where they followed the signs to Club Canaletto: a very sleek café with a large balcony which gave an incredible view across London. The lights were beginning to spark up as the city moved to evening time.

They sat inside, and both ordered open sandwiches and beer.

'So what's next, Detective?'

'We eat this and then I'm going to find a vantage point to site the laser,' he said through a mouthful of sandwich.

'How are you going to do that?'

'I'm going to test the theory that half of these apartments are empty because of foreign investors.'

'How are you going to manage that?'

'By knocking on the door, of course. How's the sandwich?'

'It's a good sandwich, but you're being deliberately obtuse.'

Tom said nothing but kept chewing and took a swig of his beer. He was going to try to do something he hadn't done since Iraq. He needed to hear what the Brankos were talking about if the next part of his plan was to work. He was getting bored of being hunted.

It was time to go hunting.

*

They stood outside apartment number 418, Pet clutching her computer bag. Tom confidently rapped on the door and stood waiting patiently. He waited for a further minute before knocking again. There was only silence from within.

He produced the small leather wallet from his pocket and unfolded it to reveal a set of lock picks. Selecting a torsion bar and medium pick, it took him less than one minute before the door swung open, revealing a dark interior within. He took a torch from his pocket and swung it into the property. Sure enough, the apartment was completely unfurnished: just blank walls and an untouched kitchen. There were deep carpets everywhere but not a stick of furniture.

Switching off the torch, he walked to the balcony, slid the door open, and took out some binoculars from his jacket pocket. Putting them to his eyes, he located the Brankos' flat by its floral curtains.

'Perfect,' he said. 'Wait here. I'll go and get the kit. I'll knock three times.'

He disappeared from the apartment, leaving Pet alone in the gloom. She sat on the floor, taking out her laptop and a small metal box and connecting them together with a small cable.

Tom returned within five minutes, carrying the holdall, which he began to unpack as soon as he was inside. Leaving the sliding door to the balcony partially open, he erected the two tripods and then, using his binoculars, aimed the laser at the far corner of the Brankos' window.

'Same again, Pet: tell me when you see the laser behind you.'

He made fine adjustments with the tripod until a single, small, red pinprick of light appeared on the kitchen unit behind them.

'Now,' said Pet.

Tom moved the photodiode and tripod into the laser beam and screwed the platform securely into place once the beam hit the component's centre.

'Okay, you have the laptop ready?' he asked.

'Come on now, Detective, you don't think I'm just sitting here in the dark, do you? This is my bit.'

Pet connected the small metal box into the leading cable from the photodiode and extended two stubby antennae.

'I've used this to hook into the building's Wi-Fi. I've bounced the signal to come direct into my computer without the need for us to sit here or trail wires up. We may as well get comfortable.' She busied herself on the Mac for a minute longer before saying, 'I'm done. We're good to go.'

Tom nodded and they left the apartment, closing the door behind them.

Back in apartment 618, Pet sat on the corner sofa, snapped open her laptop, and tapped at the keyboard. Lines began to dance slightly across the screen, but no discernible sounds emitted other than a hiss of static.

Tom went to the window with his binoculars and focused in on the Brankos' window, which was in total darkness.

'No one's at home just yet,' he said, looking at his watch, which showed it was just after 7pm.

'So what do we do now, Detective?'

'We wait, I guess.'

He sat down on the sofa and said, 'Thank you, Pet. I couldn't have done any of this alone.' Pet looked a little embarrassed and there was a short, awkward silence.

'No problem,' she said, finally. 'I get paid well. What are you trying to achieve, here?'

'Just to find out who is doing this to me.'

'Are you sure that is all?'

'Pretty much.'

'No desire for revenge?'

He shrugged his shoulders and kept his face impassive.

'Tom, I've been working with Spooks and soldiers for a while now. One thing I have learned is that revenge doesn't often satisfy those who seek it.' She spoke earnestly while staring straight at Tom, who averted his gaze up to the ceiling.

'I don't know, Pet. I just need to unravel this situation. I can't just leave it now. The only way back to my old life is to keep ploughing on.' He let out a deep sigh of exasperation and rubbed his face with his hands.

The moment was broken by a burst of static from the laptop, followed by a curse in Serbian and a rapid-fire burst of indecipherable voices over the laser-bug. They sat up, Pet scrabbling for the laptop and making speedy adjustments on Wavepad. The static cleared, and a voice spoke from the computer's tinny speaker.

'Mother, we need food!' in Serb. Aleks.

Tom couldn't make out the reply but heard a loud gale of laughter from at least two other males.

A voice he didn't recognise said, 'What has the solicitor said?'

Aleks said, 'He's shitting himself like a baby. Father's told him we're on it.'

'What's the pig saying?' the voice asked.

'No one knows where Novak is; he's disappeared. Apparently he has his phone intercepted, emails, bank, everything, and the bastard is still doing nothing,' Aleks replied.

'He'll come soon; he has to. All the police are looking for him and they probably think he killed Ivan. Lucky that we got to Filip before the police got into the house, but it was far too close. Father sent him to Sarajevo, so he's safe.'

Tom sat up at this news. Was he now a suspect for the murder of Ivan?

'Is this recording, Pet?' he asked.

'Yes, straight onto the hard drive,' she said. 'What are they saying?'

'Filip got away, the bastard,' Tom said.

A commotion seemed to be occurring inside the flat as new voices were heard.

A gruffer voice came across the speakers, older than the others.

'Papa, when's the pig going to come up with something? This is taking too long,' Aleks said.

'As soon as Novak puts his head up. He will call me. He'd better, anyway, or he'll have me to answer to,' the gruff voice replied.

Tom went to the sliding doors and raised his binoculars towards the window. The curtains were still partially open and he could see the movement from within. As he watched, the figure of Zjelko Branko came up to the window and looked out onto the street before him. He paused for a minute and it felt to Tom that he was staring straight at him in the half-light of apartment 618. Branko pulled the garish, flowered curtains fully shut, and the moment passed.

Tom paused. He had to prompt a response, or nothing would be accomplished. He had to force the corrupt officer out and he could think of only one way to do that without compromising their position.

'Pet, I need you to do something for me.'

'Okay,' she said, a little suspicion entering her voice.

'Take my phone. Take a train a few stops from Old Street to, say,

Moorgate, then come up to the street. Go where you can't be seen, disengage airplane mode, and let it appear on the network. That will prompt contact. I need to stay here because of the language.'

'I can do that. I'll be an hour.'

Tom tossed her his iPhone, told her the PIN code and said, 'Call me on the burner phone before you spark my phone up so I'm ready for whatever happens.'

'Sure thing, boss man.'

'And, Pet,' Tom said as she was heading to the door.

She paused and turned to face him.

'Be careful. Don't engage with anyone; these are dangerous people.' Tom spoke with a genuine concern which surprised them both.

Pet just smiled, turned on her heels, and left the apartment.

Tom continued to listen to the laser-bug feed, but they seemed to have quietened down and were watching a sports game by the sounds of it. An occasional cough or comment was all that ensued, giving him confidence that the listening device was still working.

About thirty minutes later his burner phone buzzed with a message from Pet.

'Phone going live now, Pet.'

Tom sat patiently and waited but nothing seemed to change immediately. The sports game continued with the muted crowd noise and Aleks was heard saying, 'The referee is a donkey, Papa,' which received a grunt in reply.

Ten minutes later, Tom heard a faint electronic ringing sound followed by a 'Yah,' from Zjelko.

'When? … Where is he? … How long ago? What? Not even a phone call? So, he just switched his phone on and received messages. What were they? What do you mean, you don't fucking know? What are we paying you for, Mr Pig?'

'Right. We're on it. Make sure we're not interrupted and make sure—' He stopped abruptly, the call obviously over.

Zjelko said, 'Novak is moving; he's close to Moorgate Station. Come on, let's go. I'll call Dedic.'

A further pause beset by static. 'Dedic, Novak is moving. The Shard, London Bridge Station. See you there.' The voices faded and were replaced by the tinny sounds of the television.

Tom stood and looked out of the window, down to the junction with City Road. After about three minutes, a dark Range Rover Evoque appeared and turned right onto City Road at speed. Tom could see Zjelko's buzz-cut hair at the driver's seat. He noted the registration number of the vehicle and then sat down to wait for Pet to return.

*

Pet returned forty minutes later with a soft triple knock at the door and a smile on her flushed features.

'All go okay?' she asked, walking back round to her laptop.

'They got the call minutes after you switched on and dashed out to go to London Bridge. We now need to know the number who called them: that's our bent cop.'

'Back to work, Detective. Let's see what we can find,' she said as she began attacking the keys with renewed gusto, concentration etched on her face. 'Okay. Zjelko on 219 was called by a number ending 109 just after I used your phone. Zjelko then called a new one ending 659 immediately after that,' she said.

'That would be Dedic; he despatched him to London Bridge after the call. We need cell sites and call history on 109. Can you also do open source and anything else you can think of on that number in case the bent cop has used it elsewhere, assuming it's a dirty phone?'

'I'm on it,' said Pet, tapping away at the keys.

Finally, we're making progress, thought Tom. They had the number for the dirty cop, and so they were one step closer to identifying him and blowing the whole thing wide open. None of what they were doing was evidential, nothing could be used in court: the bug was unauthorised and the phone data hacks that Pet was doing could never be admitted to either. Tom was effectively riding roughshod over the law. He just wanted to get to the bottom of it; he could figure out how to make it evidential later.

'Okay. 109 is an unregistered pre-pay with no details attached to it at all. A typical burner phone. It receives a call from 079—which was your NCA man—just after I disabled airplane on your phone. That must be to your primary bent cop who is receiving information on the intercepted calls from the NCA agent. He's made and received several calls recently to Zjelko and the 079 number; he also made other calls to other numbers a little while ago which I can look at,' she said. 'I'm running 109 through an open source software package which will find any time it's been entered into the Internet.'

Tom said nothing, impressed with her skill.

'I have a couple of hits. One is on a "sexual encounters" website. There's no photo, just an email address and a description, calling himself "Big Toni". "Forty-three-year-old, slim, professional male lives in London. Email address listed here." He sounds nice!' she said, sarcastically. 'Big Toni has also been on a freelance escort site. He's used that email to write a review on a girl he's used in the past. He was very impressed, which is nice, although he seems a bit fixated on how "young and fresh" she was. Ew!'

Tom's interest picked up a little at this news.

'Do you have the girl's profile there?'

Pet swivelled the screen round so he could see the small image of the escort. Tom stared at the picture of the young, pretty girl dressed in a tacky schoolgirl uniform, hair fashioned into pigtails, with a provocative look on her face spoiled by flat, dead eyes.

It was Ana.

23

'You know this girl?'

Tom nodded. 'She was a working girl at the brothel I was at when I was undercover. Whoever our dirty cop is, he's clearly a client. She will know who he is, and this could be a major deal. It certainly explains the hold the Brankos have over him. If he's as senior as I suspect he is, then consorting with prostitutes would finish him.'

'So where do we go from here?'

'I need to speak to Ana. She knows who the bent cop is, even if she doesn't know she knows it.'

'Is it safe to speak to her? She was with the Brankos.'

'I don't know. I always got on well with her but Aleks told me they'd packed the girls off back to Bosnia as they were getting troublesome. I don't know if that's true or not.'

That was a quandary. Ana had the information, even if she didn't consciously know it. Tom had got on well with her, but a feature of trafficked victims is they often don't feel like victims in the traditional sense. He didn't know whether she knew he was an undercover cop or not, and meeting her could land him in the hands of his enemies. Pet interrupted his chain of thought.

'Did she have a phone?'

'I think so. She was Mira's favourite.' He reached for his phone and located her number, reading it out to Pet.

'Give me a minute, I'll see what I can come up with.'

While Pet tapped away, Tom dug out the SD card and picked up a blank envelope from the rosewood desk in the corner of the room. Tucking the SD card inside, he scribbled his old friend Buster's address on the front of the envelope. Buster was now also a cop; he'd joined the year after Tom and was serving as a Detective Constable in the Met's Professional Standards branch, where he'd joined straight from the City of London Force as a 'clean skin' officer, working in anti-corruption. There had been suspicions of organised corruption in a few squads, and the Met had imported some new blood from outside forces to root out the problem.

Tom needed the SD card away from him, and a couple of days in the postal system and then in the care of his old friend would keep it as safe as could be reasonably expected. There was no link between Tom and Buster on record, despite them serving together in the SRR. The discharge papers said that Tom left the Royal Marines and Buster left the Parachute Regiment, which was a side-benefit of SRR not officially existing as far as the public were concerned. He scribbled a brief note on a Post-It note: 'Buster, guard this with your life and I'll be in touch soon. Keep it firmly under your hat. Love, Borat.'

Signing off with his old nickname, known only to Buster, was an instinctive safety measure to keep their association quiet.

'Okay, looks like Ana is still in the UK. The phone has been busy with lots of calls in and out and messages hitting cell sites in Islington, close to Upper Street. Looking at the traffic on the escort site, she is still working.'

Tom went into his phone's contact list and read out the numbers he had for Mira, Aleks and Luka.

'Any trace of those numbers on her call history?'

'Mira's number was calling it until three days ago, but no trace of the other two.'

So it would seem she wasn't working for the Brankos any longer. That wasn't unusual; working girls often changed hands between pimps for a fee.

It still didn't answer the question of whether it was safe to call Ana. She may have new pimps who wouldn't like it, and they might go straight to the Brankos. He couldn't pose as a client as that could just be walking straight into their hands if the Brankos were still controlling her. The other factor weighing heavily on Tom's mind was that he didn't want to expose Ana to risk; they'd kill her just as quickly as they killed Ivan.

'I've an idea,' Pet said, looking at Tom. 'I'm looking into her phone. It's a pre-pay, no contract, but it's linked to a Facebook account and has a Cloud password. If I can bypass those, we may be able to view her last phone backup which would include all messages, emails, photographs and videos. If they are blackmailing the corrupt cop, then she may have the compromising pictures or videos. It has to be worth a look.'

'It would certainly be safer. How confident are you that you can bypass the password?' he asked.

'Facebook will be easier: I can run a simple brute force attack on the password. I've a programme I wrote that narrows down possible passwords by scanning all social media and online information for any subject. Once I've got that password, if she's not careful, I'm betting it will be the same all over. Most people aren't security-conscious and are just plain lazy.'

'Do it. We need a break, and at least I won't get her killed this way.'

While Pet worked, Tom took the opportunity to take a short stroll to the twenty-four-hour convenience store nearby to buy a second-class stamp for the envelope containing the SD card, and two coffees. Posting the envelope, he felt pleased that it was safe and out of the way for at least a couple of days.

Returning to the apartment with the coffees, he found Pet punching the air in triumph.

'Boom! Password cracked, and she was using the same for both as I expected. People are so lax!'

'Genius is what you are, Pet. Let's have a look.'

'Okay, she has a reasonable number of photos saved in files and folders and her WhatsApp backup is available. There's very little stored in her emails or SMS so I'm guessing she doesn't really use them.'

'Can we search for messages from our bent cop?'

'Sure thing. I'm downloading the messages into Excel, so it'll be easy. I can cross-reference with all the numbers we've encountered so far and see what we get.' She typed furiously as she spoke before saying, 'Right, there are a number of messages to and from our bent cop, who she has saved in her phone as "Toni." Mostly arrangements to meet or slightly suggestive ones, and him declaring his adoration for her and how beautiful she is. Gee, what a creep.'

'Carry on,' said Tom.

'Okay. Quite a few messages from our friend at the NCA as well, asking if she can sort parties out for the two of them, plus friends. Jesus, how many bent cops are there?'

That was a bit of a revelation. So whoever it was at the NCA feeding information to the bent cop was also using the Brankos' services. That meant they had a hold over at least two cops or NCA agents.

'Can you run all the numbers alongside each other, cross-referencing and looking for anything that appears on the bills for all the numbers we have so far? I'm looking for anyone that appears between our dirty cop and dirty NCA Man. My guess is we have a group of cops or agents who share the same taste in women,' Tom said.

Pet continued to work at the computer while Tom checked the window of the flat opposite with his binoculars. The laser-listener remained quiet and there was no movement at the windows.

'Okay. I have three numbers that all seem to call each other as well as calling the Brankos and Ana. One is the dirty cop, one is dirty NCA Man, the other ends in 419. I'll check that one out now.' Her face was a picture of concentration as she typed away.

Tom was seriously impressed with her efficiency and could see why she'd be a prized asset of the CIA. The intelligence she was finding in seconds would take weeks through official channels.

'It's a burner phone again: most of its calls are to the other two plus several to the Brankos and Ana,' she said.

An idea flashed into Tom's head.

'Can you get cell sites for all the phones? Use time parameters that will give us the best indications of where the phone is during work hours and where it is first thing in the morning and last thing at night.'

That was a classic investigator's trick. The first call in the morning and last call at night generally indicated the area someone lived. During the day, if the phone was static long enough, then that would indicate where someone worked.

'It's a good job I have good e-discovery software, Mr Detective, or this would take forever. Hold on.'

A minute or so later, she ran her fingers through her hair and yawned. 'Okay, cell sites for Dirty Cop put it hitting cell sites during work hours in London NW6, Kilburn. There's a mix of masts but best guess is Salisbury Road. After-hours seems to be in Watford.'

Tom's eyes did not display the impact of this news.

'That's Kilburn nick; that's my police station. The bent bastard is a colleague. Who's next?' His matter-of-fact tone was a little unnerving.

'NCA Man's work hours we know; out-of-hours he's in Hemel Hempstead.'

Tom nodded and said nothing.

'Last man, 419 number: working hours is IG1 postcode, Ilford Town. Looks like he's sleeping at an address in St Albans.'

'That's Ilford Police Station, where Adebayo was in custody. I'm laying bets that's who erased the SD card.'

So, there it is, thought Tom. Three corrupt public officials, all living close to each other in Hertfordshire, all using the same prostitutes, all eminently corruptible because of their lifestyles, and all with the opportunity to carry out what had happened.

'We've got their phone numbers, we know where they work, we just don't know who they are yet.' Pet looked at Tom, whose face remained blank. 'I've checked the timeline and the calls between them all match the events so far,' she said. 'Your Ilford man was called by Bent Cop while Adebayo was in custody, and the other calls match what's happened so far. We have the three of them, so we just need to find out who they are. But how?'

'Let's skim through the photos and then get some rest.'

Pet brought the photo-roll up on the screen with each folder displayed.

'For a working girl, her pictures are well-organised. Look: all labelled,' Pet said.

It was true: there were eight folders, each labelled clearly.

Tom's eyes went straight to the folder marked Hackney and he tapped the screen. 'That one.'

Pet opened the folder and a series of thumbnail pictures appeared on the screen. She enlarged the first which showed three girls, all dressed in lingerie, arm-in-arm. Tom recognised them all as the three girls from the brothel.

'Scroll through steadily.'

The pictures were a mix of the girls with each other, alone or with various males at some type of party. Inane drunken grins appeared all over, and the seediness was evident even through the screen.

Pet scrolled through mostly similar photographs until Tom shouted, 'Stop, go back!'

Pet clicked back to the previous image, showing a lurid picture of Ana and one of the girls arm-in-arm, both dressed in skimpy underwear, clutching joints and glasses of champagne. They were stood in front of a dressing table laden with cosmetics, contraceptives and a large vibrator. But it wasn't the items or even the girls that drew his attention, it was the reflection of the half-dressed person taking the photograph. Tom took in the thinning hair, the weak chin, the pallid cheeks.

Detective Chief Inspector Simon Taylor's blotched and puffy face leered back at him, holding the camera phone in front of his pale, bare chest.

24

Tom felt the rage rising within him. It was a colleague. His boss had tried as hard as he could to provide the information which would have him killed and had also been indirectly responsible for Ivan being brutally slaughtered.

He felt the fury build, threatening to engulf him, but he forced it back down. He had to remain focused. He still had a job to do, but he knew one thing: Taylor would pay for this. They would all pay for this.

'Tom?' Pet's voiced pierced the fog that was filling Tom's head.

'That's my boss: DCI Simon Taylor. He's working for the Brankos and trying to have me killed.'

Pet paused for a second, thinking of the impact of this information.

'What can we do?'

'We need some rest and I need some time to think. I can't confront him as this is all off-the-books. It's illegal and none of it is evidence. Christ, I could end up in jail for what I've done so far. I'm going to have to do this my way, nothing official, and I'm keeping everything to myself until I know who all the bent bastards are.'

'So what do you suggest?'

'I need to speak to Stan and my old friend, Buster. I also need to be sure that Taylor is as corrupt as I think he is and not just someone who uses prostitutes. I suggest some sleep and we can start again when fresh tomorrow.'

'Sounds fine to me, Detective. I'm exhausted.' Pet stretched and yawned, her arms raised above her head. 'We should sleep.'

'Sure. Let's do that.' Tom moved towards the bathroom.

He took stock of where he was. If it wasn't clear before that he had no way back, then it was crystal-clear now. He was being chased by the Serb mafia, who were being fed live, intrusive intelligence by a corrupt police officer aided by an NCA agent who was using resources normally used to fight terrorism. The destruction of the SD card at Ilford showed that there was also at least one other corrupt asset he did not yet know about. He had only one option: keep fighting forward. He was going to bring these people down.

*

He woke early and lay in bed for a few moments, thinking through what lay ahead.

Pet stirred in her bed. 'Can we get a nice breakfast before we start work? I'm hungry,' she said, smiling through sleepy eyes.

'You know, Pet, you don't have to be here. You've done so much for me so far. If you needed to go, I would understand.' Tom spoke earnestly: it made him a little uncomfortable to be relying on another person, even in a case like that. But, in reality, another part of him realised he still needed her.

'You don't get rid of me that easily. Mike told me I was with you until this is resolved.'

'Well, as long as you're sure. I really appreciate the help. I'm going to take a shower first and then I have a plan.'

'Care to enlighten me?' she smiled.

Tom returned her smile. 'I'm going to need to find out what is on Taylor's computers. Can you help me with that?'

'Of course, depending on how close you can get to them. If you can get direct access to his hard drive, I can give you everything. If it's remote access I will be a bit more limited in what I can do. It'll cost you a cooked breakfast, either way.'

'Deal,' said Tom, throwing off the sheets and making for the bathroom.

As he showered, he realised he was going to have to seek a favour from not only Stan, but Buster as well. He couldn't take Pet to those meetings as he was probably going to ask them to do something not strictly legal, and neither of them would want a witness.

He quickly dried off and got dressed again before rejoining Pet. They left the apartment and headed up to the restaurant, where they both ordered scrambled eggs on toast, and coffee.

The Brankos were currently missing; he didn't know where, but he didn't feel he would learn much more from listening to them in any case. He could ask Pet to track them by their phones and monitor the laser-listening device while he did what he had to do.

One thing was for sure; he needed some help in identifying Simon Taylor's cohorts and the only two people he knew he could trust were Buster and Stan.

'I have to go off on my own for a bit,' he said.

'Why alone?'

'I need to meet a couple of guys. They're friends and I trust them, but I may be asking them to do something questionable and they'd be more comfortable without a stranger in tow.'

'Okay. So what do I do?'

'Can you monitor cell sites on all the phones we know about? I need to make sure I'm not going to bump into the Brankos, and I also need the laser-listener monitored just in case something comes up.'

'I can do that, but are those really all the reasons why you want me out of the way?' She fixed him with a piercing stare.

He shrugged. 'I don't want you getting hurt, Pet. I'm going to have to confront these guys soon, and Ivan was killed because of me.'

'I can look after myself. I'm a big girl. But I understand you have to do what you have to do. Just make sure you come back; you're a good guy.' She smiled but there wasn't much humour in her green eyes.

Tom smiled back. 'Come on, let's go. We've work to do, and I can't do it without you.'

Tom paid the bill, and they went back to apartment 618, Pet settling straight in front of her laptop.

'I have to go,' Tom said. 'Can I take the satellite phone? I need to make untraceable calls while I'm out and about.'

'Take what you need, Detective. I'll be here waiting for you and you need to call me regularly.' She programmed her number into the phone and tossed it to Tom, who caught and pocketed it. 'Don't do anything stupid, like getting killed.'

'I'll try my very best,' he replied and left the apartment, taking just his burner and satellite phones, leaving the Sig in the grab-bag. He really didn't want to be caught in possession of it; he had enough problems without risking a firearms charge as well.

*

Tom sat in the Passat in the Canaletto's car park and took a moment to compose his thoughts. He snapped open his burner phone and dialled the number for Stan, who answered with his usual cheery, 'CID office Kilburn, how may I help you?'

'Stan, it's Tom. I need to speak to you as soon as I can, there's been a big development.'

'I'm sorry, my dear. The officer is on annual leave. May I take a message and ask him to contact you when he's back...? Of course... You're welcome. Goodbye.' The phone went dead.

He didn't have to wait long until Stan called him back; the burner phone buzzed in his hand almost straight away.

'Talk to me, Royal,' said Stan.

'Right, this is going to sound mental, but I've every reason to believe that Simon Taylor is bent as a nine-bob-note. He also has two others helping him: one on the NCA in SW1, the other at Ilford nick.'

'Jesus, what a turn-up. What do you want from me?'

'You have contacts all over, but I need you to be discreet. Can you pull whatever strings you need to pull? I need to find out who he has a link to at those places. It may be in personnel files and it could be that some of your mysterious contacts may have some idea. I know Taylor was on SOCA in the past and I'd like to find out who he worked with there and where they are now. Just get your ear to the ground.'

'Okay. I've a few people I can call up. There may be rumours floating around, you never know. Leave it with me, dear boy. Are you okay, by the way? Glenda is going bloody mad not knowing where you are. A dead body with a slit throat turned up in Willesden, some kind of Serb mafia nonsense. Nothing to do with you I take it? You are listed as a person of interest.' Stan's voice gave nothing away, but Tom could feel the probing.

'It's all crap,' Tom said. 'I'm getting closer, but I need to find out who Taylor's working with before I blow this thing out of the water, okay?'

'Leave it with me and take care. I've got to run, Royal. Keep your head down.'

And with that, he was gone. Tom knew that Stan would be discreet and, along with Buster and Mike, there was no one he trusted more.

He picked up the phone again and tapped in another number.

'Hello, DC Pete Rhymes speaking,' said a chirpy, cockney voice on the other end.

'Buster, it's Tom. Don't say my name out loud if you're in company.'

'You're fine, mate. I'm at home on-call, and I'm also hearing some fucking bullshit rumours about you being of interest in a murder in Willesden,' he said in his familiar machine-gun-speed voice.

'Can we meet? I need some help.'

'Of course, buddy. Where?'

'Usual place, about midday?'

'I'll be there. Stay safe, my little Polish friend.' And with that, he was gone.

The 'usual place' was the Punch and Judy in Covent Garden, a busy pub in the centre of the square. Its attraction was its popularity with tourists: two people could speak freely and never be noticed amongst the throngs of visitors buying over-priced food and drink.

Tom arrived slightly after midday and saw his old friend sat in a corner booth in the darkest corner of the hostelry, nursing a drink. He ordered two pints of lager at the bar and went and sat in front of Buster. There was no handshake or hug, just a knowing smile that was more than adequate as he placed the beer in front of him.

'I love it when you give me beer, Borat,' smiled Buster.

'I know you well, cockney wanker.' And they both giggled like schoolchildren.

'So, what's going down? I'm hearing stories about a UC going rogue and getting his informant killed.'

Tom sighed and brought Buster up to speed on events.

'Jesus fucking Christ!' Buster's voice was a shocked and forced whisper, his meaty face screwed up with the news. 'I knew there was a lot more to it but no one's saying much. No one knows of our history at SRR, so I've not been asked anything: it's just the usual police rumour mill.'

'I'm ninety-nine percent sure that the main man is DCI Simon Taylor, my boss at Kilburn,' said Tom. 'The second is someone at Ilford nick, where the solicitor was taken and some evidence wiped. The third, I think, is NCA at SW1. They've had my phone and bank hooked up and I only managed to escape getting kidnapped because the guy had a slightly moody-looking warrant card.' Tom paused again, aware that the story was ridiculous when said out loud.

'Do you have evidence of this?'

'Nothing admissible. I've had a bit of help along the way which I'll tell you about another time. I'm hoping you can do some research on the Professional Standards' intelligence systems to see if there's anything known about Taylor and accomplices. I've got the Serbian Mafia after me, backed up with access to all the law enforcement databases and resources. I need to identify the lot of them before I can plan my next move.'

Buster gave a long sigh. 'Jesus, Tom, this is unbelievable. A DCI using intercepts and bank monitoring to get a serving DS wiped-out?' The detective paused, worry etched in the lines on his forehead. 'You know I trust you and I owe you more favours than I can ever repay from our SRR days, so I'll do it. One thing though.' He paused, raising his eyebrows while taking a sip of his lager. 'Don't go killing anyone. I know how good you are at it. We may be able to make some of this official if the evidence can be parallel-proved, and we may be able to use whistle-blower rules to protect you. Just don't kill anyone, okay? You kill someone then I can do fuck all to help you, Borat.'

'I'll try. I promise.' Tom took a deep swig of his drink.

'Another thing,' Buster said.

'Go on.'

'What happened with Ivan: the dead bloke in Willesden?'

'I went there to see him to find out what he knew. Someone got there before me and slit his throat. One of the Serbs turned up and I knocked him out and legged it. A bullet may have gone through the ceiling, but I didn't fire it.' Tom said.

'Hmm. Well there are loads of people on the Murder Squad who want to speak to you. Neil Wilkinson is keeping a bit of heat off you after the kidnap attempt, but they will start calling you a suspect rather than a person of interest unless they get hold of you soon.'

'Not yet. No way. I have genuinely no idea who I can trust. Apart from you, Buster.'

The two men clinked glasses before Buster said, 'Right, I have to get out of here. I've got your number and I'll get back to you once I know something, so stay local. I'll pop into Charing Cross nick as I can access everything from there.' Buster nodded, finished his beer, stood and walked off with a wink.

Tom sat for a moment longer to give Buster time to get well

away before he left the pub. His thoughts were interrupted by his phone vibrating.

'It's Stan, old boy. I've asked about and no one knows too much, although one or two people seem to know of a rather bad smell about Glenda from the time he was on the NCA. One thing my sources were clear about is that he's never going to get promoted again, which probably accounts for his bitterness.'

'Nothing concrete, then. Just rumours?' Tom asked.

'Just that, although he's not well-liked and is thought of as a little creepy, trying to live a bachelor life with his flash car and daft suits.'

'Okay. Thanks, Stan.'

'One more thing, Royal. I've been keeping an eye on him and he's been very jumpy since all this broke. He keeps making frequent trips down to his beloved Jag where he just sits inside talking on the phone. Very strange.'

'Okay, mate, thanks for everything,' said Tom.

'Always a pleasure, never a chore, old son. Take care of yourself,' Stan said and rang off.

Tom felt a little better after speaking to Buster and Stan. Although he did feel a little bad for the slight mistruth he'd just told Buster. He would certainly try his best not to kill anyone. Apart from Zjelko Branko. Zjelko was a dead man walking.

*

He left the pub and walked slowly around Covent Garden, pausing by a street entertainer who was amusing a clutch of tourists with a juggling act. He watched with mild interest, happy to let his mind wander away from current events.

He noticed the surveillance team almost immediately. His eyes were drawn first to a youngish-looking guy who he immediately pegged as a cop. The man was wearing a North Face fleece and Timberland boots: almost a uniform for plain-clothes cops. To make things worse, he could see the guy's lips moving as he touched his finger to his ear. Tom picked up his pace a little, walking towards Leicester Square before turning left along Long Acre by a large coffee shop which had a plate-glass window on both sides of the corner. A classic 'window trap' used in anti-surveillance: glancing back would enable Tom to see through the glass corner. As Tom turned, he saw the guy in the North Face fleece start jogging to close the distance between them. He sighed. That was another schoolboy error.

He made a snap decision and quickly diverted into the coffee shop, going straight to the counter and ordering a coffee. As he waited, he used the large mirror on the back wall to observe the street outside. A man in a grey hooded sweatshirt walked past the shop and went across the road where he paused, apparently interested in the window display of an upmarket dress shop. He was clearly using the glass to try to keep watch on the door of the coffee shop. Tom knew there would be at least another two surveillance officers on foot nearby, probably taking cover in shops ready for him to move on.

He paid for his coffee with cash and sat at a table at the back of the shop. He didn't have to wait long. The cop in the blue North Face entered within three minutes and made for the counter, making a big show of looking everywhere apart from at Tom. He quickly got a coffee and sat at a table by the door, using the same mirror Tom had used to observe the interior of the shop.

Tom couldn't help but smile. He wasn't worried; it was definitely a police team, as he recognised the tactics, and it was obvious who had put them onto him. He stood suddenly and made his way to the door, watching the barely-concealed look of alarm on his observer's face. At the very last second, Tom diverted and sat down on the chair opposite North Face.

'Hello,' Tom said to the young officer with a smile. Alarm flashed across the man's face as he stuttered a greeting.

'Listen, mate,' said Tom in a friendly, non-confrontational voice. 'You lot really need to work on your tactics and tradecraft. I'm not being too critical as I reckon you're not long qualified.

Why are you following me?'

'Errm, I'm just having a coffee...' the officer stuttered in a Midlands accent.

'Look, I don't have time for this. I'm really fucking busy. Now, can you bugger off and leave me alone before I make a really big scene and publicly blow-out all of your foot units outside, starting with your man in the grey hoodie over the road looking into the dress shop window.' He grinned as the man's eyes flitted to his colleague outside. 'Now you've not done too much wrong, but I am very good at this; I've been doing it for years. I'm assuming Buster sorted this to protect me, but can you please piss off and tell him to come back and see me, right now. Tell him I'll buy him a tea.'

The man hesitated just a second and Tom could almost see the cogs turning.

'Go on: chop-chop,' said Tom, with as much sarcasm as he could muster.

Clearly defeated, the officer stood up and left the coffee shop, pulling his phone out of his pocket as he did so.

About ten minutes later, Buster sat down with a sigh in the chair the surveillance officer had recently vacated, a rueful grin on his face.

'Why?' asked Tom.

'Because we're all worried you're going to get topped. My boss wouldn't let you just walk away, mate. I'm sorry.'

Tom was unable to be angry at his old friend. He accepted that he was only doing what he thought was right; Buster was the most honest person he knew, despite all the bluster, and it would have almost killed him to go behind his back.

'They're a shit surveillance team. Who trained them?' Tom asked.

'They are a new one. Recruited from all over so we have some unknown faces on the teams. I must admit they are a bit green.'

'They are shite. Don't use them against proper villains. You managed to find anything out about Taylor yet?' Tom asked.

'Fuck me, mate,' said Buster. 'We only met twenty minutes ago!'

'Well then you shouldn't have distracted me by setting your Keystone Cops on me, should you?' grinned Tom. 'Anyway, I know you: twenty minutes is more than enough for you to dig out intel. So come on: spill what you've found out.'

Buster grinned in defeat. 'There is a very bad smell about Taylor, mate. You may be onto something.'

'Go on.' Tom felt his pulse quickening.

'Taylor left SOCA under a bit of a cloud in 2010 when he was a DS. Apparently, him and two others were running a trafficking job that was all looking good until it totally collapsed in somewhat suspicious circumstances. I can't find anything concrete, but the suspicion was that one of the three tipped-off the targets and all the trafficked girls disappeared back to Eastern Europe just before the arrests went down. Totally smashed the job to bits, and two years of work went down the crapper.'

'Jesus, that sounds bad. Was anything ever proved?'

'Nope. SOCA was a bit of a joke at the time. Management were totally incompetent and just decided to send the two cops back to the Force and transfer the SOCA guy elsewhere. Want to guess where to?'

'No, I want you to tell me, you daft bastard.'

'The SOCA bloke, Gareth Jones, was transferred to the fucking line room in London. They sent him to listen to intercepted phone calls, where he's still working to this day.'

So that was clear. Taylor's link to phone taps was currently sitting a few miles away, listening in to intercepted phone calls.

'What about the other?'

'DC Graham Albrechtsen retired from the Met in 2015, where he finished his career on the Crime Management Unit at Tower Hamlets. He never got promoted, was always in the shit, and was suspected of all sorts of capers, none of which were ever proved.'

'Not him, then.'

'Want something else, Borat?' Buster asked with the same

teasing note in his voice.

'I'm going to punch you in the face if you don't stop winding me up.'

'Graham returned as Dedicated Detention Officer Albrechtsen at an East London nick. Want to guess which one?'

'Let me take a wild stab in the dark: maybe Ilford?'

'Boom! Spot on. Somehow, despite all the clouds over his head, the Met took the fucker back as a gaoler. Apparently, he suffered the detective's disease of lots of divorces and needs the money, so he takes care of prisoners for twenty grand a year. Listen, mate, this is big news and probably provable with some work. Let me speak to my boss about it.' Buster's tone quickly switched to a serious one.

'No way. I've no idea how far this goes. I have no one to trust apart from you; they could have friends anywhere.'

'Listen, mate, my boss was recruited direct from Manchester. She's untouched by the Met, just like me. I trust her one hundred percent and she's a very good lateral thinker. We can sort this; come and see her.'

'I can't, Buster. Not until I've sorted this out properly. Taylor could have others working for him, too much has happened for me to not rule that out. I'm sorry, mate. I gotta run. Don't bother with the surveillance team, I'd only embarrass them.' Tom stood, clapped Buster on the shoulder and walked out of the coffee shop.

He felt bad leaving his friend like that, but he wasn't ready to come in just yet. So many bad things had occurred, and he couldn't assess the impact, the potential risks. Could they try to pin the murder of Ivan on him? Who knew what else was at stake?

25

Simon Taylor sat in his office, wondering what he should do with the information he'd just received.

He'd managed to elicit some information from Novak's file by convincing the clerk he needed it for safety reasons, given that Tom was absent without leave.

Every method he'd employed to try and trace Novak had failed. His bank accounts were silent, his phone switched off, and the CCTV camera which a contact at Camden Council had trained on Novak's apartment had come up with nothing. Not a single sighting had been reported, and the Serbs were getting more and more impatient.

Adebayo had also been on the phone trying to sweeten the deal by offering him more money to make it all go away. Probably hoping to cut the Brankos out of the deal. He was an oily bastard, Adebayo, but Taylor had said he'd look into it. He'd managed to get the update on the rape from his contact at Ilford; it seemed the girl had left the shelter and hadn't been seen since. So without the undercover recording and without the girl, the case was dead. That just left the immigration and trafficking case that, as he understood it, wasn't solid either. All they needed was the SD card, and then the whole problem would go away, and it wouldn't hurt if Novak disappeared off the face of the Earth either.

In a flash of resolution, he decided he had to use the information he'd just received. He picked up his burner phone and composed a text message, his fingers tapping out an address into the message field.

'Cameron and Shona Ferguson, Cregganmore Farm Cottage, Duthill Burn, Near Carrbridge.'

Taylor hesitated for just a second. By sending the message to Branko, he would be an accessory to whatever befell Novak's foster parents. Could he live with that?

He got up from his desk and strode down the corridor, descended the stairs and emerged into the sunlight of the police station backyard. He didn't want to make any more calls inside. He didn't think anyone would be listening, but he felt he couldn't be too careful, and his car was as secure as anywhere. Fishing in his pocket for his car key, he unlocked his Jaguar F-Pace SUV and climbed in. He'd been forced to use his own personal car since Stan had taken the Passat he normally used, which had annoyed him intensely. Nestling into the plush cream leather seats, he keyed a number into his phone. The call was answered almost immediately.

'Hello, my little policeman friend,' said Zjelko Branko in his low growl. 'I hope you have some information for me?' Taylor could picture the unpleasant grin on the Serb's face.

'Look, I have the address of Novak's foster family here now. I can send it to you, but you must keep my name out of this, and you must promise they won't be harmed. They're innocents in all this.'

'Mr Policeman, I'm hurt you think I'm such a monster who would hurt the innocents. But you're giving us nothing to catch Novak, so we have to go proactive on him. We won't hurt a hair on their heads, my friend. As long as Novak comes up with the goods.'

'Okay. I'll send it to you after I finish this call. Novak is too careful, and I can't see him popping his head up for you, so you'll have to see what this brings. By the way, they live miles away: in Scotland.'

'Never mind that; we have associates in Scotland who can at least get proceedings underway while we get up there. Give me the address and keep us informed of any developments. Your career and your liberty depend on it.' The line went dead.

Taylor felt he had no choice. His fingers hovered over the smartphone in a last vestige of hesitation before he pressed Send. He placed the handset back in his pocket and sat with his fingers massaging his temple, utterly ashamed at what he'd become.

*

Zjelko Branko sat with his sons in an empty café in the centre of Islington, eating a large breakfast of eggs and bacon as he contemplated the message that Taylor had just sent. He smiled to himself, realising that this was the way to tip the scales back in their favour. Novak's only family had to be good leverage to get him out into the open and finish it all for good. He'd been involved in organised crime long enough to know that it could only end one way. Novak had to die and, by involving the foster family, Taylor had just signed their death warrants too.

He checked their postcode on Google Maps, noting grimly that it was a ten-hour drive to the property in Scotland.

Branko had no qualms about using murder to resolve the situation. He'd killed countless times during the Balkan conflict and couldn't deny the big thrill he gained from exercising the ultimate power over other people. He felt no pity for his victims, feeling no more than when he used to kill the vermin that ate his father's chickens.

He turned to Aleks and Luka. 'My boys, you need to get yourselves to Scotland as soon as possible. I will get an associate to secure the packages, and you can take over when you arrive. I want to keep it within the family as much as we can. It's just a babysitting job until we have Novak.'

'How far is it?' asked Aleks through a mouthful of egg.

'Over five hundred miles. Take the BMW and buy a new phone on the way. Leave yours here. The police must not be able to trace you to the scene, as I'm sure there will be a big investigation.'

Both men stood and made ready to go without questioning his orders. Aleks caught the car key tossed by his father.

'Items are in the boot under the carpet,' he said, referring to the two Glock 17 automatic pistols secreted in the spare wheel space. 'There are false plates as well; put them on so ANPR doesn't catch you. Also, collect Boris on the way. I will tell him to expect you.' Boris was a proven operator and another ex-paramilitary who he knew would have no hesitation putting a bullet in any head. His boys had no kills to their name, and so he couldn't completely trust their ruthlessness. He had no such doubts about Boris.

'Do me proud, my boys. This is a big responsibility. Call me with the new phone and we will talk on the way. Stay off all CCTV; there must be no trace of you in Scotland.' He fixed them with his pale blue eyes.

Both men nodded and turned, leaving the café.

He picked up his phone once more and selected a number from the contacts list. Danilo Arken was another paramilitary associate from the old days. He was a vicious bastard who headed up the Serb mafia in Glasgow and beyond. He also had no scruples or empathy and could be trusted to do a good job for a price.

'Danilo, it's Zjelko,' he boomed, a huge grin etched across his craggy features. 'How are you, my friend? Good, good. How is your family?' He paused, pretending to be interested in the reply given.

'Anyway, old friend, to business. I may have some work for you in Bonnie Scotland, if you could do an old Chetnik comrade an urgent favour. I assure you it will pay very well.'

26

Michael Adebayo sat in the office of his friend and solicitor, a worried look on his face.

'So, my friend, where are we?' asked Asif Khan.

'Novak is nowhere to be seen, despite me offering one hundred grand to see him silenced. Those incompetent fools, the Brankos, can't find him anywhere, and Taylor is having no luck. I'm worried he's making plans to reveal the footage. If he does that, I'm in major trouble.' He rubbed his hands across his tired-looking face, tension evident in his features.

Khan paused for a moment, a contemplative look on his handsome face. He straightened his already-immaculate tie knot and spoke. 'As I understand it from my police source, the female is nowhere to be found. She fled the women's refuge and the police think she's back in her homeland. If that's the case, you only have the immigration offence left and, without knowing what's on the SD card, it's difficult to advise you properly. If you've told me everything that could be on it then you're going to get convicted and you will almost certainly be going to jail for a number of years.'

Adebayo sighed deeply. Jail would also mean that the Solicitors Regulatory Authority would strike him off, leaving him disgraced and unemployable.

Khan continued. 'In addition, the Home Office would do a financial investigation into your businesses and may seize all your assets if they can argue they are the proceeds of crime. If I understand correctly what the Home Office are saying, they can evidence that you processed all the corrupt visa applications on the basis of sham marriages introduced by the Brankos.'

'How can they prove I knew it?'

'They had the Brankos under surveillance and Novak had infiltrated them for a month at least. They also have all the statistical data of the obviously corrupt applications. Added to the evidence they seized from your office, they have a strong case. You should have been more careful, my friend.'

Adebayo knew he had been careless, made worse by the fact that he'd felt invincible in his own community for so long. He had been feared and respected in equal measures, and he'd never thought that anyone would give evidence against him.

'So, what's my best-case scenario, then?'

'That the SD card, Novak, and the girl never surface again. We can then argue entrapment; but it's hard to argue the previous month away when you have personally signed over twenty patently sham marriage visa applications. My advice, as your solicitor, is to wait this thing out and see what we can plea bargain, but the reality is you're finished as a solicitor. I also suspect you will go to jail for a number of years, and you will lose hundreds of thousands of pounds at least. They can look at the last six years of your earnings and income and they will assume it's all from crime. Don't forget, my friend, that the burden of proof in proceeds of crime hearings shifts to you. You—not the prosecution—have to prove that all your money and assets are lawful.'

Adebayo sat back in the leather chair and stared at the ceiling, stunned at the reality of the situation. This could amount to millions of pounds. His business was corrupt to the core, and it wouldn't take a genius to unpick the extent of it. The money laundering teams had forensic accountants who could unravel his accounts and investments, all of which came from his legal practice.

'What would you do if you were me?' Adebayo asked.

'You have many assets in Nigeria, and your home in Lagos is wonderful. You could make a new life there, leave all this behind. You'll never get extradited from Nigeria, you have far too much influence.'

Adebayo paused. He'd been clever: learning the lesson of another solicitor friend who had been convicted of corruption and lost over a million pounds when the police seized all his assets, he had transferred many assets to Nigeria. There had been an added incentive, with taxation in the UK being so extortionate. Not only that, but the UK's money laundering regulations also made it more than worth his while to use money-brokers to get his cash into safe investments and property in Lagos.

As a result, he owned a palatial detached property in an upmarket, gated development in Lagos. He also had investments in Nigerian banks and some gold reserves in safe deposit boxes. He could live comfortably forever and never have to face the shame of a criminal trial, jail, and the loss of his UK assets.

'The police have my passport. I also have many assets in the UK. Will they all be lost?'

'I'm sure you know someone at the Nigerian Embassy, so a new passport won't be difficult. The police or Home Office haven't restrained your bank accounts yet. To be honest, I don't think it has occurred to them, what with all the issues with Novak. This may be the perfect time to go. Shall I speak to Syed?'

Syed Shafiq was Adebayo's accountant, a bright and inventive man who could always come up with a plan to move money quickly from anywhere to anywhere.

'Do it. I'm not giving a penny to the fucking government and I'm not going to jail. The house is in my wife's name. She and the kids can follow me later. I've sold several properties recently so I'm cash-rich and only have the two houses left in London, including my home.' Resolve gripped him. He could make a new life for himself so easily in Lagos; he had many contacts and friends and a good home waiting for him. He smiled triumphantly at his friend, showing his capped, white teeth. He would win once again.

'And your brother, Michael?' Khan asked.

'Fuck him. He can look after himself.' Adebayo waved a hand dismissively. 'One more thing: the contract on Novak stays. The

SD card doesn't matter, I just want him dead.'

'As you wish, my friend. I will call the Brankos and accelerate things.'

Adebayo didn't reply, instead looking out of his office window and down at the drab, rain-soaked Ilford streets. He would miss the place, but not enough to risk jail and dishonour. He smiled at the prospect of his new life in Lagos.

27

B ack at the Canaletto, Tom let himself into the apartment to find Pet hunched over her laptop, exactly as she had been when he'd left. She looked up and offered up a dazzling smile at his arrival. The detritus of a takeaway meal was scattered about her feet.

'All good, Detective?'

'As good as can be expected,' he replied. 'Any movements at the Brankos?'

'None. Quiet as a grave, but I've been busy.'

'How so?'

'Taylor sent a text to Branko which went through iMessage on the phone system. I managed to get an IP address and link it into his Cloud account. I'm running the password hack I used for Ana; I'm hoping that will get us into his last backup, which will give us everything on that phone. I'm being even more clever than that, though,' she teased.

'Go on, then,' Tom smiled.

'I've managed to remotely jailbreak his phone and I've planted some malware I designed onto it. It will hopefully give us full access to his phone. He's not been clever as he's not been updating his software.'

'Could be useful, even though it's not been a busy phone.'

'I also tracked a call between Taylor and Branko just before the message was sent, which may make it important. Branko called a new number straight after the iMessage which is registered to a Danilo Arken in Glasgow. Cell site puts Branko in Islington and

Arken in Glasgow. Any ideas on that?'

'The name's unfamiliar. There is a Serb population in Glasgow and the mafia have the vice trade sewn up. Can you run the name through your databases?'

'Sure thing, Detective. Have you learnt any more?'

'I'm good. I know who the bent cops are; I now just need to prove it.'

'I can't help you with admissible evidence,' she said, her fingers tapping at the keys. 'But I've just fully hacked his phone.'

'You've done what?'

'The malware has worked. I can mirror his phone onto my laptop. You can look at his photos, emails, messages, and everything really. Won't even have to wait for it to backup to the Cloud. I impress myself sometimes. I've not managed to do this before, but thankfully it's an old phone and old software. High-five, Detective.' Pet held her hand aloft and Tom lightly slapped it.

'I'll load all messages into a spreadsheet for easy searching.' She continued typing.

Tom sat next to her in front of the computer, watching as she opened Excel. There were very few messages and his eyes were drawn to the most recent one sent just four hours ago to someone listed as 'Z' with the number he recognised for Zjelko. The message content simply listed a name and address. Tom's stomach lurched and rage gripped him like a vice.

The familiar Highlands address jumped off the screen and hit Tom in the face like a thunderbolt. His face darkened as the anger boiled, showing only as a hardening of his features and tenseness in the jawline.

Pet noticed the shift in his demeanour and asked, 'Tom, what is it?'

'That's my foster family's address. Taylor has sold them out to get to me. This changes everything.' He voice was flat and emotionless but something in the delivery of the words conveyed the fury behind them.

Tom picked up the satellite phone and dialled a number from

memory, holding it to his ear and walking around the apartment as he listened to the tone until the answer machine kicked in. He hung up without leaving a message and dialled another number, but that also went straight to answerphone. He dialled one more number: again, straight to answerphone.

'No reply on their landline and both of their mobiles are switched off. That's unheard of: Cameron is always on-call for mountain rescue and Shona is never without her phone. Something's happened, I know it.'

'Give me their numbers; I'll run them through.'

Her fingers blurred across the keyboard and, after only a couple of minutes, she said, 'Both phones were hitting a cell mast close to their home address until about thirty minutes ago. They were clearly switched off at the same time as they both lost the signal at about three-thirty. As they're on different networks, it's unlikely they lost signal at exactly the same time.'

'No. It means someone else switched them off. There's only one explanation: Branko despatched Arken from Glasgow to get to them. He will want to get in contact to make his demands. I'll have to switch my phone back on in case I have a message. Start clearing everything up, we need to get out of here.'

Pet nodded and began packing her equipment up as Tom grabbed his iPhone and switched it out of airplane mode. Its connection was indicated by a buzz as a text message arrived from a number he knew to be Zjelko's. With a sense of dread, Tom opened the message and saw that a video clip was attached.

Wordlessly, he pressed Play and the clip immediately filled the handset's screen in sharp clarity, showing four figures in the kitchen of Cameron and Shona's home. Cameron was blindfolded, his hands pinned behind him, secured by some means to the radiator at the side of the room. Shona was on the floor on her knees, facing away from the camera. Her wrists were fixed behind her back by what looked like zip-ties. Her wrists were pulled upwards and her head forced down by a burly male, who was wearing a balaclava. Another masked man towered over Shona with an automatic pistol tucked into his belt. Tom's heart sank when he saw that the man had a pair of pruning secateurs in his hand.

'No!' Tom screamed pointlessly at the small screen, realising with horror what was about to happen. The man with the secateurs grabbed Shona's left little finger and, without hesitation, closed the blades around the digit. He then paused to stare at the camera and, even through the balaclava, Tom could see the grin on his face. He clamped the blades shut and Shona emitted a piercing scream, bucking in agony as blood flowed and the severed digit dropped to the carpet. Cameron started to thrash against his bonds at the sound of his wife's scream. Suddenly, the clip was over.

A mix of fear, rage, and hatred rose in Tom, almost threatening to overwhelm him. He forced it down, aware that it was a time to think clearly, not emotionally. He breathed deeply, trying to organise his thoughts, as he spoke quickly and decisively.

'I'll have to call Branko but he's going to want the SD card. I need to buy some time as it's in the post to Buster. I can always burn another copy from my phone, but I don't intend handing it over in any case. There's no way they're going to let any of us live, whether they get the card or not.

'I'm going to phone Zjelko now. Can you cell site Arken's phone and get me any intel you guys have on him or his associates?'

Pet nodded and retrieved her laptop from its bag.

Tom punched the number for Zjelko into his iPhone and was answered almost immediately.

'Detective Sergeant, so kind of you to call.' His voice was gruff with a hint of menace.

'You fucking bastard, you fucking animal. She's a fucking innocent.'

Branko chuckled. 'We wanted you to know that we were serious, Novak. We want the card and all copies. If we get it, your family lives. If not, they die. But they won't die easily, Novak. My men will use your mother's shears and will cut pieces off them until they beg to be shot. The men who are with your parents are very dangerous and won't hesitate in putting a bullet in each of their heads. You will bring the card to me at a place of my choosing in London. You will come alone, and I will know immediately if you tell anyone in law enforcement. You have four hours to comply.' His voice was level, but there was no mistaking the malevolence behind it.

'I can't get it by then. It's in a safe deposit box and by the time I get there it will be closed. They don't open until nine in the morning. I'll get it then and bring it to you.'

'Where is this safety box? You'd better not be shitting me, Novak.'

'I've had a safe deposit box for years. Why wouldn't I put something so important in there? Your tame policeman must have told you I have one. Come on, be logical.' This was a calculated risk. Taylor and his people had obviously done a financial profile on Tom when tracking him, and that would have revealed the Holborn bank branch where he had the box. His thoughts briefly turned to the two remaining diamonds tucked safely away there.

There was a pause at the end of the line that seemed interminable.

'Eleven tomorrow at a place of my choosing. Just remember, Novak: I own you. I will be tracking this phone, so you must leave it on. If you try anything stupid, your mother will lose another finger. I will call you every so often to make sure you're in London and not trying to do anything stupid. Remember, I will know everything you're doing. Your family is being held by men who would enjoy killing them and your cooperation is the only way to keep them alive. Now, do you understand, Novak?'

'I understand,' said Tom, quietly.

The phone beeped as the call was finished.

Pet looked at him. 'I think I got the gist of that. Arken is hitting a cell mast close to your family's place. I've run him through the CIA database and he's a nasty piece of work: ex-White Eagle, suspected of multiple murders, and an active and dangerous criminal in Scotland and Bosnia.' A photograph of a Slavic-featured man in his fifties with dark hair and a broken nose filled the screen. Tom stared at it, committing the image to memory.

'Right, let's pack up and get out of here, and I need Mike Brogan on the phone.'

*

Minutes later they left the basement car park in the Passat and exited onto City Road. All the equipment, including the laser-listener, were stowed in the boot.

'What are you planning?'

'I have no choice; I have to get to my family. There's no way Branko is going to let them live, not a chance in hell. As soon as I hand over the card, we all get killed.'

'But what can you do? Why not just call it in? Let the professionals handle it.'

'I can't. Taylor would be bound to hear about it and then they're dead. I have to do this on my own.' He rubbed his forehead. 'If I leave my phone with you in London, will you be able to divert calls to me on the satellite without anyone knowing?'

'I'm sure I can. I would need to route the call via VOIP into a sat-com. I'm sure it would be achievable. Your iPhone would hit the London cell sites and, to all intents and purposes, it would be as if you were speaking on your phone.'

'Right. I just need to get to the Highlands sooner than they could ever expect. Can you get Mike on the line for me over speakerphone?'

When Mike answered the call, Tom brought him up to speed without preamble.

'Jesus, Tom. This is bad. What do you need?'

'I need to get to Inverness airport urgently. I need to be there much faster than they would expect me to get there. Can you help?'

'Possibly. But are you sure you want to go dashing up there alone? Can't the kidnap squad lead this?'

'No way. Simon Taylor is corrupt and has influence; he would hear of it immediately and then my family is dead. They're all I have left, Mike.' Despite his even tone, there was no hiding the desperation in his voice.

'Wait by this line and I'll call back in ten minutes.'

Tom pulled into a side street just short of Upper Street and stopped the car.

'What are you going to do?' asked Pet.

'I'm hoping Mike has some resource that can get me to their house quickly. I can watch without being expected and then figure out a way to take the gunmen out. If I was going to drive up there, it would take at least ten hours; but a flight is just over an hour. It would give me the element of surprise I badly need.'

'You only have the Sig, and you can't take that on a flight.'

'I'll improvise; I'm good at that.'

The sat-phone buzzed.

'Mike?'

'Where are you?'

'Islington, in a car with blue lights and a siren.'

'Okay. Get yourself to RAF Northolt, go to the main gate and get Pet to take the car away. You're expected. There's a jet ready to take you on a priority flight path to Inverness airport; it'll take less than an hour. You have some photo ID?'

'A driving licence in my cover name.'

'Okay. You'll need to show that. You can't take any weapons through the gate or on the flight so lose whatever you have. I've arranged for a tactical package to be made available for you. I know I said I couldn't give you any equipment, but this has gone up to a level where I am gonna pull some strings. My representative on the flight has access to some irregular resources that we tend to reserve for special circumstances. I think we can call this a special circumstance, Tom. Use the flight to acquaint yourself with the contents. It's nothing you've not seen before, but my representative on the flight can answer any questions. Sorry, my friend, I can't give you any manpower on the ground.'

'That's no problem, Mike. You're doing more than I expected. Thanks, man,' he said, the gratitude heartfelt in his voice.

'We can get you to the airport, but after that it's over to you.'

'That'll be enough. I've another favour to call in elsewhere.'

'I want you to stay in constant contact with Pet: there's a communications kit in the tactical package. We may also be able to offer some real-time support, technically. I may be able to divert a satellite or two.'

'I will, Mike, and thanks.'

'Best of luck, man.' And he was gone.

Tom looked at his watch, it was 1645 hours. Branko would be expecting him to hand over the SD card in eighteen-and-a-quarter hours.

'We will need to secrete my phone somewhere en route and leave it switched on. I don't want them seeing it close to the RAF base. I know a place, but you'll need to retrieve it as quick as you can after you've dropped me off, in case he calls. I think we are safe for an hour or two, though.'

Pet nodded in agreement as Tom started the engine and then pressed two hidden switches just below the steering column. A wailing noise erupted from the bonnet area and he engaged the automatic gearbox, speeding off west, weaving through the dense traffic. His face was a mask of pure concentration as the city at rush hour flew past, the blue strobe lights concealed within the grille flashing urgently.

*

The journey to RAF Northolt took just under half-an-hour, the only sound inside the car the wail of the sirens. At Hanger Lane on the A40, Tom pulled into a small cul-de-sac and stashed his iPhone under a loose paving slab beneath a bush. Once at the RAF base he pulled over in the visitor parking bays, removed the keys, and handed them to Pet.

'Take the car and go somewhere safe where we can stay in contact, and retrieve my phone as quick as you can,' he said, his eyes fixed on the barrier.

'Are you sure this is what you want? You know it's almost

certainly a suicide mission.' She looked at him, her eyes moist.

'I've no choice. My foster family is all I have, and without them I'm all alone. There is no way Branko will let them go, even if I give him what he wants.'

'But—'

'There's no other way, Pet. Take the Sig and go somewhere safe. Be ready for me when I start; I will need your help.' He grabbed her hand and squeezed it tight for a fraction of a second before opening the door. Pet pulled him towards her and threw her arms around his neck, burying her head against his chest.

'Promise me you'll be careful, Tom,' she said in a faltering voice.

'Always careful, Pet,' he said, disentangling himself and fixing her with a smile. The smile didn't reach his flinty hard eyes, though.

He got out, carrying nothing but the sat-phone, and strode up to the main gate, which was manned by a uniformed MPGS guard armed with an SA80 assault rifle. The guard viewed him with mild interest.

'My name is Tom Johnson,' he said, giving his cover name. 'I understand I'm expected.'

'Go into the guardroom, sir, and speak to the duty RAF Police.'

Tom went up to the small window of the guardroom at the side of the barrier, where a middle-aged man dressed in the petrol-blue of the RAF sat. Tom noted the epaulette-mounted rank slides of a sergeant, with the red-and-black insignia of the RAF Police.

'My name is Tom Johnson. Are you expecting me?' He proffered the driving licence and the sergeant took it wordlessly.

'Wait one moment please, sir,' he said in a broad Yorkshire accent.

Tom heard the barking of orders from within the guardroom, shortly followed by the sergeant striding out of the door wearing the white-topped flat cap which gave the RAF Police their nickname: 'Snowdrops'.

'Follow me please,' he said, nodding at the armed guard, who in turn raised the vehicle barrier. They walked to a nearby battered Land Rover Defender, which bore the same black-and-red RAF

Police insignia.

'Jump in and I'll take you straight to the terminal. Someone is waiting for you there.'

The journey took no more than five minutes and was taken in absolute silence. Tom suspected that the sergeant had been warned to ask no questions, owing to the irregular nature of the encounter. His manner was not one of interest or excitement and it seemed that 'Ask no questions' visitors were not uncommon, given it was an airfield used regularly by Special Forces from varying countries. Tom himself had deployed over to Northern Ireland on more than one occasion from that base on SRR assignments.

The Land Rover pulled up alongside a low, white art deco building, which Tom recalled was the small terminal that housed passengers and processed the security procedures. As well as being a fully-functioning RAF base, Northolt handled a large amount of civilian flights, particularly smaller business jets, within the UK and Europe.

'Gentleman to meet you is here now, sir,' said the sergeant. 'Have a good trip,' he added, almost as an afterthought but with a smile touching his lips.

Tom nodded his thanks and got out of the vehicle, watching as his greeter approached. He was a tall, well-fleshed serviceman wearing CS95 fatigues bearing the chest-mounted rank insignia of a Squadron Leader. He wore no headdress and had a wide smile on his face.

'I'm Roy McKenzie,' he said in a light but confident Scottish accent. 'I run 32 Squadron. I look after all the flights that come and go from this place. I've no idea who you are, Tom, but someone in a very high place wants you looked after and on your flight. Immediately.'

'Thanks for everything, Roy.'

'If you follow me, I'll get you on your flight straight away, lucky bugger. You're on a HS215.'

'Should I be impressed?'

'It's the RAF business jet taxi. Whatever clout you have, mate, can you pass some my way?' He smiled again, showing even, white teeth.

Tom said nothing but followed in the officer's wake as he strode through the terminal building and straight to security.

'No luggage or anything you shouldn't have on a plane, Tom?'

'Nothing: just a phone and driving licence.'

'Right. Whizz through security and you're on your way, mate.'

Tom passed through the metal detector arch, having put his phone, belt, and watch through the X-Ray machine. Having cleared security, the Squadron Leader led him at breakneck speed through to the exit gate and out onto the aircraft pan.

A small twin-engine business jet with red and white decals was waiting, engines already humming. A set of steps that were part of the cabin door were in position, with a suited attendant waiting at the top to greet him.

'Have a good trip and take care of yourself, Tom.' The Squadron Leader extended his hand, which Tom shook with a firm grip, before smiling, turning on his heels, and striding off.

Tom ascended the steps, two at a time, and came face-to-face with the man waiting by the door.

'Tom, I assume,' the man said. He was in his thirties, fit-looking, of average height and build with neat dark hair, dressed in a dark suit and an open-necked shirt. He had a soft New York accent and an open, smiling face.

'I'm Bill Kowalski, an associate of Mike Brogan. He's asked me to offer you every courtesy. Please, welcome aboard, Tom.' He extended his hand which Tom shook; there was no trial of strength, just a genuine warmth.

'Thank you for your hospitality, Bill. Are we ready to go?'

'Yep, fuelled up and ready to rock-and-roll. We'll have you in Scotland in less than an hour. I've also got some kit to talk you through once we're up; I'm told you will be familiar with most of it. Come on: let's get going.'

The aircraft interior was functional and had a military feel in the décor and furnishings.

'Mike didn't say why, but he said you needed to get to Inverness ASAP. He must like you, Tom,' said Bill, fixing Tom with a searching stare before turning to deal with the jet's steps and door, securing them tight.

'We go way back.'

They sat opposite each other on the leather seats and both fastened their seat belts.

'We have a priority take-off in place, so we'll get going now. No stewardesses, I'm afraid, but I'll fix you a coffee once we get going and there's a sandwich somewhere. No safety briefing, either, but I'm guessing we'll be fine.'

The cockpit door was shut and Tom imagined it would stay that way, bearing in mind the unofficial nature of this flight.

'Who does the jet belong to?'

'Your Royal Air Force. Someone senior from our end has put in a phone call to someone senior in the RAF and they've very kindly lent us a jet. I came along from Northwood with the tactical package.

'Well, I'm very grateful. The quicker I'm in Scotland, the better.'

Within seven minutes, the engines roared and they were away. Tom looked out of the window and watched West London disappear below him, his mind turning over what lay ahead. He looked at his watch: 1735 hours.

*

As soon as they'd reached cruising altitude Tom asked Bill, 'Am I good to make a sat-call on here?'

'Go ahead. Something important?'

'I just need to plan my onward journey,' Tom said, punching in a number.

'Hello?' a broad Highland accent barked down the phone.

'Donnie, it's Tom.'

'Tommy, my boy, where have you been? We were supposed to

all go fishing last month; what happened?'

Donnie was an old family friend. He'd served with Cameron over many years in the Marines, both rising through the ranks together. He was a legendary character: joined at sixteen, fought in the Falklands War, highly decorated, and eventually commissioned as a helicopter pilot. He'd stayed in the Corps for over thirty years, retiring a couple of years previously when he managed to get employment with Bristow Group in Inverness as a search-and-rescue pilot. It was a perfect home-from-home for Donnie, as almost all the pilots and crew were ex-Navy or RAF. He lived close by Cameron and Shona and they remained good friends, often going out on the hills and fishing together. He was also a big character who didn't suffer fools gladly but would do anything for Cameron and Tom.

'Listen, Donnie, I don't have time to explain. I'm on my way up now and will be at Inverness airport in about forty-five minutes. Please tell me you're on duty?'

'Certainly am, mate: on all night. What's going on?'

'For reasons I don't want to go into right now, I urgently need a lift up to the bothy as soon as I land. It is, quite literally, a matter of life-and-death. Can you help?'

'Possibly, son. But I'll need a little more than that.'

'It's to do with Cam and Shona and it's urgent—as in life-and-death urgent—and I can't call it in officially or it will all go bad. I'll explain as much as I can once I get there. Can you trust me that much at least?'

'Tom, I trust you, of course, and I owe Cameron everything. I'll meet you off the plane; what flight are you on?'

'It won't be on the flight list. It's a standard RAF business jet: I think it's an HS215. It will be there in about forty minutes.'

'Jesus, are you on a private jet now? I'm intrigued. I'll meet you there.'

Bill looked quizzically at Tom, one eyebrow raised slightly.

'I seem to be calling in a lot of favours at the moment.'

Bill reached behind him and pulled out a plain, matte black, vulcanised Pelican case. 'Shall I brief you on the tactical package Mike asked me to leave you with?'

'Please do.'

Bill snapped the case open, revealing that it was inlaid with dense foam with cut-outs storing various items. Bill reached inside and pulled out a short machine pistol.

'Heckler and Koch MP7 personal defence weapon, telescopic stock, folding front-hand grip. It has 4.6 x 30mm ammunition, and this one has an Armasight NYX 3 third generation night-scope with eight-times magnification. Are you familiar with this weapon?' Bill was clipped and business-like in his delivery.

Tom nodded. 'I used it in the military but not with this sight.'

'It's a great sight, can be used without magnification and it's the latest generation of night vision tech. Ideally it would be zeroed before operational use.'

That was generally the case with many firearms. They needed to be test-fired and adjusted to suit the individual user, owing to natural variances in eyesight.

Bill pulled out a long, black, flat metallic box from one of the cut-outs and screwed it on the front of the MP7.

'Gemtech 4.6mm brick suppressor. It's really effective but, if you're firing the normal high-velocity rounds, it won't be that effective against the noise. You have four magazines, plus three forty-round boxes with standard copper-jacketed, armour-piercing rounds that will make short work of anyone in body armour. You also have one twenty-round magazine containing some made-to-measure subsonic rounds that will be all but inaudible if shot from any kind of distance. A hundred metre headshot would take out an enemy and no one would hear anything. Okay so far?'

Tom was impressed; the MP7 was a fearsome weapon, up to 950 rounds-per-minute rate of fire. It had an effective range of up to two-hundred metres, with devastating stopping power in something not much bigger than a large handgun. It was light, at just over four pounds fully-loaded, and only twenty-five inches long with the stock extended.

'No problem,' said Tom.

Bill pulled out a standard-looking Glock pistol. 'I take it you're familiar with Glocks?'

Tom nodded. 'Police and British military use them.'

'Bomb-proof, reliable weapons. This is a fourth generation Glock 17, as good as it gets, and you have four magazines and a further box of fifty in the case. Should be enough unless you're planning a war?'

'I certainly hope not.'

'You have a chest harness rig for the MP7 and magazines and a thigh or pancake hip holster for the Glock and a spare magazine,' said Bill, positively buzzing. 'We also have some communications kit here,' he continued, pulling out a six-inch-long rectangular box with a short aerial and covert microphone attachment and earpiece.

'This uses GSM technology, so you'll be able to speak directly to Pet or Mike on an open mic or using the transmitter button here. It's real simple and the transmissions are fully scrambled, with an algorithm at each end so you won't be overheard.' He handed the rig over to Tom. It seemed simple and was comprised of the main unit and a wireless microphone and earpiece, with an on/off switch and volume control. Tom was well aware that the encryption would be entered using a 'fill gun' that loaded the encryption and frequency data on the screen.

'You've a covert chest harness for this which will fit in with the MP7 sling,' Bill said as he reached for another piece of kit from the Pelican case.

'There is a standard German-issued tactical body armour vest here which can be worn overtly or covertly depending on what you're looking for. Latest Kevlar formation: won't stop a big, high-velocity round but it will stop most handguns. I'd certainly wear it if doing something dangerous.'

'I'll bear that in mind.'

'Last thing is this.' He handed over a small, seven-inch tablet that looked similar to a mini iPad, other than it had a chunky, robust-looking black surround making it resilient.

'It's a direct communications tablet which will allow Pet or Mike to send you documentation or link you into various types of imagery. It has its own GSM transmitter that can either use cellular phone systems or satellite communication if necessary. If you can use an iPad, you can use this.'

Tom turned the tablet over in his hands, feeling slightly overwhelmed by the equipment that had been handed over to him. It was favour payback like he'd never seen. He now had two powerful firearms, 140 rounds of sub-machinegun ammunition, and 118 rounds of 9mm handgun ammunition. If the Brankos wanted a war, he was now armed to take part.

He fixed Bill with a direct, even gaze. 'Thanks for this. And send my thanks to Mike. I don't know what I would have done without him.'

'Don't worry about it. Just don't lose it, we'd like it back. Everything you have is untraceable and will either show up as lost or stolen, so Uncle Sam can deny it and you. Now buckle up: we're landing any time now.'

As Tom sat back into the luxury of the leather chair with its endless legroom, Bill reached into an overhead locker and produced a couple of pre-packed sandwiches.

'You want these?'

'Sure,' said Tom, ever aware of the military doctrine: eat when you can, drink when you can, sleep when you can. You never know when your next meal is coming.

Tom ate the cheese and chicken sandwiches as the plane descended. He looked out of the window at the familiar sights of the small Highland airport. He checked his watch, which showed 1830 hours: less than two hours since he had received the call from Branko, and at least eight hours sooner than he could ever have been expected to get to Scotland. He just had to hope that Donnie could come through and get him to Cameron and Shona's as quickly as possible. He wanted to see the house in daylight to do a close-target recce before planning an assault and rescue.

*

The HS215 landed smoothly and quickly taxied to the terminal. Tom was conscious that, since getting on the plane, he'd heard nothing from the pilot or anyone from the crew: probably as he was on a fully-deniable flight. He wondered what had been done to keep the aircraft off any official records.

Bill opened the cabin door and folded it down. 'Thank you for flying Air Deniable, we hope you enjoyed your flight. Please have a safe onward journey,' he said in a slightly tinny voice, mimicking a pilot's patter.

Tom stood and shook hands with the American agent. 'Thanks, Bill.'

'Stay safe and stay in touch with Pet; she has your back.'

Tom descended the steps, which Bill immediately closed behind him. The aircraft note changed, and it lurched off again. Clearly there was no waiting for a return take off slot either.

Tom noticed the difference in air temperature compared to London. He estimated that it was about ten degrees Centigrade, making a mental note of the clothing he would require given the altitude up in the Cairngorms.

He strode across the pan towards the familiar terminal. There wouldn't be any Customs or Border Force activity, given that it was a non-domestic flight, but he was aware of the multiple CCTV cameras that would be tracking him.

As he approached the door, he heard a familiar voice shout, 'Tom!' He turned to the source of the greeting to see the large frame of Donnie, dressed in orange flight overalls, walking towards him. He was a tall man, well over six feet, and of powerful yet lean build. He had short, grey hair and humorous blue eyes, a smile never far from his mouth. He was a big character who had never quite pulled off being a Major in the Royal Marines, remaining close to the NCOs and Marines despite his rank.

'Good to see you, Donnie,' Tom said as they hugged.

'Come on, man. Helicopter's warmed up and ready to go.'

Tom followed Donnie to a waiting Ford Mondeo airfield maintenance vehicle with a flashing orange strobe light on the top. They got in and set off towards the nearby helicopter pan, where a red and white liveried helicopter sat waiting with two crew members stood by. The logo 'Coastguard Rescue' was emblazoned on the helicopter's flanks. Tom recognised it as a Sikorsky S-92, almost identical to the US Black Hawk helicopter used in many Special Forces deployments. It was now used by a civilian firm to perform the role that was traditionally performed by the RAF and Navy. Most of the pilots, like Donnie, were ex-military.

As he drove, Donnie said, 'Go on then, I need to know something before I send a multimillion-pound aircraft on a taxi mission. I have enough influence to get this done without too many questions, but I at least need a clue.'

'I'll tell you, Donnie, because I trust you, but we cannot go to the police. You'll have to trust me on that one. Cameron and Shona are being held hostage up at the cottage by armed Serbian gangsters. It's because of something I've done in my work; they've got them to get to me and some evidence I have.'

Donnie let out a long sigh. 'Jesus, man. What the fuck are you going to do?'

Tom paused. If he told Donnie the whole truth, he probably wouldn't drop him off, thinking it was a suicide mission. A little white lie was required.

'I've managed to get up here hours before they could expect me. If you can take me up to the bothy, I can kit-up and put in a close-target recce ahead of a rescue which I'm being helped with by the Americans. I can't trust anyone in the police as there's a corrupt cell that will blow it all up and get Cameron and Shona killed.'

'What do they want from you?'

'They want a memory card that shows a corrupt solicitor raping a woman as well as his involvement in organised crime. I filmed him while undercover.'

'Why not give it to them, then?'

'They'll kill Cameron and Shona whatever happens, then they'll kill me. They can't leave us alive: the lawyer is a multi-millionaire and I know too much. These bastards are ruthless monsters, Donnie.'

Donnie turned to look at the Pelican case that Tom had tossed on the back seat of the Mondeo.

'I take it that suspicious-looking peli-case you have there doesn't contain your clothes?'

'The American friend who organised the flight has sorted me out with more than I need to defend myself. I also have satellite cover and communications equipment. I need some kit and clothes from the bothy for the CTR before the rescue. I'll freeze in what I'm wearing right now.'

For a full minute Donnie was silent before he eventually said, 'Cameron pulled my arse out of the fire on more than one occasion. I owe him everything.' He stared at the airfield in front of them. 'Come on, Tommy-boy. The helo is waiting for us.'

*

Tom and Donnie approached the helicopter, which had a line mechanic attending to the front wheel assembly.

'All set to go, Jim-boy?' Donnie said to the mechanic.

'All set, boss,' replied Jim-boy.

Donnie tossed the Mondeo keys to him, saying, 'We won't be long; just up to the Cairngorms for a wee drop-off, pal.'

'She's full of fuel and all systems are looking good.'

'Never expected anything else, Jim-boy. See you in a bit.'

They approached the open cabin side door, where a crew member in an orange flight suit and helmet sat waiting for them. As they walked, Donnie said, 'We'll head in and set you down by the base at Bynack More, which doesn't take us over the farmhouse. There's no need to give the enemy a free look at us. That's only a short hop to the bothy. You worked out how you're going to get to the farmhouse?'

'Yeah, I can get there in about forty minutes, I reckon. Gives me plenty of time to set up for a CTR.'

Donnie stopped walking and fixed Tom with a stare. 'Well, I hope you know what you're doing, my friend. I wouldn't want anything to happen to you or your family. You all mean a lot to me,' he said, his eyes meeting Tom's. Both men paused for a minute, looking directly into each other's eyes.

The moment broke, and Donnie turned to nod at a member of the crew.

'Tom, this is Tiny, our winch-man. My co-pilot over there is Adam and our wonderful winch-op, Gavin, is sat by the monitor over there.' He nodded briefly at each crew member in turn.

All nodded and smiled but said nothing.

Tiny directed Tom to a bench-seat on the side of the aircraft. 'Sit here and strap in. We're cleared for an immediate lift. Put these on.' He handed over a set of headphones with an attached microphone.

Tom nodded his thanks and began to strap in, settling the headset over his ears and ensuring the microphone was correctly positioned by his mouth. He set the peli-case on the floor in front of him and held it tight into the aircraft with his lower legs.

Tom had travelled in helicopters on many occasions during his military service, both in the Gulf States and the UK, so he settled immediately into the familiar routine.

Donnie's voice crackled in his headset. 'Okay, gents, we're ready to rock-and-roll. For the benefit of all, we're heading off south: quick scoot adjacent to the A9, taking as quick a route as possible. We will infiltrate from the west side of Bynack More on the north-eastern ridge of the range and set our passenger down there. Flight time should be about fifteen minutes.'

The engines started to whine as the helicopter blades began to rotate, building to the deafening roar Tom knew so well, before he felt the aircraft lurch forwards and ascend.

The journey took just over twenty minutes, with the Sikorsky flying at its cruising speed of 280km-per-hour. The crew were a hive of activity during the flight, constantly running a series of checks and monitoring the systems. Tom tried his best to tune out the almost incessant stream of dialogue between the team until Donnie's voice came over the headset saying, 'Five minutes to landing, Tom.'

Tom felt the aircraft descending as Donnie's distorted voice crackled in his ear once more. 'Thirty seconds to landing. Get ready, Tommy-boy.'

The winch-op slid the door open and hung out, secured by a tether, to check the landing site for any obstructions. He quickly announced it safe to land.

Tom felt the helicopter wheels kiss the floor in a gentle landing and then the winch-op slid the door open while nodding to Tom.

'Thanks, Donnie, I appreciate the lift,' Tom said into the microphone.

'Take care. Call me when you can.'

Tom unbuckled his harness, removed his headphones, and jumped out of the Sikorsky, clutching the peli-case. He jogged to a nearby small outcrop of rocks, which he squatted behind to shield himself from the rotor-wash that was beating hurricane force winds and whipping debris about. The note of the helicopter's engines changed and roared as it ascended again, turning as it did so and moving off in a tactical take off, gaining height rapidly and speeding out of sight.

Other than the wind there was no noise as Tom assessed his surroundings on a small plateau in the shadow of Bynack More that jutted over a thousand metres up. The silence was a relief to Tom, comforting and peaceful, given he'd moved in very little time from London to a jet aircraft to a helicopter.

Tom had climbed the Munro on many occasions over the years and, despite the grave situation, he immediately felt at home. It was his turf and he knew it intimately, something which he hoped he could turn to his advantage against the intruders. It was a popular Munro with walkers, but they mostly ascended the opposite side by the popular Loch Morlich. The side Tom was on was rarely used, other than by the more intrepid of the many climbers. Tom checked his watch: just approaching 19:00.

He shivered; it had been about ten degrees Celsius at the airport, but he estimated that up there it was closer to five. Not problematic, but not comfortable in his lightweight clothing and trainers.

He hefted the peli-case and headed across the plateau to the bothy.

*

The bothy sat in the shadow of Bynack More: a small, one-roomed structure made of local stone and believed to be well over a hundred years old. Tom had bought it a few years before from Auld Willie, a man who farmed nearby and whose family had owned it for as long as anyone could remember. It had fallen into disrepair over the years through neglect and didn't appear in any of the guidebooks.

Tom and Cameron had repaired the corrugated iron roof and windows, made it watertight, and fitted a log burner which they had lit and left burning for two weeks solid just to dry the place out.

After that, they'd managed to damp-proof it and lay a suspended floor over a waterproof membrane. Once that work was complete, they had a readymade, cosy bolthole in the Cairngorms that was the envy of many. There was no running water, no toilet, no decorations, no soft furnishings, and no home comforts. It was just a bothy they could use to light a fire, get warm, and shelter from the elements. A sleeping platform with a foam roll-mat occupied one corner and an old armchair by the stove also doubled as a hot plate for cooking on.

Tom did not immediately enter the bothy but circled around it, depositing the peli-case by the locked lean-to storage shed that butted onto the side of the building. He crouched low and crept up to the window at the rear, peering in to make sure it was empty. It appeared that it was, so he collected the case and approached the property's only door.

It was unlocked, as was the tradition, offering refuge against the worst of the weather to walkers, whoever they may be.

Tom entered, feeling the usual sense of excitement he felt when coming back to what he considered his real home. The wood burner was set with paper and kindling, and there was a large stack of logs to the side of it ready for cold or stranded walkers.

Within a minute Tom had the beginnings of a fire crackling away. He added a few logs and soon the fire was roaring, filling the small room with warmth and turning the place from cold and uninviting to warm and welcoming. He took a small kettle from the rack above the stove and went outside to the small burn that ran towards the River Avon, where he filled the kettle before returning to the bothy and setting the kettle to boil.

Despite the urgency of the situation, Tom did not feel the need to rush to the cottage. He did not want to move until last-light, which was about an hour away, to avail himself of the advantage of the cover of darkness.

In true British military tradition, he was not going to begin his mission without a hot tea inside him. He did not have a firm plan other than getting eyes on the cottage and trying to get usable intelligence as to what he was facing. He had one advantage: surprise. The Brankos still believed he was five hundred miles away, back in London.

The satellite phone buzzed in Tom's pocket which he answered with a, 'Hello?'

'It's Pet. You have a call coming in from Branko. I'm patching him through to you, he will think you're somewhere near Camden, which is where your phone is.'

Her voice was replaced by a gruff one which barked, 'Where are you?'

'Camden.'

'I hope you're not trying anything stupid. Not if you want your family to live.'

Tom said nothing.

'I will call you again. You'd better still be in Camden. I'm going to be checking with my friends where you are, and I have people everywhere: just remember that.'

Pet's voice replaced that of Branko.

'Are you okay?'

'I'm fine. I'm close by and safe at the bothy. I'm also well-armed thanks to the CIA, so I'm leaving at last-light to move up and get eyes on the cottage.'

'I had a satellite pass over the property twenty minutes ago: there were two cars there, an old Land Rover Defender and a new looking Mercedes SUV.'

'The Defender is Cameron's; the Mercedes must be the kidnappers.'

'Makes sense. I've been checking on the Brankos' phone signals. All are still in North London and there is no trace of their vehicles on ANPR, so I suspect it's just the Glasgow crew you have to deal with.'

Tom digested this information. If there was only one vehicle, it meant a maximum of five individuals at the cottage, if the Brankos were still in London. Tom couldn't see that they would commit more resources to what was, essentially, a babysitting job.

'Anything from our corrupt police friends?'

'Branko has been calling Taylor, probably making sure you're still in London.'

'I guess so. Listen, I have to go; I've got stuff to do.'

'Be careful and stay safe.'

'Always,' said Tom, and he rang off.

The kettle began to whistle and Tom took a tea bag from a jar on the unit to make himself a cup of black tea. In his mind he was back in a war zone, preparing for whatever may come next.

He opened the peli-case and withdrew the MP7, checked the action and ensured that the weapon was unloaded, more by habit than necessity.

It was immaculately clean, but he still stripped and examined all the components in any case, fully aware that his life depended on its reliability. Once satisfied, he reassembled the weapon and set it to one side. He screwed on the square-shaped suppressor, ensuring it was tight.

He took one of the magazines and loaded it with thirty-five high-velocity rounds but topped it off with five of the subsonic low-velocity ones. The remaining fifteen low-velocity rounds he loaded into the remaining magazine.

He checked the workings of the Armasight scope, which was secured onto the weapon's Picatinny sight-mounting rail. It seemed simple enough to use and similar to other optics he'd used in the past. There was a rubberised menu button on the top of the sight, with directional buttons that would adjust the sight's directions minutely once the operator had ascertained how true the weapon fired when testing. He fully intended to use ten of the low-velocity rounds to give at least a basic zeroing, living as always by the military rule of the Seven Ps.

He went to the large, heavy, metal cupboard in the corner of the room which was secured with a stout combination padlock. He always kept a spare set of warm clothes in the bothy after one occasion when, soaked after an unsuccessful deer stalk, he had to endure cold and soaking clothing for hours while they slowly dried on him by the fire.

Opening the lock, he withdrew an old set of CS95 multi-terrain pattern camouflage trousers and a windproof smock that he'd kept hold of after leaving the military. He also dug out an old chunky green fleece, hunting gloves, and his camouflage cap. He was glad of the well-used pair of brown Meindl walking boots and thick socks that sat at the bottom of the cupboard. He would now be far more appropriately dressed for what he was about to undertake.

He quickly changed, leaving his discarded clothes in the cupboard, apart from his T-shirt, which he kept on. He strapped on the Kevlar vest and adjusted the straps to make sure it fitted well and close to the body to offer the best protection. He was impressed at how light and comfortable the vest was: far better than anything he'd worn in the past.

He pulled the windproof smock over the vest and picked up the harness that Bill had mentioned. He found that it was a fairly simple bit of kit, but not one he'd seen before.

Under the left arm, there was webbing strap storage for three magazines to be secured with a clip fastener; the fourth magazine would remain in the weapon. This harness appeared to be a bespoke item, probably commissioned covertly by CIA field teams as, with the butt folded, the whole rig wouldn't be visible beneath a loose-fitting jacket.

He secured the three high-velocity-filled magazines in the harness and snapped the remaining magazine, loaded with the fifteen subsonic rounds, onto the weapon.

He took a long swig of his cooling tea and grimaced at the bitter liquid before topping it up from the kettle.

He slammed a magazine into the Glock, racked the slide, and slotted it into the thigh holster without checking it. Glocks were bomb-proof, hence being one of the most commonly-used handguns.

He checked his watch: 19:32. Still at least a full ninety minutes of light left. He wanted to be in position immediately after dark, giving him a little more time for some essential preparation.

He left the bothy and walked back up to the plateau where Donnie had dropped him off. It was a long, flat area with a slight uphill gradient heading towards the steep ascent to the summit.

He walked up to the rocky outcrop where he'd sheltered against the helicopter's blade-wash and picked up a small piece of soft stone, using it to scratch a small square mark onto the side of the rock to give himself a rudimentary aiming point. He then turned and paced back fifty metres. He extended the telescopic stock of the MP7, took up a kneeling firing position and activated the scope, noting that it was set on day-mode as he adjusted it to two-times magnification. He squinted through the reticule at the rock; aiming at the scratched square and selecting single-shot on the weapon, he squeezed the trigger. The report from the MP7 was eerily quiet: no tell-tale crack as would have been given off by the standard high-velocity weapon, more of a metallic 'Thunk' as the working parts recoiled and another round was fed into the chamber.

He squeezed the trigger three more times in quick succession. Through the scope he could see that the standard zero on the sights was not too bad for his eyesight. The four rounds had struck slightly high and left of his aiming points. He made minor adjustments on the sights to correct the inaccuracy.

Pulling the MP7 back into the aim, he squeezed off a further three rounds at the makeshift target. Checking his grouping through the scope, he noted that the new marks were central on the rock: as good as could be expected for that type of weapon.

He stood and engaged the safety catch and let the weapon drop on its harness before squatting to locate the seven spent shellcases, which he pocketed. He had no intention of leaving any evidence of his presence.

He walked back down to the bothy for his final preparations before the trip to Cregganmore Farm Cottage.

Once back in, he slid the kettle back onto the stove. While he waited for the water to boil, he took out the communications device, switching it on and turning it over in his hands. It was grey in colour, the same size and weight as an average smartphone, but with no screen and only an on/off button and volume switch. He located the small earpiece, which was similar to ones he'd used in the past, and slotted it in his ear.

He heard a light hiss and then a tinny voice sparked up.

'You took your time, Detective,' said Pet.

Tom picked out the wireless pressel switch, depressed it and said, 'Sorry, Pet. Been busy.'

'No problem. You have some unpleasant weather coming in. Heavy rain and a forty-mile-per-hour easterly wind.'

'Perfect. I like bad weather.'

'Mad Englishman.'

'I'm not English.'

'You got me there, Detective. I have nothing new on the

Brankos: they still appear to be in London. He's not tried to call you and he's not used the phone apart from one call to Arken about ten minutes ago. There's been no movement at the house, but we think one of them went out for a cigarette a few minutes ago. I can send you a screen grab to your tablet.'

Tom reached for the tablet and saw a mail icon appear on the screen. Selecting it, he saw a blurred image, zoomed in on the farmhouse. Tom took in the sight of Cameron's battered Land Rover and the smarter-looking Mercedes both at the front of the house, a two-bedroom place set well back from a small farm track, about half a mile from the nearest road. He saw smoke drifting from the chimney and the top of a figure stood outside the door, a glow in front of his face.

His approach would have to be stealthy and he was thankful of the forthcoming inclement weather. He did not fear rain. 'If it ain't raining, it ain't training': the words of his old troop sergeant rang in his ears.

'Thanks, Pet,' he said and then, as an afterthought, 'If Branko calls, will you be able to patch him in to this comms system?'

'No problem.'

'That's great; means I don't need to carry the satellite. I still have to prepare so I'm signing off. I will call in again later.'

He appreciated the help he was being given, but he was conscious that it was now down to him, although the thought didn't make him nervous, it made him determined. He switched off the communications set and removed the earpiece, tucking both items into his inside jacket zipped pocket.

He took the boiling kettle and made another black tea.

Once more it was him, on his own: the little boy from Sarajevo.

*

He retrieved a small camouflaged day-sack from the locked cupboard in the bothy, another item that he'd held onto after leaving the military. Digging through it he found a folding pocketknife, a tactical pocket-torch, and a stick of camouflage cream which resembled a matt green double-ended, large lipstick.

He smeared the green and brown camouflage cream across his face, making sure that the pattern he daubed roughly corresponded with the pattern on his CS95 combat smock. He ensured that his ears, back of his neck, hands, and arms up to his elbows were appropriately covered. Concealment was going to be his best friend that night: he needed to stay invisible even if he did not believe they would be expecting him. He had left London almost three hours ago: that was only long enough to drive as far as Birmingham on a good day.

He stood and began a physical check of all his kit.

He ensured the Glock was loaded with a round in the breach, ditto for the MP7, and he did a quick check on the optic sights, setting them to two-times magnification. He checked all his spare ammunition and placed the box of fifty 9mm rounds into a zipped pouch on the day-sack.

The satellite phone he put into the day-sack, secured within the main top-flap zip pocket.

The torch he jammed into the pen pocket on the right sleeve of his smock, and the pocket knife he tucked into the top of his walking boot, using the clip to secure it in place.

He ensured all his pockets were securely fastened and that the covert communications kit was secure and switched on, then took the tablet and tucked it into the day-sack, along with a small bottle of water which he'd already filled at the burn. He fixed the earpiece in his right ear and ensured that the covert microphone was well-positioned.

He checked his watch: almost 20:00. Perfect. That gave him enough time to advance to the cottage and get there just before last-light.

He hefted his day-sack onto his back and adjusted the shoulder straps so it was as comfortable as possible, before leaving the bothy, his shoulders squared and his jaw set in determination.

He was ready. Game on.

The cottage sat about five miles north of the bothy, which meant Tom would have to traverse the foot of Bynack More and follow the river to the forest block. He could then follow the track to the cottage. A portion of the forest that sat at the front of the cottage had been harvested, leaving it open for about two-hundred metres, which afforded plenty of cover but also good vision.

He planned to set up his initial O.P. at the edge of the cleared forest block using the wood piles as cover, which would give him a good view of the front of the building.

Tom pressed the communications pressel. 'Pet, you getting me?'

'Loud and clear, Tom. What gives?'

'I'm setting off to the cottage now. Only contact me if it's urgent, especially if Branko calls.'

'Sure thing. Last satellite about twenty minutes ago showed no changes.'

'Thanks, Pet. Speak later.'

He walked around the bothy to the lean-to at the side of the structure. It had been built by him and Cameron as a shelter and also as somewhere to hang carcasses after a successful shoot.

The wind was picking up and Tom shivered as it blew the cold, northern air across the plateau.

The door was locked with another combination padlock that Tom thumbed open. Inside sat a green quad bike: a Yamaha Grizzly 4500 four-wheel drive machine, the same as was often used by the military.

Tom sat on the machine, which still had its keys in the ignition, and pressed the electric start button. The first turns were slow but then the quad barked into life with a muted roar. He eased the machine out of the lean-to and headed off north into the cold, wild Cairngorm wilderness in the shadow of the dark, foreboding peak of Bynack More, the wind picking up and ominous clouds forming.

*

Tom made his way down, following the contours of the river whch he knew would take him to the forestry block opposite the farmhouse. The rear of the cottage was bordered by livestock grazing, usually Auld Willie's sheep in one of the fields and a pedigree herd of Highland cattle in the others.

He was able to maintain a brisk enough speed without revving the life out of the quad. The wind was brisk and blowing from the east, which Tom was grateful for as it meant that he would have the wind in his face as he approached the farmhouse, carrying any sounds away from the enemy within. He was well-practised in infiltration and exfiltration from CTRs, having done both in hostile environments right under the nose of the enemy, but any advantage was to be utilised: including being able to take the quad up close for a speedy getaway if necessary.

He hit the road as he left the Bynack approach and entered the forestry block through an open gate which led onto a wide, well-maintained forest track.

He was able to make good progress for the final mile and then pulled off the track through a gap in the trees where he continued at walking pace, negotiating the moss hillocks and fallen branches, the revs kept low on the quad's engine. Having got far enough, he killed the engine, leaving the keys in the ignition slot as he quickly gathered some fallen boughs, criss-crossing them across the quad in a rudimentary camouflage. He finished it off with some sphagnum moss slabs and a few ferns, making it all but invisible from the forest track, but visible enough for him to find.

He paused for a moment and re-checked all his pockets and equipment to ensure that nothing had loosened during the bumping and lurching of the quad bike ride. He extended the telescopic stock of the MP7 and squatted, putting the sight to his eye and scanning his route. He switched the night vision on but there was still too much light to make it of any use. He was confident that his approach had not been audible with the stiff breeze that was blowing into his face, which he estimated to be twenty to thirty miles-per-hour, and would therefore carry any sound nicely away from the farmhouse.

He reached into his pocket and pressed the communications pressel. 'Pet, you hearing me?'

'Loud and clear, Tom.'

'No words from Branko? I'm about to deploy close-in.'

'Nothing. His phone made and received a few calls: at least one to Arken and one from a number in Nigeria. Want to guess who?'

'Let me guess. Adebayo?'

'Boom! He's run off. He must have got a false passport as there's no trace of him leaving with his own. I guess he didn't fancy his chances.'

Damn, Tom thought. That made the solicitor untouchable if he'd fled. He pushed the thought out of his mind; there was nothing he could do about it now.

'Anything else to report?'

'I managed to trace the Mercedes. There's not so many of that model registered in Glasgow, so I ran all the possibles from the PNC through the ANPR database. We got just the one that hit all the ANPR cameras between Glasgow and Aviemore, where it turned off.' She sounded pleased with herself as she reeled off the registration plate number.

'It's not registered to Arken, but I did manage to get an image of it on the A9 at the Perth roundabout, and I'm as sure as I can be that there were three people on board. So that's how many there are for you to deal with,' she said, still sounding quite smug.

'Thanks, Pet, that's useful. You are a magician.'

'Other than that, Branko and his boys' phones are all still hitting the same cell mast as before, so I guess they're waiting for you to hand over the card tomorrow. Unless they are using untraceable communications as well.'

'I have to go, Pet. I'm going quiet now unless I have to speak to Branko. Are you familiar with the click system?'

'I ask a question, you answer two clicks for yes, one for no, right? Three deliberate separate clicks for ask-me-questions?'

'Spot on.'

'Be careful, Tom.'

'I'm always careful,' Tom said as he began to move towards the farmhouse.

He moved carefully as he approached Cregganmore Farmhouse, in full patrol mode: eyes scanning, senses tuned in. He listened as intently as the wind would allow, the butt of the MP7 tucked firmly into his shoulder. He was entirely familiar with the environment, having played in those same woods as a child. The forest smells were familiar to him: the heady, resinous pine scent and the soft earthy smell of the fertile soil. The ground was soft underfoot, and he tried as best as he could to be as silent and stealthy as his surroundings would allow. Even with the wind masking his movements, the covert approach was as natural to him as breathing.

Every twenty steps or so, he adopted a crouched stance and scanned a full 360 degrees, observing for anything alien to the environment: the muscle-memory of patrol skills as strong as ever.

He soon came to the edge of the forest and the clearing in front of the farmhouse, which sat about two-hundred metres in front of him, a large log pile immediately in front obscuring his view and, hopefully, that of any watchers as well.

He tucked himself down behind the log pile and took stock of his situation, again with close observations to his sides and rear, taking in the view in the half-light. His plan was to get to a viewpoint from the edge of the forest and observe until the light had completely gone, whereupon he would move up to his close observation point, which he was estimating to be about fifty metres from the farmhouse. From there, it was a case of a few hours CTR and then he would make an assault plan, depending on the intelligence obtained from the previous observations.

He took his water bottle from his day-sack and took a long drink before stowing it away again, ready to go.

*

He lay down behind the log pile and slowly leopard-crawled to its edge, giving himself his first view of the front of the farmhouse. It was a long single-storey building with a slate-tiled roof and parking for four cars on a block-paved area to the front. It had three bedrooms, a single bathroom and a large kitchen diner with a log burner that was also used as a sitting room. The small lounge was rarely used. The front door sat squarely in the middle of the building but, like most houses in rural areas, it was never used, remaining locked and bolted with a heavy curtain drawn across on the inside. Tom could never remember anyone accessing the building using the front door; all visitors naturally would go over the hard-standing and along the path to the back door, where the house had a large garden that backed onto livestock fields. The garden was put to good use by his foster parents, with chickens in a large run and coop at the rear, and vegetable plots that kept the family in fresh produce most of the year. A small decked area with a table and chairs sat at the rear of the house, accessed by a set of French windows that were used infrequently.

From his position he could see the front of the house and the leading edge that led to the back door, where any enemies would most likely emerge from.

He ideally wanted a viewing point that would give him a visual on the back door. This meant that, once it was fully dark, he would move about a hundred metres across and adjacent to the track to give him a side-view of the house with a profile-view of the back door. This would also protect him from any casual glances that anyone may take from any of the windows.

As the photograph that had been messaged to Tom showed Cameron and Shona in the kitchen, he was going to assume they were still there. It was cold and the smell of wood smoke in the air indicated that the log burner was lit, as the central heating in the property was not efficient, to say the least. The kitchen was a double-aspect room with windows at the front and rear, which gave Tom options he was grateful for.

The farmhouse was accessed by a half-mile track of compacted earth and type one shingle that had to be regularly replaced when the heavy rains came. It was the only dwelling for miles and its isolation was complete and reassuring in good times.

As expected, he could see Cameron's old battered Land Rover at the front of the house and a smart, black Mercedes M-Class SUV parked next to it. Raising the MP7 night-sight he could easily pick out the licence plate in the greenish gloom: the number was the same as Pet had dictated to him earlier.

Just another half-an-hour now, he thought. Last-light was approaching, and it was time to go to work.

28

He remained statue-like for the next thirty minutes as the last of the light ebbed away. The wind picked up, gusting hard, and he felt a few specks of rain. While he didn't welcome the discomfort of being wet, the extra concealment that poor weather offered would be helpful. In his Marine basic training, much of the efforts of the staff were geared to getting the recruits wet, cold, and miserable. Not out of any sadistic urges, but to reinforce the need for them to learn to look after themselves in poor conditions and yet still be operationally effective, no matter how bad the weather. It was impressed on them that often the difference between good soldiers and great soldiers was who could operate in harsh environments.

He started to feel the cold seeping into his bones and decided that it was time to move forwards and across to his CTR location. He back-crawled to the cover of the log pile and stood, shaking the stiffness out of his limbs. From his day-sack he retrieved his fleece pullover, stripped off his combat smock and pulled the fleece over his head. He quickly zipped his smock back up and resettled the day-sack on his back.

He moved carefully and slowly in a half-crouch between the areas of cover, picking points ahead of him to move to, taking him closer to the house in a clockwise direction to give a better viewpoint of the side of the property. As he moved, he stopped frequently to use the night-sight to check the farmhouse for any signs of movement.

He soon found himself in a deep rut in the soft earth, where one of the massive logging tractors had passed at some point. Crawling to the lip of the rut, he saw that he was about sixty metres from the side of the house, giving him a good view of the vehicle hard-standing, rear garden, and the path to the back door.

Squinting through the MP7 sight, the house was bathed in a greenish glow as the optic enhanced the natural light present in the windows. He surmised that the curtains were closed but the lights were on, as the optic was not overwhelmed by the artificial light coming from the property.

Satisfied with his position, he settled down to wait. He was patient and could wait as long as it took; sniper training had taught him that as much as how to shoot straight.

Pet's voice erupted in his ear. 'Tom, are you there?'

'Yes.'

'Branko is ringing now, can I patch him in?'

'Yes, do it. I take it my phone is in the same area as last time?' He didn't want to speak so close to the house, but he felt that the wind was strong enough to mask his voice. He ducked down into the ditch a little to get out of the elements.

'Novak?' the gruff voice barked.

'Yes.'

'I hope you're being sensible.'

'I'm still here. Is that all?'

'I'll know if you're not. I can even tell what fucking room you're in if I so choose.'

'Couldn't be more pleased for you, Branko. Is that all?'

'Remember: it's nine o'clock now. I want that card by eleven in the morning or people will be hurt.'

'I remember.' Tom resisted the urge to finish with a threat of vengeance.

Tom heard nothing more until Pet spoke.

'He's gone,' she said.

'Thanks, Pet. I have to be quiet now.'

'Sure. Take care and don't do anything silly. I'm going to put your communications on open mic so we can monitor what's going on.'

Tom didn't reply but tapped the pressel twice and crawled back up to his viewing point, turned the scope back on the farmhouse, and settled back down while ignoring the creeping dampness in his legs.

A flash of light erupted from the back door as it was opened by someone from within, who then stepped out onto the back path. The flare from the overexposed light made him shift his eye away from the night-sight as the individual slowly walked down the path. Tom adjusted the scope to take account of the extra light emanating from the doorway. The figure walked slowly onwards and then another burst of light, magnified by the image-intensifying properties of the scope, blotted out his view briefly. It settled, and Tom realised that the individual was lighting a cigarette as he ambled down the path in Tom's direction. The man was clearly not aware of his surroundings and very tactically unaware: no professional would paint such a big arrow on their face by openly smoking in an unknown environment. He increased the magnification on the scope and focused on the figure's face, which he did not recognise.

The man was wearing a light-coloured, hooded sweatshirt, and light trousers; he was shaven-headed and of powerful build and walked in the graceless way of a seasoned bodybuilder. His face was etched with a bored scowl as he stood and smoked on the path, staring mostly at his feet but also glancing around at his surroundings. It didn't appear to be any type of patrol or check for anyone, it was simply a smoke break. Tom smiled to himself and wondered if Shona's aversion to smoking had forced the kidnapper to smoke outside in the cold. Shona was no shrinking violet and Tom couldn't imagine her allowing anyone to smoke in the farmhouse, whatever the circumstances.

The light at the doorway flared once again as another man came to the threshold and seemed to shout at the smoker, who turned to face him. Smoker walked back to the door and handed the cigarette pack over to his colleague, who cupped his hands to his face as the sight flared once again with the lighting of the cigarette.

Tom zoomed in on the pair as they smoked and chatted, an opportunity forming in his head. If there were only three kidnappers then he could take out sixty-six percent of their manpower with just two silenced rounds, leaving him only one other to deal with. Those were odds he would take any time.

He quickly weighed up all the implications in his mind, a clock beginning to tick in his head as he did so.

If he took them out now, he would then have fifty metres to cover to get to the house, which would take at the very least thirty seconds bearing in mind the terrain and fence at the boundary. He also didn't know for sure that there were only three opponents. He needed more information and more intelligence to come up with a plan. There had been one smoke break and logic said that there would be others. He had time: the longer it went on, the more likely that the Serbs would relax, offering a greater element of surprise.

He decided to wait, continuing to study the two smokers. The newer of the two was very similar to his friend in terms of build and gait. He was perhaps even bigger, with a bull-neck and shaved head, and was wearing baggy sports gear. Tom couldn't be sure if either man was wearing body armour, such was the looseness of their clothing. He filed that fact away for future reference.

They finished their cigarettes and tossed them on the path, the embers flaring away on the ground as both turned on their heels and re-entered the farmhouse, closing the door as they did so.

*

Tom remained utterly focused on the farmhouse despite the stiffness and cold that permeated his clothing and into his bones. Discomfort was a feature of CTR that every soldier knew only too well.

The past three hours had demonstrated something of a pattern of behaviour of the captors within. Every forty minutes or so, the two Tom had previously seen would come to the back door, smoke a cigarette, and appear to converse in a calm manner for as long as it took to do so. He checked his watch again: nearly midnight. He would probably see the men again within the next twenty minutes. It was time to act.

He crawled slowly forwards, keeping his belly low in the dirt as he edged inch by inch with the night-sight glued to his eye. He intended to get within twenty metres of the fence that separated the cleared forest from the track.

When he was fifteen metres away from the fence, he found another rut left by the forestry tractor which he crawled into. That gave him an ideal firing position with a clear view of the back door. He settled and looked through the sight once again, checking that his view was clear and he was ready to engage. He knew what he had to do: he had no choice, these people were his enemy. He was back in sniper mode, ready for the moment, ever-patient, waiting for the target to appear, ready to engage. He had been in that situation on many occasions in Afghanistan: twenty-eight times to be precise, with twenty-eight confirmed kills. This was no different, he told himself, knowing it to be a lie.

He didn't have to wait long. The familiar flaring of the scope brightened the scene before him, and he tightened his grip on the MP7 as time began to slow for him imperceptibly. The first figure came into view, a cigarette already pursed in his lips, the lighter sparking as he raised it up to his mouth, exaggerated greatly by the image-intensifying properties of the sight. He was immediately followed by his comrade who was laughing, his hand extended and waiting for the cigarette to be handed over to him. The first man was having difficulty lighting the cigarette, owing to the wind that had picked up and was howling down the pathway, his hands cupped around the end of the lighter as it formed a bright flare in Tom's vision. He lit it and then handed the cigarette pack and lighter to his friend, who repeated the process, managing to light his much quicker. They both stood just away from the door, smoking and talking, the ends of their lit cigarettes like torches in their mouths.

Picking up a stone the size of a marble, Tom tossed it at the rubbish bin close to the fence, striking the empty receptacle with a resounding and hollow-sounding 'thunk'.

Both men's heads turned sharply towards the noise. The larger of the two reached into the back of his trousers, producing an automatic pistol and holding it by his waist. After a brief exchange they slowly walked towards the bin, their eyes scanning all round. They moved stiffly and without tactical awareness; again, Tom detected no serious military training.

They approached the bin carefully, the other male also reaching into his waistband and producing a pistol, which he held out slightly in front of him. They stopped a couple of metres short of the bin.

Tom slowly moved the sight so the red dot hovered in the centre of the bigger man's forehead, time inching by as he controlled his breathing and cleared his thoughts. He took up the tension in the trigger and flicked the safety catch one notch down into single-shot mode.

A further pound of pressure and the weapon lightly bucked in his grip, emitting a soft report and metallic click as the working parts, re-cocked by the gases from the shot, injected a new round into the chamber. The bigger man's head rocked back, the cigarette arcing into the air above him like a firework.

Tom shifted his aim while calculating the trajectory. Deliberately, and in what felt like a relaxed motion, he shot the other man straight in the forehead. Both fell to the ground as if their legs had suddenly disappeared, one a fraction of a second before the other. The wind carried any noise away from the cottage and Tom doubted that anything at all had been heard by those inside.

He paused for a full minute to check that there was no activity from within the farmhouse following the two shots. The subsonic ammunition and large suppressor had done their job; the report was as quiet as Tom had heard from a weapon and, while it was not silent, it certainly did not sound like a gunshot.

He advanced on the two bodies, the MP7 held on his shoulder, slowly and deliberately aware that the low-calibre, low-velocity round may not have immediately killed the men. Unless they were dead, they were still a danger.

He needn't have worried: he didn't need to be a doctor to see that both men were dead. He had seen many dead bodies—he'd killed more than most, as many snipers of his generation had— and those guys were as dead as any he'd seen.

Both had small entry wounds, one centre-forehead, the other had gone straight through his left eye. Neither had exit wounds and Tom could well imagine the small round bouncing around inside their craniums, smashing their frontal lobes and destroying the central cortex of their brains. He took their handguns, one of which was still clasped by its now-deceased owner, and tossed them over the fence. He quickly patted them down, finding nothing else of value but noting that neither wore body armour or had a mobile phone on them.

Nearly two minutes had passed since they had left the back door and Tom had no time to waste, so he grabbed hold of the bigger man by the shoulder of his jacket and dragged him behind the large rhododendron bush at the edge of the parking area, about four metres away. He repeated the process with the other body, breathing heavily with the exertion.

He took a moment to regain his breath and prepare for his next move. Three minutes gone; nearly enough time to finish a cigarette. Whoever was left inside would be expecting them back soon.

*

He advanced to the farmhouse at a steady pace, not bothering to try to be silent as he strode down the path towards the back door. As he arrived in the storm porch, he squatted down and opened the small wooden box door that Cameron had made to shield the electricity fuse box. It had been replaced with a modern circuit breaker a couple of years before and was now simply a bank of switches which isolated various circuits in the house. He could hear the TV booming away from inside the house with what sounded like a sports game.

He readied himself for his final assault. He just needed an edge: darkness and surprise would give him that. He flicked the isolation switch and the house was plunged into darkness, the sudden silence overpowering.

He entered the utility room with his eye pressed against the scope, the room bathed in the pale green and black shades of the image-intensified light.

'What the fuck is going on?' shouted a voice in Serb.

'Power cut,' shouted Tom in Serb, not expecting to fool anyone but maybe to introduce some confusion.

He advanced along the hall towards the kitchen with his eye glued to the night-sight on the MP7. As he approached the open door, the flames from the wood burner caused the sight to flare and, momentarily, it was useless. Making an instant decision he allowed the MP7 to drop and catch on the harness under his arm. He moved to his thigh holster and drew the Glock, extending his arms out and pointing the sidearm towards the doorway. He entered the kitchen without hesitation, ready to engage.

He immediately saw the giant Serb—Arken—in the middle of the room, his colossal, meaty arm encircling Cameron's chest and pulling him tightly in to his body. He was a massive man who dwarfed Tom's foster father, the man's head only coming up to chin-height on the Serb. Tom also saw the automatic pistol jammed against Cameron's temple. The light from the roaring stove bathed the room in an eerie yellow half-light, making their faces dark with dancing shadows.

'Move one step closer and I'll put a bullet in his head,' Arken hissed through his teeth.

Tom froze to the spot. 'Don't do anything stupid, Arken. No one needs to get shot here.' His calm delivery was measured, but unusually, he felt real fear. He couldn't lose Cameron.

'Drop the weapon, Novak. Drop it now or they die.' Arken shook as he spoke, his voice rough as he spat out the words in glottal Serb.

'Okay, Arken, I'm throwing the pistol now. Don't do anything stupid.' Tom tossed the Glock onto the nearby leather armchair.

'Now the machine gun: get rid of it.'

Tom reached under his arm and unclipped the MP7 sling, the weapon falling to the floor with a clatter.

'Kick it away towards me,' the big man said.

Tom propelled the MP7 across the tiled floor with his boot.

'Arken, we can all walk away from this, but I'm not alone. Your men are dead, and I have backup coming soon.'

'You're lying, you fucking pig.'

'I'm not lying, Arken, how do you think I got up here so quickly?' Tom's voice had settled, and he felt a strange calm envelop him. 'Cameron, Shona, are you okay?'

Both his foster parents' hands were bound, and both had duct tape across their mouths, but both nodded. Cameron fixed Tom with a direct stare and Tom was sure that he could read something in his eyes, which sparkled in the dancing light from the fire. Almost a trace of fatalistic humour. Cameron was short and wiry, but he was teak-tough after all those years in the Commandos. Shona looked utterly terrified, the shock and horror of events clearly etched across her face.

Cameron dropped his knees slightly and then drove upwards and backwards, smashing the back of his skull into Arken's nose and mouth with a sickening crunch. Blood spurted as Arken's head flew backwards with the force of the impact and instinctively his hands came up, releasing Cameron who dived away from the big gangster.

Tom flew forwards and crashed into Arken's midriff with his shoulder in a head-on rugby tackle. It was like running into a brick wall, but he felt the breath explode from the Serbian with a whoosh. He fell backwards with Tom landing square on top of him, and Tom grabbed for the arm that still held the pistol, trying to pin it to the floor. Arken, though, was too strong and, regaining some of his composure, began to fight back, clubbing Tom across the back of his head with his free fist. The pain was ferocious, but Tom grimly held on, realising that if Arken got his gun hand free it was all over.

Out of nowhere Cameron appeared and stamped down on Arken's hand. He was still wearing his work boots and the Serb cried out as the bones crunched against the metal of the pistol. He released the weapon, which Cameron kicked away to slide across the shiny floor. Arken, now alive to the new threat, kicked out blindly from his prone position towards Cameron, catching him square in the side and sending him flying across the room, where he crashed into the coffee table.

Arken let out a roar of fury and unleashed a volley of punches with his good hand at Tom, who had tucked his head into the man's side to try to avoid the blows. Arken tried to roll over onto his side, trying to stand. That was a big mistake, despite the enormous size disparity between him and Tom. Tom immediately released Arken and slid across his body, locking onto his now-exposed back and encircling the man's massive bull-neck with his left arm. He locked that in place by gripping onto his own right arm, inflicting a rear naked choke on the big Serb. Tom's right hand snaked to the back of Arken's head, driving it forwards, and he squeezed with all his strength, compressing the man's carotid arteries and driving his wrist bones into his throat.

It was like holding onto an angry bear as the man bucked and struggled and fought for his life, but Tom's technique and strength were too good and he soon began to flag. No one can survive long once the blood supply to the brain is interrupted. After forty seconds he had stopped struggling. Tom held on for a further minute until he could feel nothing and then released his arms to fall back onto the tiles, exhausted and gasping for breath.

After another minute he stood and returned to the back door, flicking the circuit breaker switch to switch all the lights back on.

He returned to the kitchen which was now bathed in soft light from the side lamps.

'You guys okay?'

Cameron nodded from his prone position on top of the destroyed table, looking at him with relief in his eyes.

Taking his knife from his boot top, he released their hands from the zip-tie bindings. Shona's hand was tightly wrapped in a bandage, a red stain evident where the blood from her severed finger had seeped through.

As he got closer, he saw the relief in Cameron's eyes turn once more to fear, the man bucking and attempting to shout, his voice muffled by the tape as he looked behind Tom. Tom began to straighten up, a sinking feeling of dread in his stomach, while reaching for his MP7. He turned and was stunned to see Aleks and Luka Branko walking into the room.

Aleks was already pointing a Glock at Tom; it was too late for him to raise the MP7. The Glock roared in Aleks's hand and Tom felt a fantastic impact in his chest, like being hit with a sledgehammer. All the breath left his body with a whoosh and he was flung back, violently landing on top of Cameron. His vision went black.

29

A lot of nonsense is often spouted about the effectiveness of body armour. Kevlar is great at preventing certain bullets from entering the body, but they don't stop the trauma caused by a projectile hitting you at three-hundred-and-seventy-five metres-per-second.

All that force has to go somewhere, and it all went straight into Tom.

The bullet had struck him dead-centre of his chest: on the sternum which, fortunately, had absorbed most of the impact. Some of that force had also fortunately been absorbed in his being knocked backwards.

Tom was gasping for breath, aware through the fog in his brain of shouting and rough hands dragging him across the floor, his hands being secured behind his back. He managed to breathe a couple of rasping breaths, replacing the wind that had been knocked out of his lungs by the impact of the 9mm round.

Words filtered through the fog. 'Jesus, he's killed Danilo. Where are the others?' He couldn't identify who had spoken.

He looked up, wincing at the pain in his chest, and looked up at the three men. Aleks still had the Glock pointed at him, Luka was stood to his side, while the third man he didn't recognise. He was much older than the Brankos—in his fifties, Tom estimated—and was dressed in jeans and a leather jacket. He had short, cropped grey hair and his face was lined and weather beaten; he looked uncompromising and tough, with the latent aggression he'd seen in far too many others on many occasions.

'How the fuck did you get up here so fast, Novak?' Aleks said.

Tom sank his head back into the carpeted floor but did not reply, already entering resistance-to-interrogation mode following the shock of capture. He had completed a very unpleasant course in this when with the SRR; all the instructors had been SAS members who had taken their job very seriously. The main lesson of the course had been how to turn into the 'grey man': not being aggressive, playing up the seriousness of your injuries, and biding your time.

Despite the communications device that was being monitored, Tom said nothing.

'Answer me, pig!' one of them yelled, fury in his voice, and a kick was delivered to the side of his torso. Pain exploded in his already-shocked ribcage.

Tom coughed and spat out blood on the carpet; he'd bitten his tongue when he was shot. He feigned confusion greater than he was feeling. More than anything, he needed his captors to underestimate him.

'Search him,' said a voice he didn't recognise: presumably grey-hair.

Tom felt one of the men begin to go through his pockets, retrieving the weapons, ammunition, and communications device. The lifesaving body armour was torn from him.

'Jesus, he's got a radio,' said Luka. 'Who is listening?'

'No one. You're holding the transmit button and you've ripped off the microphone,' Tom replied. He had to get them to believe that no one was coming to the farmhouse or they would cut their losses and kill all of them.

'How did you get up here? Who is helping you?' he was asked again.

'I hitched a lift on a private jet from Northolt that was coming up here. A buddy works there, and he sorted it out.'

'What about the guns? Where did you get those?' asked Luka.

'Police armoury: a mate of mine is in charge and I persuaded him to give them to me.' He didn't know if that was believable, but he had no choice.

'We'd better call Papa,' said Aleks.

'I'll do it,' said the grey-haired man, and he walked out of the room.

Aleks and Luka were very nervous, panic seeming close to the surface. Their lack of experience was evident, and that concerned Tom; he could imagine them starting to shoot just out of fright.

Tom turned slightly onto his side, giving him a better view of the room. Aleks still had the Glock pointed at him, but he was looking at the corpse of Danilo rather than him.

Grey-hair walked back into the room clutching a mobile phone in his hand.

'The boss wants to speak to you,' he growled, holding the phone to Tom's ear.

'What have you fucking done, pig? You've killed my friend, and that's going to get your parents killed too.'

'Branko, no. There's a way out of this. No one else has to die. You still want the SD card, right?'

'I'm listening.'

'The card is in a security box, but I can get it to you. I can phone the bank in the morning: it's a numbered box and I can authorise the contents to be released to you once the office opens. After you have it, let my family go and you can do what you like with me.' Tom knew he had to buy time if he was to get an opportunity to escape.

'You have a communications device. Who knows of this? I know it's not police as my contact knows nothing and he is well-placed.'

'The flight was organised by an American who owes me a big favour. He gave me the communications device, but no one knows I've been captured. He just thought I was watching the farmhouse. He works for the US government and they cannot get involved. I'm on my own here, you have to believe me,' he said with exaggerated desperation.

'How did you keep your phone signal in London?'

'It is in London, I just set up a divert to another phone.'

'Where is the card?'

'At my bank in Camden. It opens in the morning and I can call them and arrange for emergency access. It can be done.'

There was a pause, which seemed to stretch out forever. 'Okay, you can stay alive a little while longer. If you come up with the card, I will spare your parents and you will be quickly despatched.'

Tom knew that was nonsense; Branko had no intention of letting any of them live. Of that, he was absolutely sure.

'Ten o'clock tomorrow morning you call the deposit company and arrange access. If you fail to do so you will witness my men shoot both of your parents. You will then die, but not quickly or easily. You haven't met Boris before, have you? He has peculiar talents for inflicting pain that I witnessed many times during the war.'

Tom shuddered at the prospect and wondered if Pet or Mike were listening.

Boris snatched the phone away from Tom's ear and walked out of the room once more, speaking quietly into the handset.

*

Tom lay quietly on the floor, slightly on his side, the Branko boys scowling on the sofa and Boris in the armchair, his eyes half-closed. The grey-haired man seemed the picture of calm, and Tom could tell that he was someone who had been in many violent situations in the past.

Once the decision to wait had been made, the three captors had established a routine: one of them resting while the others watched them, pistols always to hand.

Tom's bindings were secure but did not restrict blood-flow, so he was able to get comfortable and rest, to some degree. He had even managed to doze for a few snatched moments.

They'd managed to organise bathroom breaks for the three of them with a great deal of care, one at a time and covered by two of the captors, one from a little more distance using the captured MP7. Other than that, it had all been peaceable.

They'd been in that position for a few hours and, by looking just to his left, Tom could see that the old carriage clock on the fireplace showed 5am. It would soon be light.

Tom looked over at Cameron and Shona, who were sat back to back, resting against the wall. He gave them an almost imperceptible wink which was returned by Cameron. He didn't frighten easily but Shona looked terrified and weary and Tom wondered about the long-term effects of their ordeal on her. He felt an enormous pull of affection for them; they'd opened their home to a twelve-year-old Bosnian boy and treated him as if he were their own child. They were his rock, his touchstone, and he would do anything at all to protect them.

The situation remained unchanged for another hour until the grey tendrils of a Highland morning began to filter through the windows. Tom felt utter exhaustion in every fibre of his body; his sternum ached horribly, and his ribs were sore from being kicked, any hope of escape fading fast as time passed by.

30

Zjelko Branko sat in the armchair in the living room of his apartment, having returned earlier that evening. Mira was asleep in bed and had been for some time, traipsing off without a word in her stained housecoat. He shook his head at the thought of her: it was only business and family honour that kept him from walking away from her forever. When the whole sorry situation was over, they could go their separate ways. He wanted out of the prostitution and trafficking game: it was just too risky.

He picked up his phone and selected a number from his call history.

It was answered after about ten rings with a sleepy, 'Yes?'

'We have Novak,' Branko said.

'Thank God for that. Where is he?' said Simon Taylor.

'In Scotland. He killed three of my associates but fortunately my boys managed to arrive and disable him.'

'What? How did he get to Scotland? It's at least ten hours away.'

'He says he got a plane, but he was well armed with sophisticated weapons and had communications equipment. Do you know how he got them?'

'It's nothing to do with law enforcement; we couldn't organise that, and I've heard nothing at all. I would know. I don't like this, Branko.'

'He says a friend did him a favour, and he managed to get him on the plane, and he got the weapons from the police armoury.'

'That's nonsense, there's no way could he do that. He's bullshitting you. He needs taking out, now. We can manage this, but he needs to disappear forever.' Taylor was almost babbling.

'What about his parents?'

Taylor paused, stunned at what he'd become a part of. He was going to be an accessory to a multiple murder, but it was too late to back out now.

'Just make sure they're never found, and you'd better get out of the country as well.'

'I just have to get the SD card from his safe deposit box. I need Adebayo's money,' Branko said, all matter-of-fact.

'Are you crazy? That's mad. Just how are you going to get the SD card?'

'He's going to arrange it with the bank,' Branko said.

'Then you're being really fucking stupid, Branko. They'll never allow you access. And as Adebayo has fled to Nigeria, how are you going to get the money? You'll never get paid. Get rid of them, and get out of the country,' Taylor said, all of a sudden assertive.

'If you call me stupid again, I will see to it that you never enjoy your pension, Mr Police Inspector. When did Adebayo go?'

'I'm sorry. He went earlier today, and he's apparently shifted all his money and gone, forever. He has assets and a home in Lagos. You'll never see that money.'

Branko sighed: a deep, rage-filled sigh. So, no money and no way of extracting it from Adebayo now he'd fled.

'Okay, so it's a tidy-up operation. The three that Novak killed won't be missed. There won't be any evidence of my people going to Scotland: there were false plates on the car and they didn't take their phones. We can dispose of the bodies and we will all go back to Serbia until this blows over. You need to come up with a way to distance us.' Branko was all efficient planning now.

'Just get it done and I can make sure no suspicion falls on you. I can claim that Novak was depressed and suicidal or something. Just make sure the bodies aren't found.'

'They won't be found, my friend: it's the middle of nowhere up there.' And Branko hung up.

He paused for a second before dialling another number.

Going Dark

'Boris, change of plan. Get rid of them all.'

31

Boris stood in the hallway of the cottage with his mobile phone clamped to his ear and a grim, determined look on his face. 'No problem. It will be done, my friend,' he said quietly. He returned to the kitchen and fixed a serious eye on Aleks. 'Aleks, with me,' he said.

Aleks stood and walked out into the hall where Boris waited; there was a quick whispered exchange before Aleks returned to the kitchen, nodding for his brother to go and join the older Serb.

There was a further exchange and then all three men came back into the room once more. Boris hefted the MP7 and pointed it directly at Tom.

'Stand up!' he commanded. 'Now listen and listen well; we're all going to take a little drive. We're going in your Land Rover. If you resist, I will shoot the lady first: do you understand?'

Tom nodded. 'Where are we going?'

'That doesn't concern you. If you cooperate, then no one will be harmed. If not, it will be bad for you. We will shoot your mother in the stomach and torture your father and make you watch.'

Boris was good: Tom had to give him that. He was careful to never get within grabbing distance and he kept the MP7 trained on him throughout. There was simply no opportunity for Tom to try to disarm any of their captors. The Branko brothers kept Cameron and Shona in a similar manner as they all made their way out of the farmhouse.

Tom was positive they had no intention of going for a drive. It was rather the case that they didn't want to shoot them in the house, leaving unnecessary evidence of their demise behind. He figured they planned to create just enough breathing space to get out of the country, once he and his foster family were all dead. Try as he might, he couldn't figure any way in which he could overpower the three of them. Shona and Cameron were shackled, as was he. He began to face up to the fact that this might finally be it. He didn't fear death, he never had, but he felt desolate for Cameron and Shona. They were good, honest people who didn't deserve this.

'You don't have to do this, Boris. Kill me but leave them alone, they're innocents,' Tom said in Serb as they came to the front of the house.

Boris didn't take his eyes from Tom's, keeping the MP7 pointed at him, a cruel smile splitting his face. 'Shut the fuck up. There is nothing for you to say right now. Just know that, if you try anything, then your family will suffer. Cooperate and you will all die quickly and cleanly.'

Tom took a strange comfort from the sunlight warming his back as it rose above the horizon behind him. He had spent so much time in deadly situations in foul weather, so he found it oddly pleasing that he would die with the sun warming his body. He took in the vast expanse of forest, the huge Scots pines swaying in the now gentle breeze. If he looked left, he could see the jutting peak of Bynack More. The air was sharp and clear with the usual distinct smell of pine in the air and he breathed in deeply, drinking it in like a fine wine. There are worse places to die, he thought.

'We will all walk into the clearing. If you don't cooperate you all die where you stand,' Boris said, still fixing Tom with his blank-eyed stare. Tom could detect no doubt or nerves, just utter conviction from the Serb.

He heard a muffled sob from Shona and a muted growl from Cameron as they all shuffled across the track and through the gap in the fence into the cleared forest.

As Tom crossed the boundary, a flash of reflection flickered from the woodpile he'd hidden behind just a few hours ago, a slight but definitely visible blink. Tom felt a glimmer of hope rise in his chest. Only one thing could have caused that, and he thought of the radio transmitter sitting in the kitchen of the farmhouse.

They carried on stumbling over the rough terrain for about twenty metres before Boris said, 'Stop there.' He began to circle clockwise around the three of them, the weapon never leaving Tom.

'Your father wants to watch this. Luka, get your phone and videocall him. All three of you kneel, now. If you don't, I shoot the bitch in the gut and you watch her die.'

Shona's sobbing intensified but Cameron just glowered, tears running down his granite cheeks and spilling over the duct tape that still secured his mouth. Tom looked at them both in turn, nodded and gave a slight wink and a smile. 'Do it, guys. Just do it,' he said, something in his voice making Cameron's eyebrows rise just a little.

Tom turned his head to the right to look at Boris, then turned to look left at Luka, who stood with a smartphone in his outstretched hand, clearly recording them. He could hear rustling behind him: about five metres away he estimated, mentally noting the position where Aleks stood.

He heard the distinctive sound of a handgun being cocked behind him and smiled before he said, 'You know, Boris, old boy, this isn't the first time I've had a gun pointed at me. Not the first time at all. I wasn't scared then and I'm not scared now. Would you like to know why?' His voice was measured, low, and even.

He saw the merest flicker of doubt and puzzlement cross Boris's face as the large-calibre bullet from a sniper rifle smashed into the back of the grey-haired man's head, causing it to explode in a violent shower of blood, skull, and brain matter.

'Shona, DOWN!' he screamed, as the rifle's report roared and cracked. Tom realised that he was obstructing the sniper's view of Aleks, who was bringing the Glock to bear on him, and threw himself to the left, clearing the way for their unseen saviour. He rolled into a tyre rut and raised his head just enough to hear the second explosion from the rifle. Aleks was thrown backwards as the next shot hit him centre-mass, hurling him back with the terrible force of a large-calibre impact.

Two down, one to go, thought Tom as he began to move, striding with force across the uneven ground to the spot he'd marked Luka as last occupying. Shona was screaming on the ground, with Cameron laying protectively over her, as Tom lunged past them towards Luka.

Tom figured no more than three seconds had passed since the last shot and he bolted towards Luka, who was squatting on the ground, the phone falling from his grip as he reached for the pistol secured in the front of his trousers. There was a look of utter confusion, panic, and horror on his face. Tom's reactions were far too quick for him and it seemed as if Luka was wading through treacle, his body yet to catch up with what his eyes had just witnessed.

Tom did not give him a chance to recover, kicking him with a brutal Muay Thai right-footed front-kick that caught the still-rising Luka square on the cheekbone. Flesh split and bones cracked. Luka was stunned and bleeding, but he was strong. He swayed but did not fall, just slumped to his knees.

Tom had no intention of leaving it there, not while he was still cuffed. Luka had signed his own death warrant when he had pointed a gun at his family. Tom stepped over the kneeling Luka so that the man's head and neck were between his thighs. He picked his right leg up, secured his foot behind his left calf, and fell to the ground onto his back. He tightened the triangle chokehold on Luka's neck and squeezed as tight as he could. Luka began to buck and thrash, but Tom tightened the choke even more and sharply bucked his hips, jerking his leg upwards. There was a muffled click from Luka's neck and he died immediately, his neck snapped.

Tom raised himself onto his haunches and reached into his boot top to retrieve the folding knife that had remained there during his captivity. He'd not been able to come up with a feasible way of deploying it until that moment. He opened the blade behind his back and the keen edge bit through the restraints, quickly freeing his wrists.

He looked at Luka, his eyes open but dead and lifeless. A faint tinny voice came from the dropped smartphone, close to the body.

Tom picked up the phone and looked at the screen, which was filled with the ugly face of Zjelko Branko. The man was shouting, 'Luka, Luka! What is happening?'

Tom operated the icon on the screen to reverse the camera so it focused on his own face, still smeared in camouflage cream. The shock at the sight of Tom's cam-cream-smeared image was clear on Branko's face. 'Novak!'

Tom spoke, his voice even, deadpan and emotionless. 'Branko, you don't need to say anything. There is nothing you can say. Your sons are dead. All your people are dead. I would advise that you try and enjoy the rest of your life, Branko. Live every day as it is your last, knowing that wherever you go, wherever you try and hide, I am coming for you.' Tom finished the call and dropped the phone onto Luka's corpse.

He ran over to Cameron and Shona, cut their restraints and removed the duct tape as gently as he could from their mouths.

'It's over,' he said and the three of them sat and hugged each other on the damp earth in the dawn sunshine, Shona sobbing quietly.

*

They sat there for a few minutes, just gathering their thoughts and letting the horror of what had happened sink in, before Cameron said, 'You got some friends helping you then, boy?' The relief was evident on his face.

'It would seem so,' he said, looking in the direction of the sniper.

Almost on cue the bark of the quad bike's engine jumped out from the direction Tom had left it. The noise increased, and it could be heard coming along the forest track five-hundred metres away. Tom was grateful for the departed high winds that had masked his arrival on the quad bike the night before.

Cameron broke the silence once again. 'Come on, love, let's get you in the house and get the kettle on,' he said, standing and offering his hand to Shona. He pulled her upright and she looked directly at Tom. Her eyes were full of terror and tears rolled down her cheeks. She was deathly pale and looked older than her years.

'I knew you'd come, darling. I knew it,' she smiled with tears in her eyes.

'Both of you go inside while I see who's coming. Cameron, take a look at Shona's finger. We will need to get her to the hospital as soon as we can, but we really don't want cops up here right now.' said Tom. There was some clearing up to do; it suddenly struck him that they had six dead bodies to deal with.

The quad's engine grew louder as it approached the cottage, having traversed the forest track, eventually reaching the main road which led to the farmhouse access track.

Tom turned to watch as the Yamaha appeared around the bend, a ghillie-suit clad sniper at the controls with a long-barrelled rifle slung over his shoulder. Tom recognised the rifle as an Accuracy International 338. It was a little overkill for the job bearing in mind he had only shot from about two-hundred metres away. Tom recalled that, in 2009 in Helmand, a sniper from the Life Guards had killed a Taliban fighter at a range of over 2,400 metres with that weapon; still, he had no complaints about this sniper's weapon systems choice.

He pulled up alongside Tom and shut off the engine. 'Mr Brogan sends his regards, sir. He would like to speak with you.' He handed a satellite phone over to Tom but remained on the quad; he was a small, wiry, black man in his early forties and had the look of a seasoned veteran. He was dressed in a fully-camouflaged sniper suit while he cradled the rifle reverentially, staring at Tom with a half-smile.

'I never let a favour go unreturned, my friend,' Mike said down the phone.

'Well, all I can say is thank you, Mike. I thought that was the end for all of us.'

'My man is disappointed that he got so close. He likened it to shooting fish in a barrel. He probably won't want to talk very much, he's a slightly shy freelancer,' Mike said. 'What do we have to deal with there, man? There's a clear-up team en route.'

'Six bodies, unfortunately,' said Tom. 'Three in the clearing, plus another two in the bush by the house, and one inside. I didn't have much choice, sorry.'

'No problems. The clear-up team will be there soon. Your folks okay?'

'They will be. Cameron has seen it all before, but Shona has had the tip of her finger removed,' Tom said.

'There's a medic with the clear-up team. Get him to have a look at it, but you will have to come up with a reasonable story to explain how it happened. We really can't have cops there any time soon until we have cleared up. We have very little time; I had to call in some favours to pull this off and I want to get it all cleared up as soon as we can. Also, we'll need to get our tactical kit back. I'd rather it didn't fall into the wrong hands and I guess you don't want to look after it.'

'The three corpses in the clearing have the weapons. The comms kit and spare ammo is in the house, and the case is up at the bothy,' Tom said.

'That's cool. My guys can retrieve at the clear-up. Is there much of a mess inside?'

'None, really: just a broken table and maybe a bit of blood from a busted nose. We just need to get rid of the cars,' Tom said.

'No problems. If you could get the BMW back down to London and lose it somewhere, one of my guys will get rid of the Merc. We'll take care of the stiffs and we're good to go. I think the crows will take care of the detritus the sniper rifle caused,' he said in an amused tone. Tom realised that, despite the pristine good manners, Mike was a ruthless operator who had obviously organised clear-ups after similar incidents over the years.

A faint thump-thump of helicopter blades became audible

from the north.

'Okay, the clear-up team will be with you in minutes. They may be a little shy: they are all freelancers as well. I'll call you back once things get sorted your end,' Mike said, and he ended the call. Tom handed the satellite phone back to the sniper, who nodded his thanks.

Within a few minutes, a Sikorsky UH60 Black Hawk, painted in plain, dark green, tore into view over the treeline, its rotor-wash sending the branches into a fury as it came in low and fast.

Tom noted that the engine tone was identical to his coastguard taxi earlier, which meant it wouldn't attract too much comment at that early hour; he wondered if that was a deliberate strategy.

The helicopter landed in the clearing and a civilian-clad man with a flat-top haircut and a pistol on his hip exited and jogged up to Tom. 'Good morning, sir. I understand you have a casualty. We have a medic who can assist.'

'Yes. My mother has had the tip of her finger removed.' Tom said.

The man returned to the helicopter and a similarly dressed individual exited and jogged over, holding a compact rucksack.

'Is your mom in the house? I will be able to help.'

'Yes. Thanks, she'll be in the kitchen.' Tom said, watching as the man jogged off towards the house.

The other man spoke. 'Can you direct us to where the items for removal are located?'

Tom explained the location of all the corpses and weaponry to the man, who nodded his understanding and turned to jog back to the helicopter, where hand signals summoned some unseen occupants. He was joined by three other men, all similarly dressed, one of whom was carrying several black bodybags. The whole appearance of the new arrivals was one of complete efficiency and practised unity of purpose. Tom wondered how many times similar things had happened in the UK.

Tom looked at the still-silent sniper and simply said, 'Thanks, man.' There was real gratitude in his voice.

The man just smiled widely, turned on his heels, and jogged to the helicopter, his job done.

The rotors eased to a stop and silence once more enveloped them. The first man approached Tom and said, 'Why don't you go and join your folks while my guys sort this situation out, sir? They've done it before and probably wouldn't appreciate extra and unnecessary witnesses. Make them a cup of tea. That's what you English do, right?' He showed white teeth in a pleasant smile.

'I'm not English,' Tom said, returning his smile.

*

The clear-up team worked with predictable efficiency, transferring all six corpses to the Black Hawk on a stretcher once they'd been body-bagged. The only trace that anything untoward had occurred in the farmhouse was the damaged coffee table. The medic was extremely efficient, if taciturn. He cleaned and thoroughly dressed the severed digit, which fortunately had been cut at the point of the nailbed so had not caused any tendon damage. He also gave Shona a shot of antibiotics but advised that she would need to seek medical attention in due course.

Tom took a moment to assess his reaction to personally killing four people over the past hour. In essence, he felt the same as the twenty-eight times he'd snuffed out lives before, when employed as a sniper in the Middle East.

Nothing.

He had no demons, no dark thoughts, no guilt, and he knew he wouldn't dwell on it. They had to die, they deserved to die: they chose to imprison his family with intent to kill them, so Tom felt nothing other than relief that Cameron and Shona were safe. He wasn't malicious and he didn't enjoy killing, but neither did he feel bad about it.

Tom turned to his foster parents, feeling a tug of affection towards them. It made him feel a little more human and possibly normal, having such emotions that he rarely felt otherwise.

'Are you guys going to be okay?' he asked.

'I'll be honest, Tom: my finger hurts like fuck,' Shona said. Tom was amazed to see that there was a touch of humour in her voice, despite the events of the past few hours. Once again, he was amazed by the inner strength of this tough, Highland woman.

'I'm sorry that I brought this to your door, guys,' Tom said.

'Shut up, boy.' Cameron spoke forcefully. 'You brought nothing to our door. Those individuals being loaded on the helicopter brought this to our door. You did what you had to do and risked everything for us. Just promise me one thing.'

'I'm listening,' Tom said, feeling emotion rising in his chest.

'Make sure that every one of the bastards who did this, organised it or allowed it to happen pays an appropriate price. Remember what I always said to you when you were growing up? Whatever you do, always do right!' Tears coursed down the cheeks of the rough, tough ex-Bootneck, and his eyes glistened with anger.

Once again, all three of them hugged.

Within forty minutes, all the bodies were on board the helicopter, together with Mike's clear-up team and the sniper. Tom had not exchanged so much as a word with any of them and it was clear by their actions and body language that they wanted no interaction at all. He imagined that staying as invisible as possible was essential in their line of business.

Tom sat in the kitchen with Cameron and Shona, all of them clutching mugs of tea but no one speaking. A mixture of exhaustion and the stress of the previous hours were clearly taking their toll and Tom wondered what effects this would have on them. Cameron was an old campaigner who had seen his own share of violence and combat, but he was not getting any younger. Shona was tougher than she looked, but no one needed to see and experience the things she'd had forced upon her by evil men with evil intents. Her quiet, Highland life had been shattered, albeit temporarily, and Tom hoped she'd get over it in time.

The satellite phone buzzed in Tom's pocket.

'You guys okay?' Mike said.

'We'll be grand, Mike. I want to thank you for everything. We'd all be dead if it wasn't for you,' Tom said.

'You know something. You once did the biggest favour a man can do many years ago, so me being here right now is all thanks to you.'

'I think we can call it even now,' Tom said.

'My friend, I now have twin daughters and a beautiful wife, and we live in a vineyard in Southern California. None of that would have happened if it wasn't for what you did in Basra when you risked your hide to save mine. I'll never repay the favour as far as I'm concerned.' Mike paused and there was a brief silence before he continued.

'My guys have left the keys in the BMW, if you can deal with that. The Brankos drove up from London in it so it's your ride back down. It's on false plates. You may want to leave them on and avoid all the cameras you can. Maybe you could park it up near Heathrow somewhere. We will lay a trail of computer breadcrumbs suggesting they've all gone back to Serbia, so it should kill off any missing person enquiries. One of my guys is doing the same with Arken's Mercedes and he's on his way to Glasgow with it now. The only trace of anything untoward here will be gone once the crows have finished their meals.'

Tom could hear the Black Hawk's engines warming up outside.

'No problem. And thanks once again. I have some things to sort in London, but I reckon I can handle it from now on, maybe with a little help from Pet,' said Tom.

'Yeah, I think you have a few corrupt cops to bring down. Good luck.'

'Let's go fishing soon,' said Mike.

'I'd like that; I can teach your arse how to catch a salmon.' With that, Mike hung up.

The helicopter engine-note changed as the blades whirled and it took off. Tom watched out of the window until it disappeared over the treeline. He needed a shower, a change of clothes and some breakfast before setting off to London.

Going Dark

The next phase of the plan was already forming in his mind.

32

The Next Morning

Tom woke early, glad to be in his Kentish Town apartment after the rigours of the past few days. He rubbed at his sternum, which still throbbed thanks to the trauma inflicted by the 9mm bullet.

The journey down from Scotland had taken over ten hours once he'd fuelled up at the tiny local petrol garage, which had the benefit of no security cameras. He'd paid in cash and didn't need to refuel again, as the BMW X5 was surprisingly economical for such a big, powerful car. Shona had prepared some food and a flask of tea for the journey, so he didn't need to stop other than to relieve himself at quiet locations off the motorway.

He had driven straight to Heathrow airport, arriving just after 6pm. He drove straight to the medium-term parking close to Terminal One, being careful to keep his face away from the many CCTV cameras in the area. The tinted windows would have made any images of limited value, but he wanted to have as little connection to the vehicle as possible, as all its previous occupants were now dead and, most probably, at the bottom of the North Sea.

He had parked on the second level in the darkest recess he could find, where he quickly switched the number plates, putting the genuine ones back on the vehicle and stowing the false ones in the small rucksack he carried that contained only the remainder of his food, flask and passport.

Finally, he had used baby wipes to clean all the surfaces he'd touched to remove any DNA or fingerprint traces. Satisfied, he had then set off in search of a cab back to Kentish Town.

It was unlikely anyone would take any notice of the BMW for a number of weeks and, if Mike had laid the trail of breadcrumbs he'd referred to, it would all add to the picture of the Brankos fleeing the UK.

The switch of plates also had the advantage that, if Tom had hit any ANPR cameras throughout the journey down, the false plates would take the enquiry no further. He had broken the plates into numerous pieces which he'd disposed of in multiple dustbins on his walk from the Tube station to his apartment.

He wasn't worried about Branko; Tom was the hunter now, not Zjelko Branko, so he had felt safe to go home and sleep in his own bed.

He finally got home at eight o'clock, clutching a takeaway curry which he ate sitting at his breakfast bar, relishing the spicy and delicious meal and washing it down with a bottle of beer. He'd had a long, hot shower to get rid of all the grime and sweat of the preceding hours and climbed into his bed, where he'd slept like a baby.

Turning all the events over in his mind the next morning, he surmised that he was clean, with nothing to link him to the events in Scotland. The job was not over yet though, as thoughts of Simon Taylor and his cohorts flared in his mind.

He got out of bed and dressed in a plain white T-shirt and blue jeans. The bruise on his chest was beginning to bloom in varying colours. He went through to the kitchen where he prepared himself coffee and toast while thinking about his next move.

Picking up his burner phone he dialled Pet. She answered immediately.

'You took your time, Detective. You wait until now to speak to me?'

'Yeah, I know. I didn't want to use the burner phone outside of

London and I was too knackered when I got home.'

'You're at your apartment?' she asked incredulously.

'I wanted my own bed. There's only one Branko left and Adebayo's out of the country.'

'Branko has left the country as well; I just pinged his phone in France. I think he ran as soon as he realised what had happened. He used one of his cards to buy a Eurostar ticket. I imagine he's on his way back to Serbia.'

Tom turned this over in his mind. For the moment, he was happy to have Branko out of his hair; he could wait. His priority was Taylor and the dirty, corrupt bastards he'd been working with.

'So, what's your next move?' Pet asked.

'Anything new on Taylor and the others?' Tom asked, ignoring the question.

'Taylor was speaking to Branko during the night: no new texts or WhatsApp messages. He's hitting cell masts at the police station as far as I can see. No other contact with anyone. I doubt Branko would tell him he was fleeing.'

That made sense: he couldn't see why Branko would tell a serving police officer, no matter how corrupt, what his plans were. The whole criminal network was shattered, but that didn't mean he could stop: he was just beginning.

'My priority is to get evidence we can use against them. I want them in jail.'

'How do you propose you do that, Detective? Everything you have so far you can't use because of its slightly irregular source.'

'I'll tell you later. I have a plan forming, I just need to speak to a few people to get it moving. Stay out of sight and I'll call you later.'

'You're not giving much away here,' she said, sounding slightly hurt.

'Not over the phone, Pet. You've done so much for me, I don't want to expose you any more. Taylor will do anything to get off the hook and the evidence needs to be watertight.'

'I was so worried about you, Tom. Is your mother okay?'

'She seems more together about it than Cameron; she is very

tough. She's going to the hospital with a story of an accident with an axe and some firewood. I also want to say, Pet, from the bottom of my heart: thank you. Without you I think my family would be dead by now.' Once again, Tom surprised himself with a slight jolt of emotion. Was this normal, he wondered?'

'Tom, I'm just glad you are all safe. I couldn't have lived with myself if I hadn't done everything I could. You're a good man, Tom.' There was a pause that seemed like an eternity but, in reality, was probably just a few seconds.

Eventually Tom spoke, all business once again. 'One last thing: I need a number from my phone. Can you get it for me? Look up a number for "Lucky D" in my contacts.'

Pet sighed, presumably at Tom's slightly abrupt tone, but she read the number out to him anyway.

'Thanks, Pet. Speak soon.' He ended the call.

He immediately dialled the number he'd written down which was answered with a cheery, 'Hello, who's that phoning Lucky D?' in a light, cockney accent.

'Lucky, my man. It's Tom Novak.'

'Tommy-boy, how you been? You've been out of sight for months! What's up? You don't need the services of your best-ever snitch, eh?'

Lucky D was a career criminal. A car thief par excellence, who Tom had arrested long ago but had managed to turn into a valuable informant. He knew everyone and everything that went on in the Islington area and was happy to pass on anything he didn't like the look of to Tom when it suited him. Lucky had a big problem with drugs and drug dealers: he couldn't stand them, probably due to his own mother's long-term addiction. He wouldn't grass on anyone other than drug dealers or people connected to murders, but he'd given Tom many good leads in the past that had seen some big dealers locked up and netted many big seizures. That was not the purpose of his call, however.

'I need to get into a new Jaguar F-Pace without anyone knowing I've been in it. Is that something you would know about?'

'Blimey, you don't fuck about, Tommy, not even: "How are you, Lucky?" You always were a direct twat, weren't you, Tom?'

'Sorry, Lucky, I've had a few bad days. And it's really urgent, as in life-and-death, so what do you reckon?'

'Just teasing, mate. A new F-Pace? Big old security on them, but where there's a will there's a way, me old china. You want to drive away or just get in the motor?' asked Lucky.

'I just want to get in the car without setting off the alarm.'

'Easiest way is to use a signal jammer. You need to be close by: when your man locks the car, you jam the signal from the key and the car won't lock. The only problem is if the car makes a noise or your man notices. You also won't be able to lock the car afterwards,' Lucky said, warming to the task. He was proud of his expertise in vehicle theft, something which Tom always found amusing.

'That's not ideal; I need to lock up afterwards.'

'Can you get hold of the key? 'Cos if you can then I could clone it and you could do whatever you want with it then.'

'I don't want to, it would take too long and would be too risky.'

'In that case, I'd use a roll-jam. It's a Jag so it will use a rolling radio code for every press of the key fob.'

'I'm assuming that has nothing to do with sandwiches. Come on, man, I'm busy,' said Tom, a degree of levity in his voice.

'It's a lovely bit of kit. It's basically three radio transmitters in a box which you hide on or near the car while your owner is away. When he returns and blips the lock, it won't work because one of the transmitters has jammed and simultaneously recorded the signal. When he presses it again, thinking there's a glitch, it will lock or unlock as normal and he won't think a thing about the unsuccessful blip. What he won't know is that you have an unused code stored in the roll-jam that you jammed which you can use at any time. It won't start a Jag, but it will get you inside and you can lock up afterwards,' Lucky said, unable to keep the glee out of his voice at his own perceived genius.

'That sounds perfect, Lucky. Can you get your hands on one?'

'Depends on the usual, Tommy-Boy: what's in it for old Lucky

D?'

'My eternal gratitude and the knowledge that I owe you one.'

'Chuck in a ton and it's a deal, as long as I get it back afterwards.'

He always cut to the chase, but Tom figured £100 was reasonable in the circumstances. Usually Tom could have sourced informant rewards from central police funds, but it took a whole heap of applications and reports and would take time he didn't have.

'It's a deal. When can I get it? Bear in mind that the answer I want to hear is "right away". I'm in a hurry.'

'How about the café on Chapel Market in an hour? You can buy me a tea?' Lucky said cheerfully.

'One hour. See you then,' Tom said and hung up.

He dialled another number on the burner phone, which was answered quickly. 'My dear boy, I thought you'd never call!' boomed Stan.

'Can you speak?'

'Fire away. I'm nearly at work, just in the car.'

'Is Taylor in today?'

'He should be. Diary says he's in all week and he's on-call as well.'

'Is he still using the Jag?'

'Yes. Especially since you nicked the Passat.'

It suddenly hit Tom that the VW was still with Pet. He guessed he should sort that, as well as his own car in Shepherds Bush, soon.

'Can you text me when he gets in? I need to have two minutes in the back yard with the car and I need you to keep him occupied and out of sight of the car.'

'No problems. Soon as I see him,' Stan said.

'Thanks, speak later.'

*

The café was a typical North London establishment: nothing flash, no lattes, no flat whites, no pastries; just tea, coffee and fry-ups. The place was about half-full of office staff and hi-vis-clad construction workers, all enjoying the tantalisingly tasty repast that flowed over the counter all day.

Lucky was already sitting at a booth when Tom arrived, a cup of tea and a half-eaten bacon sandwich in front of him. He nodded as Tom sat in front of him and smiled. He was a scrawny man in his early forties with sharp features and deep blue eyes that shone with intelligence and cunning. He was a good thief but deplored violence and was liked by all, which was what made him such good value as a source of intelligence.

Tom ordered a tea from the wordless and scowling owner, who wore a stained apron and a purple rinse hair-do.

'So, will this work then, Lucky?' Tom asked.

'On my baby's life, yes, Tommy-boy. It's a cracking bit of kit as long as all you want is to get in the car without damage.'

'Last I checked, you don't have any kids, Lucky. Who'd want your genetics?' Tom asked with a grin.

'Ouch! A dagger through my heart, Tom. You are a cruel man. You got something for me?'

Tom reached into his jacket pocket and pushed an envelope across the table and then took a swig of the strong, almost bitter, tea.

Lucky crammed the envelope in his pocket without checking and then slid across the table to Tom a mobile phone-sized device that resembled a small walkie-talkie with a short, stubby antenna.

'It's got a small magnet on one side. Just push the button, stick it on, and the battery is good for a few hours. I'd get straight to it, though, once the car's been locked, so another key doesn't override it.'

'So how you been, then?'

'Not so bad. Staying out of trouble, keeping quiet and not stealing shit, Detective.'

'Good to hear. I'll get this back to you once I'm done with it.'

'Make sure you do, Tommy-boy,' he said with an impish grin.

Tom drained his tea and left the café, walking towards Angel Station five minutes away.

He took the Tube to Tottenham Court Road, which boasted many audio-visual and electrical stores. It wasn't a new stereo that Tom was looking for, however, as he pushed open the door of a small, grimy store and strode in.

It was a dirty, uninviting place with a solitary staff member sat behind the counter using a magnifier to inspect a small piece of circuitry. Glass cases lined the walls displaying varying types of cameras, bug finders, bugs, and other types of surveillance material.

'Can I help you, squire?' the worker said in Middle East-accented English. He was a thick-set man with a full beard and open-necked shirt straining against a bulging stomach that a thick, leather belt was fighting to contain.

'I'm looking for a small GSM listening device. It needs to be voice-activated, have a good battery life, and preferably records as a backup to an internal memory,' said Tom.

'Best is this one, squire. Takes any SIM, just dial-in. It's got a 16GB memory card, will do five days in stand-by mode, twenty hours talk-time, and only a hundred-and-eighty quid.' He handed Tom a small box the size of an average wallet.

'How big is the actual unit?'

'A bit bigger than a fifty-pence-piece, mate. You won't find a better one.'

'I'll take it. You have any SIM cards?' said Tom as he handed over the cash from his wallet.

'I'll chuck in a SIM, gratis. Nice doing business with you.' The man grinned, showing gold-capped teeth.

Tom walked out of the shop, the bug in his pocket. The whole transaction had taken about two minutes. He retrieved his phone and sent a message to Stan.

'Glenda in?'

The reply was almost instantaneous. 'Yes. Been to the car twice already.'

Tom dialled the number for Pet. It was time.

33

Tom took the Tube from Tottenham Court Road, changed at Oxford Circus, and headed up the Bakerloo line towards Queens Park Station, which was only about a hundred metres from Kilburn Police Station. Walking out of the Tube, he felt the sun break out from behind the clouds and warm his face. He felt good. For the first time in a while he felt in control and in charge of his own destiny. He'd still need a bit of luck if his plan was to pan out, but he was a firm believer in making his own luck, which he hoped he was doing now.

He sent a text to Stan as he walked. 'Still there?'

The response was immediate. 'In his office, doesn't want to be disturbed car parked by the back gate in a response bay.'

Tom typed a reply. 'Am I clear to swipe in?'

'My mate assures me you're good to go.'

Tom had been worried about gaining entry to the nick if his card had been deactivated. The entry card system was pretty basic and carried no other information other than entry and exit controls. He was happy that there would be no marker alerting his superiors if he entered the building.

Tom typed a reply. 'Nice one, mate. Tell Glenda his car needs moving; maybe get a mate to tell him.'

Tom was well aware how many mates Stan could call up to get that done, and he needed Taylor to unlock the car while he was in range.

Stan replied. 'Give me 5.'

Tom turned left into Harvist Road along the side of the red-bricked police station and towards the back yard. Ignoring the main vehicle gate, he walked further up and used his warrant card to swipe in at the staff access gate at the rear. The backyard was full of parked vehicles and he immediately spotted the large, grey Jaguar SUV, slap bang in the middle of the response vehicle bays by the back door. Parking there was heavily frowned upon, and the Borough Commander would occasionally get a bee in his bonnet about it.

Tom walked to the back of the yard by the tall fence and got into an unlocked, marked police carrier, the type often referred to as a 'riot van', and sat low in one of the back seats. Tom thought it was likely that the Territorial Support Group, who used the carriers, were in the nick, probably with a prisoner. He put on a discarded Gore-Tex jacket and jammed a slightly too large police cap on his head. There was an empty space directly in front of the carrier that Tom was confident was the obvious choice of parking space for Taylor.

His phone buzzed in his pocket.

'On his way down, Chief Super just given him a bollocking, lol!'

Tom smiled to himself, shaking his head at Stan's abilities.

The back door to the police station flew open and Taylor stormed out in shirt sleeves, his gaudy tie loosened. Anger was written all over his face as he walked to his Jaguar. The indicator lights flashed as he pointed the key at the car, then he climbed inside and reversed the car out of the response bay, straight to the space in front of Tom. Tom kept himself low but was confident that the uniform would mean that Taylor wouldn't even offer him a glance.

Taylor swung the door open and stepped out, slamming it violently while pointing the key at the car: Tom's cue to press the rubberised button on the roll-jam. Nothing happened: no flashing indicators and no noise from the Jaguar. Taylor paused for a moment and then pressed again, a frustrated look on his face, and the Jag's lights flashed with a 'blip' noise. Taylor didn't miss a beat and strode angrily towards the back door of the nick.

Tom watched him return to the police station and disappear back inside, leaving the yard all peaceful once more.

Tom removed the borrowed uniform items and got out of the carrier, pointing the roll-jam at the Jag as he did so. The lights flashed, and the blip indicated that the kit had worked perfectly. Tom didn't skulk or hesitate as that would have just attracted more attention than if he was brazen and obvious. He walked straight up to the car, pocketing the roll-jam and pulling out the GSM bug in a smooth motion. Opening the door, he squatted on his haunches and took out the bug, snapping it onto the underside of one of the seats. It attached with a reassuring metallic click. Taking out the roll-jam again, he pressed the button once more and the familiar blip told him that the car was now locked and secure. Perfect!

He tucked the device back in his pocket and took his burner phone out and dialled Pet, who answered immediately. 'Give me good news, Detective.'

'I'm going to give you a number for a GSM bug I've just planted in Taylor's car. It's voice-activated, but I want you to dial into it and set it to record via your computer once I give you the word. Also, make sure any text messages he sends are forwarded over to me as well.'

Tom read the phone number out from the SIM packaging. A tone from the phone in his ear told him that another text had arrived.

'Got it. Ready when you are.'

'Good girl, speak soon.' Tom hung up and checked the screen on his phone.

'Back in his office and he looks pissed off!' read Stan's message.

Tom walked quickly down to the rear door of the police station and used his warrant card to swipe into the building. He quickly covered the corridor, glad that the station seemed quiet. He nodded at one uniformed constable who was hurrying out of the nick, clearly responding to a call by the general chatter he could hear from the personal radios.

Tom ascended to the second floor and walked along the corridor, directly to the office with the laminated sign taped to the door: DCI Taylor.

Tom grabbed the door handle, twisted it, and walked in without knocking.

Taylor was busy studying his computer screen but looked up with a slight start when he heard the door open. Unused to the lack of a knock, he was clearly preparing for a rebuke at whoever the visitor was.

His face registered shock as Tom strode confidently into the room, shutting the door behind him.

'Tom,' the DCI spluttered. 'You're safe! Thank goodness. Where have you been? People have been so concerned.' The look of concern on his face was genuine but Tom knew it wasn't concern for him.

Tom said nothing but walked slowly to the chair in front of his senior manager and sat down, not taking his eyes off the man for a second. His dark, almost black eyes seemed to bore right into Taylor's soul.

'Tom, people have been looking for you, you must know this, and I've had all sorts of resources out looking—'

'I know what you did, Simon: you and your friends. I know it all.'

34

'Tom, what on Earth? I've no idea what you're talking about!' Taylor stammered, his lips quivering, and a sheen of light perspiration dotting his top lip. Fear shone out of his eyes like a beacon and his shoulders slumped.

'Shut up, Simon. I know all of it. I know you've been blackmailed by the Brankos and Adebayo. I know you got Albrechtsen to steal the SD card from Ilford. I know that you got Gareth Jones, your mate from the NCA, to bug my phone and intercept my banks. I know about your taste for little girls, you sick, fucking pervert. I can forgive all of that. I know Branko and Adebayo pushed or paid you to do it all.' Tom paused a moment, his eyes firmly fixed on Taylor's pale and weak ones.

'But, Tom, I—'

'Shut up, Taylor,' Tom yelled in a fair impression of a rage that he didn't really feel, but he wanted Taylor to think he was unhinged and dangerous.

'But what I can't forgive,' he continued, 'what I will bring you down for, is giving my foster family's home address to those bastards, who you knew would kill them. To silence me and get the footage of that sick fuck Adebayo back, you were willing to murder my family. I know it all, so don't fucking dare deny it, or I'll snap your skinny little fucking neck right here.'

Tom sat back in the chair, his legs crossed, and his fingertips steepled in front of his face, a sudden picture of calm as his eyes locked unblinkingly on Taylor.

They held that position for a full minute before Taylor eventually broke the silence.

'I assume you have proof of all this? I guess not, or it would be the IPCC here now, not you,' Taylor said, a little confidence coming back into him.

Tom said nothing but just continued to stare without moving a muscle or even changing his expression. He wasn't expecting a confession, inadmissible as it would be in any case, as Taylor couldn't be sure that Tom was not recording the conversation.

'I have a photo of you snorting coke off a prostitute's belly. It's nice but you look a little saggy: you may want to work on your abs,' Tom said with a smirk.

A hint of a smile came across Taylor's face. 'How did you get those? I assume in a manner which complies with all the evidential requirements that a leading QC would be unable to challenge?'

'I know you sent the text to Branko with my parent's address on,' Tom said, feigning a slight fluster of his own.

'And how do you know about that, DS Novak? I assume any invasion of my privacy was properly authorised by a superintendent at least?' Taylor was warming to his task now, enjoying the apparent turning of the tables.

'I'm going to bring you down, all of you; especially now my family are safe. I wonder what happened to the Brankos and all the Serb mafia you sent to me. Where's Adebayo? Everyone has vanished, I hear; it's just you and your cronies left. Just think, Taylor, just think to yourself, "I wonder what Tom Novak is capable of?" I hope you sleep soundly in your lovely place in Watford.' Tom smiled, but the menace was obvious and evident in his voice which had lowered to a growl.

Alarm flashed in Taylor's eyes. 'How dare you threaten me, you odious little man? Who the fuck do you think you are? Your career is finished, you little refugee rat,' he spat with a mix of fury and fear.

Tom paused, the silence almost congealing the atmosphere in the stuffy office.

Suddenly he stood, causing Taylor to jump, just slightly, in fright. Tom took two steps around the desk and moved his face to within an inch of Taylor's. 'Be seeing you very soon, Simon.' He smiled, exuding a latent violence that he didn't really feel, but he wanted to leave a lasting impression.

Tom turned on his heels and walked out of the office, slamming the door behind him.

As he walked down the corridor, he pulled out his phone and sent a message to Pet. Game on, he thought grimly.

*

Simon Taylor sat, stunned, in his office, unable to organise his thoughts enough to decide what to do next.

He'd been unable to raise any of the Brankos since they'd captured Novak. He couldn't think what had happened and the thought of it concerned him.

He felt incredibly vulnerable and couldn't come up with any set of circumstances that could have landed him in the situation he was now in. Clearly the kidnap of Novak's family hadn't worked, but where was Branko and his wretched family? He wasn't answering his phone since their last conversation in the night.

Adebayo had gone, that much he knew; one of his contacts in Special Branch had let him know about that. Gareth, who had been monitoring his accounts, had watched him clear them.

Best-case was that the Brankos had fled back to Serbia and, with Adebayo back in Nigeria, he and his friends may now finally be in the clear. Taylor was sure that Novak had nothing admissible or IPCC would have been there instead.

Perhaps just keeping his head down would be the best way forward, but he had to speak to Jones and Albrechtsen to see what they thought. Jones had access to everything at the NCA and could see if the Brankos had indeed fled.

He needed to speak to them right away: it was urgent. He pulled out his burner phone and composed a message to their WhatsApp group.

'We need to meet. No details on phones, I'll call you both in five mins.'

He pressed Send on the old iPhone and received blue ticks indicating that the messages had been read.

He needed to be careful: nothing written down, no messages that could be read if the phone was ever seized, not that he could see that happening. He decided to ditch his burner phone after meeting the others and would get them to do the same.

He wasn't taking any chances, especially as he had no idea how Novak knew what he knew. He was sure of one thing, though: there was no way Novak could have heard any phone calls, as Gareth Jones was at the centre of the NCA intercepting mechanism.

Taylor always thought that he, Jones, and Albrechtsen were a formidable unit. When on the NCA, they had brought down some serious criminals and managed to feather their own nests and enjoy the fruits of their labour. A stupid Bosnian immigrant wasn't going to stop them; he had no idea who he was dealing with.

Tucking his phone into his pocket, he stood and walked along the corridor towards the car park to call the boys; they had plans to make regarding Novak. He wasn't worried anymore and began to smile as he felt his confidence rising, knowing that others had tried to bring him down in the past and all had failed. Because he was so smart.

35

Tom sat in the café around the corner from the nick, a large cappuccino and a half-eaten bruschetta on the stainless-steel table in front of him. It was one of the new types of establishments that had been springing up in the Kilburn area since the chic and cool families had started moving in, once they could no longer afford the property prices in Maida Vale or Notting Hill. The walls were lined with shelves of produce full of expensive pastas, antipasti, and Italian wines. No single chair matched another and the whole place had a shabby-chic feel that was as false as it was welcoming. The exodus of the traditional working-class population had also led to the exodus of the traditional greasy spoon café, to be replaced by delicatessens that served paninis, focaccia, and fifteen different types of coffee. Tom was unsure what he felt about that as he enjoyed a good, old-fashioned fry-up as much as the next man. He was fussy about his coffee, however, and very much enjoyed well-made Italian snacks, so it was honours-even as far as he was concerned.

The café was bustling with a large group of middle-class mums, sat gossiping on a large sofa while their kids played happily on the rug by their feet; posh accents mixed with the babble of the children resulting in a happy buzz.

Tom felt the phone vibrate in his pocket and, checking the display, saw it was Pet calling.

'Hi, Pet, what can you tell me?'

'Taylor is calling one of his buddies, clear as a bell. You want to listen? I can patch you in?'

'Do it.'

There was a clicking in his ear that was then replaced by the voice of the man he had, just fifteen minutes ago, been having a confrontation with.

'Gareth, it's Si. We have a problem with Novak,' Taylor said.

Tom could only hear Taylor's half of the conversation. He hoped it would be enough.

'I know, I know, but we need to meet: the three of us, it's important. I don't want to talk on the phone but it's important. I don't know where the Brankos have gone and Adebayo has legged it to Nigeria. I need you to double-check that as well.'

A short silence followed with the slight hiss of static in the background, but the quality of the bug's transmission was impressive and as clear as a bell.

'Okay, tonight at about seven, usual place. At least we can get something to eat and, if we sit outside under the burners, we won't be overheard. See you then.'

Tom digested this information. He wanted a specific location if his plan was to work as he intended.

Tom heard Taylor coughing slightly before the DCI said, 'Graham, it's Si. You okay to speak?'

There was a short pause before he said, 'We need to meet, mate, urgently. There's a problem with Novak and we need to sort it, for good. I don't want to talk on the phone. I'm meeting with Jonesey later at seven. Can you get there?'

Once again there was a short pause before he said. 'Yeah, that's the one, big place by HMS Belfast. We can sit outside, get a bite, and talk it through. Okay, see you later. Don't worry, man: we can sort it.'

There was another pause before Taylor said, 'Stop worrying, mate! We can sort it between us. Novak is no one. I'll see you at seven.'

There were muted shuffling sounds followed by the sounds of the car door opening and then being slammed shut.

Pet's voice emanated from the phone. 'You get all that?'

'Clear as a bell. Thank you, Pet.'

Tom put his phone back into his pocket and smiled to himself. They'd described a large pub with outside seating under gas heaters and in the shadow of HMS Belfast. Tom knew that pub: he'd been to it a good few times for a beer and a burger. The Horniman by Hays Galleria on the banks of the Thames, directly opposite HMS Belfast: the old WW2 warship which had been preserved as a tourist attraction.

The pub was huge and bustling and, if you could get a seat outside, it would be the ideal place for a quiet meeting about nefarious activity. He'd even met informants himself there in the past, as it was nice and public and allowed for a discreet chat in an environment where you wouldn't be overheard.

He sipped his coffee and checked his watch: it was only 11am. Plenty of time.

He picked up his phone and dialled, listening as the phone rang in his ear for about ten seconds before a familiar cockney voice answered. 'I wondered when you were gonna call me, you cheeky bastard, Borat.'

'Hello, Buster.'

*

Simon Taylor arrived at The Horniman just before 7pm and saw that the terrace was absolutely packed out with early-evening drinkers enjoying the unseasonably good weather. He had been unable to concentrate at work after Novak's visit and had quietly fumed at the man's insolence all day. He'd had to work hard to avoid the Borough Commander, who was gunning for him about the domestic violence clear-up rate having slipped badly recently. He just couldn't bear the day-to-day drudgery of borough policing, but it seemed the only way he may be able to climb the promotion ladder any further.

Despite everything he'd done, the hours he'd put in, and the general improvements in the borough's performance, he'd been rejected at the last two promotion processes. He couldn't figure out why; they just seemed to flounder with very little feedback as to why he was not getting promoted. 'Just keep plugging away, Simon,' the Chief Super had said, without giving him anything concrete. It was so frustrating.

He looked inside the pub but couldn't see the other two anywhere, which was annoying; he hated any kind of lateness, particularly in circumstances like this. He went to the bar and bought himself a pint of lager together with a large whisky chaser to settle his nerves. That would be his fourth pint, as he'd stopped off nearby for a couple of liveners before the meeting. He'd found himself drinking far too much recently, certainly since his unfortunate dealings with those bastard Brankos.

Taylor wandered outside onto the terrace once more to see if any spaces had cleared, but it was still jam-packed with revellers and groups of drunken office workers, still in their business attire with loosened ties and discarded stilettos.

He was on the point of giving up and going back inside to find a seat when a shaven-headed, short, stocky man with a pretty blonde companion said, 'We're just leaving, mate, take this one,' in a cockney voice, indicating to the table they were vacating. It was littered with empty glasses and two cleared plates. A condiment box fashioned like a small, vintage wine box sat in the middle of the table holding a menu, napkins, cutlery, and sauces.

'Thank you,' Taylor said, relieved. The table was perfect: not too close to any of the other tables, and right next to the river wall overlooking the Thames. He sat down and got his phone out to see if the other two had called. They hadn't.

He took a long swig of beer and took a sip of his whisky, savouring the warmth and smoky taste.

A young and pretty waitress appeared and said with a bright smile, 'Can I just clear this please, sir?'

'Please do,' he replied, and she began to take the remains of the meal away.

As she wiped the table down she said, 'Will you be eating

tonight?'

'I'm expecting a couple of friends. I suspect we will eat something.'

'I'll just replenish your sauces and things then, sir,' she said.

She cleared the table and disappeared for a moment before returning with a freshly-filled condiment box that had new bottles of sauce and more napkins.

'Just let me know when you'd like to order, sir.' She smiled as she put the box on the table.

Simon couldn't stand places like that with their faux rustic themes. It was all so pretentious, but the location was perfect for his purposes that evening.

Taylor yawned and checked his watch again: 7:10. He sighed in frustration and looked at the diners on the next table: a foursome of two men and two women, all casually dressed, all quite young, and all tucking into average looking burgers with chips served in wire baskets reminiscent of chip fryers. He shook his head ever so slightly at the whole ridiculousness of it all.

His thoughts were halted at the sight of Jones and Albrechtsen stood looking around on the terrace, scanning for him. Albrechtsen was a huge man, overweight and sporting a bushy, greying beard. He was casually dressed in jeans and a bomber jacket. Jones was much smaller, almost petite, and was smartly dressed in a blue suit sporting small, round spectacles. He looked every inch the accountant, which had worked well for him over the years as he was a skilled investigator and ruthless operator.

Taylor gave the pair a brief wave and they walked over, serious-faced, and sat directly opposite Taylor. Neither looked happy and both looked concerned.

'So, what's the deal then, Simon? You've got us worried,' Albrechtsen said in his deep, rich voice.

'Come on, boys, drinks first. I'll have another pint.' Taylor smiled, keen to establish control of the meeting. They had been equals at SOCA but Albrechtsen and Jones had not gone further whereas he'd been promoted.

They scowled and went off together to the bar to get the drinks, whispering conspiratorially as they walked.

Taylor allowed himself a small, satisfied smile at this minor display of power. It was likely that they would be a bit pissed off when they learnt the extent of the situation, so a display of control early on would prove essential.

They reappeared after about five minutes, both clutching drinks. Albrechtsen also carried Taylor's pint, which he set down in front of him.

All of them took sips of their pints and then Albrechtsen and Jones sat back in their chairs expectantly.

Taylor took another long pull on his beer, set it down on the table, and fixed each man with a brief stare.

'Okay, we have a possible situation. Novak managed to rescue his parents in Scotland. I don't know how. The Brankos took them hostage in order to get the SD card but, somehow, he managed to get from London to the Highlands in just a few hours and free them. I can't get hold of anyone and earlier today Novak showed up in my office threatening me. He knows about you two and says he is bringing us all down,' Taylor said.

'Whoa, whoa! Back up, Simon! When did taking hostages become part of the plan? I just got the fucking SD card, and that's it. I know fuck-all about hostages. What have you got me into?' Albrechtsen was stunned. His beefy face flushed almost scarlet and his eyes were wide with alarm.

'I know, I know. But Novak knows all about that. I've no idea how. He's obviously got serious help, and he managed to get to Scotland in a matter of hours and get his hands on high-end weaponry.'

'Oh, for fuck's sake!' said Albrechtsen scrubbing his face with his hands. He sat back, desolate, in his chair, staring up at the parasol they were sitting under.

'Jonesy, do you know what's happened to the Brankos and Adebayo?' Taylor asked.

Jones appeared calmer as he paused, taking a sip of his drink.

He knew he was far more implicated than Albrechtsen, having been tracking Novak all along using highly illegal means.

'Border targeting shows that all the Brankos apart from Mira have left the country. Zjelko got on the Eurostar earlier today and Aleks and Luka both got a flight out to Belgrade this afternoon. It's not confirmed and is intelligence only, but it should be reliable.' He spoke in a light Welsh accent and seemed completely calm. 'Adebayo, we think left yesterday, not using his own passport but possibly using an associate's. The CCTV has been pulled, and he got on a flight to Lagos at 3pm. He's also moving most of his financial assets. He's not coming back.'

Taylor nodded at this information, expected as it was.

'This, at least, is good news. They're out of the way all apart from Mira and I don't think she knows anything about us.'

'Any ideas on who's helping Novak?' asked Jones.

'Not a clue. They're obviously well-placed and resourceful but also obviously not entirely lawful. He has a picture of me with one of Branko's girls that he couldn't have got legitimately. He's obviously had access to phone data, which will also be illegal. If he grasses on us, then he gets himself in the shit. I can't see any admissible evidence he has on us or it would have been IPCC not him that visited me this morning. Now that the Brankos and Adebayo are gone, I reckon we're nearly home and dry.' He paused for effect, taking a drink from his pint.

'Well that's a relief then at least. But where the fuck did you get off sending a kill team up to the Scottish Highlands to take out a family to get that SD card?'

'Branko is an evil bastard. I had no choice; he'd have sold us all down the river. Novak would have got all of us thrown in jail for fucking ten years, minimum. I don't know about you, Graham, but I don't fancy that much,' Taylor said, his voice dripping with sarcasm.

'So, what next, then? We just can't leave Novak storming around with big guns, where will it end? He could decide to bloody kill us, he could get something admissible, he could land us all in jail.'

Jones spoke forcefully and somewhat surprisingly, thought Taylor.

'Hang on, hang on, you're talking about killing a cop? Please tell me that's not what you're saying,' said Albrechtsen.

'What do you suggest, Graham? I'm all ears.'

The big man just sat, staring blankly ahead for a moment before saying, 'I never thought it would come to this. I know we pulled some bad shit capers on SOCA. But Christ, never murder!'

Taylor spoke, 'If this comes out, best-case scenario we're up for misconduct in a public office and conspiracy to pervert the course of justice. Worst-case scenario, it would be conspiracy to kidnap and murder: especially if Novak talks about the attempt to abduct him at Holborn nick. You knew all about Graham: there's phone records between us on that and it was your contact at the Yard who got us the warrant card for the hit man.'

Albrechtsen sighed once more at the knowledge that he was more involved than he'd first thought. He had made some calls to a mate at Scotland Yard and smoothed the waters to issue a warrant card with less scrutiny than usual.

Jones stirred in his seat. 'I have a contact. He is very efficient, he has had lots of practise, and he owes me a great big favour. He's ex-Russian military and would probably sort this problem for us for a reasonable fee.' He spoke evenly and calmly as if discussing a car repair, not the execution of a serving police officer.

The silence between them now was palpable, each man realising what they were discussing.

Albrechtsen broke the silence. 'What will he charge?' he said with a resigned look on his face.

'He's a professional, so he won't be cheap, especially as it's a serving cop. It will be at least twenty grand, and that's mates' rates.'

'So that's over six grand each. Can we do that?' Taylor asked both men.

'I don't have anything like that, otherwise why would I be working as a fucking jailer at a police station?' Albrechtsen said.

'Look, let's not talk cash now, Jonesy. Call your man and set up a meet. We can talk about the finances once we know how much he wants. You're sure he's capable? Novak has shown us he's more than competent at staying alive,' Taylor said.

Jones nodded and then drained his beer saying, 'Another?' as if they'd been discussing football.

A new voice came out of the general hubbub on the terrace, and the three realised that they had company.

A tall, slim, well-dressed, middle-aged woman stood next to their table, a half-smile on her face. She was accompanied by a casually-dressed, short, stocky man with a shaved head, who Taylor recognised as the man who had vacated the table for him.

'Gentlemen, allow me to introduce myself. My name is Detective Superintendent Jane Milligan, and this is my colleague, Detective Constable Peter Rymes. We're from Directorate Professional Standards.' As she spoke, the table in front of them with the foursome Taylor had earlier observed all stood and positioned themselves strategically around their table, cutting off all avenues of escape. One of them produced a small camera and began to record the proceedings, while the diners from the other tables turned to watch.

Milligan spoke again. 'These are also colleagues who have been enjoying dinner while you spoke. You are all being arrested for conspiracy to murder, conspiracy to abduct, blackmail, and attempting to pervert the course of justice. You do not have to say anything unless you wish to do so, but it may harm your defence if you do not mention, when questioned, something you may rely on in court. Anything you do say may be given in evidence.' She checked her watch and then looked at each of them in turn.

All three men seemed to shrink within their own clothes as the familiar caution was read out to them, each word a body-blow as the shock hit them like a train.

'Come on, fellas,' said Buster. 'Let's get you lot out of here. We've warm cells with your names on them.' A wide grin split his face.

Taylor stood and almost fainted as he did so, feeling his world fall apart, especially when he saw Buster lean forwards to pick up the condiments box and wink at him. It was all pre-planned; they'd been set up, and he knew for sure that every single word the three of them had just exchanged had been recorded.

None of them said anything. The one thing they knew, with all those years of policing experience, was that nothing they could say at that moment would help.

36

Two Days Later

Tom sat back in his chair in the interview room at Jubilee House in Putney, the HQ of the Met Police Directorate of Professional Standards.

It was a typical police interview room, small and square with screwed down furniture, a camera in the corner and a digital recorder at the back of the room.

Detective Superintendent Jane Milligan switched off the interview recording and smiled just slightly while her assistant, who had introduced himself as DS Naz Patel, began to secure the master disc in a numbered sticky seal, which Tom signed.

'Thanks for coming in, Tom. We needed to get your account and, as the most significant of witnesses in this sorry affair, we needed to record it,' she said.

Tom had stayed out of the way for a little while after the arrests of Taylor, Albrechtsen, and Jones, just to let the dust settle. He'd needed to sleep properly and try to clear his mind after the events of the past week or so, as he felt seriously wrung-out and, frankly, exhausted.

Milligan and her team had been keen to interview him straight away, making it very plain that they were only looking at him as a witness who was the victim of serious police corruption. Tom had in turn made it perfectly clear that he wanted to wait a couple of days to get his head straight and, in reality, to decide what he would tell DPS and what he wouldn't.

He obviously could say absolutely nothing about the CIA assistance; they would rightfully deny anything, and he could hardly confess to the five killings in Scotland and the numerous counts of illegal surveillance and computer hacking he'd been a party to.

He kept as close to the truth as he could, starting with his undercover deployment, his cover being blown and the failed kidnap attempt on him. He then moved on to his decision to go dark as he didn't know who had been selling him out. He did tell them about his efforts to draw his chasers to Ealing, and furnished the DPS with the photos he had taken of his chasers which he hoped would help link everything together for them.

The main difficulty was in explaining how he had worked out that Taylor was the corrupt officer, as he couldn't allude to his relationship with Mike or Pet. He concocted a reasonably believable story that one of the working girls he'd engaged with while undercover had shown him a photo of Taylor with her, describing the image to them in detail. When asked about why he had been speaking to the girl, he claimed that he'd bumped into her in Hackney after he'd gone dark and thought she may have had some information, given she'd worked for the Brankos. She'd as a result told him that one of her clients had been a cop, and she'd shown him the photo, leading to the link being established.

He explained that he'd approached Buster as he felt he was the only person he could truly trust.

Tom found it quite strange that his account was accepted almost without challenge, despite the numerous holes that littered it. Superintendent Milligan was clearly nobody's fool and, from the look she gave him with her piercing blue eyes, she clearly did not believe he was furnishing them with the whole truth.

Once the discs were sealed Tom asked, 'So, where are we?'

Milligan regarded him with those intelligent and knowing eyes that seemed to bore into his very core.

'Are you telling me that Buster hasn't kept you in the loop?' she asked, daring him with a half-smile to deny it.

'He told me a bit. He said that Albrechtsen has rolled-over and squealed, and that the evidence was looking good, but that's about it; he said he didn't know details.'

'That's about right. Albrechtsen has come on-board as an "assisting offender" and he is singing like a canary about everything but putting all the blame on Taylor, claiming he knew nothing about the plans to murder you or your family. He's even talked about their time together on SOCA a few years ago and about de-railing a major enquiry. We have damning phone evidence, photos on Taylor's computer, and we have Taylor messaging your family address to Branko. We also have large amounts of unexplained assets for Taylor and Jones that seem to have no legal basis or source. I can safely say that I've rarely had so much evidence against such serious offenders,' she said.

'Well, that sounds promising.'

'They've all been charged with conspiracy to murder, conspiracy to kidnap, blackmail, and misconduct in a public office. We've already had tentative offers of plea bargains from all parties, such is the strength of the evidence. It's just a shame that all the Serbians have mysteriously disappeared: the computers all seem to suggest they are back in Serbia.' She stared her icy stare straight at Tom once again.

Tom's face remained blank and expressionless.

'Is there anything you'd like to add, Detective Sergeant?' She raised a well-teased eyebrow and Tom thought he could detect a touch of gentle sarcastic humour.

Tom was about to answer when she held up a hand to silence him. 'Before you answer, I should say that the CPS will be looking for a simple resolution to this case. They are probably going to offer to plead guilty to misconduct in a public office and conspiracy to pervert the course of justice. We may also get conspiracy to kidnap for Jones and Taylor, but I don't think we will push too hard. I think everyone is keen to avoid a trial, particularly with the undercover aspect to this case. I'm sure you would rather not appear as a witness at court?'

'I can think of other things I would rather do,' Tom said, averting his gaze, which he imagined told volumes.

'Well, all good then. As long as you're happy I know everything I need to know?'

'I think I've said everything appropriate, ma'am.'

'Ugh, don't call me that! I hate being called "ma'am",' she said with disgust. 'It makes me feel old and like a lower grade crusty royal, call me "boss", please.'

'Sure thing, boss.'

'Right, Tom, we'll be in touch. Now, I believe that you're expected back at Kilburn. I think the Borough Commander is expecting you, as well as Stan,' she said with a straight face.

'Stan? How do you know Stan?'

'Doesn't everyone know Stan, Sergeant Novak?' Her smile this time was warm and genuine.

37

A Week Later

Zjelko Branko left the small bar at about 11pm, walking out onto a grimy back street in Belgrade to begin the slow journey back to his dingy hotel room in the most insalubrious area of the once great city. He had drunk far too much beer and vodka, as had been the pattern since arriving in the city over a week ago, and he staggered slightly as he negotiated the rough footway, cursing his failure to secure a woman to while away the evening with.

For the first time ever, he felt a little lost in his home city, being, as he was, very short of available funds. The city felt claustrophobic and down-at-heel to him and he'd resolved that, as soon as his situation improved, he would move on to somewhere new.

He had managed to hook-up with an old associate from his White Eagle days, who owned the hotel and had offered him the use of it for a few weeks until he could sort out some funds. Once they were secured, he should be good to go for a considerable time; maybe he could buy a nice Alpine retreat in the old country.

He'd watched his incompetent boys get killed by that bastard Novak, but he couldn't see how the man had got to Scotland so quickly: he was like the proverbial bad penny, that man. Zjelko swore revenge once his situation improved, although that was more for his shame at having failed than any particular love or affection for his stupid offspring. He realised he wasn't even particularly upset at their presumed demise; they should have been better at their jobs, and his main emotion was one of shame at their incompetence given it had been such a simple job.

His wife—the stupid, dowdy Mira—was still in London and she could stay there as far as he was concerned.

His main concern was the lack of funds which was restricting his status and opportunities to build him back to where he had been before his incarceration. The trafficking game was not worth the bother and dealing with whores was far too much of a headache. He needed to get away from anywhere within the EU because of the bastard European arrest warrants that, no doubt, the UK would be seeking for him while they still could.

He had enough contacts to avoid arrest and extradition to the UK while in Serbia, but he would need more cash if that situation was to stay permanent. He cursed Novak for causing him all those problems.

All he had now was the stashed jewellery that he'd secreted in a rural hide in Switzerland after one of the heists he and some others had pulled just before his arrest. The gems and watches he'd buried would be able to set him up in a new venture; he just needed the dust to settle before he could travel to retrieve them. He smiled; once he had the money then there would be many good business opportunities coming his way.

Arriving back at his hotel, he yawned and checked his watch; it was just after midnight as he walked through the glazed doors into the grimy and dowdy reception area and nodded at the concierge, a grey-haired, yellow-skinned man called Yuri who barely spoke to anyone.

He staggered up the stained, carpeted staircase to his small, impersonal room which overlooked the car park at the rear of the building. Searching through his pockets, he located the room key which was attached to a large wooden fob upon which the hotel's logo was printed in chipped gold paint. Putting the key in the door and pushing, he entered sleepily, desperate to slip between the faded floral sheets, fraying though they were.

Taking his jacket off as he entered, he back-heeled the door behind him, closing it with a loud slam. He fumbled for the light switch and flicked it on, bathing the room in a dim, yellow light.

The impact he felt against the side of his neck was sudden and agonising and he fell to the floor as if electrocuted, his vision failing as he fell. He felt like he'd been shot and couldn't organise his thoughts as his limbs refused to work. He felt himself being dragged along the floor and his wrist being secured as his vision went black.

Branko had no idea how long he was unconscious for, as he slowly began to come around. He was confused that he couldn't move his right hand to try to stand up. Looking around, he could see that it had been secured to the radiator he was sitting against, his legs extended out in front of him.

The room wasn't empty; a white clad figure wearing a face mask sat on the threadbare armchair in the corner of the room, appraising him coolly.

'I told you I was coming for you,' Tom said in a low voice that managed to combine calmness and menace in equal quantities.

Tom was dressed in a white, paper, forensic overall with the hood up, a face mask, blue nitrile gloves, and black plastic overshoes. He looked just like the crime scene examiners Branko had seen on the TV after murders or other serious crimes.

He seemed utterly calm and completely in control. Branko couldn't see his features but the dark, almost black eyes and calm, low voice were unmistakeable. Branko's heart sank; he knew what was about to follow.

'What do you want?'

'Only one thing. To kill you. You die tonight, Branko. But before I kill you I want you to hear something, so you know why I'm here.'

Branko tried to speak but Tom silenced him with a raised hand.

'You don't need to talk, you just need to listen. I know everything that has happened and everything that you have done. You know what, that's not even the reason I am here. The reason I'm here now is down to what you did to a little boy once in 1992 back in Bosnia, when you were a murdering White Eagle. You deprived that twelve-year-old boy of his father, you brutalised his mother, and you forced that boy to lose his childhood and flee his homeland. You murdered my father, Branko—my father, Jacov Novak—because he wouldn't join your White Eagles, and you raped my mother, Aishe. And that's why I'm here today. To kill you for costing me my childhood and making me the man I am here today who has killed over and over again. I killed your sons and your friends, and do you know how I feel about that? I'll tell you: I don't care. I feel nothing, and you did that to me. You robbed me of the ability to feel. That's why I'm here and that's why you die today.' Tom spoke evenly, quietly, almost a whisper, but the raw hatred for the man before him shone out despite his clothing and the slight muffling of the mask.

Branko didn't say anything straight away. A heavy, thick silence enveloped the room, almost like a palpable gas, before Branko broke it with a light chuckle.

It began as a low snigger, his shoulders moving almost imperceptibly, and an unpleasant smile began to creep across his pock-marked face, his scar visible like a vivid white slash.

'You think your father was a hero, Novak? The great Jacov Novak? Yugoslavia's Olympic hero.' The sarcasm was redolent in his voice. 'My goodness, Tomo, you are naïve. Your father was a thief; he stole from me, diamonds that were to secure me forever. Your father was a killer, he worked for Tito's secret police and he would eliminate his opponents for him,' he continued, still chuckling.

Novak didn't waver, instead remaining impassive. 'My father was a government interpreter; you are a liar.'

Branko's chuckle became louder, almost a guffaw.

'An interpreter? Don't be so naïve, boy. Your father loved Tito. He worked for him for years and would do anything for him; the blood on his hands is real. Only after Tito's death did he begin his silly work. He believed in Yugoslavia, the deluded fool, when Milosevic was showing us the true way of Serbian superiority. He had his chance to be a great patriot but then he met your Roma mother and became soft, especially once you were born. He lost his balls and became a subservient pussy.' Branko's unpleasant chuckling continued. 'I would have let him live but he stole from me and wouldn't fight on the right side. That's why he died; I shot him between the eyes and laughed as I did it.' He began to laugh hysterically now, tears coursing down his scarred cheeks, his eyes shining with manic, unhinged fury and mirth.

Novak's expression and demeanour had not changed at all as he watched the big Serb's hysterics.

Branko composed himself and looked at Tom, 'You should be thanking me, Novak. By killing your weak father and having my fun with your whore of a Roma mother I gave you the gift of strength. Not for us the weakness of compassion, but the strength and power of ruthlessness. The weak deserve to die and leave the strong behind, Novak, you must realise this. We are the same, Novak. It is us, and those like us who will triumph,' Branko hissed through gritted teeth, his red-rimmed eyes blazing with hate.

Tom paused and his eyes betrayed a smile that had appeared behind the mask.

'We're not the same,' Tom said in a hoarse whisper as he stood.

Tom's extended fingers flashed towards Branko and drove into the cartilaginous tissue of his windpipe, just below the Adam's apple, crushing it completely. Branko's free hand clutched at the ruined trachea, but it was too late and the damage was too devastating. Unable to draw in air he began to panic and thrash, clutching at his throat and trying to clear the destroyed airway. The more he thrashed and panicked the greater his need for oxygen. His legs kicked and he tried to pull away from the radiator, his eyes beginning to bulge and his tongue lolling. His struggles soon weakened as his face grew red. Soon he lay still. Tom sat back down on the chair and waited.

'We. Are. Not. The. Same.' Tom spat every word at the corpse.

He quickly removed Branko's watch and freed his wrist from the radiator. He took his wallet and mobile phone from his trouser pockets, which he put in a small carrier bag he'd picked up from the floor.

Opening the door to the hotel room, he put the 'Do Not Disturb' sign on the door handle. With luck, housekeeping wouldn't find Branko until late morning at best and even then, the cause of death probably wouldn't be ascertained until after a post-mortem.

Without a glance at the corpse, he opened the sliding balcony door and exited the room onto a small, tiled space occupied by two plastic chairs and a broken table. The car park behind the hotel was almost empty apart from half-a-dozen cars. There was no sign of life anywhere, so Tom quickly climbed over the balcony wall and lowered himself over the edge. Using the balcony below, he silently dropped to the ground and walked away calmly.

He quickly stripped off the forensic suit, mask, gloves and overshoes and stuffed them in the bag, together with the items taken from Branko. He then picked up a rucksack he'd left on the balcony when making his entrance into the hotel room, put all the items inside and hefted the bag onto his back.

He walked a block away, to where his rented Hyundai was parked in a side street. He unlocked it and got into the car, stowing the rucksack in the passenger footwell. He would dispose of the forensic protective gear and items taken from Branko en route back to the airport, where he had a plane to London leaving in just over five hours.

The US passport and credit card he carried in the name of Thomas Chandler had been secured by an associate of Lucky D in London in exchange for five hundred pounds. Fortunately for Tom, Branko had not been careful in Belgrade, leaving electronic traces of his presence that were easy to find.

Tom searched for any adverse feelings he was experiencing, either negative or positive, and was once again a little disturbed to find no trace of what may be referred to as normal emotion after the events he'd just experienced.

There would be no trace of Tom having left the UK, let alone entering Serbia or travelling to a seedy hotel in backstreet Belgrade and killing Branko. Not a computer trace, not a CCTV image, not a forensic fibre or fingerprint.

Tom smiled as he began the short journey to the airport. He was hungry and fancied a bite to eat and a cold beer, and hoped somewhere would be open after he'd checked-in.

38

Michael Adebayo had enjoyed a fine evening at a fundraiser for a children's charity at the mosque affiliated to the housing development his new home occupied. He was a fairly observant Muslim, as many converts were, but he had to admit that his reasons for worshipping at present were more about finding useful contacts and associates than being close to Allah.

He was keen to imbed himself in the community of fellow wealthy residents and had been generous with his donations at the fundraiser, making some good new business contacts with mosque elders as well as some of the more up-and-coming members as well. All a good investment for his future, especially as it looked like he wouldn't be returning to London.

He had settled into Lagos quite nicely and quickly, helped by the fact that he already had a comfortable, well-furnished home in the gated suburb community which was well-managed, affluent, and immaculately maintained. Not for him the dire slums and grinding poverty of downtown Lagos.

Adebayo had a sneaking suspicion that the charity, Lagos Community Mosque for Syrian Orphan Relief was a cover for ISIS, but he didn't give it too much thought. He wasn't politically active and certainly had no desire to live under the restrictive Sharia laws, enjoying, as he did, the finer things in life.

He missed London and his wife and children, but not so much that he wanted to return and risk prison and asset confiscation. His wife had point-blank refused to accompany him, citing the children's education, which he understood, but he did not enjoy the dishonour it brought him in his new community. He hated the pitying eyes of his new friends when they learnt that his family were still in London, no matter how much he assured them that they would be joining him in due course.

He had no shortage of female company, however. Men of his means rarely did, and he often entertained lady guests at his mansion. Not that night though; he had an early meeting with an important businessman who he hoped would offer him some opportunities to grow his nest egg with a possibility that was very interesting.

Pulling his Range Rover up to his house, he pressed the remote control on his keyring and the iron gates swung open, revealing a sweeping drive that led to his modern, single-storey home. The double garage door was already rolling open as he approached, the lights automatically activated. He edged the big car into the immaculate space with its red-painted, glossy, concrete floor and parked next to his sleek Mercedes.

He was yawning as he exited the car, having to pull the hem of his kameez robe up as it caught on the gearstick. He had taken to wearing traditional Islamic dress more and more often, as it seemed appropriate and many of his neighbours dressed the same.

A voice in English cut through the silence behind him, causing him to almost jump out of his skin, 'Mr Adebayo, may I have a moment of your time please, sir?' A tall, heavily built bearded man stood at the entrance to his garage. He was distinguished looking with a neatly trimmed beard and was wearing an immaculate tailored suit that Adebayo could tell was not off the peg.

'You startled the life out of me. Who the hell are you?' he replied.

'State Security Service. My name is Major Okafor. I would like to speak to you, Mr Adebayo,' he smiled, showing perfect, white teeth.

The man came a little closer, flipping open an identity document which depicted a photograph together with the logo of the SSS depicting an owl on a green crest.

Adebayo reeled nervously: the SSS were the national intelligence agency for Nigeria, universally feared by all.

'What, err, what can I do for you, sir?' Adebayo stuttered, trying to keep the real and naked fear from his voice.

'Perhaps you could accompany us to our local office. I have a gentleman who would dearly love to have a conversation with you. Something to do with your charitable donations here and back in the UK.' He spoke with charm that carried an undercurrent of menace and utter confidence that, frankly terrified Adebayo.

'Well it's not convenient right now, Major Okafor.'

Major Okafor held up a manicured hand and smiled. 'Mr Adebayo, I'm afraid I must insist.'

Two headlights pierced the darkness from the far side of Adebayo's sweeping drive and a dark VW van slowly eased from its parking spot towards the men.

The van pulled alongside them and the side door slid open, allowing an enormous, bulky man to unfurl himself from within. He was dressed in black combat trousers and a black leather jacket. He was shaven-headed, bearded and looked tough and dangerous as he stood to the side of the van door, his hand directing Adebayo inside.

'Major, please. I haven't done anything wrong,' Adebayo stuttered again, a fleck of spittle flying from his lips as the terror began to take hold.

'Mr Adebayo, please, let us not create a scene. My colleague, Captain Oni, is not a patient man; he really wants to go home to his wife as he recently got married, you see. If you delay him unnecessarily, he will be very displeased.' Okafor smiled without even a trace of humour.

39

Six Weeks Later

Tom ran at pace through the Camden streets and onto Hampstead Heath, enjoying the burn as he pushed himself round the perimeter of the park and along past the bathing ponds, his breath escaping in clouds of vapour in the chilly morning air.

He ran for a solid hour, stopping frequently to perform press-ups and sit-ups, even performing a set of pull-ups from the low bough of a sycamore tree.

Once he was happy he'd done enough, he queued at the Parliament Hill coffee stall to get himself a large, black Americano and a bottle of water.

His drinks in hand, he walked over to a nearby bench, feeling his body cool as he took several long gulps of the water. Sitting down, he warmed his hands on the coffee cup and enjoyed the view in the early morning: the crisp, clear sun.

He sat back and closed his eyes, feeling the sun warming his face, enjoying the post-exercise burn that he was so used to after all these years of habitual workouts.

'You're looking fit, my friend,' said a familiar American voice to his right on the bench.

'Getting fitter, Mike, always getting fitter,' Tom said without opening his eyes.

Mike was sat next to him on the bench, neither of them acknowledging each other's presence, as was the etiquette in meetings such as these.

Both men remained silent for a few moments as a young mother pushing a child in an expensive-looking pushchair sauntered by, before Mike asked, 'How's Cam and Shona?'

'They're okay. Cam is tough as old boots and Shona is a proper Highlander: they're a resilient breed, you know. She's managing fine with a slightly shorter finger, as well.' Tom said with a smile.

'That's good. Any problems with the police?'

'None. They told them that three guys turned up masked and held them for a while before getting a phone call in the middle of the night and leaving without a word. Police seem to have accepted it. They seem a bit perplexed about the finger, even with Shona being firm that it was a wood-chopping accident.'

'What about your corrupt colleagues?'

'In prison, apart from Albrechtsen who is somewhere secure and secret, being that he's a super-grass now. There won't be a trial: all have accepted early plea bargains and they'll be sentenced next month. Everyone is baffled about how the Brankos got back to Serbia under their noses. It caused a bit of head scratching. Your breadcrumb trail did the job, Mike.'

'Hey, it's what we do, my friend. Branko Senior's death was widely reported in local papers in Belgrade as a gangland killing and robbery between rival Serb mafia factions. Tragic, huh?'

'Hey, it's a jungle out there.'

Mike snorted a laugh by way of answer.

'So, it's pretty much all over, right?' Mike asked.

'Not quite. There's still Adebayo; he's lording it up in Nigeria I imagine.' Tom spoke with just a small amount of bitterness detectable in his voice.

'Do you believe in fate, Tom?'

'No, not really, I think stuff just happens. Bad stuff to bad people, bad stuff to good people, and vice versa. It's just all circumstances and luck, there's no grand plan. Not as far as I'm concerned, anyway.'

'I kind of agree with you, but I do believe that bad things

happen to bad people more than they do to good people. Adebayo is a bad person; something bad will happen sometime. It's bound to. Rule of averages. Do more bad stuff then more will come your way, I reckon.'

The two men just stared for a full minute at the morning scene in the London park.

Mike's mobile phone made a distinctive 'Ping' as they sat and, after a few moments, Tom heard a soft chuckle come from the American.

'Check this out,' he said and slid his mobile phone across the bench to Tom, who picked it up and looked at the screen. Two pretty blonde girls, aged about eight, grinned out from the screen: both had bunny ears, sparkly eyes, and stars seemed to be circling their heads, all obviously computer generated onto the twins' picture. Tom recognised Mike's kids, having met them once during a trip to California a few years before.

Tom smiled and slid the phone back across the bench. 'They've grown so much, mate. Cute kids,' he said, suddenly envious of Mike.

'It's a Snapchat. Do you have it? I'll get them to send you some, they still talk about you,' Mike said.

'I don't have it. I'm not much one for social media apart from as an investigative tool.'

'Don't be a grouch. Download it, my kids want to send you messages.'

'Maybe,' Tom said. Then added, 'How's Pet?'

'She's good, she's in Berlin for a while. She said to say hi and that you should call her.'

'Maybe I will,' Tom said, not knowing if he meant it or not. He'd not seen Pet, other than at a very brief meeting after the arrests of Taylor and the others. He'd figured it was safer to keep a distance between them until things were resolved, but he couldn't say he didn't think of her a lot. Relationships were not something that Tom could quite get his head around, though, and he couldn't see how anything could work with both of their itinerant lifestyles.

'I've been asked to offer you a job by my superiors; they reckon that someone who can do what you pulled off would be an asset to the Agency as a UK resource. You interested?'

'It's flattering and interesting, but I work for the UK. Britain gave me a life and I would never reveal anything that may harm this country. I owe them everything.'

'I told them that's what you'd say. Honour is a rare commodity these days, old friend and you have it. You'd be a valuable resource and we'd pay very well, but I doubt that would make a difference.'

Tom didn't reply, just turned and looked at Mike for the first time during the meeting and flashed him a warm smile.

'I gotta go, Tom. I have a flight back to the States later today. I'm reassigned: I start in Washington next week.'

'Well, best of luck, mate. I think I can now say that we're even in the favour stakes.'

'Never. I'll always owe you, as you probably know after seeing my daughters. Be lucky, man. And if you change your mind about the job, just holler.'

Tom smiled once more and watched Mike stroll off towards Highgate Hill without a backwards glance.

Tom finished his coffee, dumped the cup in the trash and began his light jog back home through the bustling Camden streets.

Once home, he flicked through his iPhone, went to the app store, downloaded Snapchat and created a basic profile. He figured a bit of banter with Mike's kids would be quite amusing, so what was the harm?

He showered quickly, dressed in a clean pair of jeans and a white polo shirt and pulled his shoes on, getting ready to go to work. He'd been moved from the main office into the proactive team and he had a planning meeting at 9am.

A tone he didn't recognise from his phone indicated some activity required his attention. He picked it up and saw that he had a Snapchat message. It took him a few moments to familiarise himself with the new app but soon it came up with a message from 'Mike B'.

He opened the message and stared at the image in front of him.

Michael Adebayo was pictured, a haunted look on a face which now sported a long, unkempt beard. He wore orange overalls and leg and wrist restraints and had clearly lost a great deal of weight. His sunken cheeks and deep-set eyes radiated desperation and hopelessness. A 'No Smoking' sign behind Adebayo was underwritten in Cyrillic script. The picture suddenly disappeared into thin air as quickly as it had appeared, to be replaced with a text message which simply said, 'Bad things happen to bad people.'

Did You Enjoy This Book?

If so, you can make a HUGE difference

For any author, the single most important way we have of getting our books noticed is a really simple one—and one which you can help with.

Yes, you.

Us indie authors and publishers don't have the financial muscle of the big guys to take out full-page ads in the newspaper or put posters on the subway.

But we do have something much more powerful and effective than that, and it's something that those big publishers would kill to get their hands on.

A committed and loyal bunch of readers.

Honest reviews of our books help bring them to the attention of other readers.

If you've enjoyed this book I would be really grateful if you could spend just a couple of minutes leaving a review (it can be as short as you like) on this book's page on your favourite store and website.

Thank you so much—you're awesome, each and every one of you!

Warm regards

Neil

Acknowledgements

Writing a first draft of a book is a long and lonely process involving many hours of procrastination, frustration, brain racking and head-scratching. Getting a book ready to publish, however is very much a team effort. My eternal gratitude goes to all those who have encouraged me in my quest to write a book and get it published into the world, where strangers will hopefully read and enjoy it.

To the friends and family who read the earliest drafts of the book: Angela Rowbottom, Gail Wilson-Kenny, Matt O'Neill and Andy Scripture, your encouragement gave me the impetus I needed to keep plugging away. To my good friend Simon Hammock for keeping me straight on all things relating to search-and-rescue helicopters.

A number of very talented authors kindly read the manuscript and gave vital critique, observations and the belief that I could do this. Huge thanks, therefore are due to Margaret Kirk, Alex Walters, Ian Patrick and Michael Jenkins. Your support and friendship has been of such value and without your help I wouldn't be writing these words right now.

A special thanks goes to the wonderful editor, Emma Mitchell, who turned 103,000 words of gibberish into 95,000 words that a publisher wouldn't delete at first sight. You taught me that less is more, a lesson every author needs to listen to.

Thanks also to my beta readers for their invaluable feedback: Andreas Rausch, Ami Agner, Kirsti Wenn, Alison Belding, and David and Joyce Oxley. And to our amazing proof reader, Paula

Beaton.

To Si and Pete at Burning Chair for believing in the book and taking the chance on a washed-up ex-cop with an urge to tell a story. I hope this is the beginning of something brilliant.

Of course, thanks to my lovely wife, Clare and my kids, Alec, Richard and Ollie for all your love and support. You all make it all worthwhile.

Finally, thanks to you, the reader, for taking a chance with your cold, hard cash on a debut author. Stay tuned; there's more where this came from.

Neil

About the Author

Neil Lancaster served over thirty years in law enforcement in the both military and Metropolitan Police, working in a number of detective roles investigating serious and organised crime. During his career he chased murderers, human traffickers, fraudsters and drug dealers.

Neil now lives in the Scottish Highlands where he spends his time writing crime fiction, influenced by his experiences.

You can follow him at www.neillancastercrime.co.uk

Or on Twitter - @NeilLancaster66

About Burning Chair

Burning Chair is an independent publishing company based in the UK, but covering readers and authors around the globe. We are passionate about both writing and reading books and, at our core, we just want to get great books out to the world.

Our aim is to offer something exciting; something innovative; something that puts the author and their book first. From first class editing to cutting edge marketing and promotion, we provide the care and attention that makes sure that every book fulfils its potential.

We are:

- Different
- Passionate
- Nimble and cutting edge
- Invested in our authors' success

If you're an author and would like to know more, visit
www.burningchairpublishing.com
for our submissions requirements and our free guide to book publishing.

If you're a reader and are interested in becoming a beta reader for us, helping us to create yet more awesome books (and getting to read them for free in the process!), please visit
www.burningchairpublishing.com/beta-readers.

Other Books by Burning Chair Publishing:

Beyond, by Georgia Springate

Burning: An Anthology of Thriller Shorts, edited by Simon
Finnie and Peter Oxley

The Infernal Aether Series, by Peter Oxley
The Infernal Aether
A Christmas Aether
The Demon Inside
Beyond the Aether

The Wedding Speech Manual: The Complete Guide to Preparing,
Writing and Performing Your Wedding Speech, by Peter Oxley

www.burningchairpublishing.com

Printed in Great Britain
by Amazon